# NEVADA SON

## ...A FAMILY ODYSSEY

by

Rob Robertson

Basque Original Series #32

# NEVADA SON

## ...A FAMILY ODYSSEY

by

Rob Robertson

**CENTER FOR BASQUE STUDIES
UNIVERSITY OF NEVADA, RENO
2024**

This book was published with generous financial support from the Basque Government.

Center for Basque Studies
University of Nevada, Reno
1664 North Virginia St,
Reno, Nevada 89557 usa
http://basque.unr.edu

Copyright © 2024 by the Center for Basque Studies and the University of Nevada, Reno
ISBN-13: 978-19-49805-86-4
All rights reserved.

Library of Congress Cataloging-in-Publication Data

Names: Robertson, Rob, 1951- author.
Title: Nevada son : a family odyssey / by Rob Robertson.
Other titles: Basque originals ; 32.
Description: [Reno, Nevada] : [Center for Basque Studies Press], [2024] |Series: Basque originals ; 32 | Summary: "This novel is a fictional account of a native Nevadan and his relationships with Basque friends in search of their ancestry"-- Provided by publisher.
Identifiers: LCCN 2024011430 (print) | LCCN 2024011431 (ebook) | ISBN 9781949805864 (paperback) | ISBN 9781949805864 (epub)
Subjects: LCSH: Friendship--Fiction. | LCGFT: Novels.
Classification: LCC PS3618.O3174 N48 2024  (print) | LCC PS3618.O3174 (ebook) | DDC 813/.6--dc23/eng/20240506
LC record available at https://lccn.loc.gov/2024011430
LC ebook record available at https://lccn.loc.gov/2024011431

Printed in the United States of America

*for Joyce*

*She taught us how to live.*

# PART I
# LOST DIASPORA

# 1

# FRANK AND THE DUST DEVIL

The four riders pushed quietly along on horseback, two each on either side of a small gathering of Angus cows and calves. A pair of black and white Border Collies were doing the real work this morning, racing back and forth behind the cattle; nobody was watching them, as they required no supervision. The youngest among the riders was glad that the sun was at last visible over the peaks of the Toiyabe Range. It had been a chilly start to the morning, and he welcomed the warming rays. Frank McClelland was riding next to his mother, side-by-side as they traveled below the impressive canyons that rise up from the northeast playas of the Desatoya Mountains. They were on the Smith Creek side of the range.

Frank was seven years old, and he was wearing a felt cowboy hat that was too big for him. Everything was too big for him, chaps and hat especially, because they had been passed down to him from his older brother Robby. He was transfixed this morning on the image of his mother's beautiful face, now fully illuminated in the morning sunlight. The crown of her head was wrapped in a silk wild rag, and he imagined for a moment that she was a gypsy fortune-teller, even though her western hat (secured with a woven horsehair loop) was visible behind her neck and shoulders. She too wore chaps for protection from the sharp juniper and sage branches that they navigated.

He found himself staring at the deep red hues reflecting within her ebony hair. It was the first time he had noticed this phenomenon and he wondered to himself, *How can there be red in the color black?* He always understood that his mother was actually of Basque descent, because she often talked proudly about that fact; he would learn some years later that she had come to Nevada with her parents in their dreams of raising sheep on their own land. She was from one of the northern provinces of Spain, located high in the Pyrenees Mountains of southwest Europe; it was the rugged expanse that stands as a natural boundary between France and Spain. That steep range of mountains ultimately isolated the entire Iberian Peninsula from the rest of continental Europe, so it had sequestered the Basque people for generations.

When she finally glanced over and noticed Frank staring at her hair, she smiled and sidled up next to his horse. Reaching out with both hands, she cupped his face tightly between them and smiled her radiant smile, "You are so *handsome*, my young Francis! One day, a beautiful girl will steal your heart and you will stare at your mother no more," and she poured out the entirety of her adoration upon him. *"Mom!"*, he protested, "Please call me *Frank!*" "Oh, *'please'* . . .", she affectionately teased and then continued, "Someday you will also know that you were named for Saint Francis, a Patron Saint, and that is a name to honor and to be proud of."

They continued to ride along together and she beamed at her youngest son, *"Look!"* she interjected and pointed down, "Indian Paint Brush . . . so beautiful, growing right out of the rocks . . . See them?" And then later, "There, to your left. Remember(?) . . . that's Prickly Pear." This happy routine of riding along together while his mother talked to him about everything under the sun was one of young Frank's great joys, and ultimately these moments would endure as his most treasured memories of her . . .

❀ ❀ ❀

Their peaceful ride this morning was interrupted by a shrill whistle, directed at them by his father; he and Robby were riding on the opposite side of the group of cows and calves. Robert McClelland was pointing up the hill toward an Angus cow that had strayed from the rest while being shepherded across their range. "Ahh . . . Of course!" his mother exclaimed when she saw that the cow appeared to be grazing alone, "She forgot where her calf is." Frank and his mother nudged their horses in that direction and spread out as they approached the cow from two sides. His mother instructed, "I'll turn her back toward the others. You see if you can find her calf . . . I know it must be around here somewhere."

Frank began weaving in and out of the sagebrush in the surrounding area of about fifty yards which bordered the small gathering of cows. Sure enough, Frank saw the tiny calf curled up beside a juniper bush that almost hid her entirely. Wow . . . She's a little one (!), he thought. He dismounted and leaned down to pick up the calf. Cradling it with both forearms, Frank then walked her over to his horse.

He struggled to place the McCarty lead rope in his teeth, and he stepped up onto a nearby rock to gain the height necessary to transfer the calf. Finally balanced in one stirrup, he lifted her over his saddle horn, so she might rest safely across the horse's neck. Using caution now, he guided his horse back downhill while steering only with his knees; in so doing he delivered the calf back to its Angus mother, who was now baying bloody murder in the panic of seeing her lost calf.

❀ ❀ ❀

Frank's mother proudly smiled at her son as she watched his every move. But then she erupted into a fierce tirade, reflecting her exasperation at having to repeatedly search during these gatherings for calves lost by their Angus mothers. Her husband knew the speech, and he quickly looked off in another direction, pretending not to hear. It was well known in the auction houses of Nevada that other breeds of cattle require more care at elevations above five thousand feet. Many of the white-faced breeds (particularly Herefords) are vulnerable to eye irritation in the higher UV exposure; the ensuing conjunctivitis, which requires labor-intensive doctoring, is never practical.

Angus cattle do much better at high elevations, and they (of course) are known for the quality of their meat, which commands higher prices. But they are also notorious for being 'Houdinis', and that ability to break out of fences and corrals just compounded upon a penchant to forget where they last saw their calves during transit to new grazing areas.

Things settled back down again once the riders and cow dogs resumed their assigned positions, but Frank's mother continued her irritated lecture in his general direction. She at last turned to Frank and looked into his eyes to emphatically underscore her subject, "These stupid mothers are no different than those of other species in the animal kingdom—many of them will abandon their children too, or worse, harm them! Don't ever forget this Francis, especially when you choose your bride someday. Remember these Angus mothers and find a woman who won't abandon her children! They will be *your* children as well, and they will be *my grandchildren*." Frank rode on with haunting images of women abandoning their helpless babies, and his seven year old sensibilities struggled to understand; in spite of this, he trusted his mother's vision of the world with his usual acceptance.

❀ ❀ ❀

By now the heat of the day was palpable, and Frank was the first to see the tall dust devil spiraling toward him on its diagonal path. Robby saw it too, and the brothers at once locked eyes. They also risked veiled grins, hoping that their father wouldn't notice. Robby nodded toward it as a signal to his younger brother, and they were once again two accomplished thieves, galvanized in their common purpose.

Frank needed no more encouragement than that, as he had practiced the next steps many times before, always incurring the predictable wrath of his father. That notwithstanding (and to the complete surprise of his mother), he jumped off his horse and ran at full speed toward the funnel cloud. Just as he heard his mother's cries of protest in the background, Frank jumped headlong into the center of the towering desert cyclone, which by now had grown much larger.

In each of the previous times that Frank or his brother had tried this, they would have been buffeted around a little, only to find themselves laughing wildly on the ground. Once there, they would spit out the sand and then clean debris from their ears. Up until this occasion, of course, both of them had been able to stand up and dust themselves off, so even their mother might eventually be able to laugh (however privately) at this great fun.

❀ ❀ ❀

But make no mistake about it, they were certain to face the harsh scrutiny of their father and he would not be amused, especially if the cattle were scattered even just a little; if the cattle were scattered a lot, the brothers knew that they would earn a hard swat to the backside, along with the full force of his epic disappointment. Yet, in spite of that certainty, they were time and time again entirely unable to restrain themselves.

❀ ❀ ❀

No one present (especially Frank) anticipated what would happen next: As he leaped precisely into the vortex of the growing cyclone, his seventy pound body at once became airborne amidst the powerful venturi forces concentrated within it. He spun only slightly at first, so he stretched out his arms and then his legs. He began to realize that he was being lifted upward inside the widening funnel, and he glanced back and forth. Gradually he flew higher above the ground . . . ten feet at first, and then he was lifted even more, eventually to somewhere past the height of twenty feet, where he hovered in a perfect existential balance.

From this vantage he was suddenly able to see far beyond his own location. As he peered over the spinning wall of dust which had previously blocked his view—below him was his family, silently staring upward and frozen in disbelief at what they were witnessing. When he raised his eyes beyond them and focused out over the greater distance, Frank was spellbound to discover what appeared to be a glimmering ocean far beyond the playa. Sailboats heeled there beneath towering city buildings, and enormous bridges jutted out to connect the shorelines. The vision was unlike anything he had ever before seen.

❀ ❀ ❀

At last, he felt himself float back down toward the ground, as the grasp of the upper vortex began to dissipate. Finally, when he approached the bottom of the narrowing dust devil, it grabbed at his feet and began to spin him much faster; that motion easily tumbled his small body and he was tossed out onto a thick cluster of sagebrush, which cushioned his fall entirely. There he found himself lying safely on his back, amidst fragrant sage flowers, in a state of dizzy shock. He was comfortable here as he stared up at the blue Nevada sky, which was now dotted with tranquil white clouds. A honeybee flew into close view as it hovered just above his nose, so boy and bee stared curiously at one another for an instant.

❀ ❀ ❀

His family, now accompanied by the cow dogs, surrounded him within seconds. Robby arrived first and he positioned himself as close as he could to Frank's face; his mouth was gaping as he laughed in amazement. Quickly, his father brushed Robby aside with one sweep of his long sinewy arm, and he grabbed Frank by the shoulders to assess him for damage. His furrowed brows were now just inches away, and this was as worried and as vulnerable as Frank could ever remember seeing him.

Finally his mother thrust herself into the circle, and with a ranch woman's strength, pushed everyone else away. She was horror-stricken by what she had just witnessed, and when it became evident that her son was unharmed, she nearly crushed him in the tightness of her embrace. She then kissed him repeatedly over every inch of his face. By now Robby had once more wrestled his way back to the center, and he could not contain himself for even another second when he saw his brother's dazed expression, "Look at him! Look at his goofy face!", and he doubled over laughing.

Even his mother by now could find the humor in Frank's euphoric dream-gaze, which appeared plastered onto her youngest son's face, and she too began to giggle. She looked over at her husband and prodded him out of his shocked stoicism, "Robert. Look at his silly face." When Frank's father glanced down and saw his son's glazed expression, and he too (of all people) began to laugh *hard*, pandemonium was unleashed outright among the attendees. Robby fell over, holding his gut as he laughed uncontrollably. Both dogs took this as a signal to lick Frank's face, as they too joined in the family celebration. This just fueled more affectionate laughter from his parents, who were once again pressing close to Frank.

Slowly, everyone began to recover from this interlude of hilarity, and they could now only stare down at Frank on his bed of sagebrush, shaking their heads. Robby, standing beside him, was joyous and he continued to smile at him. He summed up the moment with one of his comic voices, *"That's my little brother."* Those adoring and relieved expressions poured down upon Frank until he was finally able to smile back and engage each of them.

❋ ❋ ❋

That final image of happy faces was something he would not soon forget. It was only when his mother reached down to lift his shoulders and try to sit him upright, that his vision of the faces blurred. He began to concentrate only on the voice which urgently coaxed, "C'mon Frank, let's get up . . . *C'mon, let's go*". And, as he struggled to pull himself up, he realized he was in his favorite leather chair and ottoman, and the voice encouraging him to get up belonged to his wife, Cherice. "C'mon Frank . . . Come to bed. We have to get started early tomorrow."

❋ ❋ ❋

Those detailed images from his dream were hard to shake the next morning . . . How many years had passed since his family was together? And Robby . . . My God! His happy boyhood face had been only inches away from where Frank rested atop that bed of sage. At once he was overcome by the returning weight of his brother's brilliant, yet abbreviated legacy. Frank remembered the exact moment when a controlling portion of his own heart (devoted only to his brother) had withdrawn forever behind its fortress gate. That had been the start of his years-long journey into the world of wounded others.

❋ ❋ ❋

Entirely unprotected this morning, Frank fell once again into his conjured recollection of when he knew for certain that Robby was gone. The image of his brother's face in that memory was very different from the face he had seen in last night's dream. A lifetime ago, so it seemed, he had been trapped in that eternal instant, and it had been only a coincidence that the passage of time saved him while on his distracted path to becoming a man . . .

Frank was startled when Cherice's voice interrupted his thoughts, "Honey, *are you still shaving?* C'mon. I'm going to make my lunch, but after that we need to get going." He quickly pulled himself together when he remembered that he was riding to work with his wife today.

❋ ❋ ❋

Now, sitting shotgun in her car, he wasn't questioning the superfluous car ride (so his wife's hair and makeup might remain *perfect*), in lieu of choosing a jog or a bike ride to work. Instead, Frank found himself staring at his wife as she veered aggressively in and out of San Francisco traffic. He was thinking about his mother's litmus test in the dream which judged the suitability of a prospective *bride*. He understood on some level that his rural upbringing, where he was safe within his mother's balanced sphere of existence, had not adequately prepared him for life shared with modern women—particularly, women who ran in packs *(city women)* defied his comprehension altogether. Frank wondered now if his mother would have concluded that Cherice was a good choice for her son? Specifically, would she have been moved to determine that his wife was the type of mother capable of *abandoning her children*?

Cherice was obviously adept at deflecting public questions about having children, but why? He knew that her experiences in her own family had been awful; a despotic father, looming over a terrorized mother had left a mark. Would that reality have been sufficient to earn her an exemption in the eyes of Frank's mother? Or was the litmus test simply graded pass/fail? . . . If a prospective bride was judged capable of abandoning her children for any reason (even in the face of compelling environmental history), could Cherice have earned his mother's approval?

These questions were of course academic in the setting of the current life which Frank and his wife had built for themselves. But this morning, in the aftermath of his dream, he wondered generally to himself what his mother might have concluded about Cherice?

❀ ❀ ❀

At this juncture, Cherice looked over and realized that Frank had been staring at her, and she tilted her head, "You're kinda quiet this morning . . . One too many cocktails last night?" Before Frank could say anything, she usurped his turn, "Busy day today . . . I've got so much to do before tomorrow's meetings," and she elaborated in protracted detail about that. The couple soon enough departed the car, and then navigated through a full parking garage toward the elevators which would deliver them to their offices.

After a quick peck on the cheek from his wife (who immediately wiped off her lipstick), she said, "Love you. See you tonight." From the open elevator door, Frank watched her leave, heels clicking, and then he turned to go his separate way.

# 2

# ICARUS SAN FRANCISCO

The real differences between the couple seemed much less problematic back in 1999, when Frank McClelland was barely settled into the offices of Icarus Wealth Management. He and Cherice had been irresistibly drawn to each other in the rich cloud of pheromone ether that enveloped them anytime they got too close. Then, way too quickly, and with zero due diligence on behalf of either victim, they went straight to bed and did not look up again until sometime after their marriage.

Those events were much celebrated among their mostly male co-workers, and Frank achieved a kind of cult status among them when he became the guy who finally "nailed" the celestial flirt, Cherice. She was assistant to Larry Sewell, director of fixed income for Icarus, and office conversations would stop dead whenever she glided among the brokers to deliver one thing or another from Larry's office. Frank began hearing greetings of, "Hey Franko!" as he arrived to work, mostly from men whom he didn't yet know.

Previous to that, he had only been on the office radar as a worrisome outlier, and nobody could yet imagine that he might someday be the lasting foil to their party. "*Why is he here?*" they had asked. Everyone was still beating their chests in the era of Private Placement investments and Corporate Bonds, underwritten for mostly pie-in-the-sky Silicon Valley companies, scratching for funding to take them to some next imaginary level. It truly was an amazing juncture in history; nobody seemed to apply any historical context to *value* during those days, when even the stocks of legitimate companies reached price/earnings ratios of 1:200, and the rest of them had no real *earnings* at all. Who needed evidence of enterprise involving bricks and mortar (which was universally scorned as antiquated), nor even any reasonable perspective that those same companies might not be just moments away from going collectively down in flames?

## THE OUTSIDER

Who was this guy then, who came from East Jesus (Elko, Nevada?), where he made a name for himself as an analyst to the miners Newmont and Barrick in the remote and somnolent world of Commodities and Materials? Why should that qualify him here? And why would Icarus C-Suite Administrators decide to locate him on this floor at this precise moment, right in the middle of all these sales Superstars? He didn't even have sales experience! Certainly, he would prove to be just another novelty du jour, right?

In fact, when Larry Sewell introduced him, the audience was beyond dumbfounded to hear of Frank's path through Mining and Minerals at the University of Nevada's Mackay School of Mines, before his transfer to Stanford for an MBA. They were told about his arcane thesis (which Larry described as "celebrated"), involving something to do with ". . . the divergence of supply-side behavior within the Baltic Dry Freight Index in response to sovereign dumping of raw materials (principally by China) onto world markets."

After resisting a collective urge to stab forks in their eyes, the consensus reached in the audience that day was that the only people who were arguably bigger geeks than *techies* were *geologists*. How in the hell could you go to Stanford during that era, where students were literally inventing the internet in their dorm rooms, and have none of that stick to you?

But they were wrong about that too. Those presumptions shared about Frank's time at Stanford missed the mark completely. He was actually fascinated by a vision of the future possibilities surrounding online stock trading and the instantaneous making of markets, as well as free-flowing access to market research from sources that were yet to be invented. He had long before concluded that you can't really know anything about a publicly traded company if you have to wait for a month to study its chart in the next hard-bound issue of *The Lipper Manual!*

## STANFORD SCHOOL OF BUSINESS

Early on, Frank sought out those celebrated campus geniuses and their equally-deranged friends (many of whom had dropped out of school), and he hung with them during his every spare moment in and around Palo Alto. They were energized, and tons of fun. He often bought them as many beers and shots as he could afford, and vice versa, as the kind of euphoria which then surrounded Stanford's tech cohort made for some legendary parties.

Frank never really understood the persistent social stigma that *'geeks'* endured. Certainly, they were getting laid regularly, and partly because of his association with them, he was getting laid too (an epic sidebar considering his rural origins). He was drawn to them because it's just a fact of life that the smartest inhabitants on the planet are always the funniest (and yes, often the most tortured), and virtually all of the young men and women running in those circles fit nicely somewhere within that phenomenon.

※ ※ ※

Central to Frank's place and purview among them, he remained a devoted scholar of the reality that there exists in the world huge institutional control of money. So, from his earliest days among those Stanford friends, he knew without question that their two worlds were on a collision course of tectonic proportions. Those networks, systems and programs that they were inventing in their dorm rooms were destined to be at some future epicenter of change within his world of finance, especially given the empirical truth that *timing* and *execution* are everything in wealth accumulation.

※ ※ ※

Inevitably (as anticipated by Frank), the US Tech world began its historic free-fall shortly after his arrival in San Francisco. This collapse was poised to begin at almost the exact moment when his pivotal Icarus co-workers had suspended their judgments of him. He was actually a lot more fun than they had originally thought, and some were even saying that this *fun* reached a kind of critical mass when he drank whiskey, which revealed a striking alter ego.

Such displays were rare however, and Frank was mostly still thought of as shy or sullen as he went about his work. In fact (to Cherice's growing disappointment), he did not share her attraction to the spotlight at all; while she sought out the flowing adoration from everybody in social gatherings, he preferred to travel the outer borders of the rooms, silent and unseen.

Worst of all, and to Cherice's absolute dejection, she realized too late that he almost never wanted to dance with her. From those earliest moments together, this was unforgivable and ultimately insurmountable in their world of differences. He joked meanwhile that Cherice could find a karaoke microphone within a square mile of wherever she stood, and then be the first on the list to sing, regardless of who was listening. She was fearless, with a beautiful voice during any rendition, but whenever she and her friends looked around with some conspiratory plan to force Frank up onto the stage to join them, he would by then have mysteriously vanished.

## THE DOT COM CRASH

Alas, any hopes of growing friendship with his co-workers were short-lived, as trillions of dollars worth of equity started to evaporate from the markets comprised mostly of technology companies. Between 2000 and 2002, the NASDAQ alone fell 78 percent. The landscape within Icarus Wealth Management soon changed dramatically; it began with firings. Venture Capitalists in Silicon Valley had long since sold their positions and disappeared (as they always do), and by then nobody else wanted any part of second-tier financing, or the ridiculous corporate bond offerings that were tied to this folly.

So in all, ninety brokers and their staff eventually exited the San Francisco division, and a river of suits carrying cardboard boxes full of family photos and Bay Area sports memorabilia poured out through the doors of Icarus. Of course, thousands of brokerage jobs also disappeared around the country as nearly forty-eight hundred companies within the Silicon Valley either vanished, or were acquired for a song by bigger entities. The commercial and industrial real estate of Santa Clara, Sunnyvale and Cupertino soon shared a ghost town transformation.

❀ ❀ ❀

The burst market bubble of that era and the changes it brought to Icarus overwhelmed Cherice, to say the least. Virtually all of her friends disappeared overnight, and she watched while many of her girlfriends were forced to seek marginal employment in places located well outside of the expensive Bay Area. She frequently became sad (even weepy) during those changes, but she felt that she needed to hide her reaction from her husband and her boss; both of them had remained so characteristically stoic.

Nobody among the original office brokers who had formed the tech bond pyramid saw this coming. Only Larry Sewell had once hinted to Cherice that "Market cycles wax and wane," and it therefore would be prudent to "'. . . re-collect ourselves from time to time around those things that are real.'"

Stranger still, Larry had also observed cryptically to her, "We only appreciate what is real in our lives when we stand before the abyss . . ." Those quotes from her boss, usually as he was gazing out through his windows far above the San Francisco landscape, could not have seemed more random to her, especially considering how much fun everyone else had been having around the office . . .

❀ ❀ ❀

As the weeks went by however, Cherice found some much-needed solace in this world when Frank emerged as a leader in the new company hierarchy. She observed him thereafter re-directing the work, and educating en masse to a more traditional brokerage hybrid, which had become Icarus San Francisco. To Cherice's amazement, her husband moved into a nice office (closer to her and Larry), where she could sometimes steal kisses during those rare moments when he wasn't entirely distracted by his work.

And, although she wished he paid more attention to her, she told him often that he was her *'hero'*, and she meant it. He was a rock during those frightening times which reminded her so much of her childhood, when she and her mother were uprooted repeatedly to follow her father's Army career at military bases around the world. In each of those new locations, they had moved into yet another military house that looked eerily like the last one.

### THE MARINA DISTRICT

Frank and Cherice soon found themselves positioned to benefit financially in a brief window of time following the Tech Industry collapse. San Francisco's real estate values had always remained famously impervious to market disruptions, but for an instant in the Spring of 2001, they faltered just enough to allow the couple to buy a nice little place in the Marina District. It was really nothing like the huge estate homes that surrounded them (mostly owned by San Francisco's *Old Money*). In fact, it was just a zero lot-line home, but it had a lot of nice Spanish architectural touches, including tiled-roof dormers and wrought-iron railings that surrounded long window boxes full of overflowing Bougainvillea.

Best of all, the house had a roof-top patio, accessible from the living room, and with the home's loftier street location, it provided a truly breathtaking view of the Bay. The house had escaped, along with every other house on the street, any serious damage during the 1989 Loma Prieta Earthquake; the theory among some of the older neighbors regarding that terrifying event, was that the street had been built atop a hillside ridge of stratified rock (rare in San Francisco).

This idea comforted Frank, owing to his geologist training, and it somewhat mitigated his occasional panic attacks about the price tag that came with his new home. He of course, always felt he needed to overreach when trying to impress his wife, and the purchase was just the most dramatic example of that to date.

### INVESTMENT ACUMEN

Frank's decision to buy the home had been correctly based on his expectation that gold was just beginning a multi-year liftoff, and he was positioned perfectly for that. In fact, the price of gold per ounce did move up from the mid $200's in the year 2000, to the low $500's by 2005. Of course, the horrible World Trade Center attacks on September 11 had been the pivotal event that spiked gold even higher, and Frank's grief for two friends lost that day (at Cantor Fitzgerald) turned his prediction into a very bitter pill.

In spite of his regrets, the exponential growth of Nevada's biggest mines (Barrick and Newmont) was also inevitable, and together they helped to nearly triple his holdings during that period. At times, he marveled that only he and maybe twenty other people in the world could fully quantify the scale of the mines being developed around Carlin and Elko—Newmont's *Carlin* mine would become the fifth largest in the world, while Barrick's *Cortez* and *Goldstrike* mines would grow to become sixth and seventh largest respectively, solidly establishing Nevada's prominence in world markets. During that period, Barrick would emerge as the world's largest mining company.

❁ ❁ ❁

Frank often thought about his destiny as it had unfolded, especially considering all of the inexplicable reasons why he had benefitted on his singular path. He also frequently marveled at the surreal life which he now found himself living in San Francisco, where the crowds and the pace of the city (to this day) mostly left him unable to reconcile memories of his lost family and their ranch, high above the Reese River Valley near Austin, Nevada.

It was during those times that he could still remember his mother's kitchen, steaming and full with the aromas of her Basque dinners; she would spend hours preparing pots of red beans, meant to accompany the slow-roasted lamb that was basted in her famous Vizcaina Sauce, rich with red choricero peppers. He especially loved helping during the preparation, when he was asked to stir the caramelized onions inside her huge cast iron skillet, to be commingled (as always) with a mountain of chopped Nevada garlic. All of this would be shared during loud and happy gatherings with Fallon friends and family. Those memories were maybe the only ones that still kept him grounded in this faraway place.

### HAVING TO BELIEVE

The couple eventually arrived at something resembling a honeymoon stage in their marriage, and Frank grew hopeful when his wife immersed herself into redecorating the rooms. Her dejection (even depression) following the profound changes at Icarus did not go unnoticed, and it weighed upon him. Even though their lovemaking had changed over the months (for the better he thought) to something more connected and more deeply intimate, he understood viscerally that he alone could never rescue her from her isolation.

He felt that her sadness was tied to the disintegration of a social life which had been essential to her, and he was certain that he possessed none of the skills which might save her. She truly had belonged among those kinetic personalities of her past. Happy hours and after-work celebrations on Friday nights were few and far between now, and networking with her girlfriends in the great wine bars of The Embarcadero, or clothes shopping in excited groups around San Francisco had all but disappeared from her life.

❁ ❁ ❁

So it came as good news when Cherice took up jogging, and more and more she was dressing the part along the paths that wove through the bayfront park beneath their home. People regularly did double takes when she and Frank passed by, because they truly were a stunning couple. He often rode his bike beside her and there they learned to laugh together, especially on weekends, when they found themselves mixing with the circus of people that only San Francisco can assemble; that's when neighbors came out of the woodwork to fly their kites, or throw Frisbees and play with their happy dogs. Pipes full of Humboldt County flower were lighted among these gypsies, and the pungent cannabis clouds enveloped Frank and Cherice in more than a contact high.

There amidst the guitars and Deadheads (who still twirled in the music), the young marrieds felt amused and energized. Here they had become part of the constant amalgam of San Francisco humanity. Even on the foggiest days of summer, they were grateful to be there and to be together.

## ZINFANDEL

Favorite among their routines was to end up somewhere on a beach near Crissy Field, where they could unfold a blanket and spread out their treasures purchased from a nearby Molly Stone's Market. They often brought cheeses or pate`s to spread upon crackers, accompanied by kalamata olives and almonds. Or sometimes, maybe just a deli sandwich, or a salad that was split between the two of them would suffice.

Of course, central and ever present during any of these outings would be one amazing bottle of California wine or another; spirits which Frank found he was starting to love *way* more than he anticipated. True to his humble beginnings however, he discovered during this period (when almost nobody else could bravely agree with him), that he preferred the less expensive Zinfandels and White Barberas that were emerging from the hotter, dryer hills of Amador County; those fruit-forward varietals quickly led him to grow indifferent to the mass-marketed staples of Napa and Sonoma.

He even came to believe that the popular culture of California was forever stuck in its maya of prestige—both in the cars that they drove and in the *Chardonnays* that they pressured one another to drink. And he knew it was just a sad and inescapable trap. How could these people not appreciate, even on some artistic level, that (with a few notable exceptions) there can be no linear relationship between the *cost* of the wine and the *quality* of the wine?

He was thus conflicted between his urge to go forth to shout the rude truth, and his restraint and ultimate gratitude that these legions of people were not driving their expensive cars up *Shenandoah Valley Road* to his favorite wineries. Surely, he just needed to shut his mouth, and keep the secret to himself for as long as possible.

❊ ❊ ❊

So, amidst this backdrop, Frank and Cherice would bask in those beautiful hours—crafted in equal parts by the glow of their wine buzz and the abundant endorphins which still coursed through them following exercise. This allowed them to just sit quietly, him studying the sailboats while she stared at the Golden Gate Bridge, and their relationship (as Frank believed) appeared to be working.

During those same times he might say, "This is nice," and she might whisper back, "I know . . ." Inevitably, however, when she reached over to take Frank's hand in those moments, her eyes would remain transfixed on the taillights heading north toward Sausalito . . .

# 3

# HANK

Frank could easily lose himself in his work, but his wife could not. Cherice's boredom and distraction increasingly spilled over into their time together at home, which secretly broke his heart. His recourse was to withdraw for as long as necessary to give her the space that she seemed to want. During intervals when her bitterness spilled over, Frank mostly turned inward to indict his own failings; he knew that he wasn't good at inventing a social life in San Francisco, and he blamed himself for not being what his wife needed.

✽ ✽ ✽

Amidst the changes at work, many new (and very different) brokers began to claim the abandoned cubicles on the brokerage floor. Cherice was sure they were a lot older as a group than the previous brokers—there certainly was more gray hair visible in the workplace, and phone conversations were quieter and more concise. It was just quieter everywhere, and interestingly, it seemed hard to find evidence that any of these brokers were cold-calling or pitching anything new to strangers.

Of the numerous calls she overheard, she was able to conclude that the clients on the phone lines had long-established relationships with these brokers; there was lots of banter about alumni events, and so-and-so in college, or kids and grandchildren coming to visit. These were old stories, being shared by old friends.

By then, office language had morphed into subjects that included hard currencies (gold and silver) and their miners, as well as the dollar trade, sovereign and institutional debt, the yield curve, and of course, US Treasuries. At times, it felt to Cherice that she had been transported to a foreign country which spoke a strange dialect that she couldn't fully understand, and she felt more isolated at work than ever before.

❀ ❀ ❀

Certainly, because of these changes, Frank was feeling comfortable among the more classic brokers who had claimed their territory at Icarus. One of the recent additions to the brokerage, a relaxed and funny guy named Henry (Hank) Richman, seemed to have been on a mission from the start to introduce himself to Frank. Within moments of their first meeting he asked, "Aren't you that kid who upset the apple cart with your *Baltic Freight* thing?" Frank smirked and said, "Guilty."

Hank deadpanned, "I have to work a hell of lot harder now that you dropped that bomb on us," and he winked. Frank feigned confusion, "Oh? How so?" The old broker waded in, "It used to be that A plus B equals C when I described commodities to my clients; now A plus B has to go through your goddamn meat grinder, and I need to explain why C doesn't add up anymore."

"Come on, *it's not that hard,*" Frank countered, "If A is the pork, and B is the spice, then you just add one more spice. I promise, it still gives you sausage!" Hank conceded as he jabbed back at Frank, "Does it have to be pork? I'm Jewish!" Both of them were grateful for the icebreaker, because truth be known, they were hoping for friendship here.

Frank recognized that Hank was smart, and his razor-sharp humor reflected it. There is often a fine line for that kind of humor to be perceived as respectful (which it certainly was), and it therefore also appealed to many of the other brokers. Hank was nothing if not kind, and those early interactions were contagious, eventually forging what would become known as the *Hank and Frank Show*. Their growing public friendship and road show around the office soon made for a lighter atmosphere, which endured for some time at Icarus.

## THE GOLDMAN DAYS

Hank had "made a little money" during his years with Goldman Sachs in New York, and Frank could tell that he had truly been in the mix during the emergence of the blue chip stocks of that era. This was particularly true with the dominance of the Nifty Fifty stocks of the 60's and 70's. Frank listened as raptly as any young finance student to the firsthand history which Hank shared; he was a great storyteller, and Frank hung on every word.

Inevitably though, Hank always seemed to turn the questions back around to his young friend. Frank was certain that his own brief experience in finance was (for some reason) important to Hank. There were many questions about Frank's theories regarding "wealth preservation and management," as well as a focus on his ideas pertaining to "gold as a hedge," and there were broader questions about his "models" for trading commodities or equities.

Frank, who liked to fly under the radar where his more esoteric theories were concerned, felt confident that Hank would understand them when hearing them. So (if prompted), he would share his calculus. He had recently elaborated, "I've been looking at some work by Robert Schiller, who has theories about cyclically adjusted price/earnings ratios; he uses long-term bond rates to discount market valuations, and it looks like he predicted the Dot-Com Crash using this model. It's simple really, but disruptive at the same time; people are referring to it now as *CAPE*."

"Schiller has more recently turned his focus to the housing market; he just wrote about it in the *Wall Street Journal*, and honestly, it's kind of scary." When Hank produced one of those small notepads from his pocket and scribbled on it with a golf scorecard pencil, Frank was surprised. He was always flattered by the legitimacy that his experienced friend bestowed upon him, but he was also curious about why Hank's questions were so fucking comprehensive; the two of them were just shooting the shit, *right?*

### GIANTS BASEBALL

Happily, it wasn't all business. Hank was a huge Giants fan, dating back to when he was a kid in New York. There, he had listened to his father and his uncles talk endlessly about those great old New York rivalries between the Giants, Yankees, and Dodgers. After watching baseball for years at Candlestick Park (where I froze my ass off) during the Mays and McCovey era, he finally scored a pair of season tickets to Giants games in 2000, when the new PacBell Park opened in San Francisco. They were good seats too, which Frank soon confirmed when Hank started asking him to join him at the games.

Situated above the infield in the Club Level of the second deck (section 219 near the railing), the Giants' dugout was just below them to the left; Frank was told the first time he tagged along, "Bring your glove, because a lot of foul balls end up there." Hank had renewed the tickets every year since, even though his wife Margaret couldn't join him very often these days, following some tough knee surgeries. So, it seemed natural when Hank regularly offered both tickets to Frank and Cherice (at face value, of course), "That way I can help Margaret a little more around the house, and not throw money away on these expensive goddamn tickets."

❀ ❀ ❀

It took a while to convince Cherice to come to a game, however. At first she absently protested, "Watching baseball is like watching paint dry," but from the first time she stepped into that beautiful stadium and heard the electric cheering of 42,000 crazed fans, she was hooked; emotions run high for Giants' fans in that ballpark (especially when the Dodgers come to town), and from the very beginning, that energy appealed to her on a level she could not have anticipated.

She felt at home in the stadium. She loved the fans dressed in their Giants jerseys and hats, with their beaded necklaces and lanyards covered with pins, and especially the outrageous ensembles of orange and black that the more creative fans wore. It didn't take her long to come up to speed with her own stadium attire. She found a *perfect* black baseball cap at a boutique in Los Gatos which displayed the SF logo in dark orange Swarovski Crystals, and she rocked-it when she pulled her ponytail (with blond highlights) through its open clasp in the back.

Together with her Ray-Bans, some gold loop earrings, and an expert application of lip gloss, she scored a style homerun with everyone who saw her. Within only a few weeks, she decided that she needed a J.T. Snow jersey, not because the Giants' first baseman was a multi-year National League All-Star, but because, "He has such a great ass." Of course, the jersey she chose was a little too tight across her chest, and with the top button left open, her striking look was unforgettable whenever she traveled around the ballpark.

❁ ❁ ❁

To Frank, it was incidental that Cherice rarely sat for long in her assigned seat—she had befriended Tina who, together with her husband Dan, owned the two adjacent seats in section 219. The new friends would frequently abandon their husbands early in the games to resume extensive travels around the stadium. Frank was actually relieved at this, because he was increasingly focused on the pitching strategies as games progressed; Cherice was clearly a distraction to that.

### ROVING CAMERAS

As this routine played itself forward through the weeks ahead, it was evident that Cherice had somehow become the darling of the roving cameramen who covered fans during Giants' home games. She always seemed to be caught on the Bay Area Sports Network cameras, while jumping up and down in celebration at various locations around the stadium. Those close-up video shots would inevitably appear as a live-feed on the massive Jumbotron, located behind center field.

Dan eventually commented, "Cherice must hold some kind of stadium record for live appearances on that screen." Frank would later reflect back on this time, together with unfolding changes at Icarus, as the start of Cherice's return to her preferred social existence. He knew deep down that she had stayed with him as a flight to safety following the Dot-Com Crash, but those days were quickly receding.

## THE MORTGAGES

At the same time, products being offered within US brokerages began to change dramatically, as increased emphasis was shifting to mortgage products. Mortgage Backed Securities had been around for a long time, but they had forever been too pedestrian for most brokers. When home loans tripled through 2006, however, due to the low interest rates ("artificially low so the Bushies can pay for their war in Iraq" according to Hank), institutions started bundling those loans with others that were a lot riskier.

The industry began pushing CDO's (Collateralized Debt Obligations)—they could be sold with the lure of higher returns on investment, given the rationale that risk was diluted when spread out over a larger number of mortgages. That phenomenon substantially ratcheted up enthusiasm around Icarus. Hank from the start did not embrace this new direction, and Frank agreed. "Don't get me wrong," Hank observed, "people are going to make a hell of lot of money here, but this will become froth, and it cannot end well."

※ ※ ※

It was sometime later that Larry Sewell called Frank into his office and asked him to sit down. He began, "This mortgage thing is pretty amazing, huh? I can see in your always excellent reports (smiling at Frank) that the significance of this trend has not escaped you." Frank was sober, "It's hard to ignore . . ." Larry continued, "This thing is now sweeping the country, and management at Icarus are making it clear that they want us to run with the industry leaders on this. So like it or not Frank, we have to set a new course to highlight the mortgages."

What he had to say next was harder, "Frank, I'm bringing in someone new . . . a guy named Travis Whitsome. He's number two in mortgage securitization at Lehman Brothers, and you probably already know that Lehman has become the top US underwriter of CDO's. That lead is widening as more and more of those funds are layered with sub-prime loans."

Larry continued, "We feel lucky to have gotten him, actually. He's been at the leading edge of this thing in New York, where he apparently got stuck behind some guy at headquarters who's in there like a fat rat. He wants to be number one somewhere—you'll see, he's that kind of a personality." Cautiously, Larry glanced at Frank and tried to reassure him, "Nothing changes here for you Frank; you're the smartest broker I know, so our office chain of command will stay the same. We especially need you to hold everything together while Travis builds Icarus a new revved-up mortgage division."

※ ※ ※

It got quiet for a moment as Frank took it all in, and Larry added finally, "He's bringing three guys with him so he can hit the ground running once he gets to San Francisco, and I'm sorry, but that means we will have to move some of the fixed-income guys out to give these mortgage guys a spot." When Frank glanced up, Larry immediately headed him off, "Don't worry! We're keeping Hank. He's great for morale around here, and we're going to need plenty of that to get through these changes."

Larry smiled cautiously at Frank, "But, I have to tell you . . . if these things take off like I think they will, others out there are gonna have to leave as well." Then, as an afterthought, "Oh! . . . I almost forgot . . . I told Cherice earlier today to get on the phone and see if she can find a few of her girlfriends who worked here during the Dot-Com days; it will be helpful with the new guys coming in, and those girls fit in great back when we were more about direct sales. Jesus, for a minute there I thought she was going to cry!"

When the meeting ended and Frank walked out into the atrium, he was charged by an exultant version of his wife, "Oh my God! . . . Did he tell you?! *I get to recruit my girls back to Icarus!!*"

## WHISKEY

Frank eventually escaped his wife's clutches, where he recognized that her mind was racing with possibilities (her eyes could not focus on his), and he then went straight out to Hank's desk. He stood there for a moment, staring down at him. When Hank looked up, he was struck by the seriousness of his young friend's gaze. Frank then snapped to attention and said, "Come on, let's get out of here. I need a drink." Hank blinked and finally grinned, "Well, you're the boss."

They took Hank's car, because Frank had ridden his bike to work, and they drove to an Irish bar on Mark Street. Both men were comfortable here, framed by old walnut wainscoting and Celtic glass window. The Bank had good bar food specials listed daily on a chalkboard, along with many excellent Irish and Scottish whiskey choices.

Hank studied his young friend throughout the process of ordering drinks, while Frank stared straight ahead, hands clasped. He seemed to be searching for the words that he would use next. Finally, Hank raised his whiskey glass and toasted, "Schlange" toward his serious friend; it was his preferred toast in this establishment, which amused Frank to no end, considering the New York Jewish accent that delivered it. They both took big first swigs, then Hank inquired, "So, what gives, Slick?"

❈ ❈ ❈

Frank breathed deep and began, "Icarus is going all-in with the sub-prime mortgages." At this, Hank froze in place. Frank looked at him and continued, "Yeah, they're even bringing in a guy from Lehman New York, along with some of his buddies; they want to start pushing the same shit that Lehman has been selling in their CDO's. Are you still following this cluster fuck? Everything Lehman is pushing now is basically shit, and to make matters worse, they're now loading them up with adjustable rate mortgages which will reset sometime next year. That will mean significantly higher mortgage payments for the people who can least afford them."

"Did you read Robert Schiller's op-ed piece in the *Wall Street Journal?* He said there is now 'significant risk in the housing market, and it could threaten the world banks!' That was last month Hank, and it's only getting worse! I put a calculator to this thing, and nothing about it is sustainable. Nobody I talk to knows how the fuck they're getting the ratings on these things that they are: Most of the CDO's are being sold as Triple-A. It's a disconnected mess!"

❊ ❊ ❊

Hank kept quiet, wanting to hear more before speaking. Frank looked at his friend and more carefully proceeded, "And, Hank . . . Larry told me today that he's gonna let some of the fixed income brokers go, so he can make room for these new guys from New York. He said he'll keep letting them go, so long as the mortgage business grows." Now searching Hank's face he continued, "I'm worried about you, my friend."

Still waiting for Hank's reaction, "I'd be lying to you if I told you that I think this is going to end well for *any* of us, but in the interim . . . I see big changes coming for the brokers, and that will most likely include *you*." He continued, "When I came here at the end of the Dot-Com run-up, the garbage that those quadrupeds were selling was disgraceful; there was literally nothing in those bonds to hang your hat on, so now I'm not even sure that I can be a part of what's about to happen again at Icarus."

"This is going to be worse than the last crash, Hank . . . much worse! I keep seeing that it has the potential to destroy the world credit markets, and you know better than anyone, that outcome will end with people standing in soup lines." Frank took another deep drink, and stared down at his hands.

# 4

## HANK'S PITCH

Hank's reaction could not possibly have been anticipated by his troubled friend, as he first chuckled and then shook his head. He began to speak, "My God, you are such a *dinosaur*! Where the hell did you say you were from?" Frank, stupefied, looked over at him. Hank reached out quickly to place a hand on his friend's shoulder, "Sorry," he laughed. "I *do* mean that as my highest compliment, so just hear me out."

Then he smiled and continued, "You truly are not in this for the money, are you? That absolutely amazes me, considering everything I assume about your generation. In fact, you remind me of guys I worked with in the 1960's. Back then, it was enough to just be financial advisors on Wall Street, you know? Do the best we could for our clients, and maybe even make some friends along the way."

"We'd get together on the weekends for barbeques and pool parties. The wives were always in tow. It was a great era with great drinks, and if it so happened that we benefitted from the trends that we saw at work, and maybe even grew our own investments . . . well, that was great too. Of course, nothing we sold back then was exotic, so we just hung in there year after year, and the world was real . . . But now . . . who the fuck knows?"

❀ ❀ ❀

He turned to Frank to study his eyes. "Frank, I am much too late with this, and I'm *truly sorry* if you think I have betrayed your trust in some way. I have a confession to make (searching now), and God help me, I should have told you this a long time ago. It just kept getting more complicated." *"Jesus!"* Frank interrupted, "You're freaking me out! *Will you just fucking say it?!"*

So, Hank did exactly that, "I work for someone else, Frank." He then stopped to let that sink in. "I mean . . . I am employed at Icarus, but I am only there for the purpose of scouting you. That's all." Pausing again at seeing Frank's abject confusion, he continued, "The person I actually work for, who is my oldest and dearest friend in the world, wanted me to confirm that you are *real*. And when he first talked me into this caper, I was pretty damn sure he had already made up his mind about that."

Both men paused and stared at each other for a moment. Frank, not fully oriented to the change in direction, spoke first, "How can this guy possibly know anything about me? That's just *crazy* Hank." The old broker continued, "He's big time connected-up at Stanford . . . knows your professors even. He knows everybody there for God's sake."

"It started when you published your *Baltic Freight Thesis*, and he has been following you ever since—starting back in your analyst days for Newmont and Barrick." Frank was reeling, "So . . . you're what, a *headhunter?*" Hank bristled a bit, *"No!* That's not it at all . . . well, not as a *going concern* anyway. I'm just his friend. *Aw shit*, Frank! Given what you just told me about the changes at Icarus . . . *especially now* . . . I know that it's time for you to meet Bill. He wants you to work for him."

## THE BENNETT COMPANY

This was one of those moments when a man's presumed reality shatters under the weight of an unforeseen revelation. When he can only *hope* amidst the crashing shards around him that he won't be laid bare for everyone to see in the moments that follow. The male ego hates to appear dumbfounded; the center stage vulnerability of such a moment is just never comfortable for a practiced and cool exterior. As this new reality assumed control, Frank tried in earnest to keep his poker face, and he failed miserably.

❦ ❦ ❦

Hank stared back at him and finally broke the silence, "His name is Bill Bennett, and we worked together for years at Goldman Sachs. From the start, Bill was on a whole different trajectory than me . . . couldn't help but be. He was brilliant and charismatic and handsome. He still is, except he's getting old . . . like *me*," Hank grinned at his drink. "We became friends for some reason, probably because we got each other's jokes. I was actually content to be the comic relief as long as we stuck together. *God* we had fun back then!"

"It was obvious though, that Bill was being groomed for a top spot at Goldman. He eventually became their head of Private Banking, which threw him into the deep end among their network of wealthy clients all around the world. He made a lot of money over the next twenty years . . . I mean, *A Lot of Money*. In the middle of that, Goldman made him a partner."

Hank glanced at his riveted friend and continued, "Then, by the early 1980's, Bill was about done with those silly egos of the rich and famous, so he let it be known that he wanted to ease himself out of the day-to-day at Goldman . . . and maybe even move back to California. That's where he went to school, and he wanted to pursue some of his own interests."

"You should have heard the *whining* back in New York! Too late for them though—Bill's mind was made up. But, as a last favor to his friends at Goldman, he agreed to oversee one final *little* project for them: The merger of *Gulf Oil* and *Chevron*. Yeah! He wrapped that up in 1984."

❊ ❊ ❊

"It justified his move right away to San Francisco, and a team from Goldman followed him out here—that included *me*, by the way," Hank smiled proudly— "People who speak of that era remember Bill because of his nuances in those early merger contracts, most of them groundbreakers, and to this day they still consider him to be the *'Father of Modern M&A'*. Don't think *that* conclusion didn't get some people's attention out here in the wild west . . ."

"And true to form, after earning the respect of the principals involved, he carved out an equity stake in that newly-merged company—they even asked him to serve on the board of Chevron for a few years to help oversee the changes—Yep, you guessed it . . . *more money!* He married his wife in New York before moving out here, and they have lived happily in the Bay Area ever since . . . She's a wonderful person too . . ."

### THE MONEY

Frank took all of this in, and then finally asked, "You mentioned *interests* . . . What would someone like him pursue in California? He was on top of the financial world, right?" At this, Hank laughed, "Turned out he was interested in technology. Seems he never told anybody in New York about that. So he dabbled out here with private money, a lot of it his own. Of course, he always picked the right things. Then he parlayed that with some friends in Palo Alto; your Stanford alumni connections come to mind here."

"With those friends, he was part of the brain trust that guided Hewlett-Packard during their transition years. Word was, he helped steer them beyond the calculators, and turned their focus to desktops, and then to printers . . ."

Frank was incredulous, and he stumbled with his next question, "So . . . does he still *work?*" Hank, amused, answered, "Well, of course he still works! . . . as much as is required to manage those holdings, which are *enormous,* as I can see you now understand. I will quote Mick Jagger here: 'Managing money is a full-time job'." Hank seemed to still be marveling as he shared this story about his friend.

Frank carefully asked, "How much . . . I mean . . . How much is a guy like that worth?" To which, Hank enunciated in slo-mo, "Hun-dreds (implying hundreds of millions of dollars)." Hank then offered, "He's been backing off though, over the past few years. That's got everything to do with my questions to you about preservation of wealth. Once again Frank, I am so sorry that I waited this long to tell you. I can say that he and his wife Marion have recently moved $50 million or so over to create a charitable foundation, but beyond that, I don't know the details.

❉ ❉ ❉

Marion got to know Lucile Packard very well over the years, and she talks about that as being life-changing for her. She was very much influenced by Lucile's vision of philanthropy. The Children's Hospital at Stanford? . . . That's all Lucile Packard, as I'm sure you must know. And her lead was a good fit for Marion and Bill. Together they've become long-time benefactors to a lot of San Francisco causes. Up until now, that's been mostly within the arts, as it has been for years: She likes the Museum of Modern Art . . . He likes Davies Symphony Hall, and I'm sure there are many other causes private to them both.

They are extremely visible in The City, which is no doubt why he wanted me to do the groundwork on you when it came to getting your story. Bill likes to fly under the radar in his business dealings whenever possible, and I don't blame him for that. Now, Goddammit! Look at me! I've got such a big mouth. I know him, and these are all things that I am certain he will want to tell you himself, in his own way, and in due time. And of course, he *will* tell you everything. That is . . . if you're interested."

❉ ❉ ❉

The two men sat still for a long while. Hank was relieved to finally get this off his chest, and Frank was absolutely paralyzed to speak. By now they were both deep into their second drinks, for which Frank was grateful, given this day and his whipsaw participation in it. Hank finally broke the silence, "I know this is huge pal, and I also know that changes of this magnitude don't occur in a vacuum; this certainly has got to involve input from your wife. So, I'll just ask you to think about it for a bit . . . Talk things over, and only when you know you're good and ready . . . only *then* will we introduce you to Bill."

"That being said, let me tell you one more thing, and I hope you will take it to heart. Do you remember when I said I could see that you aren't in this for the money? Well, I meant that on an existential level which has always eluded me personally. Please consider that the only other person in the world about whom I can make that statement, after five decades in this industry by the way, is Bill. You probably believe that it cannot be possible, especially considering everything I just told you about him, but it's the God's truth: He absolutely is a force of nature, and money is not what drives him . . ."

## AFTERSHOCK

The ride home in Hank's car seemed much too quick for Frank; he knew he was going to need more time to form any kind of reasonable perspective about today's developments—and, what about having no clue *at all* about how to divulge any of this to Cherice?! How could she not feel cut off at the knees in her renewed joy for bringing her girlfriends back to Icarus? Anything he might say would be taken as an impediment to that joy . . . as in, "Here we go again: Frank the buzzkill."

More ominous yet (should he actually decide to leave Icarus), where would that leave them in their marriage? What would be left to hold them together if they no longer worked side by side, especially anticipating Cherice's unbridled return to her previous social life? There was just no way that she could possibly understand any part of what might drive him to make this career change. The couple's realities were now so divergent on these topics, that the two of them might never reconcile the changes.

❊ ❊ ❊

So, as he was utterly consumed by the weight of future days, Frank was glad to discover that he had arrived home before his wife. He thought, when he found himself alone on the deck, that he might actually have some time to *think*. Those hopes were dashed soon after he grabbed a glass of water and collapsed into one of the patio chairs; it was then that he heard his wife open the front door and come breezing in, "Hey! Where did you go today?" she asked when her husband became visible through the living room windows. She laid her purse down and pushed open the screen door to come outside for a smooch, "I have so much to tell you!"

Cherice was obviously still energized from her workday. When she leaned over and kissed Frank on the lips, however, she reeled back and wrinkled her nose, "Whoof! Someone has been drinking on the job!" She wagged her finger at him and said, "You are a bad, bad boy who needs to be punished . . . Oh wait . . . you're the boss," she giggled. Looking at her and searching, Frank offered simply, "Yeah, Hank and I needed to talk about some of the big changes we're going to be seeing at Icarus."

His wife didn't stop for even a second to inquire about those big changes, and she jumped excitedly into her news of the day, "It's just so incredible! I found everyone I was looking for today. My three favorite girls in the world all want to come back to the office! Can you believe it?! Deanna and Carol and Stella are all stuck in jobs that they can't stand! Larry got on the phone with each of them today and said he can start them at double what they're now making."

"Deanna is working at an insurance office in Walnut Creek, and Stella is working somewhere in Vallejo for an accountant . . . Stellz! She's so funny—she told me she had, 'just been thinking about stepping out in front of a bus' when I called. And finally, I found Carol this afternoon at her job in San Jose; she has gone through a *lot* of changes since she worked for us! She's at some Yoga-*slash*-Health food store, where she got certified to be a Life Coach! Isn't that *cool?!* Anyway, she doesn't have a lot of clients for that right now, so she spends way too much time working the cash register, which she hates . . . And can you believe it?! All three of them are coming in to talk with Larry on Friday. Oh my God!" she exclaimed in her entirely delirious state.

### THE GIRLS

Frank remembered all three names, and he considered each one as his wife rattled them off: Deanna was a tall, curly-haired redhead who always wanted to talk about herself; she was nice enough, but aloof, and she never really opened up to him in any meaningful way. Frank had pondered the question (more than a few times) of whether or not she even liked men?

He then recalled some things that Cherice had let slip about Carol Thomas when he met her for the first time: She had fallen for some married guy at a previous job, which eventually broke up his marriage and his family. She did later marry him, but along the way she had some kind of a legal run-in involving embezzlement accusations. The office gossip-line went nuts when word got out that a Grand Jury had been called in.

Frank remembered Carol to be ringleader of the circle of friends who ran with his wife. He thought cynically to himself, "Of course, it's *essential* to have at least one malignant legal question (preferably a felony) on your resume to qualify you as a life coach."

He did remember Stella Marie Andriossi (the name he used when he kidded about her heritage), and he fondly pictured her now: Stellz was a classic . . . A curvy, olive-skinned Italiana and consummate wise-ass from New Jersey, who never minced words about anything. She had a funny swagger too when she was on a roll. And she (like himself) was comfortable with the liberal use of F-bombs as descriptive adjuncts. He also remembered that she spent more time sitting on his desk and flirting than he suspected Cherice had ever been aware of.

In thinking about Stella now, it occurred to him that her humor was kind of like Hank's. Maybe it was that same scathing New York, in-your-face honesty that made conversations with both of them fun and funny in a similar way. In spite of Frank's beyond-overwhelming day, he managed a smile at the thought of seeing Stella again.

❁ ❁ ❁

Once Frank determined that there was no way in hell he was going to talk to Cherice about sub-prime mortgages, nor the unfathomable prospect of future employment with a Bay Area financial legend, the stress of the day dissipated easily into a beautiful evening . . . The San Francisco Bay vistas beyond him added to the effect, and together with the enveloping sunset and a large pitcher of *Sangria* (accented with infused citrus slices), Frank found that he was finally able to relax.

All of this was capped with a surprising alfresco dinner, prepared happily by his wired and chattering wife, and he concluded that he needed more time to gather information about Bill Bennett. Surely, he needed to meet him first before sharing conclusions.

And, what if Frank was just dead wrong about this mortgage protégé coming from Lehman Brothers? Could it be that he was missing some imbedded truth, or not seeing an industry sea change in the world of mortgages? Oh, *fuck no!* That was the Sangria talking. He knew he was right about the mortgages. So, all the better to just focus on the changes ahead; he would sit tight for now and get educated further before speaking about any of this.

❁ ❁ ❁

After clearing the patio table, he grabbed Cherice and stole a kiss as she continued to fly around the kitchen. He whispered, "Thank you" and told her, "Let me get this. Dinner was so amazing and unexpected, and I know you've had a big day; why don't you just get out of the kitchen and go run your bath. I'll take it from here."

She tilted her head at him and smiled, "Aren't you the best? That actually sounds perfect," and she kissed him back. So Frank, now unfettered by today's reality shift, jumped into cleaning up the mess. His wife had never been a disciple of *Julia Child's* mantra, "One should clean while one cooks," but that was okay tonight, because Frank was happy to be alone with his thoughts.

As he was putting finishing touches on the cleanup effort, Cherice appeared in a bathrobe with her hair wrapped in a towel, and she apologized, "I never got to ask you about your talk with Hank today. I'm sorry. You can never get a word in edgewise, can you?" But then (much too quickly), "I'm just going straight to bed now, if you don't mind. Along with everything else I have to do tomorrow I should put together the employment packets that my girls will need on Friday. Larry said it was as good as a done deal after talking with them." She kissed him again and made her way to their bedroom.

# 5

# THE LEHMAN CHANGES

Frank spent his morning entering the brokers' weekly numbers into an Excel spread sheet. Doing so, he would be closer to completing the final calcs needed to submit his Friday report to the C-Suite. He stared at his new calculations on a white board behind him and wondered if anyone receiving his work up the chain even recognized where quantitative algorithms entered into the report? He suspected nobody did, and just assumed that the Icarus hierarchy probably skipped ahead to his final projections.

He knew that Larry Sewell didn't understand how he reached his conclusions; nonetheless, his grafts could finally be created once the new totals were added to the document's cells. He was certain he would, without question, be distracted throughout the day tomorrow by the arrival of Cherice's girls . . . all the more reason to finish everything today.

He then concentrated on the emails which remained after deleting a long list of them earlier in the morning. He turned his focus on one from Larry (to the entire office) announcing the arrival of Travis Whitsome and his pals from Lehman Brothers New York.

❊ ❊ ❊

The pals would be welcomed next week, while "Mr. Whitsome, who is obligated to provide a longer departure timeline," would follow two weeks later. Larry used the occasion to let slip that Travis would assume leadership over the new hybrid mortgage division, which Icarus would "first introduce in San Francisco, and then clone in regional offices that share our fixed-income profile." Additionally, he confirmed that Icarus would soon offer "the same Collateralized Debt Obligations that Travis helped pioneer at Lehman." Larry waxed philosophic about these exciting times in the financial world, as well as upon the opportunity which was about to present itself in San Francisco.

He encouraged the brokers to begin doing their homework on the CDO's, especially considering their growing "incorporation of sub-prime mortgages, which now clearly defines them.'" This, he urged, "should be completed before the arrival of Travis Whitsome." Larry emphasized that there would be no change in command going forward, as brokers would continue to report to Frank; the exception being those occasions where work with the new mortgage instruments "would necessarily require the oversight of Mr. Whitsome."

※ ※ ※

Effectively, this just put an exclamation point on what Frank already knew would become reality at Icarus Wealth Management. He also knew intuitively that Larry's email to the brokers was a shot across the bow; it was his fair warning to them that everybody would be held accountable to sell the new mortgage products to their clients. If brokers were able to show enthusiasm about them, they were in. If they were reticent in any way, or worse, if they had even vague ethical concerns about the sub-prime component now included within the CDO's, they would be out.

He also knew that Larry would very quickly determine who was or wasn't on-board. Frank suspected he probably already knew who he wanted to keep at Icarus, and who he wanted to terminate. This meant that next week would likely bring the first round of lay-offs, and Frank sighed deeply as he contemplated it.

### SWAN OYSTER DEPOT

After finding a good place to pause the morning's work, he went out to the brokerage floor and reminded those who habitually ran late to get their weekly reports to him by 10:00 am tomorrow. He was met with a few sly questions about the "New York boys," but the phraseology from cubicle to cubicle just amounted to transparent attempts to learn more about what Frank knew. He easily answered that they knew as much about it as he did.

His travels eventually led him to Hank's desk, where he was surprised to find him sporting tiny reading glasses and concentrating hard on his desktop monitor. Frank was ready to fire off a sarcastic shot about how inspiring it was to witness his work ethic, *considering Hank's advancing years*, when Hank looked up (stunned) and exclaimed, "The Giants got rid of *Pierzynski!*"

"The bullpen last year was *not* happy with him; someone even called him a *'cancer on the organization*!'—that clown couldn't block a changeup in the dirt if his grandmother threw it. By the end of last season, Jason Schmidt wouldn't even pitch to him! —And are you ready for this? We signed Mike Matheny behind the dish . . . *Mike Fuckin Matheny!* . . . That, ladies and gentlemen, is an honest-to-God catcher!"

He then crossed his arms and stared up at Frank, as if anticipating his incredulous gratitude at receiving news on a scale such as this . . . Frank tried not to laugh, and he blinked his eyes repeatedly before offering, "Do you . . . *Hank*—even on some *remote* level—ever pause to consider that, at this very moment (looking around), you are surrounded by ninety or more dedicated professionals who are toiling ceaselessly for the greater good of our august corporation? . . . I mean, considering that on its face, Hank . . . do you ever worry that you might not be measuring up?"

Hank stared at him for a minute, sober as a judge and unflinching. He then leaned in closer to Frank (peering askance at his coworkers) and he whispered, "These *professionals* as you call them, don't know that I just landed the biggest asset ever to enter the front doors of Icarus." He then bent his index finger to tap it emphatically on Frank's chest, "That would be you, *Slick,* and my esteemed co-workers never even saw it happen—*Yea verily, I have come for you like a thief in the night"*—After which, he leaned back into his seat and cradled the base of his skull into locked fingers. His smirk at Frank completed a way-too-smug facial expression.

❖ ❖ ❖

Frank could only blink again while staring into his friend's eyes, "Dear, Dear Hank . . . You do live a rich fantasy life, don't you? Or is it just early-stage dementia that I am witnessing, something I will no doubt experience for myself in about a hundred years, when I'm your age?" Hank immediately fired back, "Sure, crack wise *junior*, but these gray temples of mine tell me that the businessman in you is just playing it *coy* right now. Remember me? I'm the guy who gave you a bar napkin to wipe drool from the corners of your mouth yesterday."

Frank grinned at last and said, "Yeah, well let's go talk about that in more detail. What do you say we head over to The Swan today and see what the brothers have cooked up for lunch? I'm craving oysters, or maybe some chowder and a Crab Louie . . ." Then (looking at his watch), "If we leave right now, we can be there before 11:00, and that might even put us near the front of the line." Hank mostly ended his act and stood up smiling, "Oysters, he says . . . You better get a dozen; I've seen your wife."

As they headed for the door, Frank couldn't resist, "*Thief in the night*, huh? You do realize that you just used a Christ metaphor?" To which Hank coolly fired back, "How do you know I wasn't quoting the *Rosicrucians*?" Seeing the blank expression on

Frank's face, "You know . . . '*We are among you but you don't see us?*' " Still nothing . . . So Hank muttered, "Dear God, where do you keep that turnip truck you just fell off of . . . ?" Finally, as they made their way into the parking garage, Frank retorted, "I'm a rancher by the way, not a farmer." Hank shot back, "Same difference."

❀ ❀ ❀

Hank expertly guided his old Cadillac toward Polk Street, and he soon found a parking space about a block away from the Swan. Luckily, they claimed a place in line behind the first few people—this would give them the seats at the counter they were hoping for. Following grateful salutations to today's server, orders were placed, and Hank tore off and buttered a slice of sourdough bread. He then inquired, "So, what does Cherice think about all this . . . ?"

    Frank, not ready to address the question, hedged, "That's what I need to talk about today. It's a bit more complicated than I believe you realize Hank, and I wouldn't be forthcoming if I didn't give you some background; we can get into all that soon enough, but for now, let me ask what it would take to set up that first meeting with Bill? Maybe Cherice can comprehend what's happening a little better if I have some impressions of him . . . anecdotes even, that she might sink her teeth into." Hank considered this for a moment as he studied his friend's face, then he skipped ahead, "Do you think there's a chance she won't support you in this decision?"

### THE CHASM

And there it was: The question and its requisite answer which Frank, until this moment, had not shared with another living soul. He had been staring across a chasm of differences with his wife for years now, but those dynamics remained unknown to Hank. He certainly could not be prepared to hear about them today; nobody, in fact, who saw him and his wife as a *couple* at work would be prepared for what Frank finally needed to say.

❀ ❀ ❀

He started slowly, "Our difficulties in this situation are more . . . *global* . . . I'm afraid." Feeling that Hank was focused intently, he continued, "Cherice and I sometimes don't share the same reality; I mean, we just look at the world differently. Her priorities tend to gravitate toward her *social life*, which I mostly find to be shallow . . . and . . . well, I live in a world that is just more *private*. That fact generally bores the shit out of her, and we're left with glaring differences in how we approach life; these are differences which we mostly regret, and I'm dead certain that she regrets them more than I do . . ."

He paused to assess his friend's reaction and saw that he was still locked-on. Frank continued, "Cherice will see the return of her girlfriends to Icarus—who will be back at work tomorrow, by the way—as the best of all possible realities. So, to whatever extent the atmosphere at Icarus re-boots to the *party central* theme that existed in the late 90's . . . I'm positive she will feel that she has returned to her home planet."

Frank looked down at the lunch counter and continued, "So the problem I need to disclose to you is this—and *disclosure* is the correct context—even though you know I can't stay at Icarus, you need to understand that my leaving will most likely end in my divorce . . . " He stared at Hank, "That's my vision of the future: My wife, in the absence of the fabric which holds us together as co-workers, will someday soon just *wander off*—presumably in the direction of the loudest flattery—and *'that will be that'*, as they say."

❁ ❁ ❁

Glancing at Hank, he felt the need to reassure, "Please know that you didn't create this quandary; it's been in existence for a long, long time, right there with my other visions which would be the consequences of staying at Icarus. Those, like a marriage that ends in divorce, are hard to ignore as well."

"My past experience has taught me to never ignore what I see, and what I now envision at Icarus is this: A roomful of brokers laughing it up as they sell a bunch of worthless shit to legions of San Francisco's most vulnerable—those trusting clients will be relentlessly cold-called every single day. They will be elderly people who, for the most part, desperately need to protect their savings within the confines of *fixed income,* and they won't even recognize the coming threat . . ."

"Do you know what the worst part of that dream is (staring at Hank)? It will be *me* who has to compile those sales totals every week and wrap it all up in a nice big bow, like it's some kind of a *job-well-done* for Icarus—as if it would amount to a job that any asshole should ever be proud of" Frank finished, "So, absolutely, the idea of meeting your friend Bill appeals to me on a level that I couldn't even imagine a few days ago. That prospect now even feels like a kind of salvation, considering everything I just told you."

"All of it, however, is predicated on the hope that Bill and I will actually *like* and *trust* one another, and then be able to imagine ourselves working together . . . So you must know Hank, before any of that can happen, you have to tell him that he may have set his sights on tainted goods, and that my coming to work for him will most likely steer me in the direction of a divorce . . ."

### EAT SOMETHING

Hank was obviously concerned, but his essential *Hankness* remained intact, "Here! Eat this (pushing Frank's Crab Louie toward him), and have some bread too.

Sometimes I think you might be hypoglycemic, so let me do the talking for a while." He then organized his thoughts before speaking, "I'm not sure what you imagine about my friend Bill . . . perhaps that he sits around all day in a blazer with an ascot tucked inside his lapel . . . so that he may remain *impressive* while he pronounces judgements upon the *great unwashed*?"

"You are going to discover that he is very sage in his vision of the modern world, Frank . . . and that, together with the fact that he's going to like you very much, will tap you immediately into his generosity. Where he will want to *help you* in whatever way he can imagine, through any obstacles that might lie ahead. And yes, that would even include a divorce which hasn't yet begun to play itself out. So, in the meantime, relax a little and please don't forget that you will be dealing with someone who is *truly brilliant* and *truly benevolent,* and that such people don't often stumble upon the small things."

❋ ❋ ❋

With that, Hank side-stepped immediately into damage control, "I'm not implying that an impending divorce is *small things* my friend, and I honestly couldn't feel worse for you than I do right now. I'm sad, in fact, that you even have to contemplate this. Nonetheless, I appreciate you confiding in me, and Bill will too . . . But, let me suggest to you that even this divorce, which you envision with such dread, will not be big enough to define you throughout the years, nor even during the months that lie ahead . . ."

Hank once again gripped his friend's shoulder and looked into his eyes, "You'll see soon enough Frank, that Bill will not view this as anything which could ever hold the two of you back." Frank felt relief when the words sunk in. The two men then quietly finished their lunch (which Hank was right about, by the way)—Frank had indeed been *famished*. Soon, he was feeling stronger and more focused with food onboard, and he wondered what signs his friend had recognized to conclude that he needed to eat?

❋ ❋ ❋

Back in the car he said to Hank, "I've always believed that 'bad news can't wait', so forgive me for just blurting everything out today . . . I hope you know I appreciate very much being able to confide in you." Hank looked over at him and smiled, "That's what friends are for, huh . . . ?" Then after a pause, "So, are you still convinced that you want to meet with Bill? . . . If so, what's your timeline?"

Frank immediately answered, "I just need to get on with this, Hank. I'm more certain now than ever. This might be short notice, but Cherice and her girlfriends are bound to be immersed in clothes shopping this weekend—maybe even for the next couple of weekends. So, can we try to set up a *Saturday* meeting? Do you think that would be okay with Bill?"

Hank easily concluded, "I don't see why not. I'll run it past him." "Great", said Frank, "Knowing a little more about Bill and what he has in mind actually does help me break the news to Cherice—and then, to Larry of course, if things go as you expect. Speaking of which, Mr. *'Thief in the night'* . . . what are your plans *vis a vis* your employment at Icarus?"

Hank raised his eyebrows and said, "I knew this day would come sooner or later . . . My work is actually done, isn't it?" He then stared at Frank, "I suppose when I finally put the two of you together, and the ball is at last in your court, there really will be nothing left to keep me around—except maybe some morbid fascination with these new clowns from Lehman. Probably some entertainment value in that, don't you think?"

Hank grinned, "Naw, if Larry truly is planning to let brokers go right away, I suppose the decent thing for me to do would be to just offer to go first. That might grant a reprieve to someone who actually needs the money."

Hearing Hank say this drove home the gravity of the moment for Frank—*this really was going to happen*, he could now be sure, and sometime in the very near future he would reach a point where there could be no turning back. As the two men returned to work, Hank said that sometime tomorrow he would sit down with Bill regarding the Saturday meeting. They then turned and went separately in the directions of their desks.

## STELLA

Friday didn't unfold the way that Frank had expected—Cherice first disclosed that Larry had reached out to the girls the night before, suggesting that they all meet for breakfast at 9:00, in lieu of individual meetings staggered throughout the morning. She confided in him that Larry seemed excited about having the girls back too, and it was sounding more and more like this would be a welcome home party; he even asked Cherice to reserve a table at Perry's on Union Street, which meant that Mimosas would most likely be involved.

That effectively cleared Frank's morning, and he took the opportunity to easily finish his Friday report. Sometime around 11:30, as he studied stock prices on CNBC and anticipated closing levels for the week, he was startled by an absolutely dead-on Streisand impression, directed at him from his office entry, "Well . . . hello gorgeous!"

When he peered over the top of his trading monitors, there stood *Stella* in a very dressy white blouse and a very tight black skirt. Her back was pressed against the crown molding of Frank's doorway, and she was resting there with one high heel lifted off the floor and both hands gathered behind her waist. In this expert pose, her chest was maximally accentuated; she at once nailed a *come hither* sideways glance at Frank that was both sexy and full of camp . . .

Frank grinned as he savored every subtlety of her act—*smart* and *funny* did it for him every time, and she had all of that going on right now. Plus, she was truly a sight for sore eyes; he had missed her far more than he ever anticipated in the time since her departure from Icarus.

❀ ❀ ❀

Frank jumped up, and in long strides he moved across the room. He reached out with both arms, and the pretty *Italiana* spun away from the doorway to practically leap into them. They laughed in the joy they both shared, and Frank stepped back to take inventory on a leaner, more athletic version of his long-lost friend, *"Jesus, woman* . . . Look at you!"

He took her left hand and twirled her in the only dance move he had ever learned, which slowly showcased his pretty friend, "Let's make sure I have every detail of this right," he marveled, and Stella basked in his attention. "What in the *hell* have you been doing out there in Vallejo to get yourself looking like this?"

Then, typical Stellz, dripping with New Jersey enunciation, "I got tired of waiting for your twin to call, so I finally cut a deal with Pacific Gas and Electric to hook up my treadmill to the *grid*. I've been on it ever since I left this dump. It helped my power bill, but the treadmill was the only thing that got *hooked-up* in that arrangement, if you know what I mean."

Frank laughed, "I find that extremely hard to believe . . . Look at you!" "No really!" she lamented. "Oh sure, I've dated some guys, but these west coast boys just don't *get* me, I'm pretty sure—and, if truth be known, I don't really *get* them either. I've just about given up any hope of finding a man out here who can possibly understand my idea of love and family, and the importance of now and then throwing plates of spaghetti at each other."

At this, Frank laughed hard, and he reached out to once again hug his friend, "This place has not been the same since you left, *Faccia* . . ." Frank had chosen the word that Stella taught him a long time ago, which was endearing Italian for face. "Aww . . . you *remembered,"* and she hugged him back.

❀ ❀ ❀

It was at this exact moment that Cherice appeared in the doorway, and she loudly protested, *"Hey!* Get your hands off my husband, you *Bimbo!"* She teased further, "Don't think I'm not wise to you two . . ." Stella, whose arms were still around Frank's neck, narrowed her eyes to glare at Cherice. She then dropped one hand in defiance, and grabbed Frank's butt cheek . . . Finally, she bit and pulled at his earlobe with her front teeth exposed, while she stared at Cherice in defiance.

Cherice shook her head and informed Stella as she turned and walked back to her desk, "You're up next *Bimbo.* Larry is almost done with Deanna, and it's your turn next to sign my documents. Try not to screw them up after all those free Mimosas you guzzled today."

Stella, with one arm still around Frank's neck, turned fearlessly toward him and kissed him hard on the lips. She lingered close enough to breathe him in, and looked directly into his eyes. Now barely audible (and absent the New Jersey accent), "Story of my life . . . find *Mr. Right*, after he chooses some little *twinkie* who doesn't even know what she's got."

As she pushed away, "How *did* you end up with that silly ball of fluff anyway?" Frank, still unsteady from the kiss, lamely smiled and answered, "I don't know . . . *I must like fluff?*" At this, Stella stopped and studied his eyes . . . She then leaned forward for emphasis, "No you don't, honey. You never have. You just didn't want to risk something more *consequential*." At last, she managed a sad smile and turned to walk back toward the atrium . . .

❊ ❊ ❊

Frank, genuinely in shock, remained disoriented as he stood there in his office. Finally, he remembered that he would be alone at lunch today (Hank was mysteriously off-site), so he decided to walk down the Embarcadero to clear his head. If he was lucky, he might find a bench where he could sit and think things over. Suddenly, he needed to escape the noise of this office. The inane babble, unrelenting within the artificial light and air-conditioned atmosphere, was increasingly choking him; realizing how badly he needed to get out into the sun, he pulled off his tie and put on the running shoes which he kept in his office closet.

Outside at ground level, Frank was surprised at his sudden need to run, in lieu of the walk that he had considered. He bolted across two intersections, which delivered him onto the wide concrete path that stretched out for miles in either direction past the Ferry Terminal. Continuing beside the warehouse piers which are adjacent to the bay, he passed the Bow and Arrow sculpture by Claes Oldenburg . . .

The air here was cool and clean, and he eventually found his precise gait. He began to expand his lung volumes as he arrived at a familiar balance. Sooner than expected, he found himself passing under the Bay Bridge, and then past the marina which was adjacent to Pier 40. Seeing the ballpark off in the distance, he decided to keep running.

❊ ❊ ❊

Frank was now wrestling with a profound fear that his most private conclusions were projecting across his face like a movie for everyone to see—ones that he wasn't really prepared to share. Stella (in under five minutes) had just reached deep within him to expose one of those conclusions, which only he was supposed to know was there. How could she elicit with certainty the fact that he knew he was with the *wrong woman*? Was this obvious to anyone else? . . . *To Cherice*?

Frank's control of his conscious world was unraveling, and it made him want to press on. As he neared Third and King, he couldn't help but marvel at the architectural substance of Giants' Stadium, there in the midst of tall palm trees that bent light around it. While transfixed upon that, he slowly turned to reverse course, and then he accelerated back toward the Bay Bridge. By the time he returned to the marina, he knew that he had pushed himself enough today (in work clothes), so he slowed and began to walk . . .

Breathing deeply now, with hands clasped behind him, he moved toward a bench which he had hoped he might find—there he stretched a little and felt his panic lifting. He soon concluded that those private thoughts were witnessed by only one person, *Stella*, and she obviously knew him better than he remembered.

Maybe the one other person who might be capable of knowing his thoughts to that extent would be Hank, but only because they had recently been revealed to him. As for Cherice . . . *not likely!* She was so focused upon her eye liner in the rear-view mirror that Frank doubted she had any clue at all regarding his current state of turmoil.

Accepting this more likely reality, he now needed more than ever to press forward in the direction that was being offered to him . . . He sat silently for a long time on the bench, where he tried to envision those future changes—this while gazing eastward across the bay, toward the Berkeley Hills (still mysterious to him). He was staring at the gold reflections off the windows there, and somewhere within his now quieted mind, he was able to finally reconcile what he needed to do . . .

❋ ❋ ❋

Frank started walking back toward Icarus. There was no hurry today, as his report was already finished and Friday's other routines were relaxed. Glad that quarterly charts had not also been due, he was able to languish during his sunny trip back. Somewhere along the way, it occurred to him that he hadn't heard from Hank regarding the meeting with Bill Bennett, and he presumed that his absence from work today might have something to do with that.

Returning to the office, he quickly changed into one of the laundered shirts that he kept in his coat closet. He then fired up CNBC again and logged back into his trading platform. This week, like last week, had continued a market rally which was occurring broadly across a lot of sectors. *"A rising tide lifts all boats,"* he thought to himself, repeating the age-old litany that had been pounded into his head in business school. He wondered how much longer this rally could last, so he made a mental note to drill down more closely into S&P 500 earnings on Monday.

## TIBURON MEETING

As he thought about this, he heard a loud wolf whistle aimed in his direction. If memory served him correctly, it would have come from Stellz. He smiled, and stood up to see her and the two other new-hires walking beside Cherice; they were four-abreast, and heading his way. He laughed to himself when he took it in, and thought that the only thing missing were six-shooters strapped to their hips as they walked toward him at High Noon.

Stella spoke first, "We came to get your credit card. If Lehman Brothers will be here on Monday, we can't have your wife looking like *Barbie*, while the rest of us look like extras from the cast of *Les Miserables*. So, we're going shopping. Frank (completely deadpan) agreed, "Sure," and he reached into his back pocket to grasp his wallet. When he produced a credit card, Cherice slapped his hand hard and scolded, "Yeah . . . *No!* That is *not* happening! I just realized I have to train you to ignore her." Stellz grinned and blew him a kiss. Carol and Deanna then stepped toward him and exaggerated their joy at seeing him again, and they all exchanged pleasantries.

Frank recognized the unmistakable fact that the four of them were now fully energized by being back together—this was most evident in Cherice, as she stood with a new and more distant affect. "We'll probably be late . . . We were thinking that we might get something to eat afterwards. Do you need me to bring food home for you?" Frank shook his head, "No . . . Don't worry. I've got the leftovers from last night. Have fun." Cherice gave him a kiss, and the girls all spun together to walk away from his office.

❀ ❀ ❀

As Frank watched them leave, he was drawn to the clicking of their heels on the slate floor. The precision of this seemed loudly choreographed in some compelling way, and its rhythm left him staring as they left. The *'Click-Click-Clickety-Click-Click'* of their expensive heels unearthed a distant memory of him pinning playing cards to his bicycle frame when he was just a boy. The spoked wheels fanned those cards to make as much noise as possible while he craved the attention of his family.

From his left he heard Hank's barb, "Quickly Frank! *Avert your eyes!* . . . Don't stare at the *Pumps of Power!* They will turn you into a pillar of salt. Women use them as a weapon against us Frank, and you must never look in their direction again!" Frank began laughing hard at his friend's elaborate joke, but he finally warned, "And, you say I'm the dinosaur! You know those women would filet you if they heard that?!" Hank (staying in character) raised his thick eyebrows and said, "You have been *schooled*. Just remember . . . I know my Old Testament."

❋ ❋ ❋

The two men moved back into Frank's office, where Hank began, "I met with Bill for a long time today, and he said to tell you that he is *extremely* excited to finally meet you. He said tomorrow actually works great for him too, if you don't mind meeting over in Tiburon."

Frank smiled broadly when he heard the news, "Great . . . Tiburon, huh?" Hank clarified, "Yeah, he said he has a little project on his boat that he wants to finish in the morning, but he thinks he should be done by 10:00. Does that work for you?" When Frank said "Sure," he concluded, "Why don't you let me pick you up tomorrow morning, and I'll drive us over? I'm sure after all these years that I know my way around Tiburon better than you, and you wouldn't recognize Bill's boat anyway."

Frank easily agreed to this, and they firmed up details. As an afterthought, Hank asked, "Do you own any deck shoes?" Frank frowned, "Deck shoes?"— "Yeah, Topsiders. You know . . . boat shoes?" Frank apologized, *"No* . . . No, I don't." Hank quickly dismissed it and said, "Don't worry. There's a little chandlery off the highway in Sausalito. We'll stop there tomorrow on our way and pick up a pair."

❋ ❋ ❋

Frank eventually spent the evening alone, as anticipated, and he decided later to just tell Cherice that he had scheduled a meeting the next day with a client—that would buy him enough time to meet Bill, and listen to what he had to say. He hoped he was right about the shopping spree lasting through the weekend, but he also knew that he and his wife needed to talk sometime in the next two days; those conversations were long overdue, and Frank's conclusions had changed by such magnitude that they now required her full attention.

Cherice would be blindsided, no doubt, but Frank honestly could not remember the last time she had shown any interest in listening to his thoughts about *anything*. He took a deep breath as he weighed this, but he felt invigorated at the idea of being offered a new direction.

# 6

## BILL BENNETT

Early the next morning, Frank found himself struggling with clothing choices for his meeting in Tiburon. He had searched Topsiders online the night before and discovered a surprising number of styles. He learned that the boat shoes were definitely casual in appearance, yet later today he would surely be meeting the most important and influential connection of his professional life. His dilemma was in knowing that he needed to impart a respectful first impression, which he felt required a suit coat, but the Topsiders fucked all that up.

Getting dressed was so much easier when he lived in Nevada—just find a pair of dark Wranglers and a clean western shirt, then maybe iron creases into the jeans if the occasion was *dressy*. Roper boots were good for every occasion (horse shit optional), and off you went . . .

But San Francisco attire choices for someone living life in the Financial District were complex on a level that had tormented him almost from the start. A casual occasion on the weekend really meant that you wore tight new jeans with silver filigree stitched to your ass, and a pair of formal looking loafers with no socks. All of this would be topped off with a partially unbuttoned shirt (more expensive than any you might choose for work).

If the occasion took place on a chilly day, you put on the suit-coat—taking you all the way back around again to as far from *casual* as Frank could possibly imagine. He usually deferred to Cherice for these choices (especially when the context of the social gathering baffled him), but given the clandestine nature of his meeting today, she could be of no help.

❊ ❊ ❊

So, after accepting his own vision that Bill would be working on his boat, on a Saturday, Frank settled upon a pair of khaki slacks and a dark blue polo shirt (no tie required), and a blazer. He then chose his casual watch with the brown leather band. As he readied to leave, he checked in with Cherice, who was applying her makeup in the bathroom; she indeed was preparing for day number two of power-shopping with the girls, just as he had envisioned.

When she glanced at her husband's clothes, she frowned and looked at him for an explanation. Frank shrugged and admitted that today's meeting would take place on a sailboat, and that Hank was apparently planning to stop along the way to buy him his first pair of Topsiders. *"Oh,"* Cherice now understood, "You'll be walking on teak decks, so the shoes will keep you from slipping on wet surfaces. Also, you won't scuff up the deck . . . boat owners hate that."

Frank stared at her incredulously, "How the *hell* do you know all that?" She looked at him like he was an idiot, and condescended, *"Uhh* . . . We live near the *ocean?"* Thankfully, the sound of Hank's car horn down on the street rescued him from his ineptitude for all things fashion.

He then changed the subject, "I don't know what this day will involve, so I might be home late this evening." Cherice added, "Yeah, we're meeting here first—nobody has seen our house. Then Carol wants to head down to San Jose to check out the stores in Santana Row. We might go back to the Palo Alto Center if we need to dress things up a bit . . . So, I could be late too."

❊ ❊ ❊

They both agreed to text if something came up, and then smooched before Frank headed downstairs. When he jumped into Hank's Cadillac, he immediately saw that his friend was wearing jeans and a windbreaker. Frank (exasperated) blurted out, *"Jesus Christ!* Will someone throw me a fucking bone about the dress code!?" Hank stifled his laughter and admitted, "I guess I forgot to tell you that Bill keeps it pretty laid-back most of the time, but don't worry, you look like you probably *should* look for this first meeting. You'll be fine, but I think I better stop somewhere to get you something to eat; a little cranky this morning, aren't we?"

Frank got the joke, and he worked at being more relaxed. Hank remembered, "There's actually a pretty good little coffee shop next to the chandlery in Sausalito—we'll stop there after we get your shoes. They've got egg and cheese croissants, and Danish . . . really nice pastries actually, and it would probably be wise for us to load up on food this morning anyway, given our close proximity to the bar at the San Francisco Yacht Club, and the fact that it's a Saturday."

## TIBURON

The ride from The City across the Golden Gate Bridge had started foggy, but as they continued farther north, the sun started to burn through to reveal patchy blue skies. By the time Frank was taking his new Topsiders for a spin around the chandlery parking lot, he was retrieving sunglasses from his coat pocket.

It truly was a beautiful ride over to Tiburon, and along the way Frank stared at his new shoes. He lifted them off the floorboard and proclaimed, "I could get used to these things" "That's good," Hank observed, "You'll be wearing them a lot. In fact, remind me to take you to a West Marine Products store, so you can load up on more sailing gear."

"You will discover that Bill is an early riser—he's always up to watch the overseas markets come in before the New York opens. He and Marion then spend the rest of the morning having breakfast and talking, after which he dispatches his daily agenda pretty quickly, so he can head straight to the boat . . . But Frank, don't ever underestimate the amount of business that he conducts on that sailboat."

"One of the first things you will notice when you go down into the galley, is the military grade satellite phone; it's there with all of his navigation equipment. He's always connected-up by way of his virtual meeting hardware. Those networks are proprietary and secured, by the way . . . It's kind of like being onboard Airforce One." Hank chuckled, "Don't be surprised some morning if he asks you to say 'Hi' to *Ben Bernanke* . . ." All that Frank could think of to say when he heard this was, "Holy shit!"

❋ ❋ ❋

Teak decks spilled into the wide cockpit; the stained wood swept back longitudinally, and it was accented with ribs of black *non-skid* material—those accents were encircled by inlaid brass trim. Aft, within the boat's transom, there were two huge offset tillers; the trimmed porcelain wheels had been lowered ergonomically into the deck.

Frank could see that the stunning sailboat had the tallest mast by far in the harbor, and its long boom formed a ninety-degree angle to the spar—both appeared to be constructed from the same composite alloy. With its dark metallic color, everything about the rig spoke strength and precision.

Understanding nothing at all about sailing, Frank just knew by looking at this boat that it was *fast*. As they approached it more closely, he was mesmerized by the complex engineering which had been adapted within the rigging of this beautiful boat; from this close-up vantage, it truly imparted the feel of a fighter aircraft.

❋ ❋ ❋

His concentration was suddenly broken when he saw the name *Angelina* painted across the hull in gold cursive lettering. This sailboat had been christened with *the* same name as his Basque *Mother*, and Frank could only stare after new recollections of her. Walking up to the cyclone fence, Hank yelled out toward a big man who was crouched as he worked on the bow, *"Hi there sailor!"* The man looked up and smirked at Hank, then motioned for him to continue toward the yacht club entrance to access the boat.

As Hank walked in that direction, Frank watched the man stand up and then stare menacingly at him while he followed Hank toward the building. He was over six feet tall, and Frank guessed that he weighed upwards of two hundred twenty pounds. His blond hair was pulled back tightly into a Samurai tail, but some of the hair along his temporal regions had broken free from control; it looked to be frizzed and turned platinum by the ocean's sun and wind.

The athletic man sported a goatee, into which were woven small vertical beads that imparted a tribal appearance. His broad neck featured a lightning bolt tattoo, prominent among unfamiliar symbols (Middle Eastern?), and his biceps were also covered in what appeared to be military insignias. Frank knew instantly that the man was a *lifter*, but something else about him hinted that he was agile as well.

The impression left by this combination of mass and speed, was that there could be no question about the man's ability to do damage if he was so inclined . . . Frank was relieved to finally travel behind the yacht club wall, where he felt safe for the moment from that gaze.

❄ ❄ ❄

Inside the clubhouse, Frank took in the glossy mahogany walls which framed numerous windows overlooking the harbor. The ceiling rafters were strung with Navy Signal Corps flags (connected by wires). Moving past the long and impressively-stocked bar, he heard a voice directed at Hank when he first walked into view. *"Ruh-roh . . ."* the voice warned. Hank laughed and shook hands with a distinguished gentleman in slacks, white shirt and a bow tie. Wearing a pressed apron, he had apparently been busy polishing glasses behind the counter.

Hank then turned to beckon Frank closer. He proceeded to offer a genuinely respectful introduction, "*Francis McClelland* . . . allow me to introduce *Reginald Foster*, whom you will soon discover to be the finest bartender in all of the Greater Bay Area." "Nice to meet you Francis," the distinguished man observed, "and please, call me *Reggie*." Frank replied, "Likewise . . . and please call me *Frank*." Reggie began, "I feel it is incumbent upon me to warn you, young Sir, that you are traveling in dangerous company today. Please let me know *immediately* if I need to call security on your behalf," and he grinned at Hank. He then pointed to the back door which led out to the pier, "Just flip the deadbolt to open it . . . *His Eminence* has tied-off out there . . ."

❉ ❉ ❉

The two visitors turned toward the door, and Frank quietly asked, "Who's the gorilla with the tattoos?" Hank chuckled, "That's *Steve* . . . but don't worry. He won't bite." Hank led the way out onto the pier, and then turned left toward the sailboat. When he approached the bow, he reached up to shake Steve's hand, "Greetings, formidable one . . . *Steve*, this is *Frank*. Frank, this is Steve." The big man offered his handshake, "Welcome Frank", but he gripped Frank's hand with vice-like strength, and studied his eyes. Frank focused hard so he wouldn't flinch, as he too gripped and stared right back. He answered, "Thank you Steve," and at last his hand was freed.

❉ ❉ ❉

Suddenly, a tall man sporting an impressive shock of dark silver hair appeared on the stairs leading up from the galley. He was wearing a beige Patagonia pullover with a tall collar, and he stopped mid-way to smile at the approaching men, *"Hey! Look who's here!* Come on over to these steps gentlemen and climb aboard." He then deftly jumped into the cockpit, and within the same motion, reached outboard to unfasten the stainless-steel clasps which connected the stanchion lines.

Frank took in the handsome man's appearance while Hank climbed slowly and carefully onto the sailboat. Bill Bennett was tall and angular, and his quick movements suggested a younger body than Hank's timelines would have indicated was possible. He had the kind of thick, straight hair that the wind would never conquer, and his facial features were highlighted by an unapologetic tan line; Frank recognized the sunglass borders around his eyes.

Those sunglasses appeared to be permanently secured around his neck with a frayed neoprene *'Croakie'*, and he had the prominent and ruddy cheek bones that belonged to a man who was born to be outdoors. With a quick glance, Frank also noted his olive green cargo pants, which held channel locks and a large needle-nose pliers in one of the leg pockets. Bill's Topsiders (the same model as Frank's) were water and weather-faded and scuffed deeply on every surface.

The impressive man who now stood before him exceeded every detail that Frank had previously tried to imagine from Hank's stories. Bill extended his hand and reached down to help him aboard the sailboat. Frank gripped the strong and calloused hand as he stepped aboard *Angelina* for the first time.

❉ ❉ ❉

The two men considered each other now, face to face at last, and Bill smiled with his piercing green eyes, "Great to finally meet you, *Wunderkind*." "Likewise, Sir." Frank replied as he too smiled, "It's just such an honor." Bill turned toward Hank and acknowledged, "Good work Henry! I like him already." Then back to Frank, "So . . . have you forgiven me this clandestine mission that I set upon my old friend Henry . . . ?" Hank quickly interrupted, "*He* may forgive you, *but I sure as hell won't.*"

Bill and Frank laughed at this, and Bill jabbed, "He can be such an old *curmudgeon*, can't he? I'll buy him a drink later today, and you will see him brighten up a lot." Bill then motioned, "Here, let's sit outside in the cockpit; we shouldn't waste this bluebird day." Before taking his seat, Frank glanced around to study the hardware leading back to the massive winches and pedal cranks on both sides of the transom. He marveled, "This is the most impressive boat I have ever seen. It's absolutely beautiful."

Still forward on the deck, Steve muttered, "Yeah, it's a regular *pimp palace*, isn't it?" The big man was tightening a very large turnbuckle that connected rod rigging from the top of the mast to the peak of the bow. Bill countered, "Don't mind him, Frank. Steve is still mad at me for adding extra weight to the deck when I put down this *teak.*" He leaned closer to Frank and quietly scoffed, "The total was maybe *three hundred pounds.*" Steve overheard this and he didn't miss the opportunity to object further, "That's a lot of topside weight on an eighteen- thousand-pound racer . . ."

❊ ❊ ❊

Bill (feeling obligated to bring clarity to the debate) explained, "Here's the deal . . . My lovely wife Marion, who you will soon meet, absolutely adored my old sailboat; it was a 1976 Swan 60, a Sparkman and Stevens designed, true classic built by Nautor of Finland. She's still an exquisite boat today by any stretch of the imagination. She was loaded with the finest woodwork in the industry. There was a sauna below decks . . . wine cabinets . . . a huge saloon; a genuinely beautiful sailboat."

"The problem was it weighed forty-three thousand pounds, and modern sailboat design has moved *way* beyond that over the past thirty years. Angelina here is what the sailing world calls a *ULDB* . . . for *ultralight displacement boat*. It is absolutely thrilling to be on board this baby when she's underway . . . isn't it Steve?"

"Bill Lee of Santa Cruz perfected the design, and these boats can exceed theoretical hull speed; something that designers during the America's Cup 12-meter era struggled with. A boat like this can literally surf down the backs of waves when she sails off the wind. This is the kind of sailboat, Frank, that we could race to *Hawaii.*"

"But all of that doesn't matter if my wife holds me in contempt for trading in the old Swan to build this hybrid *Santa Cruz 52* to race in the *Big Boat Series*. For that reason, she was initially reluctant even to join me onboard for an occasional glass of wine, which absolutely broke my heart. So, here I am Frank, endeavoring to make things right . . . Hence, the name Angelina, which Marion *alone* chose as a way to honor her Sister . . . and now, the teak decks with trimmed black non-skid, which she believes is beautiful."

Finally pointing to a tinted plexiglass hatch cover, Bill continued, "And that is also new at the suggestion of my wife, who finally seems to be warming up to our little project here. We happily agreed to the tint for its lovely color contrast. Right Steve?" Steve at last conceded, "*Lovely . . .*"

❊ ❊ ❊

Bill wrapped up, "At the end of the day Frank, this one-off sailboat is just an example of how I choose to travel through life. If I were concerned only with racing performance, I would have built a hundred foot *Maxi* sailboat, by way of a syndicate and corporate sponsors, and then hired sixteen crew members to sail it for me. But that's not how I choose to travel through this lifetime."

"Angelina here is truly my life's metaphor, except I am actually the vessel that is filled up and enriched by her extraordinary levels of performance. So, it's okay with me if we have to make this boat a little *prettier* just to guarantee my wife's happiness." Steve, finally sounding conciliatory, quipped, "Now he's going to start talking about '*Zen and the Art of Motorcycle Maintenance*'." "Exactly!" Bill exclaimed, and even Steve chuckled at that . . .

### APUS FOREDECKUS

"So . . .", as Frank looked around, "was this new hatch the morning project that Hank mentioned?" Bill frowned a little, "No actually, we're kind of at an impasse with that. I did some damage to the main halyard-feed up there at the top of the mast, and now we're trying to figure out how we can put a new collar in place to fix it. We were hoping that we wouldn't have to drop the mast to do that, but now I don't know. It's turning out to be a *huge* goddamn project."

Bill thought a bit, and then he cocked his head to look over at Frank—his eyes widened, and he instructed him, "Stand up for a minute . . ." Frank (amused) said, "Okay", and he stood up. Bill continued, "How tall are you, and how much do you weigh?" Frank obliged, "I'm six feet three inches, give or take, and I weigh about one ninety-five."

Bill marveled, "Can this be true, Steve? Do we actually have a *Bowman* in our midst?" Frank was confused, "Excuse me?" Bill then elaborated, "*Apus foredeckus*, my man . . . You have the perfect build to be a Foredeckman on a racing sailboat." Steve's demeanor darkened immediately, "*Bill* . . . he probably doesn't even know *fore* from *aft*.*!*" "No matter," Bill dismissed him, "These are skills that we can teach."

"Oh, for *shit sake!*" Steve exclaimed as he turned away. Bill then jumped down through the open hatch and vanished into the galley below. He appeared a moment later holding something resembling a canvas-wrapped swing seat, knotted together with ropes. He threw it onto the deck, and then disappeared again. After much rattling and banging about below decks, Bill returned with a strangely oblong, black metal device. Frank saw that it held six large stainless steel Allen bolts, which presumably would be used to attach it. He also noticed what appeared to be a tool belt with a large ratchet handle and a punch protruding from its pockets.

❀ ❀ ❀

Bill (a little out of breath) asked Frank, "Are you afraid of heights?" Hank, who had so far remained silent during this landmark first meeting, began to laugh. Frank (not yet connecting the dots) answered, "Not particularly . . . I did some rock climbing up above Donner Lake when I was going to the University of Nevada; nothing really technical, but the cliffs were high enough." Bill, in wonder at this new revelation, said, *"Amazing . . . How do you feel about fixing the mast today?"* Frank was still confused, "Pardon me?"

Hank now started to laugh hard. "Please Hank," Bill signaled to him with a raised index finger, and then he proceeded more evenly. "What I am proposing Frank, is that we have you slip into this *Boson's chair*, where we will secure you with carabiners to its leather belt. Steve will then expertly attach you to the mainsail halyard, and with all of us working together, we will hoist you safely to the top of the mast."

"We will secure you to both of these big winches here, employing redundancy for the sake of safety. Then, I would like you to remove that old halyard collar up there beneath the mast cap, and replace it with this new one." Frank considered the new device and its hardware. He contemplated it all and smiled, "Sure . . . *Why not?*"

❀ ❀ ❀

Hank and Steve exchanged a look while Bill cautioned, "There is only one part of this that makes it a little tricky, Frank. After loosening the bolts and removing that old collar, we will need you to remain *unsecured* for just a moment on top of that spreader (he pointed to it just beneath the top of the mast) to thread the new halyard into place. Then, all that will remain for you to do will be to drop its remaining coils inside the mast, after which you can fasten your new collar into place."

"We will only need a moment down here to retrieve the new halyard and reconnect it to the deck hardware." He pointed to several eyes in the mast, with the last one (just above the deck) leading back through jam-cleats above the cockpit. "After we have safely connected you to the new halyard, you can slide that old collar down to us before we deliver you back down here to join us. With that being completed, we can all go next door for a great big drink; Henry here tells me that you like Whiskey." At this, Frank smiled broadly at Bill and said, "Why *yes . . . Yes I do."*

As a nervous afterthought, Steve added, "That collar is a Kevlar composite, so feel free to crank down those new bolts. We don't want to have to do it all over again while we're traveling through swells at 20 knots." Frank agreed, "Sounds good." With that, Bill smiled from ear to ear and proclaimed, "Well, *okay* then . . . *Let's fix this bitch!*"

❊ ❊ ❊

And fix it they did. Frank, after removing his jacket, secured the tool belt and carefully counted and stowed the new mast collar bolts. He filled another pocket with the ratchet and a punch, then collected and tied the new halyard to the belt's waist. Steve took expert care to fasten the boson's chair carabiners to the wide leather belt secured above Frank's hips. Bill and Hank looped the main sail halyard around two of the massive coffee-grinder winches on the deck; they then locked it twice within the self-tailing hardware.

Frank asked as he looked up at the top of the mast *(which suddenly seemed taller),* "How high up there will I be today?" Steve smirked at him, "Sixty-four feet is all . . ." Frank, unfazed, said, "Excellent. Ready when you are." Steve shook his head and joined the other two men at the grinders.

Together, they began turning the winches that quickly lifted Frank up alongside the mast. It didn't take long for him to reach the top, where he discovered from his new vantage, that he could entirely see the shimmering Tiburon back-bay (aquatic birds and all); it was absolutely breathtaking in the morning sun . . .

❊ ❊ ❊

When he assessed the job at hand, Frank realized the *good news* was that the original Allen bolts were not corroded or seized inside the old collar. The *bad news,* however, was that the top spreader was higher on the mast than estimated. It was located just far enough above Frank's chest that he would not be able to stand on it to finish his work. He would have to do some free climbing just to throw his legs over the spreader, and then straddle the mast while he worked from a sitting position.

He looked down at the other men and informed them, "I'm going to need you to lower me four or five feet, so I have enough slack to climb into position on this spreader." They seemed confused, but reversed the winches and carefully lowered Frank. Steve yelled up, "How's that?" Frank said, "Good right there . . ." Then (completely unannounced), and while the other men remained transfixed on his location, Frank wrapped the old halyard several times around his left wrist and doubled-up around his free hand as well.

He suddenly began to walk, *one foot on top of the other,* up the side of the mast until his body extended out at a perpendicular angle from it—his deck crew gasped collectively at the sight, and Steve nervously grabbed the winch handle with both hands. Frank then continued to walk further up the mast until his feet reached the required height . . . From that position, he bent his knees and extended each leg (one at a time) over the top of the spreader on both sides of the mast.

By the end of the maneuver, Frank's head was nearly upside-down beneath the spreader, where he hung by his knees like a trapeze artist. From there, he pulled himself up using the end of the halyard, until he finally sat upright atop the spreader. *"Okay!"* he shouted, while everybody below stared in awe. "Now, take back the halyard slack a few feet." Bill chuckled in utter disbelief, as he quietly punctuated this spectacle, *"Apus foredeckus, indeed . . ."* Hank and Steve could only stare in stunned silence.

❦ ❦ ❦

Frank, now perched at the highest mast location, quickly disconnected the old collar and jarred it free using the ratchet handle and punch. He lowered it to the deck using the old halyard. After positioning the new collar, he re-connected his Boson's Chair to the new halyard and threaded it back through its guide, dropping the remaining loops inside the hollow mast; he then fastened the collar into place. "Okay!" he shouted below, "It's all yours," and he began to tighten the bolts. He cranked them hard (as Steve had instructed) while Bill threaded the new halyard in and out of the mast eye feeds.

Steve at last pulled the braided rope through its deck guides, which lead aft toward the transom. When he and Bill were finished, they took up the slack and wound the halyard around both winches, securing it anew into the self-tailing locks. By the time Frank was lowered back down to the deck, less than twenty minutes had elapsed from start to finish. Achieving it, all that the four men could do was marvel and laugh in disbelief, while they stood together beside the mast . . .

❦ ❦ ❦

Unbeknownst to any of them, a small group of tourists had gathered next to the yacht club building to watch the spectacle. They were collectively holding their breath, along with four or five sailors who had emerged from their boats to see what the hell was going on. All of the spectators broke into simultaneous applause at the completion of the job, which only spurred Angelina's crew to laugh that much harder . . .

Bill stared at Frank, who was grinning wildly beside him, and he gripped his shoulder. Still amazed, Bill shook his head and asked, "Would anyone here object if we recessed for the remainder of the day? I need to buy this acrobatic young gentleman a Manhattan . . . famously prepared by Reggie of the San Francisco Yacht Club . . ."

# 7

## THE OFFER

The joviality, which was well-shared through the morning's tasks, easily magnified as the men celebrated inside the yacht club. Reggie at first heaped on his expert ridicule, when he feigned concern about *". . . the obvious drinking problem here,* which is confirmed by your *troubling* 11:00 am start time." After which (of course), he slipped away and endeavored impressively to craft the kinds of cocktails that Bill and Hank had bragged about.

Reggie (knowing his audience) kept the drinks flowing through to the early afternoon. Frank, sometime amidst these rounds, proclaimed, *"God,* he really does make a great Manhattan, doesn't he?" At which time, his friends smiled and toasted their "learned prognostication" as an acknowledgement of Frank's whole-hearted approval . . .

Only Steve would back off early, when he began to drink water. Frank remembered that Hank had conspicuously waited for Steve to choose a location at the table before deciding upon his own. It was evident that Steve wanted to be seated with his back to the wall, so he could face out toward the open room. Frank decided he would ask about that later.

Bill chose to sit next to Frank, and their easy communication on any topic just built upon the great first impressions that both of them were forming; boil it all down, they were just long-lost school chums when they talked about Stanford and their professors from different eras in the School of Business . . .

❋ ❋ ❋

Bill had stories about school from "way back when" that seemed to fly off the pages of a period piece novel. Those images of young men wearing pleated slacks and wide, painted ties were indelibly added to Frank's own memories of the Stanford campus. Frank shared his own impressions of the energy which was palpable in the dorms during his stay there; his stories recalled a who's-who of Tech at that time, collectively imagining a world which they were certain they were re-inventing.

Talk eventually turned to the subject of finance, and Bill put into perspective how Frank had originally caught his attention, "Your jaundiced eye in that Thesis, especially where you focused on 'sovereign interference,' in otherwise free flowing commodities markets, truly impressed me. Your broad concerns about China, and especially the more opaque manipulations, like those in the Canadian timber industry, all needed to be exposed."

"Then, to quantify commodities and materials disruption when tariffs interfere . . . *Wow Frank!*" Bill laughed when he finished, "I had this image of you as the fabled boy on the parade grounds shouting, 'The Emperor is not wearing any clothes!' . . . Not bad stuff for a twenty-four-year-old student."

Frank was inebriated but energized, and his appreciation of Bill's comments was sincere. Then, probably because of the confidence that Reggie's Manhattans had built within him, he let fly, "I was taught that math at some point becomes music for the best mathematicians, but it always felt dangerous to me to just concede your faith to every algorithm that was offered. What if everyone from the beginning got those formulas wrong?! I really don't know why, but from my earliest memories I just felt better when I stepped back to have a look at the solutions myself." He and Bill then sat quietly for a minute, as they considered each other in a shared admiration . . .

The silence was broken only when Reggie appeared and quietly began to tidy up the table. Hank took the opportunity to heckle him, "Who do you have to *blow* around here to get something to eat?" Reggie (formidable as ever) answered, "Oh *Hank*, you know very well that you have to blow *me* . . ." Everyone laughed, and Reggie turned to grab menus from the bar.

❊ ❊ ❊

Their late lunch had been passed to Reggie through an open window behind the bar, and it was delicious. The four men, devoid of glucose following their impressive drink fest, quietly inhaled their meals and then languished with coffee afterwards . . .

Bill offered to Hank, "Steve and I are going to drop off the Suburban at the St. Francis after we pick up Marion's car. That gives us a way to get home tomorrow after moving the boat. If you'd like, we can take Frank with us and drop him off at his house?" Hank liked the plan and welcomed the early-out as a way to score points with his wife.

He shook hands all around and stopped at the bar to laugh briefly with Reggie. He then disappeared out the front door. Bill stood up and addressed Steve, "Will you hold down the fort my friend, while Frank and I steal away to discuss his career plans?" Steve nodded back, "Of course." Bill then turned toward the bar and pressed both of his palms together (fingers pointing upward), and he bowed impressively toward Reggie, "You are the best that ever was, Reg . . ."

"Thank you for our journey here today. As usual, let's obfuscate the details of our tab, so my darling Marion won't have to worry about how much we actually drank here today; sometimes I don't beat her to the mailbox." Reggie laughed and said, "I know the drill." Then, in the same respectful manner that Bill had demonstrated, he returned the bow . . .

## THE BUSINESS AT HAND

Bill took the lead toward the club's back door, as the two men made their way toward Angelina to climb aboard. He unlocked the new plexiglass hatch and removed its teak door. The bulkhead that spanned the opening was lined with impressive electronics, and Frank followed him down into the galley, where Bill began turning on lights. Standing beside a bench within the intricate Nav Station, Bill switched on those lights as well. Frank noticed a solid console phone, which would have to be the satellite phone that Hank had mentioned.

On the opposite side of the saloon was a gimbaled, stainless steel gas range framed by cabinets and a countertop with an imbedded cutting board. Located midway in the saloon was a stout vertical pillar which stood from floor to ceiling. Frank later learned that it was structural in design, and it "stepped" the mast to the sailboat's lead keel for reinforcement. On either side of the forward berths hung braided ropes and various hardware secured inside nylon webbing. In the peak of the boat, rested a pile of large nylon bags; full of what? . . . Frank could only guess.

Bill lit a burner on the stove, and motioned toward the table, "Here, let's sit awhile. I'm going to start a pot of coffee if you don't mind. It always sounds good to me on a sailboat, especially as the evenings turn chilly." Frank agreed, "Sounds good . . ." Then looking around, "I guess it shouldn't surprise me that this boat is beautiful down here as well." Bill chuckled and said, "Well . . . thanks, but I have to take Marion's side on that. You will see; it really doesn't measure up to the woodwork in the old Swan. Maybe one day we can go look at one to give you some perspective.

❦ ❦ ❦

Bill soon poured the coffee and took a seat close to Frank. He studied him and began, "I presume Henry has prefaced my story sufficiently to get you in the ballpark, so I'll jump ahead: First off, you need to know that it still boggles my mind when I consider how much wealth I have accumulated during all these years . . . And, if I told you that I was never in it for the *money*, I'm sure you wouldn't believe me."

"Honestly, I'm sure that money only came to me because I was having so much fun earning it every single day for all those years. The tally never really drove me from one day to the next, excepting maybe those rare occasions when quantifying some portion of it was required by a CFO somewhere to parlay the next merger or acquisition." He paused and sipped his coffee, "Someone once told me, 'Money goes where it is most loved,' but I have come to believe that it actually goes where it is most *respected*, which requires knowing why it goes where it does . . . And that, as you certainly know in these complex markets, is a scholarly discipline."

"Considering that discipline, I believe that if your gratitude lies wholly within your gift of understanding how money flows—rather than in the money for its own sake—you will naturally attract it to you. Money will always seek you out, because your safe stewardship protects it . . . I believe, without a doubt, *that* is why money came to be within my control for all these years."

"So here I am . . . turning *eighty* years old next January, and all I really know for certain about the money is that I want to do something good with it for as long as I possibly can. I don't want it to end up in the hands of the *bad guys*. Meaning, in the possession of those legions of empty and ridiculous people who are really nothing more than *glorified hoarders* . . ."

❦ ❦ ❦

Bill sipped some coffee and continued, "So, as my dear wife and I imagine the next stage of *fun* in our lives, we believe we can create a reality where we might systematically give it all away—hopefully over many, many years—and that's where *you* come into the picture, Frank . . ." Bill asked him, "Is this consistent with what Henry shared with you?"

Frank nodded his head, "Yes. He told me in fact, that you and Marion have set aside approximately fifty million dollars within a charitable foundation to begin doing exactly what you just described; he said that Marion likes the *Museum of Modern Art*, and you like *Davies Symphony Hall*, among other causes, although he didn't elaborate on what those might be."

Bill smiled at him, "Yep, that's a good start . . . But now you need to know there is a bit more to the story: My wife and I don't have family, Frank. Sadly we tried, but to Marion's eternal heartbreak, it turned out that it just wasn't possible. Therefore, we will not have a Family Estate, nor any of the legal requirements which accompany them."

"So, dispensation becomes pretty simple . . . The plan is, as soon as possible, to move the *entirety* of our holdings into the foundation, where tax consequences won't diminish the amounts we want to give to our charities—and there will be many more of those, once the funding is in place. That, of course, is complicated by what I now understand you recognize to be a mortgage juggernaut brewing in the markets; I have also felt for some time now that your prediction will be threatening in ways that I have not witnessed in my lifetime."

❋ ❋ ❋

Bill paused and studied Frank. He then continued, "But, these worsening market risks aren't the only reason why time is of the essence here—and even *Hank* is not aware of this, so I will ask that you please keep this secret just between us. Marion and I, and now *you,* are the only non-medical people to have this information . . ."

He stared at Frank, "I have a heart condition that my doctors call '*aortic stenosis*'.' In my case, the valve had some past damage, and now it's not as elastic as it needs to be to push the blood along; the flow backs up, and oxygenated blood doesn't always go where it needs to go. Among other things, any pooling of blood that results also puts me at risk to throw clots . . ."

"I have put this off for far too long, and my friends at Stanford are not happy about it. Bill continued, "That leaves *you* at the center of my plans to put all of this in order—presuming of course, that we still have enough time to position ourselves before the next market crash. And it also presumes that I won't just keel over one day in the middle of our work, and make a big mess of everything . . ."

"Then, at whatever point you and I can look back upon our work with reasonable confidence—and perhaps even celebrate with a Manhattan (smiling at Frank). We will batten down the hatches and wait for the storm to pass . . . I will also, very soon after that, submit to whichever heart procedure is recommended for me."

"Stanford's new heart valve will be placed, by the way, to the great relief of Marion—that stubborn woman won't even let me sail out past the Golden Gate Bridge until I can get myself off these goddamn *anticoagulants!*" Bill grinned at Frank, who was just now beginning to weigh the responsibilities at hand, "Until today Frank, you were the only piece of the mosaic that was still missing; maybe I waited so long to seek you out, because I refused to accept that I am not immortal . . . certainly in the grips of denial, I now understand. But then I woke up one day to find that I was turning eighty, and some really smart people told me that I have a bad heart."

"Worse yet, my sacrosanct market principles got tainted during my involvement in the Iraq War. That was where I first collided with my mortality, and it forced me to examine my life to make some honest judgements about it." Things got quiet as Bill stared at the table.

❋ ❋ ❋

He looked at Frank, "When you finally came onto the radar, and I studied your path in getting here, it became evident that you might be the one person I can trust to protect my life's work, should I suddenly disappear off the planet. Honestly Frank, I get a migraine when I study your quantified models for capital preservation." He grinned, "But I also needed to be certain that you were, more importantly, the kind of person who will continue to attract money to the Foundation, which of course had to begin with your path through the Stanford School of Business," and Bill winked at him. Frank played along, "Well, *of course* . . ."

❉ ❉ ❉

Bill wrapped it up, "So I would like to propose that we, as soon as possible, make you administrator of The Bennett Foundation. Marion and I will continue to approve decisions as *Co-Executors*. You will have the authority to trade assets, initially within my oversight, and then singularly over time. How about if we start you at $200,000 more per year than you are now making, and when things evolve as I absolutely expect them to, we will adjust that amount upward on a sliding scale, as more assets fall under your direct management."

"I anticipate that your salary will eventually be commensurate with those of the managers of comparably-sized Mutual Funds . . . And Frank, if you and I can protect these holdings through the next crisis and beyond, the size of the Foundation will actually surpass many US mutual funds in total assets under management. At today's values, I put our 'AUM' right at $1.4 billion . . . So . . . can I convince you to drop what you are now doing and come help me grapple with this considerable task?"

Frank was staggered by the sums just revealed to him, and he could barely speak, "I am so humbled right now that I can't even find words. . . ." Bill grinned and said, "Then just say 'Yes' . . . I cannot imagine anyone else who is more naturally worthy than you, Frank." At this, Frank smiled back and exclaimed, "Yes . . . Of course, yes . . ." The two energized men at last shook hands, and then began laughing together beneath the decks of Angelina.

❉ ❉ ❉

Bill said he would make arrangements right away to install the same proprietary networks and equipment in Frank's house that he employed in his own—secure live video devices and dedicated lines could then be utilized as soon as possible. He asked Frank to duplicate his own trading platform in both homes, and onto portable devices as well, anticipating future changing work locales. Bill went further, "After completing each day's business, you should then plan to meet me at the sailboat, which will mostly be kept in her slip at the St. Francis Yacht Club."

In complete seriousness, he shared, "You will learn that a sailboat is a great place to spitball ideas, after taking in the morning's business news."

❀ ❀ ❀

Frank expressed excitement that he might be able to see the boat from his home in the Marina District... "Speaking of which," Bill added, "how would you feel about helping Steve and I sail Angelina back to her slip at the St. Francis tomorrow? It's supposed to be a nice day, and that is always helpful for new sailors just getting their sea legs." Frank replied, "I would love to help, if you're sure I won't get in the way."

Bill walked over to a cabinet and retrieved an old hardbound book. He returned to the table and placed a well-worn copy of *Sail Power* by Wallace Ross in front of Frank. Spinning the book toward him, he began to leaf through the pages, "Don't worry about the size of this book—for now, just concentrate on these great pictures of sails in the wind tunnels. Then . . . you will need to understand Bernoulli's Principal, particularly as it relates to an airplane wing."

"Like a wing, the sail is also a foil, and we are just wrapping the wind around the leading edge of it to pull the boat forward. Then . . . maybe . . . try to understand laminar vs. turbulent wind flow . . . Oh, and why don't you look at 'points of sail' and 'speed-made-good'? That's probably enough for tonight," and he smiled mischievously at Frank.

"Okay", Frank half-joked, "but, is there going to be a test on this tomorrow?" "No", Bill laughed, "however, you will soon discover that Steve can be a taskmaster when we sail, so learn to *love* that book." Bill looked at his watch and said, "We better start moving; we need to make a couple of stops before we can drop you off at your house. I'll go find Steve."

# 8

## THE DISAGREEMENT

Frank texted Cherice to let her know that he was heading in her direction, but also that he had been asked to go sailing tomorrow. He hoped she would forgive him "these last-minute plans." And finally, "I really need to talk with you this evening about so many things, so let's plan for some time together."

Steve and Bill appeared through the back door of the yacht club, and quickly jumped aboard the sailboat to secure it for the night. The three men then walked together along Beach Street toward the parking lot, as they made their way to a black GMC Suburban with dark tinted windows; Steve took the driver's seat after unlocking the doors.

"Frank, why don't you sit up front with Steve," Bill suggested. "We have to quickly swing by the house to grab Marion's car, so this will be a good opportunity for you to learn the route. You'll see, it's actually pretty easy to get there. Just remember to stay on Beach Street, which leads onto Belvedere Island . . . It then continues all the way to the south end of the island, where I'll point out our driveway."

Steve drove forward, turning smoothly out of the parking lot, and then he accelerated. They passed over a small bridge and soon made their way up into Belvedere. Here the foliage began to transform into manicured landscaping, amidst the afternoon shade of impressive old-growth trees. All of this imparted a feeling of natural equilibrium, and when Frank cracked his passenger-side window, he confirmed the harmony of its bouquet.

It occurred to him that he had never asked where Bill Bennett lived, and that now seemed like a detail which would have enhanced his understanding of the man. Steve slowed the Suburban where the road narrowed, taking them closer to a security shack which sat behind a lowered gate with a stop sign. He dropped his window and greeted the man inside, "Hi Burke. How are you today?" The security officer smiled, "Hard to complain on a beautiful day like this, huh? . . . So, who's on board today?" Steve obliged, "Mr. Bennett and myself, and this is Frank McClelland."

Frank nodded to the man as Steve continued, "Frank is going to start working with Mr. Bennett, so you will be seeing a lot more of him in the future." The man smiled, "Very good . . . Welcome to Belvedere Island, Mr. McClelland. Can you give me a description of the vehicle you will be driving to and from the island?" Frank answered, "Sure. It's a 1997 Ford F-150 pickup . . . a white crew-cab, short bed."

His voice trailed off when Steve suddenly turned toward him with a confused look. "Great", the guard replied, "We'll need a photo of the truck, along with your license and registration when you drive in for the first time; then we can just wave you through in the future . . . You gentlemen have a great day."

As Steve pulled away, he grinned at Frank and quipped, "Yeah, you must blend *right in* driving that old pickup around San Francisco . . . I bet poor Burke back there thinks you're the Bennett's new gardener," and he laughed some more. Frank, a little defensive now, countered, "I bought it in a fleet sale to Newmont Mining, and just never got around to buying something else. Honestly, I ride my bicycle everywhere, so mostly it just stays parked." Bill leaned forward and patted Frank on the shoulder, "Don't let him harass you, Frank. I realize about eight times a month that I need a pickup just to haul stuff back and forth to the boat . . . Maybe we should start driving that F-150 around, huh Steve? That might throw everybody a curve . . ."

❀ ❀ ❀

Steve guided the Suburban along the east shore of Belvedere Island, and Frank took in the magnificent homes along the waterfront; they revealed themselves one after the other on both sides of Beach Street. It really didn't take long until Bill said, "Okay . . . We're coming up to Belvedere Avenue here, where we'll make a quick right . . . And then just climb up the hill for a bit more. This is us on the right." Steve drove up a short distance more onto a driveway apron and inched forward to a substantial wrought-iron gate; he stopped there next to a pillar.

Frank watched as Steve extended his left palm and placed his middle finger upon a small screen which flashed blue light while it scanned his fingerprint. He stared directly into a camera that moved to center upon his face. The gate began to open slowly along a smooth track that was imbedded in the concrete. Bill noted to Steve, "We'll have to get him programmed into that gate soon, but until then Frank, just press the intercom button and one of us will let you in."

Steve guided the Suburban up and around the left border of a parking area which faced the beautiful and compelling entrance to Bill's house. Frank considered the Thai-inspired, yet lower profile gable ends of the extraordinary home. They stopped beside a very long garage, where one of the many doors was opened to reveal a vintage Citroen; the car was beautiful, and it looked to be perfectly restored. Frank followed the two men past the garage where Bill said, "I just need to grab a key to Marion's car . . ."

❁ ❁ ❁

Through filtered sunlight, Frank took in the Zen garden accents along a natural path; this steered them beside a tranquil stream which was diverted through large bamboo culverts to cascade into a Koi pond. Bill approached a garden patio door, which also served the house as a side entrance. He cautioned Frank before stepping inside, "Marion is not here at the moment, but, *whatever you do*, please do not tell her that I brought you in through this side door to see the house for the first time . . . She takes her feng shui very, very seriously. Next time, when we introduce the two of you properly, expect that she will give you her full tour, which unfailingly begins at the front door."

Frank nodded and stepped into the exquisite home. He followed Bill while he moved toward a huge kitchen—surrounding him was evidence that cooking undertaken here was being *expertly* accomplished. Seasoned cast-iron skillets, and various functional pots and pans hung on a brick wall that climbed upward from behind the large industrial gas range and stove; the range was centered beneath a huge copper hood, where the fan's ducting (also copper) was artfully guided up through a high ceiling.

Cutting boards with professional knives and kitchen utensils at-the-ready nearby, waited beside baskets of garlic and onions and various roasted peppers—fresh herbs were either hanging just above, or laid out to dry on the nearby counter tops. Next to all of this sat a very large porcelain colander filled with fresh heirloom tomatoes and scallions that imparted a truly healthy fragrance.

❁ ❁ ❁

When Bill disappeared to gather items for their trip over to the St. Francis, Frank moved out past the expansive countertop which surrounded the kitchen. He looked around and admired the living room's distinctive settees which featured recessed bookshelves and classic paintings that were illuminated by sconce lighting; these sequestered retreats bordered a sunken living room with sofas that sat close to a ceramic fire pit.

He was then naturally drawn into a wide alcove filled with ambient light; displayed on its walls was a collection of paintings that shared a similar regional theme. Feeling that the alcove had been built to highlight the center of the living room,

Frank began to more closely study the paintings. He presumed that the works of Jose and Ramiro Arrue had been chosen by Marion for display here, as well as others by Fernando de Amarica. The latter artist's hillside landscapes now especially held Frank's focus. Taken together with the pastoral settings of the Arrue paintings, he suddenly realized that some of them resembled terrain backdrops he had first seen in his Mother's old photo album. Frank vowed to someday ask Marion about them..

He at last found himself being pulled toward a wall of afternoon light, now streaming in through windows that faced back toward San Francisco. Below him was Angel Island, and beyond it and to the right were Sausalito and Mt. Tamalpais. The distant backdrop of the Golden Gate Bridge was prominent in the sunlight, and there were numerous sailboats, gathered close in a regatta on the Bay.

He could see the Presidio and Golden Gate Park and The Palace of Fine Arts, and then nearly the entire metropolitan vista of the City of San Francisco—there was Coit Tower and the Transamerica Building amidst the late afternoon fog which was now rolling in slowly over the hills that bordered The City. Frank was absolutely spellbound to see San Francisco from this vantage, and he wondered how it must appear at night with everything lit up?

Bill suddenly stood beside him, having added a jacket and a baseball cap, and he lingered for a moment to share the view with Frank, "It's an absolute treasure, isn't it? Sometimes I think about my past life in Manhattan—with its sirens and horns and pervasive noise, and I remember forever looking up from street level to see nothing but concrete. I still have a hard time reconciling that a place like this actually exists . . ."

Silently, the two men stood for a moment more. Bill was the first to break the reverie, as he turned to grab keys from the counter and then move toward the patio door. He tossed the Suburban keys to Steve, who had re-appeared in the kitchen, and the three men exited toward the garage.

❁ ❁ ❁

Bill and Frank led in the Citroen while Steve followed close behind in the Suburban, and they made their way out of Belvedere toward Sausalito and Highway 101—Frank was impressed by the vintage car, so he asked Bill to tell him about it. Bill began, "You will soon learn that Marion has a fascination for all things 'French'; her family members were hunted relentlessly during the war, and they sought refuge in and around Paris. Even though she was very young, she grew up speaking the language, and she still has deep attachments there; I will leave it to her to elaborate on that."

"Hence, the 1966 Citroen DS Manufactur, which for some reason captured her imagination. She loves this thing, but honestly, I could have bought her several cars for the money I have spent over the years trying to restore this crazy hydraulic system—Nonetheless, she still buzzes around town in it with her girlfriends in tow, even though she now mostly drives her Chevy Tahoe."

※ ※ ※

Frank enjoyed his ride back over the bridge in the comfortable Citroen, as Bill made his way to the St. Francis Yacht Club. Once there, he pulled off to the side of the parking entrance, where Steve drove past them to park near the clubhouse. He then jogged back to join them before jumping into the back seat. Again, Frank was struck by how nimble the big man was in his movements; had he played pro football? . . . maybe a linebacker? The tattoos could be consistent with that.

After pulling away, Frank guided Bill through a few turns that pointed them toward his house in the Marina District. Steve along the way asked Bill, "What time do you want to get started tomorrow?" Bill thought out loud, "Well, Marion is going to early Mass . . . So, why don't we meet at the boat around 11:00?"

Steve then directed Frank, "So Frank, you and I should plan on being there a couple of hours before that. You need to start getting acquainted with the deck hardware and some of the instrumentation and controls before we shove off." Steve didn't phrase that in the form of a question, and Frank found himself worrying about Bill's "taskmaster" reference, which he had used to describe Steve while sailing. He gripped the book that Bill had given him and remembered he needed to study tonight.

Frank at last directed Bill onto his street, "Just there on your right . . . the one with the white stucco," and Bill pulled over to the curb. Frank stepped out and leaned down to thank Bill for the landmark day, and to say, "See you both tomorrow . . ." The Citroen then pulled away into the street and it quickly disappeared around the first corner. As Frank watched the car disappear, he glanced at his watch and saw that it was nearly 6:00 pm. He marveled at everything he had experienced in this one momentous day . . . *A life-changing day*, he thought to himself.

## CHERICE

When he entered his house, he found the hallway lined with various colorful shopping bags, and he heard Cherice clattering about in the kitchen—music was playing while she prepared dinner. When he stepped into view, she exclaimed, *"Hey,* good timing! I just threw together a chicken Caesar; it sounded kind of good tonight. Why don't you open up a bottle of white, and check on that bread for me?"

Frank quickly glanced at the broiler and decided that the bread needed another minute, so he opened a chilled bottle of Sauvignon Blanc and poured two glasses. Passing one to Cherice, who silently raised her glass to him, he joined her in a first sip. He then kidded, "Well, it looks like it was mission accomplished on your shopping trip, judging by the number of bags . . ."

Cherice laughed a little and then held up a hand, "Yes, but you will be so proud of me; I didn't buy anything today that wasn't on sale, and I even got something for you. I'll show you after dinner. I scored on some really cute things. But how about you, *mister?!* Kind of a long day for you to spend with a client, huh? . . . and sailing tomorrow too? Wow . . . must be somebody pretty important," as she donned an oven mitt to grab her tray of bruschetta.

Frank took a bigger drink of wine, because he had decided to just wade right in, "Well, that actually turned out to be something much bigger than sealing the deal with a client—and that's why I texted you earlier, hoping we could talk tonight." Frank became serious now as he stared at Cherice, "I have been offered a job, Honey . . . an *amazing* job actually, and that turned out to be what my trip to Tiburon was all about today. Hank put the meeting together; he's a long-time friend of this individual, and we just hit it off from the start."

Cherice was stunned to hear this unexpected news, "*Wow!* That's kind of out of the blue, Frank . . . Have you been shopping your resume around and not telling me? I mean, how did this guy even hear about you?" Frank stepped away to turn down the music, and then he cautioned, "This is where the story takes a turn . . . Hank came to work at Icarus only so he could recruit me," and he paused a moment to let that sink in.

"All that his friend knew about me up until that time, he had learned from my professors at Stanford; he's an alumnus, and he was shown my MBA Thesis. He continued to follow me during my time as an analyst for Newmont and Barrick, because he was interested in my experience with commodities and hard currencies. Then recently, he sent Hank to watch me in the 'fixed-income' world."

"He wants me to manage a charitable foundation for he and his wife . . ." Cherice was confused (at the minimum) by what she had just heard. Suddenly she stared at Frank like he had two heads, "How long have you known about this thing with Hank?" . . . Then incredulously, "Are you telling me that he was only at Icarus so he could *recruit* you?!"

Frank back-pedaled, "Hank only came-clean about all of this a few days ago, and I thought I needed more information about his friend before you and I sat down to talk—at the heart of it all Cherice, you need to know that I am *not* on board with the direction that Icarus is taking in the mortgage market. Those CDO's are fucking *snake oil* that will come back to hurt us all, and I don't want to be a part of it. So when I brought that up to Hank, he felt it was time to tell me about his friend. After which, it just kind of snowballed; that's why I went to Tiburon today, to listen to what this man had to say, and *no*, I haven't been shopping my resume around anywhere; I certainly would have told you if I had decided to start . . ."

❆ ❆ ❆

Cherice flashed Frank an icy stare, "When did you plan to tell me that you were this *miserable* at Icarus?" Frank returned the ice, and then he couldn't soften his intonation, "I have not been miserable at Icarus! This mortgage thing is recent, and you know it as well as anyone. But when do you imagine that we might have talked about it, Cherice? You never give me an opening to tell you anything about myself! . . . If and when you finally do listen, I can always count on you to yawn, or to be distracted in some way!"

He stopped to hold eye contact, but it now felt like he was on a runaway train, "Half the time, I don't think you're interested at all in what I have to say. In fact, I think that mostly I just bore the shit out of you." Seeing her indignation, he quickly continued, "You know that I'm not making this up!" Now there was no turning back, "Day in and day out, I just listen to you talk, which is fine, right up until the moment when I actually have something important to say . . . Then, how do you suggest that I break into the conversation?"

He glared at her, "I can mostly take the constant focus on yourself. In fact, I tell myself that it's just the way you are—maybe because of your childhood, or maybe it's just something you need to do to boost your confidence—but from the very start, I have not been able to get past the fact that you never seem interested to know how I feel about *anything*." . . . Frank stared at Cherice, who was at once hurt and angered by these accusations.

She didn't wait this time, "Can you possibly *imagine* that there might be some other reason why I don't want to hear what you have to say?" Cherice challenged him as her tears welled up, "Maybe I just got tired of being *corrected* by you every time we talk. Like the Stanford *genius* deserves to have the final word on every subject. Do you honestly think I don't know that you believe I'm a trivial person? . . . That doesn't leave much of an opening to share a conversation with you, does it genius?!"

❈ ❈ ❈

Now Frank was the one who was taken aback—but Cherice kept coming at him— "The problem is, you never give it a rest . . . And, if I ever hope to escape our roles at work, it takes some miracle of persuasion to convince you even to go out with me. Then, the only thing keeping you from disappearing and leaving me alone entirely, is that we can always count on some dipshit broker to stop you at the door, so you can tell him one more time about the 'Copper/Gold Ratio', or . . . or . . . the 'Inverted Yield Curve', and 'What possibly can it all mean Frank?' . . . like, 'Thank God you are so brilliant, Frank, so the rest of us know how to think!' . . ."

Frank shot back, "I am not correcting you! . . . On those rare occasions when you're not entirely self-absorbed, you talk about other subjects without any regard for the facts; I'm just trying to keep you from embarrassing yourself on topics which don't center on you!" Cherice now had tears streaming down her face as she and her husband stared at each other, lost suddenly in a desolate place that they had not visited together before tonight. In disgust, she finally marveled, "When have I *ever* needed to rely on the *facts* to win someone else's approval?!"

She broke away first, leaving a now speechless Frank to stare at the kitchen floor. At some point he realized that his wife still believed dinner was possible, and he watched her place their two salads on the table. Mechanically, Frank organized the bruschetta within a basket set out for that purpose. He then poured more wine and balanced the glasses between the fingers of one hand.

With deliberate movements, he delivered bread and wine to the dinner table, where he sat down quietly next to his wife. Frank sipped wine only once and continued to stare at the salad, while Cherice picked slowly at lettuce around the borders of her plate. A lot of time passed while they sat there in silence.

❀ ❀ ❀

Finally, Cherice turned toward Frank and more softly asked, "So, are you going to take the job?" Frank looked at her and answered matter-of-factly, "Yes . . . *I am*", and silence returned for another minute. She sighed and looked back toward her salad. He continued, "This is a great opportunity Cherice, and I meant what I said earlier about this mortgage thing; I've come to realize that I can't be a part of it . . . I have to tell Larry tomorrow. He needs to know that I will stay at Icarus only long enough to orient this new Lehman guy; after that, I'm gone . . ."

Cherice now looked more worried, "You know that everyone there is going to assume that you got forced out so *Travis Whitsome* can take over . . . I would think you might worry about that a little bit more, and also that you might want to stay longer, if only to defend your reputation . . . your *career* even."

"I mean, how is this going to look Frank? . . . Here you are leaving your job at a legit brokerage, to work for some Mom and Pop somewhere in their charitable foundation." *Classic Cherice*, Frank thought . . . sweeping conclusions, with zero information. He weighed the futility of any possible retorts, and decided only to say, "I don't care what those people think . . . This sub-prime mortgage thing is professional suicide; it's going to bring down markets everywhere. And Cherice . . . knowing this beforehand will make it *impossible* for me to sell those products to our clients . . . I have to leave Icarus."

Cherice once again became defensive, and she stood up to seethe at him, "So, you've decided that it's okay to just run for the exit, even though your wife will be left behind while all of those markets come crashing down around her? Did you have a plan for *me* in this Frank?!" and she picked up her plate to spin away. She then flew past the kitchen counter and dropped her plate hard when she passed. Frank tried to stop her, *"Cherice!"* but she was already gone.

❁ ❁ ❁

Certainly, Frank knew that his wife and Larry Sewell would survive the next *Ice Age* together—believing with absolute certainty that Icarus would just pivot once again around some next "Big Thing," exactly as they had done following the Dot-Com crash. But to forecast that conclusion for Cherice's sake (especially now, as an afterthought), would only sound feeble to her . . . He was just about to jump up and go try to make his case anyway, when he heard her bathwater pouring into the tub. He stopped and sat down again, trying to piece together what had just happened between him and his wife.

At some point he finally cleared the table, but disheartened as he was, he could only rinse the dishes and leave them in the sink. He pulled on a coat from the entryway, then grabbed his glass and the remaining wine bottle—opening the patio slider, he stepped out into the chilly evening air. He placed the wine on a nearby table and walked toward the patio railing.

He stood there gazing out across the Bay. His eyes began to follow a supertanker during its gradual exit out of the mouth of San Francisco Bay, and he wondered where it was headed tonight? Someone once told him that those tankers (when they are fully loaded) take *six miles to stop* once the decision had been made by the captain, and Frank considered momentum on a scale such as that. He thought about the momentum of the choices he had unleashed tonight into his own life. Standing there watching, he at last came to accept the futility of any attempt to reverse course.

## IMPASSE

How long had Cherice harbored that kind of resentment for him? . . . years maybe? Thinking back upon it now, he couldn't honestly remember if they had ever shared a vision rising from anything akin to a common purpose. Instead of commitment, it was always "parry and feint" in a circle of avoidance with them, putting off shared choices for another day. Where did their commitments exist then, if everything originated in foundations lacking even any kind of cogent direction?

He let go a prolonged exhalation and concluded that he and his wife would never find their safe haven together; there were just too many moving parts interfering with steerage, and it had forever kept them apart. Frank considered this as he drank more wine. Knowing that his wife would surely want space after tonight's nuclear detonation, he decided to stay outside in a deck chair for a while more. As he did so, he pulled his coat tighter around his neck and chest. It was still early March, and even though breezes now returning to the Bay Area were gentle, they had not yet separated themselves entirely from the colder winter jet stream which travels down from the Aleutian Islands.

He saw that the night was clear however, and it likely meant that the next day would be clear as well. Better still, he knew that temperate spring days in California's Central Valley meant that fog would not roll up along the coast (as it did on most summer days). So, in spite of feeling more than a little guilty about his hopes for a beautiful day tomorrow, Frank began looking forward to sailing for his first time ever.

❀ ❀ ❀

After an unknown passage of time, he realized that he had dozed off in the chair and he was suddenly cold. He returned inside the warm house, where he locked doors and turned off lights. Hearing no sound from the bedroom, he made his way past a sleeping Cherice to his shower, where he turned up the water temperature to a hotter setting than usual.

Finally emerging from the steam and drying off, he carefully lifted the covers on his side of the bed and climbed in next to his wife. From that warm place, he quietly sighed and stared at the ceiling. After feeling Cherice turn onto her side to face him, he turned as well, and he was struck by her despondent gaze. Her eyes told him that she had cried more since leaving him at the dinner table; this only magnified his own dejection, and it was suddenly impossible to gauge in either face who had been hurt more by tonight's discourse. The two of them remained silent as they became transfixed in each other's up-close eyes, and time drifted past them into the night.

Cherice finally reached over to lift Frank's right arm, and she rolled beneath it to press her back against him. He encircled her completely with both arms (as he always did) and pulled her closer. Certain not to move from this embrace, they both fell asleep while Frank was admitting to himself that he would surely miss the smell of her hair; ultimately, this only served to remind him that she would someday soon find the courage to leave . . .

## EARLY TO RISE

He awoke trying to remember why his internal clock had become so precise over the years. His eyes just popped open without fail every time a meeting or special event required his early attendance. Maybe it could be traced back to his father's regimental approach to work.

If Robert McClelland had planned something strenuous, requiring the early morning participation of Frank and his brother, you didn't want to be the son who derailed those plans—his father's harsh reprimands were just too destructive for a young boy's self-esteem. He knew and accepted this fact from his earliest recollections, while his brother Robby mostly found it impossible to wake up for *any* reason, and he repeatedly paid the price.

Over the years, Frank honed that skill into a valuable discipline for his own career, and for everything else as well which required his commitment. On this morning, he woke at 5:45 remembering that he had been asked to study the sailing book that Bill Bennett had given him. After separating himself from Cherice's interwoven arms and legs, he moved in a stealth effort to the bathroom and splashed cold water onto his face. From there he quietly made his way to the kitchen to start a cup of coffee.

He grabbed the book and settled into a living room chair, where his reading light illuminated the old pages. Frank quickly found the "wind tunnel" section that Bill had mentioned, and he then focused on "laminar and turbulent" airflow over sails. He considered what that meant to the "windward forces" being applied to the sails themselves, and ultimately what it would mean to the speed of a sailboat.

In spite of his physics training, he was still surprised by the magnitude of the forces which could be realized on a properly set sail; he now understood as well why the weaving of materials such as *Mylar* and *Kevlar* into sail fabrics had necessarily evolved over the years.

Beyond the study outline that Bill had given him, which included "points of sail," "speed-made-good," etc., Frank found a good section on "apparent wind" and sail trimming strategies, where he considered "leeward moment" in a sailboat's path forward. Lastly, he studied deck hardware diagrams, along with the requisite terminology; he was hoping for a head start this morning, anticipating that Steve would address these things first.

❋ ❋ ❋

Frank soon afterward looked up at a clock. He figured he would be in good shape if he could leave by 8:00, so he still had time. As he was preparing his second cup of coffee, Cherice appeared in the kitchen and stood beside him. From there, they faced the coffee press together. She grabbed his hand and held it tight, and then she apologized, "I'm sorry my old ghosts came back again last night; you know that being abandoned is my worst fear."

Frank squeezed her hand and looked down at her, "I'm sorry too . . . I don't like being left behind either, so I should have been more careful in my delivery last night; you didn't need to have everything dumped on you all at once." He turned her toward him and hugged her tightly, "Cherice, there is no *abandonment* happening here. I'm here with you for as long as you want me. But, I have to say this: I wish you would let me know more often that *you do still want me*."

He searched her eyes, "These future plans started with my belief that you and Larry will be safe under the Icarus umbrella—it has always protected a*dministrators* during big market changes. You're going to be fine, just like you were after the

Dot-Com crash. It's always the *brokers* who get screwed during times like these, not the bosses. You already know this to be true Cherice; you have seen them come, and you have seen them go . . ."

"And, this *'Mom and Pop'* foundation, as you phrased it? . . . These people are *billionaires* Cherice, and they eventually want to move all of their holdings into the foundation. Assets under management on that scale will make it as big as some of the top mutual funds in the US. I will be working with a man named Bill Bennett who has ties all the way to the top of Goldman Sachs. I have never in my career been closer to anyone who is more highly connected. And the best part? He and his wife *Marion* live right here in the Bay Area. I will be working out of our home here in San Francisco . . . So, I am not going anywhere."

❁ ❁ ❁

At last, Cherice sighed and leaned against Frank, "I know we'll be okay. I just don't like change, and I still don't know how I'm going to handle it when you're not there next to me at work. I like this arrangement." Frank reached around her shoulder and pulled her tight, but seeing the clock on the stove, he apologized, "I'm sorry. I really have to go. I've got to be over in Tiburon by 9:00."

With that, Cherice remembered, *"Wait* . . . I bought you something for sailing. Stay here for another second," and she retrieved a large shopping bag which she handed to her shocked husband. "Well, look inside!" she finally ordered. Frank opened the bag and pulled out a *Navy Peacoat*. Cherice beamed, "Stella had us stop at a vintage clothing shop on Union Street so she could check out the scarves and wraps, and I saw this. The guy in the store said it's the longer version, with a tall collar; the Navy called it a 'watch coat' . . . What do you think?"

Frank pulled the jacket on and felt that it was a perfect fit, "Wow! Very nice . . . Thank you." Cherice admired the jacket and then remembered, "Oh, wait . . . I found a hat to go with it too." She reached into the bottom of the shopping bag and pulled out a black stocking cap, "He tried to sell me the Navy-issue hat, but I liked this one instead—it's *slouchy*, like the ones the grunge rockers used to wear." She smiled when Frank tried it on, "That's perfect!" She at last confided, "I don't know why, but when I bought this coat, I just felt better about you drifting out there by yourself on that great big ocean . . ."

## 9

## SAILING AWAY

Leaving home that morning with a duffel that now held his new coat and hat, Frank stepped into the sun and breathed in the cool San Francisco air. He was surprised at how invigorated he suddenly felt. Last night's face-off was tough of course, but finding the beginnings to any kind of resolution with Cherice surely amounted to something good. Mostly, he counted it among the tangible evidence that he was moving forward; a reality that once seemed entirely out of his reach.

Panic attacks had been unprecedented in Frank's life until recently, and he at times now felt increasingly like a specimen caught in some careless child's bug jar, where the inviolate lid above him was twisting tighter and tighter. This, together with the compression of crowds that surrounded him in the financial district, had become his new baseline. Add upon that the mounting layers of pedestrian monotony invented at Icarus, and it topped-off a claustrophobia unlike anything Frank had previously known.

Living with Cherice once gave him sanctuary. But as that faded, he was certain the life which remained might literally suffocate him someday soon. His wife's network of banal friendships and prattle only cemented his isolation. And those empty social functions she had mentioned last night—where he repeatedly found himself cornered by people devoid of imagination—now just angered him. He considered all of this as he opened the garage door at street level, and climbed into his Ford pickup for the first time in a long time.

❁ ❁ ❁

He laughed to himself when he remembered Steve's jab about "blending right in" while driving his F-150 around San Francisco. That image, juxtaposed against the absurdity of arriving in, say, Cherice's BMW convertible at some remote Nevada mining site, was even more ludicrous to consider, and he smiled at that too.

He thought for a while about Bill Bennett, and what must have been his myriad opportunities for travel and experience all around the world. After years of seeing what he must have seen at every possible site on the planet, why would he conclude that a sailboat was "his life's metaphor"? As Frank continued north, he was excited at the prospect of someday learning that answer for himself, and it was only the growing illumination of the day's sunlight that finally brought him back to reality.

※ ※ ※

His early drive over The Bridge delivered him to the San Francisco Yacht Club sooner than anticipated, and he was actually one of the first to park close to the clubhouse. As he made his way toward Angelina, he saw Steve moving about the cockpit of the beautiful sailboat. He was dropping tightly-coiled ropes at various locales on the deck. The black canvas boom cover had been removed to reveal the top of the main sail, and Frank focused on the impressive gray Kevlar spines which reinforced the head of the sail.

Steve finally noticed him but looked past him to confirm the white Ford pickup that Frank had driven. He was cheerful in his greeting, "Hey! I've got the stanchions unhooked. Give me your duffel." He then grabbed it and threw it beside the hatch as Frank climbed aboard. "Let's have a look at what you're wearing . . ."

He quickly concluded, "You got lucky today; it's going to be a nice day with flat seas, so you're probably fine. Most of the time you will need to think about layering up, especially when we're out on the water all day; once you get a chill, you can never warm back up again. Do you own any poly-props?" Frank thought for a moment, "Yes, at home with my ski stuff." Steve smiled, "Good. Start packing them in your duffel, and also pick up some bunting pullovers. Buy the good stuff; we like Patagonia on this boat. They keep you protected in the elements. I know you don't have foulies yet, so I dug out Bill's old ones and some boots for you to wear today."

Below in the galley, Frank quickly stepped into the waterproof pants that were a part of bib overalls, and he tucked in an old pullover that had been laid out for him as well. He then adjusted the suspenders to more tightly fit his shoulders; the foulies fit pretty well actually, and they reminded him of the powder pants he used to wear while skiing on stormy days in the Sierra.

When he climbed back up to the cockpit, Steve was waiting there with a well-frayed pair of sailing gloves which he handed to Frank. The gloves were designed to protect his palms while leaving the fingers exposed. Steve looked him over and nodded his approval.

From that point on, Steve set about readying sail sheets and halyards as he enlisted Frank's help at each station. He taught him to tie bowline knots ("the rabbit comes out of the hole, around the tree and back down the hole") everywhere the wind puts "load" upon sails and hardware. Steve watched his student and heckled him while he practiced, "That bowline knot has only been used on sailboats for five hundred years Frank, so please don't be the first guy to fuck it all up."

❀ ❀ ❀

Unbeknownst to either of them, Bill Bennett had approached Angelina quietly as he admired their work, and he surprised them from the pier with an accomplished pirate's dialect, *"Ahoy Mateys!"* He was pulling a wheeled ice chest, and he marveled at the extensive preparation, *"Wow!* Look at you two . . . It appears to me that somebody here wants to go sailing today."

In the blink of an eye, Steve jumped down to assume control of the ice chest. Frank followed aft to the cockpit stanchions, where he expected to help him lift the heavy ice chest onboard. Steve apparently never considered that option, because in one fluid motion he (alone) lifted the chest and set it down precisely on the deck; Frank could only watch in awe.

Bill climbed into the cockpit and happily approved, "Hey, you found my old foulies! It's nice to see them back in action, and by God, you even look like a *sailor* Frank." Steve couldn't resist, "We'll see about that," and they chuckled. When Bill stepped toward the galley, he pointed to the ice chest and informed Steve, "I've got a bottle of Champagne inside. Let's stow it up here somewhere in the cockpit. Before shoving off, we'll need to make an offering to Neptune on behalf of our new crew member today . . . And, of course, we will need to save enough to share in a toast." He winked and disappeared below-decks.

Steve opened the ice chest to retrieve the Champagne, and then reacted, "*Nice!* It looks like Marion packed our lunch today; you will soon discover that to be a *very* good thing. Marion definitely knows her way around food!" He moved the chest back toward the galley just as Bill emerged in his foulies, ready to go. Steve then quickly stowed the chest.

Bill pulled on his gloves and moved toward the engine controls. He summoned Frank after starting the engine and asked him, "Do you have any experience with diesels?" Frank replied, "Some . . . tractors and swathers, a long time ago." "Same thing," said Bill. He then leaned over the transom and pointed to a small stream of water spurting out from the through-hull, and he continued, "That's essential—we have to know the engine is circulating water to keep it cool, and that there's no piece of kelp, or something worse gumming things up. When you see that stream of water, you know we are *dieseling* as we should be . . ."

Steve climbed out of the galley and Bill gave him a heads-up, "We appear to have a nice breeze filling in this morning; if I didn't know better, I'd say we have an easterly visiting Belvedere Island this morning." Steve was surprised, *"Really?"* Bill then clarified to Frank, "That only happens once in a great while, usually meaning that we have low pressure south of the Bay Area. This time of year, it can circle warm weather around behind us, and our usual westerly wind patterns get suppressed. If it happens to be a small system, as this one appears to be, then the winds can be very nice; that usually helps to keep the bay water flat too."

Frank nodded, "We actually have something like that in Nevada. When the wind comes out of the east, we call it a Tonopah Low, or sometimes an Inside Slider. That wind is generally colder, and when it circles down from the north, it can surprise you with snow." Steve added, "Yeah, these cells along the coast can grow bigger too while we're out on the water, so we have to stay pretty glued to the radar."

Bill took one last look around the deck and decided, "Well, I can't see a single thing that you two haven't already anticipated . . . So let's make our offering to the Gods, and with their blessing, we can shove off."

❀ ❀ ❀

The Skipper soon thereafter clapped his gloved hands together, "Very nice gentlemen! Now, what do you say we go sailing? I'll stow this bottle below in the ice chest, if you two will kindly ready our dock lines," and he disappeared into the galley.

### CAST-OFF

Steve instructed Frank, "Okay, when Bill is ready at the wheel, go ahead and free the line tied to that forward cleat, and then give the bow a strong push away from the pier. Don't forget to jump onboard in the same motion, or you will have a wet start to your day." Steve grinned at him, "I'll guide the stern beside the pier until I'm sure that Bill has steerage, then I'll push us out and jump aboard myself."

Bill took his position behind the huge wheel and then leaned down to feather the engine RPMs and get a feel for the throttle. He smiled at his crew as he engaged the gear shift and advanced the throttle slightly. He followed the momentum of the bow until his steerage began to guide the sailboat forward. Steve continued to walk behind him along the dock, keeping the transom close while Bill did this, and they effectively pivoted the sailboat to point it in the desired direction, and just like that . . . they were underway . . .

❀ ❀ ❀

Frank stood next to the mast for a moment, transfixed as the boats and slips passed by on one side, and the shoreline on the other. Making their way toward the jetty opening which framed the marina, he felt the stability of the long sailboat that Bill was carefully steering out toward the bay. When Steve felt they were clear of traffic, he said, "Okay, let's clean things up." After stowing dock lines and fenders below deck, he moved toward the galley ladder and said, "Now, let's talk about raising the sails."

Frank returned with Steve beside the mast and began coiling up the slack on the new mainsail halyard. Frank watched it tighten in the mast guides and Steve instructed, "This is where you will hoist our mainsail, with me securing it back there on the winch." Steve then moved around to the front of the mast, "Likewise, these headsail halyards raise the jibs, genoas, and spinnakers in the same way. Today, we're using this blue halyard, which I've already fastened to our genoa."

❁ ❁ ❁

Steve paused, as he too noticed the east wind filling in, "We're getting close . . . Once we start, things happen fast: Bill will bring us directly into the wind, so no forces attach to the sails. Then we'll raise the mainsail first, with you pulling down as fast as you can. When the main is set, we'll briefly fall off on a port tack. From there, Bill can bring us back up into the wind, where you and I will raise the genoa; same technique, pulling down as fast as you can."

"During that interval of neutral sails, there will be a lot of noise and flogging as the wind tries to attach to them. Always stay conscious of the boom, even using eyes in the back of your head. Those genoa sheets need to be watched as well; they can act like whips if the slack is not drawn back tight . . . Are we clear?" Frank now felt a growing excitement, "Aye, aye, Sir."

Steve smiled at him and asked, "How are your sea legs? You're going to be spending a lot of time up here on the bow until we're trimmed and fully underway." Frank grinned, "I feel great. This boat is stable, isn't it?" Steve nodded, and he looked in all directions. He at last shared, "You are going to *love* this boat." Both of them grinned, and Steve spun back toward the cockpit, from where he instructed, "Okay, now just stay ready at the main halyard until Bill gives us the signal."

Frank savored a few moments more as he felt the sailboat's sleek movement through the water. He loved this vantage from the bay, especially looking back upon those same Belvedere homes that they had driven past on Beach Street. On any other day, he would have been wondering about the people living inside those amazing houses, and maybe trying to imagine their privileged lives, but today he knew with absolute clarity that *he was the lucky one* . . .

# 10

## SAILS UP

Bill glanced around and said, "This looks like a pretty good spot, gentlemen. Shall we ready the halyard?" Steve interpreted the cue, "Okay Frank . . . wait for Bill's signal, and you and I can start raising the main sail; it helps to watch that wind vane at the top of the mast while you anticipate this."

Bill steered eastward until the freshening breeze was coming directly over the bow, and he steadied the helm. When he felt that the bow was stable, he backed off the engine throttle and announced quickly, *"Okay, let's do this!"* Frank immediately began pulling down hard on the halyard, while Steve took up the slack around a cockpit winch—the huge sail climbed up easily through the mast guides with both big men pulling in tandem. When it neared the top of the mast, Steve said, "That's good! Let me tweak it the rest of the way with this winch."

Frank watched Steve take care not to overstretch the inside edge of the sail. Bill then instructed, "Okay, let's fall off a bit Frank; stay forward of the mast." Steve quickly began to adjust the boom hardware, and Frank felt the sailboat surge forward. The hull leaned over to starboard when Bill steered back toward Belvedere.

❧ ❧ ❧

Steve finished his adjustments to the traveler and mainsheet, while Frank watched the beautiful cobalt-colored sail fully engage the wind. He was surprised to see that the mainsail did not form a triangular point at its top but was instead blunted into a perpendicular angle to the mast. With the hull now slicing through the water at increased speed, it wasn't long before Bill decided, "This helm feels good, so let's bring her up again into the wind and hoist the 'genny'."

He steered once more directly into the wind. Steve steadied the boom as he instructed Frank, "Stay ready on your genoa halyard and wait for the signal." When Steve moved forward into position, Bill decided, "Okay, let's raise it!" At this, Frank and Steve together began pulling the genoa quickly aloft; Steve once more carefully applied final tension to the luff of that sail as well.

When sail-set was complete, Steve asked Frank to join him back in the cockpit, "Here . . . let's have you sit on the low side for now, so you can trim that genny while I work the main. I've got the genoa sheet started for you there on that starboard winch. Crank slowly at first, until we see how high we point. From there, you can decide on your sail trim."

With Steve again beside the traveler, Bill said, "OK, let's fall off the wind again, staying on port tack, and we'll trim the sails as needed to point away from Belvedere. We shouldn't have to point too high, but I don't want us to get stuck in the wind shadows over there next to the shoreline. That's where it lifts up and over the island; we call that 'local knowledge' Frank, which means we have learned by our mistakes," and he chuckled a bit.

❊ ❊ ❊

Bill eased the huge wheel toward land, and as the sailboat once more angled off the direct wind, both sails snapped hard in unison and filled—in an instant, Angelina surged powerfully forward. Frank was taken by surprise, and he reached for the deck to steady himself, "*Woah!* I'm assuming that's what you meant when you talked about horsepower," and both Bill and Steve laughed.

Bill decided to punctuate Frank's reaction by taking a moment to turn off the diesel engine. Tongue in cheek, he quipped, "I guess we don't need *that* son of a bitch anymore, do we?" Frank grinned. He had gotten used to the droning of the diesel engine throughout the sailboat's launch, and the sound of it had become a dominant bottom note for his experience thus far. When the noise suddenly disappeared and he heard only the uniform splashing of water as it rolled across Angelina's hull, he was completely entranced. My God, the *quiet* of it; with the occasional protest of sail fabric, popping slightly as the hull flew up and over the tops of swells, only adding to Frank's sense of wonder.

## OPEN WATER

The sailors had by now become silent, perhaps sharing a collective reverence. This sailboat, piloted by these three men, was now being entirely self-propelled by means of some unknown origin. In fact, where had this wind begun? It certainly would have originated in some remote part of the planet, perhaps as it spun with the earth on the equatorial steppes of the African Continent? Had it taken on moisture as it departed Liberia, giving it an affinity for the northern coastline of Columbia? From there, its legitimacy would only have been quickened when Panama's narrow isthmus couldn't hold it at all.

What if this wind was always meant to be a component of Frank's destiny, now especially, as it was beckoned toward a tropical depression beneath the Hawaiian Islands? Once there, a sustained gust (directed by celestial pursed-lips) might eddy the heart of it over Baja, on a certain path toward his Aspen groves in the Desatoya Mountains of central Nevada. Arriving there at last, it would spin in place and form a Tonopah Low in the vicinity of Frank's home, from where its remnants had begun their fluid cascade down toward Belvedere Island.

Frank suddenly knew—however it had materialized today. This steady and gentle breeze out of the east was surely guiding him in a direction that he was always meant to travel. He understood with absolute clarity that he was, in this moment, a part of something much bigger than himself, and he could not resist it . . .

❀ ❀ ❀

With the hull speed now stabilized, Bill leaned out over the low-side rail to look past the genoa, and he gauged the boat's distance from Belvedere's shoreline. He then decided, "I'm going to steer up toward Point Stuart over there on Angel Island. So let's trim to that, and from there we will adjust to any changes in wind direction. Frank, did you find anything in that old book that mentioned 'telltales'?" Frank nodded, "I did . . . so if we're going to point higher, I have to start tightening the genoa sheet," and he cranked the winch when Bill began to change course.

Frank focused on the florescent pieces of yarn which were fastened (top to bottom) to the leading edge of the headsail—he continued to winch the sheet tighter until the *yarns* fluttered, and then laid completely straight in the laminar flow of wind passing over them. Frank was now wrapping the wind around the front edge of his headsail, and a second set of tiny yarns called *ticks* (located on the inside curvature of the genny) began to float up, reflecting their indifference.

Steve proudly acknowledged Frank's efforts, "That's it! . . . *Perfect!* Now let me fix this traveler and mainsheet to give us the slot that we need between our two sails, and we should look pretty good." With those adjustments, the wind velocity over the surface of both sails increased markedly, and Frank once again felt Angelina accelerate faster through the water.

❀ ❀ ❀

Bill took the moment to express his appreciation for how well the sail hoistings had gone, "Excellent work gentlemen! That went *very well*. It is always of particular importance when neighbors are judging our skills from the safety of their living rooms." He beamed, "I *told* you this guy was gonna be good, didn't I Steve?"

Steve laughed a little and then suggested to Frank, "Why don't you get used to walking around on the foredeck while we're underway? Sit up in the pulpit even and take advantage of these quiet times to study our sail shapes. It never hurts to second guess the fairlead locations of your headsail, or the halyard and sheet tensions for that matter. That should be an ongoing process, especially as the wind velocity changes . . . And don't ever forget that you are our eyes up there for traffic; a collision with the Larkspur Ferry before lunch would probably ruin our day."

Frank crouched slightly so his knees could reinforce his center of gravity, and he stood for a moment beside the mast to examine the shapes of the dark sails. When he approached the bow, he was able to clearly identify Sausalito's shoreline off in the distance. He had been stable and comfortable in all of his movements so far, and he suddenly realized that the feel and the taste of the ocean breeze was something that perfectly suited him. He even began to understand a little of Bill's insistence that he might, after all, possess the right body type to someday be a decent foredeckman.

He considered this as he got lost for a moment in the glistening sunlight across the water. Relaxed and balanced enough to sit comfortably in the bow pulpit at these speeds, Frank filled his lungs with fresh marine air, and he marveled at his beautiful vantage on San Francisco Bay.

❀ ❀ ❀

When he at last faced back toward Steve and Bill, he reflected their appreciative smiles. Seated where he was, he was now able to study both sides of the sailboat, with her proximity to Angel Island on one side, and Belvedere Island on the other. He became aware that the precisely trimmed Angelina was moving faster—increasingly so as she cleared land and traveled further out to open water. Frank considered once more the incalculable origins of the wind, and whether or not it might indeed be guiding him toward some unseen destiny. If so, *where was it taking him?*

At that moment, Bill called out to him, "Frank, let's think about falling off toward the tip of Belvedere. We're going to need to be on a 'beam reach' as we do that, so why don't you take your place again on the low side and get ready to let out your genoa sheet. Steve, will you call the homestead and inform Marion that we will soon be on approach for our fly-by? She insisted that we do so on this beautiful day. Oh! . . . and que up some Albinoni for her Ladyship as well; let's add a serenade today from our cockpit speakers." Steve asked, "The Concertos?" and Bill happily agreed, "Yes . . . Perfect! Crank up the volume."

Frank returned to the low side winch, while Steve made his phone call from the galley. When both men were again in position, Bill announced, "Okay, let's fall off . . ." Steve guided Frank, "Reverse that lever on top of your winch, and then follow Bill to let out your genoa as he steers down toward Belvedere. Remember that the wind will be coming more and more from a perpendicular direction on that point of sail, so trim until you get those telltales straight again. I'm going to let out my mainsheet at the same time, so be mindful of the boom."

❀ ❀ ❀

Bill began to steer down to just beyond the tip of the island, while Steve and Frank (in unison) played out their sails. When he had settled upon this new point of sail, Bill steadied the helm, "That looks perfect Gents. Thank you. So, why don't you both join me back here, and we can stand together to give a proper salute to the lady on the hill."

Frank watched the knot meter jump steadily higher on their way to a beam reach, and he felt the deck lowering itself down again to a flat approach upon the water—this effectively allowed for the sailboat's fastest point of sail. As he stood and moved back toward the stern, he was startled by the size of the wake which was now coursing many yards behind the speeding sailboat; all that he could think of to say was, *"Wow!"*

Bill laughed at this and added, "Yeah, the farther off the wind we go, the more fun we have on this boat. When we do this with a spinnaker up . . . it's an E-Ticket ride."

### MARION

It was soon evident to Frank, as they approached the southern tip of Belvedere Island, that the boat would be sailing much closer to Bill's home than he had first imagined. He was suddenly excited to realize that he would see Marion Bennett for the first time. The men were now standing close together in the aft cockpit, with Steve standing near Bill on the port side, and Frank more forward on the starboard side; closer to Belvedere.

At once, she came into view. Marion was standing in the center of a terraced garden, close to a redwood bench that had faded gray from years of weather. The upslope behind her was bordered with brightly-colored marine succulents, surrounding a ground cover of tiny blue flowers which carpeted the hillside . . . At her feet were rows of multi-colored irises, flourishing toward their best springtime bloom.

Frank somehow knew that this was her favorite retreat—maybe a quiet place for reflection, or meditation. The garden's locale had been chosen to rest below a meandering stone path (visible within the hilltop grass), which led down to dramatic stonework steps in a rock staircase. Burled wood handrails brought it naturally down toward the ocean. This private place had been carved into the hillside, and was accented at its uppermost corners by sculpted conifers; these particularly gave the garden its own Zen feel.

❃ ❃ ❃

As the sailboat flew closer, Marion was suddenly highlighted in the late morning sun. She wore a spring dress that was protected by a well-used painter's apron, and she held a tiny brush in one hand while shielding her eyes with the other. The striking woman was taller than Frank had imagined, and her swept-back platinum hair, now illuminated in the sunlight, was easily her most distinctive feature. It could only be her natural color, as Frank knew intuitively that it would be unique on any color spectrum.

Something about the hair continued to hold his focus. She was wearing it pulled-back, and it was thick and loosely gathered behind her neck—she was beautiful . . . *and inexplicably familiar*. Marion clearly enjoyed the healthful stature of a woman who could not possibly have been born within the era that Frank was told she belonged. Even at this distance, he could see that her facial features were regal, and that her brow and widely-set, beautiful eyes placed her upon some pinnacle of grace.

❃ ❃ ❃

When the sailboat was at last closest to her, she waved at them. Bill anticipated this and gave the signal, "Okay boys . . . *Salute!*" Instantly, he and his crew (standing at ready) braced up together and offered a sharp salute to the beautiful woman on the hillside. Marion was surprised and joyous, and she placed both palms across her heart. Bill laughed with affection as well, while the boat glided past her. Yet, even as Steve adjusted the sound system to increase volume for the string and oboe serenade by Tomaso Albinoni, Frank's eyes remained transfixed upon Marion . . .

He continued to stare . . . Even after the other two men had waved their goodbyes and turned back to face the bow, he was simply unable to take his eyes off her. He barely noticed when she reached down to trade her paintbrush for binoculars on the bench beside her. It was only when she trained them directly upon him that he realized she was continuing to stare *at him* as well . . . Marion followed Frank for another moment, then raised one elegant hand to wave at him. He felt her affection as she did this, and he smiled and waved back.

❃ ❃ ❃

Within an instant of his full appreciation of Marion's gesture toward him, Frank felt oddly (again) that he somehow *knew* her. Maybe it was her arm movements when she waved, or her familiar stature, but for whatever reason, he was utterly immobilized as he stared at her. As this sensation grew stronger, he was certain that some indiscernible memory had just been excavated from deep within him; it somehow connected him to this woman . . . It was just that . . . he remained at a complete loss to understand the *why* of it.

So, he was further spellbound when Marion lowered her binoculars at that same moment, and she too stared back with her own quizzical expression. She seemed frozen while staring at him as well, until the sailboat finally put distance enough between them to break their trance.

❊ ❊ ❊

Bill grinned at his incapacitated crewmember and joked, "So, I'm guessing you think she's kinda cute . . ." Frank snapped out of it and turned toward Bill. Seeing his ironic smirk, he chuckled, "Yeah Bill, I can see you understand that *'cute'* doesn't really sum it up." Then, "She is absolutely beautiful . . . My God . . . *that hair!*" Bill shook his head, "Yeah, I know. It's a showstopper, isn't it? We met when she was in her twenties—she was working at the Museum of Modern Art in New York. The first time I saw her, I was rendered immobile . . . Truly, my feet became cemented to the ground, and I was unable to speak."

"After mustering the courage to approach her, I eventually started bringing deli lunches that we shared during our breaks. Before long, we were meeting every day for lunch in Central Park. That was where I noticed her hair for the first time . . . when we sat in the sun."

Bill thought back, "There were days when it was the most beautiful, glossy black hair I had ever seen. But, when the sun shone directly upon it? . . . this deep *maroon color* just poured over it, and it was *miraculous*. To this day, I couldn't tell you what color her hair was back then." Bill thought and began again, "Now, all of these years later, that pearl-platinum mane of hers . . . I swear, especially on days like this, that it becomes *fiberoptic* in the sunlight and I can see every color of the spectrum in it . . ."

❊ ❊ ❊

Steve had by now suffered enough, *"Okay* . . . Are we going to actually *sail* today, or should we just anchor-off nearby so you two can talk about women?" With that, Bill and Frank started busting up. Bill collected himself and joked when he looked up, *"Jesus, Steve!* We're pointing toward *San Quentin!"* and they all laughed again. "Alright . . . if you insist. Let's tack over and aim somewhere below Sausalito. From that heading, we can practice our skills and eventually make our way south. We can peel off later today and head back to the St. Francis."

❊ ❊ ❊

From there, the remainder of the day could be characterized by its long, relaxed reaches in the sunshine and perfect breezes of San Francisco Bay. Along the way, Frank was taught the precision *tacking* maneuvers that Bill and Steve wanted him to learn aboard Angelina. In that beautiful setting, they easily made their way south.

Bill had anticipated correctly that today's easterly wind direction would mitigate the usual wave surge coming out of the west, and the two experienced sailors marveled time and time again at how extraordinary it was to sail upon flat seas in San Francisco Bay. Frank got significant time at the helm (with Steve's close tutelage), and on a day like today it seemed as simple as just steering to those telltales on the leading edge of the genoa. He felt the balance that a perfect sail-set brought to the boat, and he was humbled as he considered his opportunity.

At some point Bill disappeared into the galley, and returned with plates brimming with the lunch items that Marion had prepared for them. There were stacks of trimmed sandwiches made from last night's grilled sea bass, conjured into a spread which featured her aioli sauce (a "family secret," according to Bill). Frank thought he tasted chopped pine nuts, and maybe tiny fig pieces among complex other ingredients, but he was in *way* over his head regarding the spices and other accents; together, they were unique and delicious beyond his experience.

There were kettle potato chips seasoned with truffle salt, and a side portion of apple wedges, accompanied by slices of aged cheddar, drizzled with honey. As Steve had hinted, Marion's lunches were indeed mind-blowing. This fare, accompanied by a very cold beer (dug deep from the bottom of the ice chest), amounted to the best lunch that Frank had ever consumed.

❁ ❁ ❁

Bill seemed content to leave the "rookie" at the helm for now, but he had first inquired, "Have you noticed that the wind is starting to circle in front of us . . . more and more out of the south?" Frank acknowledged this, "Yes . . ." "Keep sailing toward it, but don't be surprised to find it eventually coming entirely out of the west" Bill cautioned, "Let's do what we can to keep steering in the direction of Treasure Island—even if we have to tack over again. Just be sure to keep us well on this side of Alcatraz; the wind and the currents get pretty squirrely over there."

Bill looked at his watch, "When we pass under the Bay Bridge, let's think about making a U-turn; that will point us back toward the St. Francis—as I recall Frank, you have to write a letter of resignation tonight" and he smiled. Frank shook his head at the sudden reality check, and he marveled, "One of the many things I completely forgot about today . . ." Bill laughed and smiled, "Then, it appears we have achieved the desired effect."

# 11

# RESIGNATION

Like every other part of the day, putting the boat away at the St. Francis Yacht Club was easy; they arrived at the harbor through the gift of a directional wind change, which had filled in entirely from the west. This allowed for another perfect beam reach on their return trip, and it gave them an illuminated view of The City, which was vivid in the late afternoon sun. The beauty of that, along with the comfort of Angelina's flat approach while she headed northward, only reinforced Frank's profound infatuation with sailing.

With the lowering of both sails outside the marina jetty, and the coordination of dock lines while they guided Angelina safely back into her slip, Frank and Steve were by now easily anticipating each other's movements. In this spirit, the two energized men worked quickly together to secure the sailboat. Steve introduced "spring lines" to balance Angelina within her slip, affixing them centrally to both siderails of the hull.

Fender placement also required a different technique here, as the sailboat was floated within a web of dock lines, ensuring protection against the rolling waves of San Francisco Bay. Bill wisely opted to delay Frank's introductions inside the much larger St. Francis clubhouse—perhaps some future weekend (and earlier in the day) might offer a better opportunity to socialize meaningfully with Bill's friends and business contacts. That decision was unanimously agreed upon, knowing with certainty that the captain and crew might lose control of time altogether, should they surrender themselves to the talents of yet another excellent bartender.

Having been steered away from that, Frank was reminiscent during his ride back to Tiburon of the body glow that he always felt while driving back to Reno after a day on the ski hills; it became apparent to him that the isometrics required during a day of sailing were considerable, and he was grateful for the comfort of the leather car seat.

## A FORTRESS BALANCE SHEET

He was, nonetheless, anxious to get started on the financial matters at hand—especially knowing that he was returning to Icarus in the morning. He began, "Bill, do you mind if we talk business here in the car?" Bill, anticipating this question, answered, "Please, always just fire away Frank . . . But before we start, you need to know that Steve's presence here is ultimately for our security, which must always include these topics."

"He and I met in Iraq in 2003, where I was lucky enough to steal him away from the Navy. Since that fortunate meeting, he has had my back in ways too numerous to count, and now he will have *your* back as well—our anticipation of threats, by the way, includes all of these discussions about the financial markets— Both Steve and I have come to believe that our biggest security risks actually exist within that sphere, and it is a sad, but modern day commentary."

Frank looked at Steve and marveled, "*Oh* . . . Okay! . . . Now I get it! That explains why his eyes burned a hole through me when we first met." Steve chuckled from the driver's seat and joked, "Yeah . . . well, I thought you looked kind of *shady;* still do actually," and they all laughed. Frank shook his head as he considered this revelation, and he began, "I had a moment to glance at the new *Barron's Magazine* early this morning, and I saw a feature article on mortgage delinquencies; they have been jumping up since January, in lockstep with the 10-year US Treasury yield."

"The article implied that it's going to get much worse when a huge number of ARM's (adjustable rate mortgages) *reset* during the next quarter—the higher interest rates will be a problem for the sub-prime borrowers, and those rising defaults won't just stop with the second quarter." Frank paused for a moment and added, "So here we are in March . . . and my fear Bill, especially if housing prices decline, is that you and I may actually be getting a much later start than I had previously hoped for . . ."

Bill sighed as he digested this, and then offered, "I remember that Goldman used to track those default rates closely, and report on them in our meetings. It seemed like those numbers stayed benign forever, and it usually just felt like one person or another was using them to brag about their lending acumen. I think it might have been the 'S&P Consumer Credit Default Indices' that they were tracking . . . I'll make some phone calls in the morning to figure out how you and I can start watching this more closely."

❊ ❊ ❊

Frank continued more boldly, "Bill, I obviously haven't studied your holdings at all, so I respectfully do not want to presume anything here . . . but I think now might be a good time for you to identify the low hanging fruit among your stocks, so we can plan where to divest first; you will need to start moving into *cash* sooner, rather than later."

"Hank once told me that you prefer to fly under the radar in your business dealings. Well, I think it might be a good idea to continue that style, especially now, given the sums involved. We have to recognize the public's belief that you are a 'market maven', worthy of following. So, maybe your trading style should occur in a manner that won't draw a lot of attention; you know, maybe some pump and fake moves as you disappear. If you'd like, we can mimic the cadence of computer-trading algorithms while you do this."

"Let's move carefully and try not to incite panic; I think we both know that panic will show up soon enough after people start getting a clue. Also, let's start imagining the bigger picture of how you will want your investment pie-chart to look going into the recession." Frank cleared his throat and continued, "You should brace yourself Bill, because I am going to argue that you will need to stockpile a lot of gold. That can be accomplished in many ways, but assuming the worst about this crash, it might total as much as *forty percent* of your holdings."

Bill laughed out loud, "*Jesus Christ!* . . . I guess that's what people mean when they talk about a 'fortress balance sheet.' Well . . . I suppose desperate times call for desperate measures, but I'm sure you must know that gold accumulation on a scale such as that will raise *huge* red flags, even among my most complacent followers."

Frank shifted gears, "If you're concerned about sounding the alarms, then you might want to move up your timeline for gifting assets into the Bennett Foundation. That will give you a plausible explanation for changes in your investment style. Holding defensive assets, by definition, is a legitimate strategy for charitable trusts."

❦ ❦ ❦

It got quiet for a moment before Frank finished, "You have to know that any decisions you make will require that you begin soon . . ." Bill contemplated all that had been said, and he finally asked, "Do you have some idea regarding your remaining timeline at Icarus?" Frank was succinct, "I'll make it clear tomorrow that I am only staying there long enough to lateral to the new guys from Lehman; maybe two or three weeks?" Bill took a deep breath, "Okay. We can work around that—and, it would appear that this might be a good time for me to rekindle my friendship with *Hank Paulson*. He's been Treasury Secretary since May of last year, so he certainly will have the lay of the land."

"Paulson and I were friends back in our early days at Goldman; he rose up from the Midwest, while I got my chops in New York . . . Our partnerships were floated at the same time, and from that point on our work overlapped a lot."

"I have immense respect for him. You will find that he is a very straight shooter, and the best possible consensus builder as we face this *shit storm*. We can also be certain that he will be sitting at the head of the table in any efforts coming out of the White House, including the Fed for that matter. I will offer our services and let him know that we will do whatever we can to help him, especially as this mortgage disaster spreads around the world."

"It's going to be helpful, by the way, when I tell him that we have eyeballs on all of this in the form of your Stanford quantitative skills—effectively, our own objective oversight. That's going to make you a 'velvet hammer' in Congressional circles Frank, and people will want to line up on your side."

## THE HOME OFFICE

After a quiet moment, Bill asked, "If I can get my IT guys to your house tomorrow afternoon, can you be there to let them in? I'd like for us to get wired up together as soon as possible." Frank confirmed, "Absolutely. Let's make sure we trade phone numbers before we part ways tonight." Steve intervened, "I'll take care of all that when we drop you off at your truck." Bill added, "Good . . . and Steve, you probably ought to be there tomorrow as well, in case IT has network questions during their visit."

"Then you guys should go buy everything else we'll need to duplicate Frank's trading platform in both houses. Frank, do you have a workstation at home?" Frank was reticent, "Not really . . . just a small cabinet that I use; a place to keep my laptop."

Bill nodded before asking, "Can we carve out a little more room there? We'll want at least a small desk, and maybe an extra chair. Both of us need to work together on these initial trades, and you are going to want more space for a secure phone and new video conferencing equipment. Steve, purchase it all through 'Bennett Accounts' and then arrange for the team to install everything in Belvedere as well."

❋ ❋ ❋

Following Frank's return to Tiburon, and his sincere expression of gratitude, he texted Cherice to let her know that he was heading home. She quickly answered back and asked him to pick up some food at Mamacita's on Chestnut Street; she said she would call it in. Frank should have anticipated this, as his wife's Sunday-night routine usually involved laying out and pressing her clothes for the week ahead. That process would be magnified tonight, given all of the new ensembles acquired over the weekend . . . *Just as well* thought Frank, as he knew that he needed time tonight to draft his letter of resignation . . .

❋ ❋ ❋

His annoyance was growing large, he entertained the idea of just walking away tomorrow . . . *Fuck it!* . . . Ultimately, however, he knew it couldn't be that easy; the shock of throwing his letter of resignation onto Larry Sewell's desk (absent any offer to stay longer in the transition) could certainly roll negatively down to Cherice . . .

## LEHMAN MOVES IN

Frank approached the next morning as he would any other, with the exception being that he asked Cherice to put him on Larry's schedule in the earliest possible time slot. When she heard the request, she seemed reluctant to help, and then reminded him, "Don't forget that the brokers from Lehman arrive this morning, so Larry will probably want to talk with them before the staff meeting . . ."

Frank considered this and said, "Okay, just call me as soon as you see him; I'll walk over to his office . . . Oh, and I'm taking my truck today so I can come back here this afternoon to show some tech guys where to install the network equipment for Bennett." Cherice tightened her lips and made clear her annoyance, "Sure . . . I guess there's no reason for you to waste any more time than necessary." Frank, confused, could only stare at her before deciding not to engage at all. He remembered instead, "Just another volley of divisive energy into what should have been a nice life." It was evident that she had flip-flopped since yesterday's rare interlude of forgiveness . . . God, he was tired of her shotgun approach in grudges!

❊ ❊ ❊

He hadn't been at work long when Cherice called him, "Larry just walked in, and it looks like he cleared his schedule for the morning." Frank thanked her and headed toward Larry's office with his letter of resignation. When he walked past the reception area, he could see that Cherice was avoiding eye contact; she was still committed to the same tense-jaw expression that she aimed at him earlier.

Before he could offer his wife any kind of reassurance, Larry noticed him and called out, "Hey Franko . . . Happy Monday!" Frank returned the greeting, "Morning Larry. I need to sit down with you for just a minute . . . I'm getting coffee. Do you want some?" Larry did, so Frank filled two cups and delivered them before closing Larry's door behind him.

The two men settled after sipping their coffee, while Frank searched Larry's eyes. When Larry saw him slide his letter across the desk and realized it was addressed to him, he tilted his head back and protested, "Oh no, Frank . . . *Say it ain't so!*" Frank wanted to be pre-emptive, so he began, "This is not about you and me Larry. Seriously, nothing personal here. It's just that I have received an offer which would be entirely foolish to turn down. So, I decided not to."

Larry studied the envelope, but before opening it he pleaded his case, "I meant what I said about nothing changing here for you after Travis Whitsome arrives. Honestly Frank, I never meant to step on your toes. And now corporate is telling me that they want to put Travis on the road as quickly as possible anyway, in some regional capacity. They're going to expand this mortgage focus into our sister offices."

Frank calmly replied, "I am truly grateful for your respect Larry, but it's not about that . . . Well, it *is* about the mortgages, but not about Travis Whitsome; these sub-prime mortgages are pieces of shit Larry, and there's no way that I can put a calculator to them where everybody doesn't get killed . . ."

❊ ❊ ❊

Larry looked blankly at him until he was finally able to ask, "So, who will you be working for?" Frank replied, "Bill Bennett." Larry ratcheted up his focus, "*The* Bill Bennett?" "Yep", said Frank, "Do you know him?" Larry laughed nervously, "Well, of course I don't fucking know him; he probably wouldn't give me the time of day, but you'd have to be comatose in San Francisco to *not* know who he is. That is *amazing*, Frank. Good for you."

Frank smiled appreciatively, "Thank you", and then pointing to his letter, he paraphrased, "That's short and sweet . . . '*Thank you profusely*' . . . '*So grateful for my time here*', etc. etc., and significantly Larry, no public ax to grind about the mortgages; I didn't even mention them."

"But I'm telling you as a friend, you better pay attention to this thing in the months ahead. When you see it all start to unravel, you need to let corporate know that disaster is looming." Larry opened the letter and read it, "There's no termination date here. How long do you plan to stay?" Frank was cool, "Only long enough to bring your new guys up to speed on Icarus reporting. Then I have to go, Larry. I need to help Bill Bennett get ahead of this."

❊ ❊ ❊

As an afterthought, Frank suggested, "I don't think there's any reason for you to announce this now—that would only throw water on today's happy theme, and it certainly will be a distraction to your agenda." Frank stood up and reached out to Larry with his extended hand. Larry (shell-shocked) stood as well, and the two men shook hands. Larry managed, "I hate this, but *all the best*" . . . Frank smiled and said, "You too Larry." Leaving the office, Frank couldn't help but add a layer upon his wife's resentment as he walked away from her. He plowed straight past her deep freeze and he was inscrutable when he passed her desk, ignoring her completely.

His anger flared once again in the face of her complete absence of support, and it only grew from there. He decided that engaging her now would be futile; even a nuanced signal, where he hoped she might feel ridiculous for doubting him, would plunge him deeper into despair. He was so bitter now about how much energy it took to live this passive-aggressive life with her . . . *"What a fucking waste of time!"* he told himself as he kept walking.

With that milestone behind him, Frank began to dread his remaining tenure at Icarus. He learned later in an email that the kickoff for those future moments of dread was scheduled this morning at 10:00 am, when the Lehman *pals* would be introduced to the office. He could only calm himself when he considered that a meaningful life was taking shape for him in a parallel universe, among the enlightened inhabitants of the Bennett Company; that fact, together with the surprise reappearance of Hank, saved him from his terminal fester . . .

❁ ❁ ❁

Hank leaned into the doorway and quipped, "Judging by your tan, I will surmise that you have been sailing upon deeper waters than are currently available here." Frank laughed, "Your timing is impeccable; I just delivered my letter of resignation to Larry." Hank raised his eyebrows and stole a look back over his shoulder. He then quietly shared, *"Interesting* . . . and considering the way that your wife just scowled at me, it would appear I will be blamed for that for some time to come. And—just so you know—things didn't get any better when I asked her to put me down for my own appointment with Larry."

### RICHIE

The office meeting started on time when Larry and the three Lehman suits walked along one side of the brokerage, past the cubicles. They all stopped midway along the wall, where Larry whistled loudly and called out *"Hey folks!* Can I have your attention up here for a moment?" Amidst a lot of chair shuffling and efforts by the brokers to end their phone conversations, Larry whistled again and held his hand above him, "Over here people! . . ."

When a sufficient number of brokers peered over the tops of their cubicles, along with a complete gathering of clerical and administrative staff near the front of the room, Larry began, "I want to introduce you to the newest members of Icarus Wealth Management . . ." First, pointing toward the two men respectively who stood to his right, "This is Herb Stevens and Elliot Stein." Then turning to the younger, more casually dressed broker (suit coat, no tie) on his left, " . . . and this is Richard Coco."

The roomful of people extended a warm round of applause, and the new brokers nodded their heads and smiled in appreciation . . . Larry continued, "This is an exciting day for Icarus: We have been following for some time the mortgage industry changes that Lehman Brothers has pioneered in New York. They, to a large extent, have reinvented the industry. So, when Corporate informed me several weeks ago that we had stolen some of Lehman's talent, and that these guys you now see standing before you would be joining us here in San Francisco, I couldn't have been more excited."

After another round of polite applause, Larry continued, "The worldwide enterprise in US Mortgage-Backed Securities has grown from $20 Billion dollars in the first quarter of 2004, to what is projected to be $180 Billion dollars by the end of this first quarter of 2007. Make no mistake about it folks, Icarus will soon be right in the middle of these huge opportunities." The roomful of people erupted into more enthusiastic cheering and applause.

❋ ❋ ❋

Larry continued, "There should be no question in anyone's mind that this is going to be a *monumental change* in direction for us here . . ." Larry glanced at the faces of his brokers, "Keeping this in mind, I want to encourage you all to spend as much time as possible in the next two weeks picking the brains of these very talented gentlemen; during that time, you will be introduced to the new mortgage instruments which we will soon be offering to our clients."

"Your access to these individuals, as well as the timing of your orientation to the mortgages, has been planned so everyone here can hit the ground running when Travis Whitsome arrives in two weeks. . . . He will then share the marketing strategies which he helped develop at Lehman, after which, we will begin to focus increasingly on sales numbers."

On that note, the room became quieter as those present weighed Larry's message. He then turned the meeting over to the young man on his left, "Richard would like to say a few words on behalf of our new Associates, and then share some of his own thoughts before you get back to work." With that, the young broker stepped confidently forward and began, "So, right out of the gate, all of my friends back home call me 'Richie' . . . And, because I'm sure that all of us will soon be friends, please call me Richie here as well."

His thick *New Jersey* accent was an immediate shock to most of the west coast brokers and staff, but there was a sincerity in his delivery that was disarming. His features were handsome and wholesome. He continued, "I want to calm any fears that you might have about these new mortgage products. You are going to learn soon enough that they are really not complicated . . ."

❋ ❋ ❋

When Frank first heard Richie's New Jersey dialect, he immediately grinned and began searching for Stella. He discovered her to be staring directly back at him from among those gathered at the front entrance. She silently mouthed to Frank in a slow and hysterical exaggeration, "Oh . . . My . . . God!" His pretty friend then grabbed at her belt and pantomimed the withdrawal of an imaginary dagger from its imaginary sheath . . . She held it up to dramatically examine it, and with clenched fingers (palms facing up), she plunged it deep into her heart to die an imaginary death.

Frank had to cover his mouth with a clenched fist to keep from losing it altogether. He forced himself to concentrate on what Richie was saying, "You all know about 'Mortgage Backed Securities', right? . . . *Bor-ing!* . . . Well, when mortgage loans tripled between 2000 and 2003 because of the low interest rates and relaxed lending rules, 'Collateralized Debt Obligations' *(CDO's)* appeared on the scene; Lehman Brothers became the leader in that trend when they started bundling Sub-Prime Mortgages—most of them containing adjustable rate loans (among all the boring stuff) and they sold them with higher rates of return."

"From there, the CDO's just exploded through 2005. Banks *loved* them because they got their money back in a hurry—and then they could loan money out again in this red-hot real estate market. Fortunate for you, Lehman's results caught the attention of your leaders at Icarus, and that is why we are with you today. And that is also why you will, in the very near future, begin making *huge* piles of money!" At this point, the brokerage erupted into boisterous applause. Richie appreciated the adulation, and both he and Larry smiled at one another.

❈ ❈ ❈

He raised his hand in an attempt to wrap things up, "So, during the next two weeks we will be sitting down with you in groups to help bring everyone up to speed on this. I asked Stella to print up some homework for you, which you will find on these tables up front.

"The details of tranches are important to understand, because those layers will determine the overall rating that each CDO receives. Thank you for doing that for me, Stella." and he waved at her near the front door. "By the way, you should know that I immediately claimed Stella as my new Administrative Assistant when I learned that she is fluent in the languages of both New Jersey and California. So if you need help understanding what I have just said, or vice versa, she can act as our interpreter."

Laughter filtered around the room as Richie finished, "I do have one last item to discuss regarding Stella . . . She has offered to bring me a welcome gift of authentic Italian 'Baked Ziti.' This is so I won't feel homesick out here on the West Coast. Unfortunately, I will not be able to *share* any of it with you here at Icarus . . . Please don't risk certain disappointment by asking me for a serving." The meeting ended in appreciative laughter, as the brokers moved forward to gather their homework from the front of the room.

## 12

## STEVE

Frank weighed the office chaos while groups of gathering employees shared introductions with the new brokers, and he saw that it was a perfect time to sneak away. He called Steve from the parking lot to let him know he was leaving work early, and that he could be ready at any time to meet the IT people. Steve treated this as happy news and informed Frank that IT would be there at 2:00 pm. "So, I'm swinging by the museum right now to guide some of Marion's crew over to your house; she wants to help with your new home office, so she has arranged to have her crew members from *MoMA* follow me and deliver your furniture."

Frank was confused, so he asked, "I'm sorry . . . What did you say?" Steve laughed and then elaborated, "Marion was worried that her husband is *dumping* on you with this home office idea, so she insisted that she was going to help you. If this was Bill advising you right now, he would tell you that there is no changing her mind once she has it set on something, so please just go along with it. Plus, I've seen those steps leading up to your house, Frank . . . Let's have someone else move the damn furniture." Steve finished, "I'm actually over on your side of The Bridge right now, so it won't take long . . ."

❀ ❀ ❀

Frank got home about half an hour before Steve arrived, and he walked around inside his house, struggling to imagine how he might re-arrange Cherice's furniture; *surely his wife will be blissfully supportive* when she discovers that he has moved her furniture out of the house and into the garage. His re-modeling for a home office in the middle of her living room will be fine, right? . . . *Surprise Honey! . . . Fuck! What a nightmare!* He might as well just bring out the extra bedding right now and throw it on the floor, because that's where he's going to sleep tonight . . . He then went quickly back down to the garage and started to clear space in the alcove beside his truck.

From a ladder, he began stowing loose items atop sheets of plywood he had positioned across the ceiling joists. At about that time, a much-too-early Steve arrived in the Suburban, and he parked next to the curb—following close behind was a surprisingly large U-Haul truck, with three men staring at him from the front seat. Steve's all-business introductions of the three crew members (in white painter's overalls), made it clear that *"Karl"* was in charge of the operation.

Frank invited everyone upstairs for a look around the living room. Karl, without asking for Frank's input regarding anything, began talking, "I think I can make this work," as he slowly gravitated toward one of the walls which featured natural light through its corner windows. "I have three central pieces," began the very fastidious Karl, "A writing desk, a corner cabinet, and a bookshelf . . . Then, various desk and sconce lighting, window treatments, and of course, the chairs which will accompany the set."

He emphasized the word "set"—like that would be his artistic approach in composing the room. Then, looking at Frank with some dread, he asked (with a clearly dismissive hand sweep), "How much of . . . *the rest of this* . . . do you absolutely need to keep?" Frank was on the defensive now, "Well, my wife is actually kind of proud of what she's done here" . . . and (looking around), "I really do need to keep that leather chair and ottoman somewhere for my reading station. But, I suppose if you can arrange the room while making a genuine effort to throw my wife a bone of *respect*" (staring hard at Karl as he said this), "then, you can move whatever else you want into the garage."

Karl nodded at the request, but with a show of exasperation, he got in the last word, "I'll do what I *can* . . . but please keep in mind that this writing desk is an *important piece*—Frank by now was rankled at the intonation, but he struggled to shake it off. "I was just clearing some space for you in the garage when you drove up." Karl was dismissive as he turned to study the corner once again, and Frank looked wide-eyed toward Steve . . . Steve tried not to laugh.

Frank (relieved at a chance to escape) established his need to vacate the premises, "Steve and I have to leave to pick up some computer equipment—our IT guys will be here this afternoon—so, unless you need something else from us, we'll get out of your hair. Please make yourselves at home; there is water in the fridge . . . bathroom is down the hall, first left. . . . We shouldn't be gone long."

❀ ❀ ❀

Frank followed Steve to the Suburban and jumped in the passenger side. As they pulled away, he mimicked Karl sardonically, *"Keep in mind, this writing desk is an important piece . . ."* Steve laughed and tried to smooth Frank's ruffled feathers, "Awe, don't be too hard on poor Karl. He's head of set design over at MoMA, and he takes his job *very* seriously; Marion thinks he's brilliant." Frank retorted, "That doesn't absolve him from being a *prick*." They drove a bit, and Frank began to cool down. Steve, still grinning, looked over at him, "It *is* an important piece, you know . . . that writing desk." Frank, suddenly alarmed, turned toward him and stared. Steve continued, "It belonged to Voltaire while he was exiled in England. He wrote a couple of books on that thing during the two years he was there . . ."

"Also during that time, he and Ben Franklin became best buddies—*wild* best buddies, or so the story goes. Anyway, Ben Franklin always admired the desk, so when Voltaire returned to France, he had it shipped to him when Ben got back to the Colonies; Marion feels that it's one of the best examples of 'Georgian Architectural Style' . . . as it was, of course, made by *Thomas Chippendale* . . . whom she absolutely loves . . ."

❀ ❀ ❀

Steve's grin became even broader when he assessed his passenger, whose face was by now devoid of color, "Kind of begs the question of what ole' Ben (himself) might have written on that desk, huh?—you know, leading up to the American Revolution?" At this, Frank exploded out of his pervasive trance, and into a panic, "Are you *fucking kidding me* right now?! Why the *fuck* is that thing coming to my house?!"

"If you don't mention this to me right now, I might come home tomorrow and toss a couple of greasy corn dogs from the 7-11 directly on top of it—and maybe I should add a giant, sweating *Big Gulp* too! Hell! . . . Why don't I just pick the very spot where Voltaire did some of his best work, and set down a nice piping-hot cup of coffee without a coaster beneath it!?" Frank was now *unhinged*, "And when I'm done with that bit of handiwork Steve, I'll just rest my shoes up there too; the same shoes that walked home across the beach, so I can scratch that desk at the same time I'm scratching my balls!"

❀ ❀ ❀

Steve laughed harder than Frank was prepared to witness. Frank shook his head in amazement, but at last he was able to shift gears, "How does this stuff not just blow you away, Steve . . . I mean, watching the world that Marion and Bill live in?" Steve chuckled some more, "I don't know, Frank . . . you just get used to it; ignore the trappings of their wealth, and you'll find that they live pretty simple lives, and I think that makes them not really so different than most people."

"I mean, all people strive for things, right?—things that are *important* to them, however big or small. They're easy to spot, especially when you understand hopes and dreams. Through it all, if you pay close enough attention, you will see in *everyone* the kinds of people that they are . . . Then it just comes down to the big question, doesn't it? . . . are they *givers*, or are they *takers*? You will learn soon enough that the Bennetts are *givers* . . ." Frank considered this, and he finally relented, "Well, I suppose in your line of work you have probably studied the lives of a lot of wealthy people, but this is all new to me . . ."

❊ ❊ ❊

Steve smiled at hearing this and countered, "As a matter of fact, you and I come from pretty similar backgrounds Frank, and the Bennetts are actually my first civilian security job; so really, I only have a three-year head start on you traveling with the rich and famous . . ." Frank was skeptical, and he looked over at Steve, *"Similar backgrounds?"*

Steve smiled, "Born in Waseca, Minnesota . . . about an hour below Minneapolis, if you count the twenty minute drive east out of the town of Waseca. I grew up on a family dairy, and by 'family' I mean my dad and his two brothers, and most of my aunts and cousins. It was a great upbringing, really, if I could have just erased the snow." Frank laughed and then asked, "So . . . how do you get from *there* to meeting Bill Bennett in Iraq?"

Steve opened up, "I went to school at Northwestern, and I was able to live nearby with my mom's brother in Evanston, Illinois." Frank interrupted, "Don't tell me . . . a football scholarship, right?" Steve laughed, "No, but that's a pretty good guess; the high school in Waseca wasn't on the Division One radar, but I was a walk-on and then a red shirt freshman as a defensive end during my first year."

"The problem was . . ." (he smiled at Frank), "my uncle had this Catalina 34 that he kept moored down at the Chicago Yacht Club, where all the best sailing days happened during the summer months, when those football boys were practicing—and truth be known, football always just seemed . . . I don't know . . . kind of *narrow* to me." Frank laughed, "Sailing . . . of course!" "Yeah," Steve chuckled, "That Catalina was just a tired old clunker that couldn't point to weather at all, but I thought it was the Queen Friggin Mary."

"We did the Mackinac Island Race every year; that's three hundred thirty miles roundtrip from Chicago, out onto Lake Michigan and around the island. Lots of boats and lots of fun. Roy Disney's Maxi boat, 'Pyewacket' still holds the elapsed time record for that race. I couldn't believe that sailboat the first time I saw it. *Jesus*, it had like fifteen crew members who showed up in matching rugby shirts . . . I was just awe-struck! There was this huge blond guy stationed at a cockpit grinder, who looked like he could have been my cousin, and he turned and waved when he saw me staring at him. That boat, by the way, was built using the same ultralight design principles as *Angelina*; it's just a bigger version."

## IRAQ

Steve smiled at those memories. "Anyway, I was drawn to Northwestern's NROTC program from the start; it happened to be one of the more legit programs in the country, which helped me feel like my life actually held purpose. Then, because of my field of study in 'International and Comparative Politics'—along with, of course, my *body habitus*—I caught the eye of the Commander at the Naval Special Warfare Preparatory School up in Great Lakes."

"I spent a year there after graduation, and my path to becoming a Navy Seal was etched in stone—Commissioned Officer . . . Two years in Coronado (first as a student and then as an instructor). All this leading up to the attack on the Twin Towers. Along with everyone else in this country, still honest enough to admit it, those first visuals just burned a scar onto my soul when I watched it play out . . . I knew absolutely from that moment on that I was born to be the guy who would become al-Qaeda's worst fucking nightmare . . ."

❊ ❊ ❊

Steve got quiet for a moment and stared ahead. He recovered, "Right after that, I spent some time in Nevada with the weapons specialists out at the Strike Warfare Center at NAS Fallon," and he grinned over at Frank, "We trained on those sandy mountains in Dixie Valley." Frank was now completely riveted, "That's my back yard!" Steve laughed, "Yeah, I know . . . I probably flew right over the top of your ranch, although your family wouldn't have heard or seen the choppers at night. The 'Bravo-16' virtual combat installations are out there at the bottom of the Desatoya Range." Frank could only shake his head in disbelief . . . Steve grinned at him for a moment, and then shared, "We're connected up, you and I . . . Aren't we?"

❊ ❊ ❊

"So the next thing I know, I'm on loan to the CIA's 'Special Activities Division', and I find myself in Northern Iraq in July of 2002; we went there to secure the help of the Kurdish *Peshmerga* forces. We needed to guarantee that Ansar al-Islam couldn't operate in the region as a threat; they had been friendly with al-Qaeda, and that whole scenario might have made the northern border a real mess. When the locals finally got to watch us in action, we were able to ferret out a couple of Northern Iraqi Generals and convince them to help us when the real fighting started. That help ultimately proved to be invaluable, given the lack of support we were getting from Turkey."

"From there, I worked a while identifying Iraqi leadership targets, but by March of the next year they pulled me away completely, so I could position our Seal teams to paint targets for the first bombing sorties over Bagdad. Do you remember that? There were *seventeen hundred* of them . . . March of 2003? . . . '*Shock and Awe*?" Frank was now mesmerized and said, "Of course I remember that; I was glued to the TV . . . me and everybody else I knew."

Steve suddenly thought to ask, "Did you ever notice those F-4's that were flying out of Reno?" Frank answered, "Sure, with the Nevada Air Guard, right? . . . big noisy fuckers, 'The High Rollers', I think they were called." Steve continued, "That's right. You might not know this, but they were a photo recon unit. Those guys were the first US planes to fly over Bagdad, taking close-up pictures of all the radar and weapons installations, and everything else really, which might have been strategic."

### BİLL'S CALLİNG

Steve continued, "I used those pictures every night in our briefings. Well, of the seventeen hundred bombing sorties—five hundred of them involving cruise missiles. My teams painted all of those targets, by the way. That's where Bill Bennett enters the picture." Steve now studied Frank, "You don't know this yet, but you *will* the moment you open his stock holdings: Bill is the largest individual shareholder of Raytheon. . . . Of course, huge blocks of the stock are owned by institutions, but Bill is Chairman of the Board . . ."

Frank could barely form the words to respond, "*Raytheon* . . . maker of the Tomahawk Cruise Missile? . . ." Steve nodded, "That's affirmative, along with the Aegis Missile Defense System, and a lot of other things, including by the way, a huge footprint now in Cyber Security; those IT guys coming to your house today? . . . they work for Raytheon, which means they work for Bill . . ."

❋ ❋ ❋

Frank was suddenly not able to link his sentient comprehension to the information he had just received, and he sat there speechless. Steve steered into a Fry's Electronics parking lot and turned off the engine; he purposely didn't open the driver's side door, and he sat for a while to study Frank for any kind of reaction. When Frank still didn't move, Steve asked him, "Are you okay? . . . I know that was a lot of information. We originally hoped to ease you into that a bit more gradually, but when you pressed me on it today, Frank, I just felt that you were ready to hear it . . . I was trained from the very beginning that, '*forewarned is forearmed*', and no single concept has protected me more." Frank broke in, "No . . . I'm good . . . I get it. Things are gonna be coming at us very fast from this point on . . . so *yes,* thank you for including me."

Steve smiled at him, "Of course. But now, given this unraveling of the world financial markets (most of which you have already predicted)—and *Frank*, you should be aware that a lot of important people are very thankful for your *early eyes* on this. It's time that you prepare yourself for some changes; you need to know that Bill's scope of responsibility in the service of his country is immense, and way beyond what you might have imagined up to this point . . . It doesn't begin or end with what I just told you about Raytheon, or the US Defense Department."

"I want you to consider in the days ahead, as the world financial markets re-boot, that Bill has been asked to step up as a leader in determining our way out of this mess. He hasn't decided whether or not he will actually do that, because his experience in the Iraq War has left him very cynical about the workings of politicians and government. That notwithstanding, he likely will be pivotal (should he agree to step up), not only with World Banks or at Defense, but particularly within the US Energy Department."

"Bill feels strongly, considering what he witnessed in the Middle East, that whatever malfeasance or stupidity has occurred within the US Banking System, it will pale by comparison to the conduct of the US Oil Companies, especially given their absolute domination of the Petroleum Futures Market . . ."

Steve continued to watch Frank, who was stunned further by these broadening revelations. Considering this, Steve decided his new friend should not be expected to assimilate everything in just one sitting, so he lightly backhanded Frank's arm and said, "Let's take a break, and go buy some computer equipment."

❁ ❁ ❁

Soon after, the two men emerged from the store and loaded their electronics haul into the Suburban. The items—gathered by a very bright Fry's Electronics techie (who had anticipated Steve's visit today)—included six new monitors, two desktop towers, as well as laptops loaded with the processors and operating systems that Steve had specified. Additionally, they picked up two keyboards of Frank's liking, one video conference console, the new version of Microsoft Office, and various high-end cables and connectors; the routers and servers that they might otherwise have needed were declined by Steve, who commented only that they would be connecting everything to "one-offs" supplied later this afternoon by an IT crew . . .

### KELLOGG, BROWN, AND ROOT

As they pulled out of the parking lot Steve said, "There's a good deli across the street. Let's go grab some lunch, so you can avoid Karl for as long as possible. Hank warned me to keep feeding you, or things can get pretty ugly", he grinned as he wheeled through the intersection. Frank could only shake his head at the perpetual joke . . . They quickly settled for outdoor seating on this nice day, and both men dove into their food.

Frank was the first to speak, hoping for some clarity about Steve's "US Oil Companies" comments, "It seems beyond cryptic to me that the price of gasoline keeps rising steadily past five dollars a gallon, apparently right up to the moment when the world markets will *crash*. That's exactly when we're going to need consumers to have as much disposable income as possible, just to keep us out of the next Great Depression. Gasoline is still climbing to historic levels, by the way, even though economic alarms have been blaring for months; this 'futures market' disconnect will be the straw that breaks the camel's back Steve, and why the hell this fact is not being reconciled is just unfathomable . . . *It's Economics 101!*"

Steve nodded at this, and also sounded intense when he chimed back, "Yeah, exactly. Believe me, there are plenty of people who now have this under their microscopes. The oil companies want to keep pretending that they don't really control the futures market, and everybody has had about enough of that bullshit. Nobody lives in a vacuum anymore, especially when they conduct business on the world stage."

❀ ❀ ❀

Steve mused for a minute before he asked, "Have you ever heard of the company Kellogg, Brown, and Root?" Frank squinted and said, "Sounds familiar, but no." Steve continued, "You don't hear much about them, because they are a wholly-owned subsidiary of Halliburton—the oil exploration company which, as you know, was headed by Dick Cheney up until he became Vice President under 'W.' Well, KBR is a military logistics company that has been around since Vietnam, and Halliburton was directing them at the time we invaded Iraq."

"After we secured the Baghdad Airport, KBR came in and set up the interim military base. They assembled the offices, the barracks, the cafeterias, etc., etc. They got $2.5 Billion for doing that, by the way, with no Budget Committee oversight of any kind."

"Soon after this, I got called into Baghdad to help with security, and that's where I first met Bill. He had requested that I be assigned directly to him, given our Raytheon connection. He told me that he felt the need to thank me personally, but that he also wanted to get my 'face-to-face' on the whole targeting experience . . . and, well . . . we just hit it off from the start."

Steve continued, "Bill spent a lot of time asking questions after the Iraqi oil fields were secured and the fires were put out—there was no sign of Al-Qaeda anywhere, not even *anecdotal evidence* pointing to them. Everyone we questioned told us that they were 'where they had always been: In Afghanistan' . . . And of course, the farce that had been the 'Weapons of Mass Destruction' became increasingly evident to everyone with each day that passed . . ."

### DICK CHENEY

"We traveled out daily to look for any tangible signs that the oil fields were being parsed to the 'Coalition Leaders,' who were supposedly waiting behind the scenes to take them over. Bill had been promised before the invasion that those entities would assume control in the post-Saddam Iraq. Most of the other defense contractors in fact, confirmed to us that they too had been given those same assurances."

"Everyone in-country expected, considering all of the lives lost and the resources spent, that the region would be stabilized with an egalitarian leadership, much like that which now exists in The United Arab Emirates—the *Kuwaitis* in particular expected it, but of course, none of that ever happened. I'll let Bill elaborate on those details, along with his own experiences, which will blow your mind . . ."

"Instead, we got Dick Cheney flying in regularly to throw his weight around wherever he went. He routinely presided over the little people while conducting court and hosting steak dinners with fellow oil men in his spacious KBR quarters. Before long, everyone was calling him 'Big Swinging Dick', and it became increasingly clear to everyone (especially those in the initial attack) that the 175,000 troops on the ground in Iraq were there for only one reason: To protect the US Oil Companies while they seized control of the Iraqi oil fields, and then melded them into their own international operations . . ."

❄ ❄ ❄

"That reality moved every Iraqi, who might still have been on the fence about our mission there, to immediately pledge allegiance to the 'Islamic State of Iraq and Syria' (ISIS), and they quickly organized any and all 'hostiles' against the United States; that of course, has proliferated into the Jihadist cells that you now see every night on your evening news . . . too many to count, really."

Steve was somber as he finished, "I didn't sign up for that *shit,* and as far as I'm concerned, it stands as the low point in our history for the use of US military force." Frank could only shake his head in amazement, while Steve became silent . . .

### KARL'S WORK

When the Suburban delivered the two men back to Frank's house, both of them were happy that neither the U-Haul, nor Karl and his crew remained. Parked one house-length further up the sidewalk however, was a white logo-less van parked beside an open manhole. Orange cones were in place, and an air compressor was humming as it ventilated through corrugated ducting, pointed down into the utility bunker. Steve quipped, "Looks like you dodged an incident with Karl, but our tech friends are here; so it appears you will soon have secure lines to your house. Why don't you go up to have a look at Karl's work, while I check in with the team; see you upstairs in a minute."

Frank welcomed his chance to react alone to the overturned world which he expected to find in his living room. When he examined the room however, he was stunned to discover a striking transformation—the character of the room remained identifiable, with many (though not all) of Cherice's accents still featured. Without question, it was a more balanced and elegant version of what had existed before, and the room now seemed bigger somehow.

There was a beautiful area rug which tied together the old and the new. Some of the previous furniture had been kept, but now occupied different and more spacious locales within the room—even Frank's leather chair and ottoman had been moved to a place that made more sense. New overhead and sconce lighting fixtures, together with window treatments that better-utilized the natural light, seemed to breathe oxygen into the room.

Perhaps most surprising, the famous writing desk and chairs, along with what turned out to be a small bookshelf, did not dominate the room; they were in fact set back subtly to co-exist within the room. *"Jesus Karl . . . nicely done,"* Frank admitted as he moved around the room to eventually stand before the writing desk. There he passed his hand over the antique wood surface, and considered its history. His eyes were then drawn upward to a vaguely familiar impressionist painting, which hung on the wall nearest to the desk . . . He quickly recognized within the painting the same color and variety of irises that Marion had planted in her garden at Belvedere.

Frank moved around the desk to approach the painting, where he leaned in and squinted at the painter's signature. From a distance, Steve surprised him, "Anyone you know?" Frank's eyes widened at solving the signature puzzle. He turned toward Steve and fumbled, "Is this? . . . Is this . . . ?" Steve finished the question with a grin that he was enjoying way too much, "A Monet? . . . Why *yes,* I believe it is", and he savored the shock on Frank's face. He then facetiously dismissed it, "But, it's . . . small . . . I'm sure that it must be one of his lesser works."

By this time, Frank's recourse could only be a weary resignation to his new circumstances—to give-in entirely to these "trappings of wealth," as Steve had described them. And just accept his new reality. So, rather than allowing Steve's enjoyment of his friend's discomfort, Frank steered him away, "Let's go out on the patio and sit in the sun. We can wait there for your Raytheon crew." He now badly needed a beer, and he was glad when Steve wanted one too.

# 13

## THE PARTING

When does a couple stop being a *couple?* Certainly, they all encounter rough patches along the way, but most of them survive. Even if episodic turbulence forces a misstep that wobbles their spinning gyroscope of purpose, the gravitational pull usually remains sufficient to hold them (at least for a bit longer). That said, they are technically still a couple in the interim, even if fewer pieces of their virtuous circle are shared.

Beyond that more common scenario however, how many couples do you know whose principals are divergent from each other to such an extent that there is no hope in *hell* of ever understanding why they stay together *at all?* . . . Yet they, without fail, will inevitably be the couple who *"tays together"* for thirty years. What the *fuck* is that about?! Certainly, that couple's flawed gyroscope of purpose is seen to wobble with such an alarming exaggeration, that you are forced to worry about collateral injury to those watching from the front rows . . . Spectators could *lose limbs*, for Christ's sake!

Frank considered all of this as he weighed his wife's reaction to seeing the transformed living room for the very first time . . . There was none of the dreaded acrimony which he had absolutely expected her to bring. Cherice instead was carelessly impressed by what she saw (*flattered* in fact) upon recognizing Karl's incorporation of her style choices into his expert reinvention . . .

Considering Frank's past experiences with his mercurial wife, he knew that this reaction was far too placid, and ultimately *disengaged* entirely, from any kind of investment in Frank's new path—*so there it clearly was:* The moment of her exit from their common purpose. She had only been able to react dispassionately to the violated living room, because her attachment to it had already been jettisoned; she then easily slipped his gravitational pull . . . A gyroscope can't hold someone once they have entered into an asymmetrical orbit.

Cherice was hurrying when she commented, "Wow . . . This is nice." She then quickly informed him that she had to rush off to her first Yoga class with Carol Thomas. Along with the Yoga, Carol would be providing *"spiritual life coaching,"* which would be incorporated (somehow) into the experience. Her efforts to share those details left no openings at all to talk about Voltaire or Monet.

So Frank, in the wake of his wife's departure, decided to continue his recent quest to craft the perfect domestic Manhattan . . . after which, he reposed himself atop the patio. There, taking in the sun and the spring brilliance of San Francisco's skyline, he wondered to himself if he had ever been more *alone*, since losing his family all those years ago? It was soon afterward that he had entered into his examination of *"coupledom,"* from where he concluded with certainty that his wife was *forever gone* . . .

❋ ❋ ❋

He awoke at 5:00 am to the sound of snoring beside him in the bed, amidst the unmistakable admixture of exhaled carbon dioxide and burned ketones—the last atmospheric remnants of his wife's excessive red wine consumption from the night before (not Frank's *favorite* as a general rule). He was at least relieved for not having to think of something nice to say to her before he was fully awake . . .

Cherice had come home after he was asleep, so spiritual life coaching must have been more arduous than anticipated . . . *Whatever* . . . he thought. He got up and splashed water onto his face, and then prepared coffee before sitting down at his new computer station. The IT crew (actually a young woman and a younger man who assisted her) had done a great job of considering the ergonomics of the workstation, while they finished their complex installation. Frank found it interesting that both of them had saluted Steve after finishing their job . . .

❋ ❋ ❋

So this morning, after entering the login and password which Steve had given him yesterday, Frank fired up the system that he anticipated was now linked to a mirror-image device, installed yesterday in Bill Bennett's house—at least that was the plan. Frank spent a half hour or so rebuilding his personal trading platform across the three new monitors; these he knew would soon be lit up with bid and ask prices, trend lines and trade alerts, as well as various other earnings news throughout the day.

In the early mornings, he could study emerging markets, as well as monitor the indexes from bourses all around the world. He could decipher options activity at this station, and get equity research and quotes, which ultimately would provide him with the controls he needed to oversee Bill's accounts; he marveled once again at the unimaginable sums that would soon be transacted from this very spot.

## TEA AND VIDEO

Just as he was securing the video conference camera to a location which he felt made more sense, he saw the flashing green "meeting" light appear on its triangular console. Frank froze for a moment, because he had not expected the video device to be used so soon after its installation. Thinking it could only be Bill or Steve, he licked his fingers to flatten his bed-head hair, and then pressed the video button.

He was startled to see the lovely face of *Marion Bennett* fill up his monitor . . . She smiled and greeted him, "Good Morning Frank." Frank sat up straight, and pulled himself together enough to smile and say, "Good Morning, Mrs. Bennett." Marion continued in a serious voice that was more formal than Frank had anticipated, given those smiling first impressions from his day of sailing. "I saw that you were logged-in this morning, and I thought it might be a good time to go over a few concerns regarding the writing desk . . . I hope you don't mind." Frank nervously replied, "Oh, *of course not* . . . This desk is really impressive, Ma'am. Thank you . . ."

She began again, and Frank thought he could discern a subtle "Queen's English" lilt to her voice, "I see that you are enjoying a cup of coffee this morning . . . Steve indicated to me that this might be a problem if you could not remember to use a coaster to protect the surface of my desk . . . Are you using a *coaster* this morning, Frank?" Frank felt a jolt of terror shoot through him, as he struggled to remember if he had in fact grabbed a coaster on his way to the computer. He was relieved (but not entirely comfortable) to see that he had placed the hot cup on top of one of Cherice's magazines, "I was able to set the cup down on a magazine, Ma'am, so I'm sure the desk will be protected," and he smiled weakly.

Marion (with her still serious expression) paused and considered what he had said, "I suppose a magazine will suffice, Frank . . . What magazine did you choose?" Frank nervously lifted his coffee cup and turned the magazine over to read the cover. Then (embarrassed), "I chose a *Glamour* Magazine, Ma'am." Marion nodded her head and reacted, *"Glamour* . . . Well, that seems like a good choice, all things considered," and she stared soberly at Frank before starting again, "I understand that you received a tour of our home when you were last here with my husband."

Frank (now genuinely relieved to move past the coffee cup) agreed, "Yes . . . what an amazing home, Mrs. Bennett." Marion continued, "Then, you must also have surmised when you saw my kitchen that I very much pride myself in my cooking skills . . . Frank, I have to say that when I learned of your preference for *corndogs* as a cuisine choice, I was more than a little disappointed; I have so been looking forward to having you stay for dinner after you and my husband begin working together."

"I must confess Frank, that I do not own a deep fryer . . . I was therefore wondering if you should mind terribly if I cook your corndogs in my *wok?* I was able to find a technique which I believe will keep them authentic." And she sipped from an elegant teacup while extending her pinky finger.

By now, Frank was beyond distressed at the downward spiral of his conversation with Bill's wife . . . Overwhelmed, he looked down to find within himself any kind of appeasement for her, *"Please,* Mrs. Bennett . . . when I mentioned corndogs to *Steve,* I was merely offering a hypothetical scenario . . . an unlikely metaphor really, wherein someone who might not actually be aware of the history of your desk—and therefore not able to fully appreciate the responsibility, which keeping it entails . . ." Still wanting to continue, he glanced up to see *Steve* standing beside Marion Bennett within the live video monitor.

Steve's eyebrows were *worried,* and he seemed to be listening intently (while nodding along), as he considered each point about *corndogs* which Frank was trying to explain . . . When Marion at last glanced at Steve and she couldn't contain herself for even a second more, she erupted into long-suppressed laughter in forced bursts; this instantly communicated tea out through her nasal sinuses, and an impressive explosion of liquid sprayed out across the viewing area, even impacting the video camera lens.

Frank was now in total shock at having actually witnessed tea particulates spray out of a billionaire's nose, and it took him another instant to understand why Marion had so abruptly begun laughing. Steve at that point broke into loud guffaws of his own laughter, which upped the ante once more beyond anything that Frank had witnessed to date. So, all that remained for the stunned Frank to do, was to shake his head back and forth as he watched Steve try unsuccessfully to recover himself . . .

❀ ❀ ❀

Finally Marion re-assumed control of the video display, while dabbing her eyes and then blowing her nose hard with the tissue . . . She glanced up at Frank, and upon seeing his distraught face once more, she threw a hard elbow into Steve's rib cage, "I am *so* sorry Frank . . . *He* put me up to that (pointing at Steve), and it may have been the cruelest thing to which I have ever been a party. *Truthfully,* if I had known that I would find myself looking into such a kind and earnest face this morning, I never would have agreed to this. You obviously could not *possibly* have deserved what we just did to you . . . Please, *please* Frank, say that you will forgive me."

Gone from Marion's voice was any pretense, or any hint of formality, and all that remained was a genuine and empathetic kindness, which left Frank feeling completely charmed. He smiled at last and offered, "You are forgiven . . . but I'm not so sure about your big blond buddy over there . . ."

Marion laughed at this and agreed, "That makes *two* of us Frank," and she squinted to scowl at Steve again. She then finished, "This was actually meant to be a call from Bill this morning, before Steve hijacked it altogether. So let's continue later when you and I both have more time to plot our revenge against Steve . . . I will turn it over to Bill now, but please Frank, do not worry about that silly writing desk; a big part of my time at the museum involves our ongoing restorations—and God only knows what *Voltaire himself* might have done upon it while he was writing. So if some damage befalls it . . . we will simply *fix it* . . . *Okay?* I will see you soon, Frank. Here's Bill."

❀ ❀ ❀

Bill Bennett slid into the chair and reached toward the camera to center his image on the screen. He glanced in the direction of Marion's exit, and then leaned in to speak softly, "I can tell you *exactly* what Voltaire did on that desk, Frank: at least one or more of his *cousins!* You can be *certain* of it"—he raised his eyebrows to emphasize his point. From off camera, Marion's protest was loud, *"I heard that!"*

Both men laughed, then Bill continued, "I just wanted to fill you in on a conversation I had yesterday with Hank Paulson. I sent him an email after you and I talked about your mortgage industry calcs. He confirmed that he has started his own work, after your projections exacerbated Treasury's fears. He in fact asked me to please *'thank you for your eyes on this'*, and to confirm that he now has his own team dedicated to keeping these mortgage excesses *'front and center'*."

"He shared industry totals that far exceed what you have heard at Icarus— particularly the sub-prime component of them. That total has increased from $140 Billion in the year 2000, to *$650 Billion* in 2006. He shared that he is now truly worried, considering the portion of that risk which will be borne by *Freddie and Fannie*; he, of course, is also watching the timing of those ARM resets, which will occur just as we head into some kind of late-cycle perfect storm."

Bill smiled and finished, "I did want to tell you that while I was organizing my video gear this morning, I was able to follow along with you during the formatting of your trading platform . . . Very impressive, Frank! I can't wait for you to show me how to take it for a spin." He chuckled, "But, *go easy on me.* You have to consider that all of my stock transactions since the 1960's have taken place over the phone with the Goldman brokers . . ."

## FINAL DAYS

Frank's remaining time at Icarus started to fly. Stella had taken the news of his leaving the worst by far, but she was increasingly radiant in her budding romance with Richie Coco—the two of them had been inseparable since day one. Frank had gone to lunch with the twosome several times (at Italian restaurants of Stella's choosing) and he found that he liked Richie very much. He was a bit younger, but smart and energetic, and he even solved a problem that Frank had not yet anticipated; he was able to acquire copies of blank brokerage reports from Lehman Brothers, which identified the new mortgage CDO's being sold there, and Stella incorporated them onto Icarus forms.

Frank barely noticed his waning attachment to Icarus, nor even his widening estrangement from his wife. Meanwhile, he was helping Bill sort the details of his equity movements (nearly two hundred sixty of them) morning and night, as both men considered the "first in/first out" tax consequences of transferring holdings to the Trust.

Cherice (for her part) was adhering to her new yoga schedule, which filled up Monday and Wednesday nights, and together with the return of happy hours on Fridays, her time during those intervals was entirely consumed. This new allocation for their separate pursuits effectively locked down their opposing vectors of travel onto entirely divergent paths . . .

❊ ❊ ❊

As Frank's Icarus tenure came down to the wire, Bill received a call from Lloyd Blankfein, whose team determined that mortgage delinquencies had jumped 8% through the first quarter of 2007, and this only fueled the urgency which now drove Frank during his long days. Bill relayed other news as he summed up the Goldman CEO's phone call—he shared that Lloyd told him it was now becoming ". . . increasingly evident who the offenders are in this sub-prime mess," and he focused bitterly on the "now tenuous positions of Bear Stearns, Merrill Lynch, and Lehman Brothers" Bill finished by saying, "All of this is going to rain down hard on the rest of us, you know . . ."

Frank was stunned to learn that Goldman, along with some of the other big banks, were now sufficiently worried about their exposure, that they were taking steps to establish their own "derivatives market" for mortgage CDO's. Lloyd had conveyed, "The only insurance now being offered anywhere on this crap, is within the darkest shadows of hedge fund trading." By the time Lloyd wrapped up his phone call with Bill, he had promised he would keep him in the loop about all of this, especially as those new markets were rolled-out.

# 14

## THE EXIT

On the day of Travis Whitsome's arrival, tension permeated the brokerage as a contagion of dread moved through brokers and staff alike. Even Larry Sewell seemed to have lost a step, as his subterranean worry finally surfaced and consumed him (presumably after further weighing Whitsome's reputation). The brokers were somber as a group, and mostly they just kept their heads down in an effort to appear busy. It was now also apparent to Frank that Cherice's early morning focus on ensemble matchings, together with her obsession to achieve immaculate hair, had been a harbinger for this day at Icarus.

Word spread that Travis would first meet with administrative support personnel, and then he wanted to address the brokers alone in a "closed-meeting" format. Stella, after her own attendance at the early meeting, was the first to appear in Frank's office to report on events thus far. She stood in his doorway, and after a quick glance behind her, she began in a hushed voice, "Wait till you get *a load of this guy*," and she peppered her observations with solid New Jersey disdain, "This one is *oily* . . . and I don't mean that in a good way. My cousin used to hang out with guys like this; I think they literally used to work in those 'boiler rooms', where they fleeced old people in those penny stock scams . . . This can't be good for us."

Frank was shocked, and suddenly worried about Stella, "What are you going to do? I assumed he was Richie's *friend*, and that's why he got invited here to San Francisco." At this, Stella shook her head, *"No.* That's not what happened at all . . . I mean, Travis did put out feelers at Lehman, letting some of his team know that Icarus was in town recruiting for bigger jobs, but Icarus did all of the interviewing and hiring themselves; eventually these three guys were the ones they picked to help Travis here at Icarus . . ."

Stella looked around again, and leaned forward to speak quietly, "Richie made me promise that I wouldn't say anything, but he thinks Travis Whitsome is a *'Wall Street Puke.'* He only hung out with the so-called 'elite' after work, and never socialized with his own team. Richie doesn't respect him at all, but Icarus told him that he will eventually step up into Travis' job here, once they send him out on the road to the other brokerages."

Frank paused to consider this new layer which had just been added to the transition, and Stella (looking worried) leaned down to kiss him on the cheek . . . She pleaded, "Please keep us in your circle after you leave here, Frank," and she then bolted quickly back to her desk. Her return proved to be good timing, because Larry appeared minutes later to introduce Travis Whitsome to Frank.

❀ ❀ ❀

First impressions start with the eyes, and the two men stared hard at one another through introductions. Frank barely heard what Larry said, right up to the moment when he excused himself from Frank's office. Travis regarded Frank with a smugness that revealed his already-formed judgements about him. Frank was just as guilty of his own prejudice however, as he sized up the expensive pointed shoes, and the pegged European-fit of the slacks and shirt. But, it was the black leather jacket (instead of a suitcoat), together with a rehearsed flashing of his *Breitling* watch, that sealed Frank's first loathings . . .

It seemed to Frank that this *poser* wanted to leave the impression that he was just passing through today, and he couldn't be bothered to stay too long. As if he might be running late, even, for a more important gathering in the Hamptons. Richie was right about this one: Travis was a "Wall Street Puke."

Frank managed to rise above these dark judgements, and he gestured toward a chair in front of his desk, "Please . . . Sit down." Travis acknowledged it, but turned back toward the office door, "Do you mind if I close the door?" Frank chuckled and answered, "That would be a *first* in this office, but by all means, close the door." Travis raised an eyebrow in surprise, "You have *never* closed your office door?" "Nope," said Frank . . . The visitor shook his head and said, "Amazing . . ." and he moved to close it. He then returned to his chair.

The two men quickly resumed their stare-down until Travis broke the silence, "So . . . I finally get to meet the *'celebrated'* commodities guru . . . the unlikely *'Quant'*, who is hidden in the rough here at Icarus." Frank smiled thinly and replied, "Is that what you've heard about me?"

Travis sized up the office and continued, "That, and a lot of other things . . . But first, tell me *this:* Why does a smart guy like you want to run away from a clear opportunity to make a *boat load* of money . . . maybe more money than you have ever made in your career?" Frank was surprised to hear his own cold response, "Let's start with my absolute conviction that these products you are about to introduce here are really nothing more than *shit* . . . Do you want me to continue?"

Travis laughed and urged him on, "By all means . . ." Frank looked at him with contempt as he pressed on, "So adding upon that, you are here in San Francisco for only one reason, which will be to hold these brokers' feet to the fire long enough to force them to sell your newest version of 'shit' to our most devoted clients—some of whom, having trusted us for more than fifty years. Travis laughed again and dismissed it, "Oh . . . *devoted.*" Frank suddenly found himself weighing the kinetics of leaping across his desk to apply a Nolan Ryan headlock on this intruder, and then to start pounding his smug face until he was forced to admit that nobody he had ever met would come to his rescue . . .

❀ ❀ ❀

Frank suppressed that impulse, and he was at last able to finish, "When I look at you now, I am certain you know that I am 100% right in my conclusions, and yet there you sit—with that smug and detached look on your face, like *conscience* is something that only applies to *suckers.* Given that, I have to assume that you will continue to sell your CDO's right up until the moment when they all come crashing down upon my friends, who will collectively look around to discover that you are nowhere to be found . . ."

Travis smirked as he thought for a minute . . . He then began to speak with his own antagonism, "I have been told more than once in my life that I am smug, but at least I'm not a *hypocrite!* . . . Can you honestly look me in the eye, and tell me that this frenzy about mortgage securities is somehow different than the herd-mentality of buying Dutch Tulips in the 1600's? You *'Quantitatives'* always miss the timing of these markets, because you can never factor in the psychology that keeps pushing them higher. That concept is somehow just too foreign for your left-sided brains! . . . This market is going to *run,* you arrogant prick! and that just leaves you and me with the age-old question of who is the *'greater fool'?* . . . *me* for already being on the train as it leaves the station, or *you,* who can't find the courage to jump from the platform?!"

Frank was overcome now with anger, and he raged, "I'm not talking about *market timing,* you *moron!* . . . I'm talking about selling *criminally fraudulent* mortgage securities to defenseless old people! . . . people who trust us to do the right thing here in San Francisco! The two enraged combatants were now leaning forward, staring hatefully at each other . . .

❀ ❀ ❀

Travis then thought of something else, and he was suddenly able to lean back, "Well, I guess you and I have reached an impasse—not surprising, given that our starting point for today's meeting was your belief that I am nothing more than *'snake oil,'* actually decided by you long before we even met." Frank was jolted from his fierce concentration, remembering that he had used that term only once before, when he coined it in an argument with *Cherice* . . .

Witnessing his epiphany, Travis now easily became the viper that Frank had expected to meet today—he was savoring this raw flash of vulnerability which he had just evoked in Frank's eyes—He hissed, "Yes . . . I met your *incredible wife* this morning, and I was very surprised to discover how eager she was to confide in me about your struggles during this difficult decision to leave Icarus . . . And, 'eager' really is the best way to characterize her as she was helping me this morning."

Frank's eyes narrowed, and he seethed in measured contempt at this *miscreant*, whose very existence summed up all of the worst traits of human failure, "You need to think about something very carefully right now: I am here at Icarus only long enough to help Larry and my friends get through this transition. Considering that, you can be sure that their culture of *'conduct and decorum'* no longer carries any weight with me. That is especially true right now, after you insult my wife and me here behind a closed door . . . So . . . *asshole* . . . you have two choices: Either get the *fuck* out of my office . . . or, sit there and be certain that I am going to climb over the top of my desk and *end you!* . . ." Frank tilted his jaw upward, and at once stood tall to broaden his body mass. As he looked down upon this intruder, he stretched out his fingers on both hands, only to curl them back again into closed fists . . .

❋ ❋ ❋

Travis watched him hold in place like a tree trunk, with a stare so cold and empty that there could be no mistaking his worldly detachment from the consequences of his actions. Now it was Travis who betrayed the flash of vulnerability. Fortunate for him, it just barely coincided with a knock on the office door, as Larry came in talking, "Sorry to cut this short gentlemen, but we have to get Travis to a few more introductions before he speaks to the brokers at 11:00 am. Frank . . . Will we see you there?" Frank continued to stare at Travis, who by now was avoiding eye contact altogether, *"Wouldn't miss it for the world* . . . I'll see you around, *Travis,"* and he watched the two men leave his office . . .

❋ ❋ ❋

Frank moved to the door in quick strides, where he closed and locked it for the first time ever. Knowing for certain that he was not fit for public observation, he returned to a corner chair in the room and sat there for a long time; his profoundly agitated state of mind needed time enough to consider the words which Travis had chosen to describe his first meeting with Cherice . . .

He found himself obsessing over the different contexts of the word 'eager'— through all of those efforts, he knew with certainty that Travis had spoken the truth about his wife's signals to him earlier in the day. He had personally witnessed her style too many times before, when she mindlessly traveled beyond the borders of respect (regardless of Frank's proximity), and then later tried to rationalize it all away in the name of 'gregariousness.' Her insatiable need for acceptance and approval from men had sadly known no limits over the entirety of their marriage . . . Frank could only keep his game face during those encounters, when he reminded himself that it was all just a sad compensation for her abysmal relationship with her father.

But, as he sat there reflecting upon all of those past incidents, he now and forever concluded that he no longer cared in any measure about the reasons *why* . . . When he finally stood up and made his way out to a brokerage doorway, he slipped into the back of the room to find that he was late to the meeting.

❊ ❊ ❊

Travis Whitsome was speaking to the silent and still brokers, "We will therefore expand upon the boundaries of your fiduciary responsibilities to clients, given the much greater security that Icarus can now offer them with these Collateralized Debt Obligations . . . One last time people, you need only to remember that they are *literally* backed by *thousands of mortgages*, so you can embrace the idea that you no longer need to park your clients' cash on the sidelines. To do so would only obstruct their access to our much more lucrative opportunities to safely grow their wealth . . ."

"So, in just a few days, we will begin viewing them as central to the paradigm shift which is now occurring in our industry. These securities have become the new foundation of fixed-income investing. That should sum up for you today your responsibilities to your clients, as well as your *new* responsibilities to Icarus Wealth Management." The brokers began a long, but measured applause while Travis looked straight at Frank, as he stood beside the distant-most exit of the brokerage.

**ENOUGH**

Frank once again felt uncontrolled anger, so he turned and slipped quietly out of the room. He found himself on a path leading directly to the office elevators. Stepping into the first one that opened, he pushed a button which would deliver him down to the ground floor. When he emerged, he had to think for a moment and remember the direction to the loading docks within the massive building. As he had anticipated, he spotted several tall stacks of cardboard boxes near the truck delivery bays.

Frank grabbed three medium-sized boxes and returned upstairs to his office. He closed his door again and quickly began filling the boxes with his personal belongings, including the running shoes and extra shirts from his closet. The office files and records were left untouched, but he kept some business supplies and a stapler which he had previously purchased. When he was done, he grabbed a battered old aluminum mail cart that had been left in the hallway, and he quickly transported the full boxes outside to his pickup.

The entire mission took less than fifteen minutes, and Frank then removed his photo I.D., which was clipped to his lapel, and he grabbed his office keys from the top desk drawer—taking one last look around, he decided to jot down a final message to Larry, which said simply, *"Goodbye Larry. Good Luck . . . Frank."* He secured the note to the alligator clip on his I.D. badge, and then he walked toward Larry's office . . .

❁ ❁ ❁

His unexpected appearance surprised Carol Thomas when he became visible in the atrium. She had been giggling quietly with his wife, whose back was turned toward him. When Carol alerted her to Frank's approach, both of the women turned away and pretended to be busy with other things. Frank walked past Cherice without any acknowledgement and went straight through Larry's open door to his desk . . . He tossed his keys and badge onto Larry's desk and spun his note to face the chair.

When he turned to leave, he found that Cherice had centered herself in the atrium, and was now staring directly at him as he walked out of the office. She seemed nervous, *"What's going on?"* At this, he stopped and discovered that he had nothing left for her beyond the same vacant glare that he had leveled at Travis Whitsome. He stood there for another second before speaking, and he began walking away, *"You can figure it out, Cherice . . ."*

# PART II

# MARION

## 15

## SANCTUARY

The rush of cool air was an immediate elixir to Frank as he walked past rows of cars in the direction of his truck. All he could think of at that moment was that he somehow needed to get to Belvedere Island. He wanted to reaffirm that he really did belong to another world; one built entirely upon *respect*... and *altruism*... and *hope*. He tilted his head upward and stood with eyes closed in a patch of sunlight at the outer edge of the parking garage. After taking some deep breaths, he dialed Bill Bennett.

Bill (in good spirits) answered right away, *"Hey, is this my foredeckman?* How are they treating you over there in the corporate world?" Frank chuckled at that and replied, "Well, as a matter-of-fact Bill, I decided today that I don't much like what they're asking of me here... so I just dropped off my keys and my nametag, and I walked out the door... I was kind of hoping that you still might be offering *gainful employment* over there on Belvedere Island."

Bill began laughing hard, and he shared the news in a muffled voice to somebody standing nearby, *"Frank left Icarus today..."* He then continued with Frank, "That's a good feeling, isn't it?... walking out on a *bad* job? Isn't there a 'country' song about that?" And he broke perfectly into his rendition of the song (even adding a little *'twang'*),

*Take this job and shove it,*
*I ain't-a-workin here no more*

Both men laughed together before Bill heartily concluded, "Please immediately point yourself in this direction, *Wunderkind*... I can definitely promise you better treatment here in Belvedere." And then, *"This is a great day for us both, Frank..."*

❀ ❀ ❀

Feeling like he had been shot out of a cannon, Frank jumped into his Ford pickup and exited the parking garage toward the Golden Gate Bridge. He tried to pinpoint the origins of this sense of belonging, which grew within him as he sped north on US101. He understood that he wasn't being drawn by something new or enticing in any professional sense, but instead toward something *familiar* . . . something *known* and *comfortable*, even. It made him feel more centered, and Frank promised himself that he would someday understand why.

After a brief stop at Belvedere's security shack (where Burke took photos of the pickup, and made copies of his license and registration), Frank was sent on his way up Beach Street . . . When he pulled in close to the pillar which stood outside of the Bennetts' main gate, he pushed the intercom button and waited. He soon heard Marion's voice greet him on the speaker, *"Hello, Frank! We are so glad you are here!"* As the gate began to roll along its sturdy track, she added, "I will meet you at the front door." He remembered to turn right toward the parking circle, which gave him closer access to the entryway of the house.

❀ ❀ ❀

Frank arrived sooner at the large double doors than Marion, and he was drawn to a stunning sign which arched over the top of the beautiful entry steps—its brass piping was identical to that which framed the beveled glass in the front door sidelights—The sign featured the greeting, *SANS SOUCI* . . . Frank was contemplating this when Marion opened the front door. Her radiant face locked upon his, as they met each other in person for the first time . . .

She spoke with real joy, *"Welcome Frank!"* He was again struck with the certainty that he had known this woman from somewhere else before, and he beamed happily at the sight of her. She stepped toward him and hugged him . . . She then pointed to the arching sign that he had been studying, pronouncing the words in what he now realized was a perfect French dialect, "*Sans Souci* . . . That is French for, '*Without Worry*,' or '*Free of Care*' . . . Lovely, isn't it? It was a gift from our dear friend and neighbor Jerry, who has since passed away . . ."

Frank watched her face as a peaceful reflection passed over it . . . She smiled and then continued, "This still moves me—his passing was a great loss to the artistic world, but I am so *grateful* to have his sign here forever over our front door. I suppose, considering your developments at work today, that it might be nice for you to come to a place where you *too* are free from *worry* or *care* . . . hmm? I hope you will always remember this, each time you come here Frank . . ."

❀ ❀ ❀

Marion locked her arm through his elbow as she guided him into the great room and up the steps which rose above the tropical plants in her Asian-themed entry. They walked together toward a distant living room, and she marveled, "Did I actually hear my husband sing you a song today over the phone?!" Frank laughed and confirmed it, "Yes, I believe that may actually have happened . . . *country accent* and all." Marion laughed at this and shook her head before she began sharing details about her home.

Frank at last confirmed the subtle French origins which were woven into her spoken English, "I do not remember hearing him sound this joyful in a very long time, Frank. You don't know it yet, but you have breathed hope back into that man again; I feel as though I have my husband back . . . *Thank you!*" Frank turned his head a little to look at her, but for some reason he wasn't surprised or uncomfortable with her degree of candor. He admitted back to her, "I have to confide in you too Marion, that your husband has had the same effect on me . . . Since meeting Bill, I feel like I have returned back to where I belong, after a very long time in the wilderness," and he watched her as his words registered.

The two of them now walked along more easily, more tightly arm-in-arm as they moved down the long hallway, past an entire wing of the home which Frank had not known existed. When they reached the familiar living room and open fireplace, Frank was surprised to see Bill and Steve standing beyond the kitchen, at work together in the dining room; Steve was laying out place settings on the dining room table, and Bill was opening a bottle of Champagne.

Steve was the first to notice him, and he raised his eyebrows in a mock warning, "I hope you people realize that life here will never be the same . . . *Just sayin.*" Bill looked up and smiled. He exclaimed, *"Hey! There he is!"* . . . and he was robust in his strides toward Frank; he reached out to grasp his arms and smiled to explain the efforts that he and Steve had undertaken in the dining room, "We decided to take the rest of the day off, in honor of your landmark event. Life is too short, Frank! . . . *Landmarks must be celebrated!"*

❀ ❀ ❀

And so it was that these four happy people sat down together in the middle of the day, beginning with modest expectations that they would celebrate Frank during lunch—but they talked so comfortably and they laughed so heartily, that the afternoon soon became the evening. And *Marion,* who in fairness had not been given anything close to an adequate warning about the gathering that would ensue, rose brilliantly within her element . . . Okay, there may have been a head-start of sorts; a pureed squash bisque (which no doubt had been prepared and simmered during her morning routines), that was delectable beyond belief . . .

This was served to the grateful attendees on their path to satiety, along with another version of her sandwiches, which Frank now concluded were a unique expression of Marion's culinary genius; the entirety of which, for all Frank knew, would seem to have been prepared in just the *usual routine* of another miraculous lunchtime at her table . . .

❊ ❊ ❊

Later, when the Beaujolais and Burgundy wines appeared, it was inevitable that the party would move (as all great parties do) wholeheartedly to the kitchen. Bill and Steve knew their roles, and they were happily at Marion's disposal while retrieving ingredients and service-ware from hidden corners of the house. Her kitchen now organized, Marion drew Frank to her like a magnet, where he stayed close. At first to keep her wine glass full, and then eventually to be a vicarious witness to her breathtaking culinary skills. When he asked, she told him that she had learned to cook at an young age in a *Bouchon* in the city of Lyon, France. The owner, a celebrated woman Chef who had been a friend to her aunt, was notable for the disciples who surrounded her over the years. Marion told him that this woman was later credited with being among the originators of *Nouvelle Cuisine* in France.

❊ ❊ ❊

Frank quickly became mesmerized amidst the aromas and the blur of chopping knives and the clanging of seasoned pans, out of which came leaping flames and then filets and sauces and seared garden offerings which materialized throughout the evening. All of these ultimately were delicious beyond his imagination. Marion kept him hopping too, as he helped her present these assorted dishes *tapas-style* (on smaller plates), as eating and drinking continued while standing together in movable gatherings at the end of the kitchen counter.

Frank was in Heaven . . . The party and its laughter got loud early, and it *stayed* loud. Somehow along the way, he was literally blended into Marion's kitchen alchemy, with his own apron and stirring utensils. It was here that *The Muse* gave him the answer to his question: 'Why was he being pulled toward Belvedere Island? . . . to these people and surroundings not yet even familiar?' The answer, of course, was . . . '*This*'—simply and clearly it had come to him. '*This is the reason why*' . . . He suddenly knew that he was destined to belong among this surrogate family, encircling this beautiful and brilliant woman, who was the unmistakable Mother Sun at their center; here, she was validating forever a transcendent Universe . . .

❊ ❊ ❊

They might just as easily have been celebrating together in this manner throughout all of time . . . but at the *exact moment* of his acceptance of that certainty, Frank found himself jolted into a waking dream—back again to another time more than twenty years prior, when he also knew that he *belonged* somewhere. He became encapsulated entirely within those happy memories, where he found himself beside his Mother and his Father and his big Brother, and they were brilliant together; all of them secure in the certainty that those times would never end . . . Frank's gaze during this recollection remained locked upon Marion as she flew close before him and he suddenly knew: *It was his own Mother whom he had recognized in Marion!* . . .

That paralyzing truth (which made him gasp) happened to coincide with the pinnacle of Marion's own happiness, when she had glanced over at him for what was supposed to be only an appreciative instant. But, at seeing his eyes, she was stunned by their glistening as they remained transfixed upon her; she knew instantly that this welling had reached a threshold, which in only seconds would become irreversible. She had no recourse but to turn toward him, and reach out to place a hand upon his face . . .

Frank blinked while she searched his face, and he tried to shake off the trance; he then laughed in subdued embarrassment, and he glanced quickly toward Bill and Steve. Luckily, they were laughing hard together, perhaps recounting something which had been shared between them in some distant corner of the world. Marion, however, continued to study Frank . . .

He opened his eyes wide and then quietly apologized, *"Wow! . . . So sorry. This moment just reminded me of something that happened a long, long time ago . . . It was a good thing Marion, so please don't worry!"* Then, *"Don't burn your creation there, Chef!"* as he tried to distract her and move past it.

## THE SLEEPOVER

The night ended joyously, as Frank and Steve scrubbed pots and pans while laughing, and Bill bussed tables and countertops before stowing things where they belonged; Marion's *three boys*, as she called them, forced her to sit and watch the cleanup effort after she had been served a congratulatory glass of Port, accompanied by a piece of her favorite chocolate.

Frank was informed of the "non-negotiable" fact that he would be spending the night in Belvedere, after watching Steve disappear to hide his truck keys—he couldn't have called Cherice (even if he wanted to), because he couldn't remember where he left his phone. So, after following Marion to a room somewhere down the middle hallway of the house, he collapsed fully-clothed onto an incredibly comfortable bed, where he fell into a very deep sleep . . .

❦ ❦ ❦

He awoke the next morning in some confusion, as he stared facedown at linens and a comforter that he didn't recognize. He glanced at his watch to discover that he had slept past 8:00 am, and he regretted the later than usual hour. Then, catching a tousled version of himself in a mirror, he moved into the elegant en suite bathroom, which he hadn't noticed at all last night. Taking stock of this beautiful room, he quickly showered and brushed his teeth with supplies that had been placed there for his use . . . *How drunk was I last night?* he asked himself, when he finally began to rally.

After re-hanging towels and straightening the bed, he ventured out into the hallway which pointed him back toward the kitchen; approaching it, he began to smell very good coffee. When the kitchen came into view, he discovered that Marion was alone. She was busy arranging fresh orange juice and croissants, with a variety of cream cheeses and jams. Soft-boiled eggs and a fruit salad were already in place when Frank surprised her, *"Amazing . . . As ever."*

Marion turned around and grinned, *"You are alive!"* she laughed . . . "What a *relief!* Here, sit down. Bill is talking with our Attorneys this morning, so he told me to have you relax over breakfast. He warned that his conversation might take some time. We usually like to eat here at the kitchen counter when Bill is busy in his office. That way, he can pop out from time to time and 'graze,' as he likes to say . . ."

❄ ❄ ❄

Marion poured coffee for them both and then she sat down next to Frank. She sipped her coffee while watching him with genuine affection . . . He drank his orange juice and wolfed a considerable amount of food. When he had consumed enough breakfast to once again feel human, he sighed in relief, "Wow . . . Thank you so much—that was perfect for someone who must have put a large dent in your wine cabinet last night." Marion smiled and teased him, *"Cellar . . .* It is a wine *'cellar,'* Dear . . . and there is no chance that you will put a dent in it anytime soon." Frank looked at her and understood her amusement, "Oh . . . *right . . . cellar*, of course," and he chuckled at his still shifting perspective concerning the Bennetts' wealth.

She had been waiting for the right moment to move directly on task, "I need to talk with you about something Frank, while we have a few moments alone . . . Do you remember your day on the sailboat, when we saw each other for the first time?" He turned toward her when he felt the heightened acuity of her question, "I *do* remember that." He studied her as he anticipated this new direction. Marion nodded and continued, "I remember that you and I stared at each other for *a very long time.* Why do you feel that happened?"

Frank was relieved to at last share his secret with her, especially after his experience last night, "I have felt overwhelmingly from that first moment, that I somehow *know you,* Marion. I brushed it off a few days after sailing, because I realized there really could be no way of ever explaining *how*. Then yesterday, when you opened the front door? . . . *There it was again;* this certainty that I somehow *know* you . . . Why are you mentioning it this morning?"

Marion glanced down at her coffee and answered, *"Because, I am having the same experience, Frank* . . . I know with *certainty* that you and I are linked in some way. Bill would caution you right now, because many years ago I spent a big portion of my life trying to find family members who had been separated during the time leading up to World War II. I was hoping against hope back then to find surviving family members . . ."

❊ ❊ ❊

"Bill believes that most of my efforts were undertaken through some kind of misguided 'intuition,' probably because I was devastated for so many years at not being able to have my own children. He still reminds me from time to time that all of those searches to build a family by other means ended in disappointment. Ultimately, he was right (although I have never given up hope) that my efforts spent looking back just reinforced that I am still alone, and without my own family since the spring of 1937; that's when most of them fled from their homes and were scattered to the wind."

Marion paused to collect herself, "But, I still pay attention to those 'intuitions' Frank—in private of course. It is all that I have after so many years, so I will always continue to hope." Frank reached over to comfort her, and they sat quietly for a moment more . . .

❊ ❊ ❊

She then lifted her head, "Tell me what happened to you last night when we were at the stove?" Frank sighed and began, "Let me first say that I lost my family as well—although, for very different reasons. My mother died when I was fifteen years old, and my older brother died a year later; that was more than my father could handle, and he just withdrew from the world . . . and, as it turned out, *from me as well."*

"I was pretty young, but I now realize that I withdrew in my own ways too; that *distance* between my father and I remained until I moved away to college, and I haven't gone back home to see him since." Marion watched as this weighed upon Frank. She squeezed his hand and asked, "How did they die?" Frank straightened up a bit and said, "My mother died of a kidney ailment . . . *a rare one* . . . and my brother died in a motorcycle accident."

"All of that was nearly twenty years ago . . . Having said that, I was for some reason fixated yesterday as I drove here: I was asking myself, 'Why is there this overwhelming feeling that I am being *pulled* toward Belvedere? . . . maybe even guided toward some component of my *destiny?* By the way, you are hearing this from a *'math* and *science'* guy, so it just sounds crazy to hear myself speak in these terms." Marion shook her head and said, "Not at all . . ."

Frank continued . . . "And then, the answer came to me last night . . . I realized that being here with all of you was the first time since leaving the ranch that I felt as though I *belonged* somewhere; and it came with an overwhelming sensation that *you and I have been brought together for a reason.*"

❋ ❋ ❋

"Then . . . before you turned to catch me in my trance last night, I finally realized *what* it is that makes me believe I know you . . ." He stared at her, "I see *my Mother* in you, Marion . . . and I don't mean that in any sentimental, or idealized way . . . but profoundly, because of your *physical presence*. I see her in your *height and build*, in your *musculoskeletal movements* when you waved at me from the shoreline. I see it in your facial bone structure, your smile, and your piercing eyes *right now* . . . And I especially see it in your *hair . . .*"

"This all came to me last night when you were moving around the stove, and it took me back to a time when I was gathered with family around my mother, and she moved in our kitchen with your *exact movements*—you and she are the *same* Marion . . . and I don't know why. You speak about your *family*, but I assume that they are from France, and I know that my mother was Basque, from the mountains of Northern Spain . . . The truth is Marion, none of this adds up without me concluding that I am delusional . . ."

❋ ❋ ❋

Frank now felt vulnerable in the certainty that he had revealed too much, but he looked over to discover that Marion's expression had turned to quiet shock . . . A gasp had interrupted her breathing, and she could barely form the words, *"What was your mother's name?"*

Frank's eyes widened suddenly when he remembered that Marion had chosen the name for the sailboat, "Her name was *Angelina* . . ." Marion's hands flew up to cover her mouth, and it was now *her* eyes that welled, sufficiently so that Frank was moved to steady her. He quickly placed a hand on her back. When she finally recovered, she came at Frank with a barrage of questions that he couldn't answer about his mother's past: "What were the names of your Grandfather and Grandmother . . . ?" "When did they leave Spain . . . ?" "'How old was your mother when she immigrated to America?"

Frank apologized for his sparse recollection of the facts. He barely remembered that his mother sometimes shared an old photo album with him at bedtime.

She had pointed then to black and white pictures of her family, and Frank recalled that she shared beloved stories about them and their lives in the *Pyrenees Mountains*. "Those photos, in fact, remind me of some of the paintings that you have in your living room." He cautioned Marion however, that the bedtime stories his Mother had shared would have been told to him when he was just five or six years old.

Marion was further riveted by what she had just been told, and she reassured Frank, "Those paintings that you noticed are famous landscapes of the Basque Country of Spain . . . not of France." Now, it was Frank who was stunned. It was then she revealed that she, like Frank's Mother, was also of "Basque descent." "My Mother and my Aunt escaped from the Spanish Civil War, and they carried me with them to France."

She then quickly pivoted to approach her inquiry from a different direction, "Do you know when your mother arrived in Nevada?" Frank was certain about that, "She and her parents moved to Fallon sometime after World War II." Marion wrote down particulars of the move: the Nevada counties in which Fallon and the ranch were located . . . When and where his parents had been married, and the legal names of his parents on both sides. She smiled when she learned that Frank's mother was Catholic.

So, deciding that she had enough information for at least a start, she cautioned Frank, "Let me take it from here . . . and *please* . . . do *not* mention any of this to Bill until you and I know for certain whether or not we have anything to tell him. Marion then stood up and hugged him hard, "Something is happening here Frank, and I am certain that your Mother has her hand in this." From that moment on, Frank's sense of 'self' changed; he was now certain that he had become part of some greater momentum, and the certainty of it elevated his confidence in every other construct which had previously defined him . . .

## THE NEW JOB

Bill emerged after the long conference call with his legal team, and he shared that the decision had been made to expand the 'Charitable Foundation' to now include 100% of Bennett Company assets. All that remained in this regard was to establish new and separate accounts at Goldman Sachs, which would legally conform within the foundation bylaws. Once they were given the green light from Goldman, all assets under management could be transferred accordingly . . .

Frank breathed a sigh of relief at this news, because the problem of determining tax consequences on the sale of ages-old stocks was now solved. That didn't change the urgency of their timeline to prepare for an impending market crash, but it helped a lot. He and Bill began working into the late evenings starting then and there, and nearly every day thereafter for many weeks; occasional warning signs, like the April 2007 increase in mortgage defaults, reminded them to press on. . . .

Frank began driving to Belvedere early each morning so he could have coffee with Bill by 5:00 am. They would then watch CNBC and talk during their time leading up to the opening of US markets. That changing time commitment, which felt seamless to Frank, was a *big change* for Cherice. There had been two drama-filled days when she gave him the cold shoulder following his "no-call/no-show" on the night of his Belvedere celebration.

After that however, Cherice realized Frank wasn't engaging (at all) in her drama. True to form, she could only hold him in contempt when she was certain that he couldn't live without her. During periodic episodes over the years, when Frank had reached the limit of his patience and he couldn't stand her narcissism for even a second more, she would panic; a person can't pretend to be *indifferent* in a relationship *if they are afraid of being alone* . . .

So as their lives together sped toward summer, all that remained of them was a little couch time on rare evenings (when there really wasn't much left to say), while Frank remained so busy with his work that he still couldn't imagine how he might end the relationship once and for all . . .

# 16

## GAME DAY

Arcane financial realities were not on the horizon at all back at Icarus Wealth Management. The New York Yankees were coming to town in June to play the San Francisco Giants in two interleague baseball games, and that was an opportunity for a party; the expatriate Yankees' fans around Icarus ran with it, and plans developed in a hurry.

It was decided that as many co-workers as possible would attend the game, scheduled for Saturday, June 23$^{rd,}$ at 1:00 pm. A block of tickets was purchased in the visitors section, along the first base line, and it was decided that everyone would then leave for Lefty O'Doul's following the game; once there, they could take over the bar. Stella reached out early to Frank, and she urged him to attend; he had actually been missing her, and now Richie as well . . . He wanted to go to the game, but sitting anywhere near Travis Whitsome was not an option, so he called Hank and made plans to attend with him . . .

❀ ❀ ❀

Coinciding with that time in June, Bill had made plans to travel to Zurich, Switzerland with a commodities broker from Goldman—this being the result of his decision to transact a large purchase of gold bullion from institutions of Goldman's choosing. Marion decided to travel with them as well, but she would then "spin off" on a trip of her own to Spain, while Bill conducted his business. She and Bill planned to then reconnect afterwards and travel to a few of their favorite places, during a short vacation.

Marion winked at Frank when her destination was revealed, and she talked cryptically of her historical interest in Northern Spain, "I'll be doing a little genealogy research there in some of the churches near the Pays Basque region . . ."

❈ ❈ ❈

The day of the Yankees' game arrived, and Frank was actually feeling good about taking a break from work. It was supposed to be a nice day, so the idea of sitting in the sun and laughing again with Hank sounded great. Cherice had disappeared early, presumably to connect with her friends and help coordinate the delivery of tickets to the Icarus attendees . . . Hank, as usual, drove Frank to AT&T Park in his Cadillac; the two friends caught up on current events as they made their way to the already-busy Lot-A parking area.

Soon after he and Hank arrived in Section 219, Frank left to find Stella and Richie. They wanted to meet him on the first base side, above the visiting team dugout. When Frank found the excited couple, Stella spun around to show off her new 'Jeter' jersey with the number '2' printed across the back; she and Richie were obviously having fun in their Yankees caps and pin-striped jerseys, and Frank was happy knowing that the two of them had found one another . . .

As batting practice wound down, Stella told Frank they would give him a ride after the game, knowing that Cherice was leaving early to save seats at Lefty O'Doul's; the friends agreed to meet in front of the stadium by the Willie Mays statue, and then walk from there to the car.

❈ ❈ ❈

Frank would look back on the events of the day and remember that it had been a game which lived up to the hype of the longstanding rivalry between the Giants and Yankees. The Yankees struck first when they put up three runs in the third. The Giants could only answer back with one run, and then the Yankees added to their lead with another run in the fifth.

AT&T Park was rocking throughout the game, as an impressive number of Yankees jerseys appeared in the seats. This of course just made everything louder. The Giants never seemed deterred by the deficits, however, and with one more run scored in the sixth and another three runs in the seventh (to finally take the lead), pandemonium spread exponentially among the Giants' faithful.

### THE JUMBOTRON

Maybe it was a coincidence that the Giants had taken the lead in those late innings— Frank would never know for sure—but Cherice had chosen those moments to tell friends that she needed to leave for Lefty O'Doul's. Just after that, the roving cameraman found her in the stadium. Hank was the first to see her on the Jumbotron, and then Dan and Tina in their adjoining seats saw her too. Frank even remembered hearing loud and concentrated cheering near the Yankees' dugout when her image appeared on-screen.

He focused on his wife in the live video feed, this time filmed at an angle which was shot from slightly behind her—certainly if she had noticed the camera, she would have turned directly toward it and jumped up and down as usual . . . *but not today*. Just as Frank was admitting to himself that she truly did possess a beautiful profile, another image entered the video frame: It was the image of a man in a Yankees jersey, and he moved in confidently behind her to wrap his arms tightly beneath her chest. He then leaned down and kissed her on her neck . . . Cherice arched her head back and closed her eyes, as she reached up to place one of her hands onto the side of the man's face. With the other, she lifted his hand and pulled it hard against her breast . . .

❀ ❀ ❀

The whole video lasted less than twenty seconds, but it rendered Frank unable to move or speak. From the corner of his eye, he saw Tina get up in a hurry and bolt down the row, away from him. Her husband Dan was incredulous, and he was left only to stare at Frank. Hank turned toward Frank to grab his forearm and search his eyes before trying to console him, *"I'm so sorry, my friend . . ."*

### LEFTY O'DOUL'S

The term, *humiliation* will never come close to describing the moment in that kind of public betrayal, and all that Frank wanted to do now was excuse himself and disappear. Hank certainly anticipated this, so he offered, "Why don't we get out of here, Frank." That sounded good to someone who just needed to hide somewhere and try to find meaning in what had just happened . . . His phone, however, was suddenly ringing non-stop from his pocket.

When he finally grabbed it, hoping to switch it off, he realized that it was Stella calling. Her panicked voice when he answered was a surprise. *"Frank! . . . Richie just ran out of here to go to Lefty O'Doul's!* He didn't say it, but I know he's going to beat the shit out of Travis . . . We have to stop him, Frank! If we don't, *I think he might kill him!"*

Stella was crying, and clearly terrified, "Please Frank, meet me outside by the statue. We have to stop him!" She then hung up. Frank was left staring at his phone, but he knew that he had to help in spite of everything. He turned to Hank and said, "I have to go. I've got another ride, so please don't worry about me, Hank . . . *I'll get through this.* Let's talk in a couple of days . . ." Frank managed an appreciative smile and then he shot toward the stairs . . .

❊ ❊ ❊

As he ran down the exit ramps, he was gasping in shallow breaths (barely obtainable to him) from the upper remnants of his tight chest—this was a limit upon his breathing that he had never felt before. When he at last saw the Willie Mays statue, he broke into a sprint toward it. Beyond some milling fans, he saw Stella arrive just ahead of him. She finally saw him and lunged forward in a desperate effort to cling to him.

She was sobbing less now, and she managed to wipe away tears, *"We have to go now!"* she urged, "Richie said he was going to jump in a cab, and go straight to the bar." The two of them ran all the way to Stella's car, and then quickly exited the parking lot. Frank gave her directions, while she worried out loud about having seen Richie work out with a heavy bag at the gym, and she began to cry again . . .

When they arrived at Lefty O'Doul's, Stella veered diagonally into a red 'No Parking' space and her car screeched to a stop. Frank jumped out and immediately ran into the bar—just in time to see chairs topple and a large table fall sideways in Richie's wake. His friend had lunged forward and was now tightening his grip with both hands around Travis Whitsome's neck; the momentum propelled both of them, and Richie followed Travis to the floor in a sliding fall. From that position, Richie began pummeling Travis' face with thunderous right-fisted blows, and he yelled, *"You sucker-punching piece of shit!"*

Frank saw one of the blows hit Travis' nose so hard that it was laid flat beside the midline of his face; his Yankee jersey was instantly spattered with blood . . . Patrons scrambled, and there were shouts and screams from everywhere inside the bar. Frank's reflex was to lower his head and fly at full speed toward Richie. The direct impact of his shoulder hitting Richie's torso toppled him from his position on top of Travis, and in an instant Frank pinned his friend to the floor. From there he kept repeating to him, *"That's enough, Richie! . . . It's not worth it, Richie! . . . He's not worth it! . . ."*

❊ ❊ ❊

A bartender suddenly appeared, after shoving patrons aside on his way to reach Frank, *"I just called the police! . . . I want you people out of here!"* That was sufficient to get Richie to stand up, and Frank grabbed his arm to turn him toward the front door—on the way out, Frank stopped abruptly when he saw Stella leaning in close to Cherice's face. Carol Thomas was there too, with her arms protecting the inconsolable Cherice.

He heard his wife tell Stella through her tears, *"I haven't loved him for two years . . ."* and when she realized that Frank was standing there, she cried harder and then faded in her follow-up to him, *"I haven't loved you for two years . . ."* She then quickly turned away to hide her face in Carol's shoulder. Upon hearing her, Stella moved in (only inches away) and seethed at her, "That doesn't justify what you did! . . . *It only proves that you're a coward!*"

Stella spun away and moved to catch up with Richie, who was staring back from the front door. This left Frank standing alone before Cherice and Carol. His wife hid deeper in Carol's arms and she wouldn't look at him again . . . He wasn't sure that words were possible, but he turned to face Carol and say, "Well . . . at least you know where to start on her spiritual path: Teach her the *karmic law* that it's not good *to steal someone else's time* while she's here . . ."

❀ ❀ ❀

Frank walked out of the bar and slumped into the back seat of Stella's car. She looked over her shoulder for any sign of police, then quickly sped away in a series of random turns down the connected side streets . . . After a long interval of silence, she eventually looked back at him through her tears, "Where do you want to go, Frank?" He answered quietly, *"Let's go to Crissy Field* . . . We can sit there for a while."

When he was finally able to speak again, he said, *"I am so sorry* . . . I never wanted Richie to end up in the middle of this." Richie was still taking deep breaths and his face was flushed, but he reassured Frank, "It's not like that *at all* . . . This thing between me and Travis goes back a long, long time. *He's not a good person*, Frank—I've watched him hurt more friends than I can even count. If he's not fucking with you behind your back, he's ridiculing you in public because you won't sell your soul for the almighty dollar . . . I just wasn't raised like that . . ."

❀ ❀ ❀

A picnic table at Crissy Field proved to be a good place to calm racing minds, and the three friends sat there for a long time without speaking—that eventually proved to be enough for each of them. At some point, when darkness descended and the park lights flickered on, Frank stood up and said, "I have to go home now. That's where I need to be."

So, the three of them returned to the car, and Stella drove slowly back through the streets of the Marina District. She stopped in front of Frank's house, and everyone got out. Both Richie and Stella hugged him, and they said their goodbyes . . . Stella wasn't comfortable with leaving him alone, but Frank reassured her, "This is going to be okay, Stellz," and he stood tall there on the sidewalk until she drove away.

❀ ❀ ❀

When her car disappeared, Frank climbed the steps to his house and let himself in. It felt eerie to walk into the dark house, so he turned on lights along the way, which eventually led him on a search of all the rooms. At each stop, he felt a growing sense that he was returning to a familiar place in time (when he was sixteen years old). Back then, he had been forced to embrace his new existential certainty: *Despite finding himself alone, he knew that being alive would now be more vivid* . . . The familiarity of this once again calibrated him within a context of certainty.

When he at last turned on the lights in the master bedroom, he could only stand for a time and stare at the bed. Eventually he knew that he needed to turn those lights off as well, and only then was he able to move toward the living room. He was drawn again to the writing desk, where he sat down and examined it more closely. He crossed his arms on top of the desk, and rested his head upon them . . . Exhausted, he closed his eyes and fell asleep . . .

# 17

## MT. GORBEIA

Aboard the Dassault/Falcon7 corporate jet, now in mid-flight to Zurich, Marion Bennett was as encouraged as she could ever remember. A large portion of her adult life had been spent searching for lost family, but until now, that quest had been confined to finding her mother's people, descendants of the *Aguirre* family. She never knew the full identity of her father, as her mother had died before sharing those details with her.

Years earlier, Marion had given up on the possibility of learning about him when she discovered that her birth certificate, along with most other family records kept in the Basque Provinces of Spain, had been destroyed by bombings. Now, after all these years, she was once again feeling the stirrings of hope . . .

❀ ❀ ❀

By her own choice today, she was seated alone in the last row of the plane, while her husband's business was being conducted forward in the aircraft. From this private place, Marion examined an old black and white photograph of a tall man with black hair; he was cradling an infant wrapped in a receiving blanket. The man was standing on the porch of a sturdy home, smiling down at the baby. Mountainous terrain in the background climbed up to a distinctive granite peak, which framed the photo's upper borders. She turned the photograph over to look at the reverse side, and she read her mother's handwriting for the first time in a very long time, *Ando and baby Angelina* . . .

Marion had first seen this photo on her twelfth birthday, several years after the death of her mother. Her aunt had given her the photo, along with some unique jewelry and a rosary which had been special to her mother. That was when Marion heard about her father for the first time. Her mother, "Bixentia" met "Ando" at church services in Algorta, within the Basque Country of Spain . . . Ando was from a neighboring province, and he had come to find work in their town.

Bixentia's brothers were prominent political figures in Biscaye Province, and they became suspicious of Ando, whose home province of Alava remained a stronghold for Carlists; the wealthy and powerful supporters of Francisco Franco, who were secure in their backing by the Catholic Church.

Marion's aunt explained, "After Franco's coup d'etat which led to the Spanish Civil War, these things were important to men, but that didn't stop Bixentia and Ando from falling in love." When recounting this for the first time, she revealed to Marion, ". . . and this is how you came to be born."

❀ ❀ ❀

According to her aunt, the threats to Ando by Marion's uncles only worsened as the Civil War loomed larger. Bixentia eventually pleaded with Ando to leave (for his own safety). Soon after that, Hitler bombed Northern Spain *when Franco pledged his Fascist support to the Nazis.* This sealed the fate of Spain, after which most of the surviving members of the Aguirre family fled to France. The Fascist armies continued to hunt the Aguirres relentlessly, and Marion (in the care of her mother and her aunt) hid in Paris. There they spoke only French for the entirety of World War II.

❀ ❀ ❀

Her aunt told her that while she was in Paris, *"A letter from Ando somehow found your mother, two years after she left Algorta;* he had written that he hoped she was safe, and that he often thought about her. He regretted only that their time together had been *'star-crossed,'* and therefore could not be . . ." The letter also informed Bixentia that he had eventually found love again, and he prayed that she *too* would someday have love in her own life.

He ended his letter by revealing the birth of his daughter, Angelina, and he included the picture which Marion now held. To this day, she vividly remembered the talk with her aunt, and in particular hearing her say, "Your father escaped Spain and remained in hiding throughout the war, so that was the only time Bixentia heard from him . . . She never again had a chance to tell Ando that *you* were *also* his daughter." Marion turned the picture over once more, and she stared for a long time at the handsome man who was holding the *Sister* she had never met . . .

Now, all these years later, Marion felt that she had been lucky to find Robert and Angelina McClellan's marriage certificate in the records of Churchill County, Nevada. She discovered right away that Frank's mother's maiden name had been Angelina Cenarrusa. This would have been enough for her to continue her search, but her heart almost stopped when she read that the 'Witness to the Marriage' had been Andere Cenarrusa, whose relationship to the betrothed was listed as Father of the Bride. So it was with this information in hand, that Marion made her secret plans to find the Basque home of Andere Cenarrusa; she prayed that somehow along the way, she might also learn that his nick-name had been "Ando."

### AMAIA

After delivering Bill and the Goldman Sachs commodities specialist in Zurich, the plane would then fly to Madrid for refueling, before carrying Marion to the Vitoria Airport in Northern Spain. Here, she would meet a Basque Heritage Agent named Amaia, whom she had hired to accompany her the rest of the way to Vitoria-Gasteiz. Once there, they would begin their search for Cenarrusa family records.

Amaia had reassured Marion that the census records and vital statistics stored at the Heritage Center would be a good starting point; here they could research people born within the seven historic Basque provinces.

The only hitch in Marion's otherwise perfect plan was that Steve, in spite of her protests, had arranged for a security contractor to accompany her in Spain (after Bill and his entourage went their separate ways in Zurich). This was unacceptable to her, given the clandestine nature of her trip, so she had already confirmed plans to ditch this guy long before their jet approached the private tarmac. The pilot, who recognized Marion from previous Goldman Sachs business trips, conspired with her to taxi back out onto the runway immediately after she dispatched the security agent on a spurious mission to "retrieve her passport" from Bill's luggage.

As the Falcon pulled away from the corporate facilities in Zurich, Marion saw Steve running (too late) onto the tarmac, in a frantic effort to stop the plane. She laughed at him through a rear porthole window of the aircraft, from where she waved at him in the style of a parade Queen. He was left only to admonish her with a wagging finger and the shaking of his head, while she continued on toward Madrid.

It was late morning when Marion arrived in Vitoria, Spain. Before departing the jet at the smaller airport, she high-fived the grinning Captain and thanked him for his connivery. After confirming the time of her return in three days for her flight back to Zurich, she descended the stairs.

Amaia was there holding a sign to identify herself, and the two women happily greeted one another. In her late twenties and very pretty, Amaia looked the part with her dark hair and eyes, and her clear olive complexion. She spoke excellent English and French, and Marion was impressed to learn that she was also fluent in the more difficult *Euskara*—the ancient language of the Basque people. She shared with Marion that "languages" had been part of her curriculum at Barcelona University.

Traveling in Amaia's car through Vitoria-Gasteiz, the two women decided first to check Marion into her hotel, and then get acquainted over a cup of tea. That would leave them the remainder of the afternoon to begin their work at the Heritage Center. Amaia warned Marion that cursory inquiries had not produced much to date; nothing she had yet seen established that the Cenarrusa family once lived in Alava Province— Seeing Marion's disappointment, she tried to reassure her that there were still many more substantive documents to examine, including government Census Reports and Postal Records, which usually were the best sources of information.

❊ ❊ ❊

If the Basque Heritage Center had not displayed an official sign on the outside of the building, it might have been mistaken for a small library, but Marion was happy to find that it was quiet and comfortable inside. She sat close beside Amaia, and marveled as the young woman flew through the various government records that appeared on her computer.

Amaia at some point shook her head in frustration, "I was certain that the Alava Census Reports would show something." She then decided to expand her search to include the records for both Alava and Biscaye Provinces . . . and immediately the Cenarrusa name popped up onto the screen. Amaia was encouraged when only one family file appeared for both provinces, and she wrote down an address. She then accessed a map which highlighted the town of Ubide, and zoomed out from that image to show the Basque province border lines.

Relieved now as she removed her glasses, she turned to face Marion, *"Okay . . . I think I figured it out. Your family received mail here at the post office in this little town of Ubide—which is in a very isolated area. If the Cenarrusa physical address was up on this mountain above Ubide, then that would place them somewhere just inside the southern borders of Biscaye Province . . . not Alava Province . . . This is a more common mistake than you might think for people living in the mountains of Spain."*

Remembering her aunt's description of Ando's neighboring home, Marion was hoping for something more conclusive, but she acquiesced when she saw how close the Cenarrusa home had been to the Alava border. Amaia turned back to the reports, but she now pulled up the Biscaye Province documents as well. In under a minute, she produced all of the records for the Cenarrusa family, dating back to 1901. *"Here we go,"* she said as she made copies of each census report, compiled at ten-year-forward intervals. Significantly, the Cenarrusa name disappeared entirely from the 1941 census reports.

Marion and Amaia were excited to quickly find within the 1931 records the census entry for "Andere Cenarrusa," together with both of his parents. Marion had not expected to learn that Andere also had two younger brothers, "Matia" and "Domeka." With the site still open, Amaia offered to search back into the 1800's if Marion was interested, but she declined, "Let's save that for later."

Marion's fixation at seeing Andere's name on an official Basque document was soon interrupted when Amaia observed, "Look at these Census Reports. Each one of them going back to 1901 lists the Cenarrusa's physical address as "Gorbeia," with no numeric delineation. Now, let me pull back on this map of Ubide . . . See it?" and she pointed to the computer screen, "Gorbeia is this mountain to the northwest of Ubide; *it appears that your family lived on this mountain . . .*"

❁ ❁ ❁

The two women gathered up their Cenarrusa family documents, along with postal records which included the Ubide map. After making a donation to the Heritage Center, they returned to Amaia's car, where Marion asked her, "Is there a backpacking store nearby? I would like to find a topographical map of Mt. Gorbeia." Amaia turned toward her (in some alarm) and said, "I think you may want to look at that terrain first, before you decide to venture out; it's pretty rugged up there Marion, and it would appear that we have a storm coming . . ." Marion laughed and reassured, *"No,* don't worry . . . This is just for my own research. But you do bring up a good point; I will eventually want to hike up Mt. Gorbeia if we believe it to be where we will find the Cenarrusa home."

"Do you suppose we might be able to find someone, a *guide* who knows the area?—or better yet, perhaps someone who knows the local history as well?" Amaia considered this, and during their drive to a backpacking store (which she had remembered seeing), the two women formulated a plan for the morning: Following breakfast, they would set out for the Postal Center in Ubide. There they could also look around a bit, and perhaps question locals who might know anything about the Cenarrusa family . . .

## THE AGUIRRE CONNECTION

The backpacking store turned out to be impressive, which made sense to Marion when she visualized its proximity to the Pyrenees Mountains. A young store clerk had easily produced the correct topo map for the area that included *Mt. Gorbeia.* As they were returning to the car, Marion decided, "You know Amaia . . . all work and no play makes for dull girls, and *jetlag* only makes matters worse . . . So I propose that we stop working *immediately* and find a nice place to enjoy a glass of wine." Amaia laughed at this and said, "I know *just* the place; my family used to vacation nearby . . . *Ooh!* and they have great tapas there as well . . ." Marion was impressed, *"My kind of girl!"*

❀ ❀ ❀

Amaia soon pulled into the parking lot of a building which was located on the outskirts of town. The bright yellow structure with its tile roof was more a restaurant than a tavern, and it was nicely cared for, with fresh paint and planter boxes full of healthy flowers. Amaia used her *Euskara* dialect to greet the woman who met them at the front door; she appeared to be part of a family enterprise, and it was a good guess that the smiling man (staring at them from behind the bar) would be her husband. The framed cabinets behind him amounted to deep lattice compartments which honeycombed the entirety of the back wall, and the spate of dark bottles held within them confirmed that *wine* was the spirit of choice here . . .

Marion smiled when she stepped upon the birchwood shavings spread out across the floor, and past picnic-style tables (for 'family dining') which were adorned with checkered tablecloths. Amaia asked her, "White or red today?" Hearing that red was Marion's choice, she spoke to the woman again while they were led along one side of the dining room. The woman then gestured toward two upholstered stools, placed on either side of a taller, more private table.

❀ ❀ ❀

Once seated, Amaia said, "I took the liberty of ordering two glasses of wine from the *Chacoli* appellation . . . It's really more of a *table wine*, but it probably is the most traditional of our Basque wines." She laughed a little and warned, "Be *careful* though . . . it can sneak up on you, especially when the tapas come out and you find yourself drinking more. Try it and tell me what you think."

The very nice bartender delivered their wine, and he asked a casual question of Amaia. After smiling at Marion, he returned to the bar. Amaia explained, "He asked why the "pretty lady" was in Basque Country? I told him that you had family who once lived here." Both of them raised their glasses, and Amaia toasted, *"Eskerriska!"* which she interpreted to mean, *"Cheers and good health"* . . . and they tasted their first glasses of wine.

❊ ❊ ❊

They hadn't been seated long before Amaia asked the question which had been weighing on her since their first introductions, "You mentioned that your mother was an "Aguirre" . . . Is that the *Aguirre family* from our history books?" Marion smiled at her and said, "Yes, I'm afraid so . . . Jose Antonio Aguirre was my Uncle. He was my mother's brother."—Amaia's eyes got big, and she couldn't contain herself, "Marion! . . . He was a great man, and a *hero* to us in this part of Spain: *He was our first President of Euskadi!* I took a history class in my fourth year at University which was devoted to *only Jose Aguirre* . . ."

Marion chose her next words carefully, "I am so honored by your respect for my Uncle. Thank you, Amaia . . . but having said that, I wish his efforts had served your people better; the Spanish Civil War ended so *horribly* for the Basque Provinces." In spite of this concern, Amaia continued to gush, "He was a *visionary*, Marion! . . . If you consider the reforms that he proposed 70 years ago: Free health care and state-sponsored housing, and before that, he was the leader of *profit-sharing* for employees working in his family's business. Those are ideals that have *endured through modern times."*

Amaia continued to be his champion, "His enemies spread lies and fear about supposed connections to the *Soviets,* but all of that was untrue; he never relinquished authority to *anyone*—and history proved that authority during the war was *usurped* by the *Soviets* because they wanted to control Spain, especially in the face of the advance by *Mussolini,* who invaded with *seventy thousand troops!* No . . . *Jose Aguirre* was his own man . . . *He was a man of the Basque people!"*

Marion hesitated, "Please know that I agree with everything you just said, but you have to understand that my uncle's bid for *democracy* was doomed from the very start . . . *Italy* and *Germany* saw to that . . . Now, all these years later, I have come to believe that even *Ernest Hemmingway's* presence in Spain *muddled* those early hopes for a *"Spanish Republic"* . . . Everyone wanted to drink with the *famous* man, and share his stage—especially the Soviet leaders; they being the most regrettable. *Political rantings* and *booze* are a bad combination, Amaia, and it *certainly attracted the autocrats that surrounded Hemmingway . . ."*

❊ ❊ ❊

Marion continued, "Sadly, everything you just mentioned about him is ultimately what led your people into war against the Fascists. Those ideals were *disrupters* of the status quo, and it made powerful people mad. For instance, my uncle's vision of an ecumenical Catholicism in that era *amazes* me even to this day! . . . He suggested those ideas in the *1930's!* By supporting them, Jose Aguirre incurred the wrath of the Catholic Church, and therefore the wealthy and powerful *Carlists* who controlled Spain."

"So ask yourself this question: 'Did his efforts *help* or *hurt* the Basque people, if ultimately, it was *he* who opened the door for *Franco* and the monsters who followed him?' I think this is at the heart of what destroyed the Basque Country dreams of democracy. It has always been so, my dear, that idealists are quick to rally us to war, but they are the least prepared to fight the wars, and especially, to fight the *monsters* that they will certainly encounter . . ."

## GUERNICA

Amaia was less animated now, and she carefully phrased her next question, "Was your mother affected by the bombing of *Guernica?*" Marion knew this question was coming, *"Yes,* she was . . . but thankfully, as I learned when I was older, it was only because I was ill that day that she and her sister survived at all."

"You were most likely taught that it happened on a Monday; that was 'Market Day' in the town square when the German Luftwaffe bombed the city. Hitler agreed to the day and time of course, even though he knew it was when most of the women and children from the region would be present there. That decision to strike literally at the heart of the Basque resistance, and at Jose Aguirre's followers in particular, was engineered by Franco himself . . ."

"I learned years later that the bombing of Guernica was the first time ever that Germany used its Condor Legion air force in a 'Blitzkrieg' over a civilian population . . . They unleashed their new incendiary bombs that day as well. Blitzkrieg was conceived by them to leave a 'scorched earth' path, prior to rapid invasion. Most unforgivable of all, Franco knew that there would be those terrible casualties to his own people, even though Guernica was many miles behind the front lines of the Spanish Civil War . . ."

❦ ❦ ❦

Marion stared at her wine . . . "I was just a few months old, and I had developed a fever that day. My mother and my aunt decided to stay at home to care for me there on the outskirts of Algorta. But they had arranged to have other family members buy food for us in Guernica."

Amaia watched as Marion struggled now to continue her story, "More than a thousand people were killed in and around the market that day, most of them women and children and the elderly—just a portion of the *six thousand* who were killed in the region. After the bombing, Franco's troops went house-to-house, shooting any known supporters of the *'Republicans'.*"

"You probably read in your schoolbooks that the number of casualties at Guernica was eventually disputed . . . but be assured, that was just an early attempt at revisionist history. When Charles de Gaulle and the United States decided to back Franco's regime in the early 1950's, the historical accounts of that day began to change—They had decided that if Franco was going to be recognized as their ally, he needed to possess a better legacy in Spain . . .

❁ ❁ ❁

The two women sat quietly together and didn't speak for some time. At last, the bartender broke the silence when he brought them two more glasses of wine—he engaged Amaia in a brief conversation, and she translated that this new wine was from the '*Rioja*' appellation, where the mostly *Tempranillo* grapes are grown at higher elevations—She added, "He said this will be a better pairing for the tapas which will soon be served, and he reminded me that '*Tapas*' in Basque Country are actually called '*Pintxos*'. . ."

The arrival of the food proved to be a good addition for Marion and Amaia, and the second glass of wine lightened their spirits. They watched as groups of friendly locals arrived and sat together at the nearby tables, as well as around the bar . . . Nice music had begun playing, and the distinct *accordion* themes built upon a happy atmosphere. The *pintxos* were delicious, and Marion acquired recipe details for more than one of them . . .

❁ ❁ ❁

Later in the evening, Amaia asked for a final detail to Marion's story, "How did you and your mother escape from Spain after the bombing?" . . . Marion said she learned that one of her uncles had run to the house that day to gather them, so the women quickly bundled her and followed him up into a nearby forest.

They hid there with a group of remaining family members, until Jose Aguirre himself joined them later that night; he had been warned by his ranks that Franco's troops were waiting on the roads below which entered and exited the town of *Bilbao*. There, the troops planned to ambush anyone trying to escape.

"Because of this, my family left that same night on a path which took us up into the mountains. The group continued to travel only at night for weeks, until we reached *Paris*; it had been secretly arranged that supporters of the Aguirres would help us along the way. Upon our arrival there, family members were divided and hidden in safe-houses scattered around the city." Marion revealed, "We never again saw those separated from us . . . We received word later that two groups of them had been discovered in Paris, and they were killed by the Germans."

❁ ❁ ❁

"Eventually, my aunt moved us to *Lyon* near the end of World War II, and I was old enough by then to remember that secrecy was still very much required during our travels . . ." Marion was more wistful now, "I can't remember with certainty having met *Jose Aguirre* before he sponsored my immigration to New York, in the guardianship of my aunt . . . He spoke to me then of his love for my mother, who had died of pneumonia in France."

"By this time, my uncle had been given a post at Columbia University, and his prominence there as a lecturer eventually helped me to gain admission and complete my college education. During those years, I remember that he was seeking asylum elsewhere, after the United States joined de Gaulle in supporting the Franco dictatorship."

❀ ❀ ❀

"The only time I can remember talking with him at length was during a trip together to see 'Guernica,' the famous painting by Picasso; it was on display at New York's Museum of Modern Art, and it was being protected there in its own room on the third floor. I was just sixteen years old then, and at some point only he and I were standing before the painting. It was perfectly lit up, and I was spellbound by the *size* of it! . . . The Curator had suspended it from the ceiling, where visitors could fully appreciate that it was eleven feet tall by twenty five feet wide . . . *I could not turn my eyes away from it.*"

"I had, of course, grown up hearing so many horrific stories about the day of the bombing . . . but to suddenly understand the scope of the tragedy for the first time—when I could feel the abject despair that Picasso captured in his painting. Well . . . I truly wasn't *prepared* for it, and it just impaled my unprotected soul . . . I began to weep, and my uncle turned to stare at me, I suppose because he was astonished by my connection to the piece; his face then contorted, and his own eyes teared-up. He grabbed my hand, to comfort me I am sure, but I can still remember looking into his eyes at that exact moment, and realizing *the enormity of his personal loss . . .*"

# 18

## UBIDE

The following morning was rainy and gray. Marion had gone early to the restaurant beside the hotel lobby. In her style, she had ordered numerous items from the breakfast menu. By the time Amaia met her there, the colorful fare was spread out across the entire table. Marion joked, "I hope this will be enough", and she poured coffee for her young friend. "I don't know why a leisurely breakfast has always appealed to me; maybe because I have never liked getting up and *rushing off* anywhere first thing in the morning."

She removed serving dish lids and inventoried the choices for Amaia, "These lemon pastries with custard are really special, and we also have some nice Basque chorizo . . . Poached eggs and toast are here . . ." They then talked easily about their plans for the day and confirmed that they would travel directly to the *Postal Center in Ubide* to begin their search.

Amaia added, "Your 'leisurely breakfast' is probably a good idea today, because this storm is not supposed to clear until mid-morning; we are going to be traveling through some very beautiful countryside, and you will appreciate it more if we wait for these clouds to lift . . ."

She then took a deep breath, and apologized to Marion, "I want to ask that you please *forgive my naiveté* last night . . . Had I considered my questions more thoughtfully, I would not have taken you down that path to *Guernica*. Seeing you react as you did last night, I realized what a terrible memory it must still be, and that it should not be something I ever approach carelessly again."

Marion was touched, but she reassured, "Oh, *nonsense!* . . . Life has to go on Amaia, and sometimes we cry, hmm? I could certainly say to you as well that I am sorry if I cast *disillusionment* upon your ideals last night . . . Jose Aguirre stood for so many good things, and I shouldn't let my misery about lost family diminish the fact that I am still very proud of my Aguirre heritage . . ."

Both women smiled and sipped their coffee before Marion asked, "Are you close to your family, Amaia?" She answered, "Yes . . . Well, we live in separate cities, but we remain very close—I stay with them during the holidays; they are in *San Sebastian*, and I am here—My father is a Physician there, and my mother is a Teacher. I have a sister who is eight years younger than me." Marion smiled as she considered this, "That's good. I hope you will always cherish them . . ."

❀ ❀ ❀

The clouds did indeed lift as the morning progressed, and Amaia studied the map that she had printed yesterday, "We just need to stay on N-240, which will take us through *Legutio*; that's within the lake country that I mentioned is so beautiful . . ." Marion eased herself into her car seat, and she watched as the passing countryside became more lushly wooded.

After climbing for a while, they crossed a long bridge which spanned an impressive gorge, and they emerged onto a shoreline road; this carried them for miles beside a glistening lake. Marion read a sign which appeared to be a *scenic highway marker* for this beautiful mountain reservoir, "Embalse de Urrunaga" She then opened her passenger-side window and breathed in the pristine atmosphere of the earth with its ancient conifers and deciduous trees from this remote part of the world.

Everything had been washed clean in the recent downpour, and Marion was becoming aware that she recognized a convergence within this bouquet from some indiscernible past. Amaia pointed to a sign which directed them toward *Ubide*, and she steered her car in that direction. It was clear that they were gaining elevation, as the highway wound upward through a series of switchbacks and long S-turns. Everywhere around them were tiny streams of water runoff, a lingering testimony to the morning rain.

## SASHA

At last, the road leveled out within the small hamlet of Ubide. The town was situated at the base of surrounding mountains, which hinted at higher elevations beyond them to the northwest—today, a thick cloud layer blocked any possible view of those taller peaks—Amaia turned her head a bit and pointed, *"There! . . .* That's the *Postal Center,"* and she parked close to a curb on the narrow town street. The two women walked a short distance to the building and went inside.

It appeared that the office was closed, because it was so dimly lit, and silent. Marion rang a bell which had been left on the counter—from upstairs, they heard the sound of steps that made the floorboards creak, and then someone opened a door and began to descend the small flight of wooden stairs. A stocky, 50ish woman wearing a house dress and a cardigan, turned on a light and greeted them in her Euskara dialect. Amaia greeted her in kind.

Amaia then entered into a long dialogue, most of which regarded Marion, as she motioned toward her and variously pronounced the names "Cenarrusa" and "Aguirre." Marion also recognized "Gorbeia," but not much else. When Amaia completed her inquiry, the postal agent took her turn. After a long discourse, she began pointing toward the road and attempted to give directions (which included a lot of conflicting hand movements).

Amaia eventually talked the woman into drawing a map of driving instructions, which was completed on a lined piece of notebook paper. The woman enunciated the name, "Sahats Belasko," and Amaia restated it to make sure that she had the correct spelling—"Sasha" was finally offered as an apparent nickname to make matters easier. She and Amaia exchanged pleasantries, and Amaia directed Marion toward the door as they started to leave. Before exiting the front door, however, the woman appeared to be reminding Amaia (one more time) about the "*txakur,*" in what seemed to be a concerned warning . . .

❃ ❃ ❃

In the car, Amaia sounded encouraged when she shared her recent conversation, "I think we might have just gotten lucky back there . . . It turns out that her grandfather is well known in this area as a local historian, and also as a guide for the surrounding mountains." Marion smiled when she considered this, but then caught herself, "Wait . . . '*grandfather?*' . . . Did you say *grandfather?!*—that can't possibly be right! . . . The woman was in her 60's!" Amaia laughed and said, "I know. Maybe we stumbled upon one of those *Basque enclaves* that has a higher population of *centenarians* . . ." and she gave the hand-drawn map to Marion for navigational help.

After a couple of U-turns, and one stop to decipher a damaged street sign, the two travelers found their way onto a long gravel drive which climbed toward a distant canopy of old-growth trees. Blended into those surroundings, was a neat little cabin with rough cut board-and- batt siding, and a cedar shake roof; they only recognized the cabin when they were practically on top of it.

A remnant of wood smoke barely streamed out of the metal stovepipe on the roof. The juniper smoke was mixed with the unmistakable spice of pine needles after a rainstorm, and it carried Marion to a place of calmness . . . Fortunately for her, she was enjoying those calming effects through the small and protected opening at the top of her car window, because *(from out of nowhere)* she was charged by a massive creature, which slammed at full speed into her side of the car!

The hairy paws of this beast eclipsed nearly half the surface area of her passenger-side window. She immediately screamed at the top of her lungs, causing Amaia to shriek with her own piercing scream; this duet resulted in a discordance which actually hurt their ears. If they hadn't heard the loud barking that ensued, or seen the broad, tri-colored face of the *Great Pyrenees* dog next to Marion's window, they might have mistaken it for a bear.

❀ ❀ ❀

Marion calmed herself as she watched the dog continue to bark beside her window . . . Amaia recovered as well, and then she remembered, "Oh my Gosh! . . . *'Txakur'!* . . . She tried to warn me about the *dog!*" Marion struggled to understand, as she looked at Amaia and asked, "What?" Amaia explained it more slowly, "Txakur is the Basque word for 'dog' . . . The woman at the Postal Center said that *her grandfather has a dog."*

Marion was considering a joke about that inadequate warning, when she turned back toward her window to discover the wizened face of an old man, staring at her from *only inches away*. Marion screamed loudly again, and that caused Amaia to scream once more as well, which caused the huge dog to bark louder . . .

The tiny old man, who was only marginally taller than his dog, began laughing uncontrollably; he laughed so hard in fact, that tears came to his eyes. Through all of this, at no time did he move any further back than the few inches which separated him from Marion. He was peering into the passenger-side window as if it were a snow globe meant for only his enjoyment.

❀ ❀ ❀

Amaia grabbed Marion's arm while the two women attempted to catch their breath, and they were eventually able to laugh at their reaction. When she looked back toward her window however, Marion realized that the old man had disappeared—only the barking dog remained beside their car. She puzzled, "Where did he go?" Amaia ducked below her rear-view mirror and searched forward. She answered, *"I don't know* . . . but I hope he comes back to rescue us from '*Cujo*' here." More than a few minutes passed, and they looked at each other as they tried to understand the apparition.

At last, the old man appeared on his front porch, and the screen door slammed behind him. He began unwrapping something inside a large piece of white butcher paper, and he finally produced part of a beef leg bone, with sizeable scraps still adhering. The huge dog, at the first sight of the butcher paper, flew onto the porch and obediently assumed a sitting position before the old man.

Marion heard the man instructing his dog which included a series of unusual glottal clicks, and she watched the huge animal spin around and trot toward the opposite end of the porch. Once there, it sat its huge body down in the middle of a round throw-rug, next to an old rocking chair. After the wizened man delivered the leg bone, he leaned down to pull on his dog's ears and offer verbal affection. He then turned fully toward Amaia's car and he signaled for the two women to come up onto the porch . . .

❁ ❁ ❁

After exchanging a look, they both opened their car doors and carefully moved toward the old man. He greeted them and smiled broadly. Amaia returned the greeting, and after the man confirmed that he was *'Sahats Belasko,'* he asked her to call him "*Sasha.*" He then opened his front door and motioned for them to enter his home. Both women glanced warily at the huge dog as they climbed the steps up to the porch, but the animal now seemed oblivious to their presence.

The house was dark when Marion first entered the living space, which included a small functional kitchen on her left. Living room furniture, centered around a wood stove, filled up the better part of the adjacent room—just beyond the wood stove, there appeared to be one very narrow bedroom, and beside it a tiny bathroom. The free-standing wood stove had a modern feel to it, with a trimmed door that featured glass for viewing the fire; it had been expertly placed upon a raised hearth of flat quartzite stones.

The old man gestured toward a worn loveseat which was angled toward the wood stove, and the two women sat down. He then moved around the room to open some modest curtains, and more light streamed into the area. The light revealed that the cabin walls were surfaced with planks of varnished pine, and that brightened the daytime feel of the room.

When he returned to his large chair and footrest, he angled them to face the women more directly. Before sitting, he asked Amaia if he could make them some tea. They thanked him but declined . . . Amaia began describing the *purpose* of their visit, and Marion recognized some familiar words, remembering that she had just heard them at the postal center.

She found herself staring in amazement at the face of this man, who was at least in his nineties. She concluded that it becomes more difficult to determine the ethnicity of people as they approach one hundred years of age. It was no doubt the deep facial wrinkles (more like furrows really) that become visors above the eyes, which makes it impossible to know if old humans are Asian, or Aboriginal, or Spanish . . .

Maybe time is the final equalizer. When we reach one hundred years of age, all of us will have returned to where we started—once more we will resemble *everyone else on earth*. Marion was still admiring his great face, when Sasha turned toward her and smiled. Somewhere deep within those furrows she caught a laser-flash of wise brilliance from his eyes, which instantly made her smile back.

❦ ❦ ❦

She heard Amaia enunciate the 'Cenarrusa' and 'Aguirre' names again, and then ponder any possible connections to 'Gorbeia', but Sasha just smiled and continued to listen. Finally, he spoke in a kind and lyrical cadence. After asking him to reiterate several statements, she turned to Marion and confessed, "He sometimes incorporates a type of slang which is tough to follow."

"He does help clarify my questions by answering in my version of *Euskara*, however. He confirmed that the Cenarrusas lived for many years on Gorbeia, although he told me that he does not remember the names of the *sons* . . . He often saw their parents in town however, up until the time that the entire family moved away, anticipating the start of World War II . . ."

Marion felt encouraged as she weighed this information, but asked, "Does he remember where their house was located on Mt. Gorbeia?" Amaia asked the question, and Sasha quickly nodded, *"Yes."* Marion then asked, "Does he know someone who might be able to *guide* me up there to see the house? . . ."

When Sasha heard the question, he glanced at Marion and grinned. He then began speaking to Amaia. She hesitated before interpreting, but she eventually repeated, "He says that he is *the only one left* who knows where the Cenarrusas lived, but he won't be able to take you up to the site." This surprised Marion and she asked, *"Why?"* Amaia reluctantly articulated, "He . . . He says that you are *too old* to climb that mountain with him." Marion immediately braced up and glared at Sasha, *"Pfff (!) . . . You old goat!* Who are you to call me *old?!"* Sasha didn't need translation for this, and he began laughing *hard;* even Amaia started to giggle at Marion's indignation.

Sasha quickly jumped up and pointed to the footstool at the base of his chair; he then spoke brusquely as he engaged Marion. Amaia interpreted, "He wants you to put your foot up on that step and *flex* your leg muscle." Marion did not hesitate. She jutted her jaw and moved quickly to place her foot where he was pointing. Sasha then growled as he flexed his arms. Amaia coached, "Now, harden your calf muscle . . ." When Marion did that, Sasha grabbed it with his hand, which he had shaped like a *claw*.

Marion didn't flinch, and she glared down at the old man who was squeezing her calf. Sasha let go and shook his head while he dismissed her. Amaia giggled some more, "He says it feels like an *old leg of mutton*, and that you probably won't make it a hundred meters up that mountain . . ."

Marion spun toward Sasha (whose enjoyment in this game was now barely disguised) and she ordered him, *"Okay . . .* You put *your* leg up there, *Methuselah!"* He laughed heartily at this, knowing that Marion had taken the bait. He then stepped onto the footrest and rolled up his pant leg to display his own calf muscle. Marion squeezed it hard, and she was secretly impressed to feel the strength in the old man's leg, but she now played along with his joke: "Amaia, we need to find someplace that will rent him a *wheelchair* before we start our climb." At this, Sasha laughed hard again, and the interlude was wildly contagious for some time among the three participants . . .

## MAKING PLANS

Marion decided that she would like some tea in this house after all, and without asking, she moved into the kitchen to take charge. Sasha smiled as he watched her, and he eventually talked in detail about what it would take (and what supplies would be necessary) for a climb up Mt. Gorbeia. The peak was not so prohibitive because of its *steepness*, but because it was surrounded by rugged terrain and *very thick brush*, especially at the lower elevations.

They would drive as far as "Sarria," and leave the car there overnight . . . Starting from a nearby trailhead, they could hike beside a stream located on the west side of Mt. Gorbeia. The path there was the best way to gain altitude while avoiding the thorny foliage which occupied the sunnier ridges leading up the mountain. Then, climbing along the edge of a lower canyon, up to a glade called "Arkarai," they would turn east toward the saddle known as "Berretin" near the base of Mt. Gorbeia; once there, they would make camp for the night.

Sasha then described the second leg of their trip, which would require only a short hike the next day, but it would take Marion east through Cenarrusa grazing lands, which he remembered as being, "very beautiful." Eventually they would arrive at "Pagazuri," which was close to the ancestral home of the Cenarrusa family. Marion listened raptly to every detail of Sasha's description, while Amaia translated and compiled detailed notes about the journey.

Marion communicated her intent to return in two or three weeks to begin the hike, then she asked how they might contact Sasha to confirm that he was ready to join them? Sasha didn't understand the question, but he tried to answer with varying responses to clarify that he was, "always right here", or "now here, and here then." The two women finally decided that they could always just contact his granddaughter at the Postal Center to get word to him, or perhaps they might return "right here," and give Sasha whatever time he needed to prepare for the hike . . .

❀ ❀ ❀

Before leaving Sasha's home, Marion felt that she needed to set the record straight. It had been weighing on her that all of Amaia's introductions thus far were framed by her assumption that: "Marion's family lived in this area." She was therefore moved to disclose the fact that she was not *certain* Andere Cenarrusa was her *father,* nor that Angelina Cenarrusa was her *sister* . . . In the absence of confirming that Andere's nickname had been *'Ando',* nothing during this trip so far had brought her that certainty.

This left only one remaining hope, which required climbing Mt. Gorbeia and standing before the Cenarrusa home. From that spot, she hoped to confirm that the rock formations located behind it were the same as those framing the photo which had been mailed to her mother all those years ago . . .

Amaia looked at her with a new sadness, and she carefully interpreted the message for Sasha. Marion then stood up and handed the black and white photo of 'Ando and Baby Angelina' to him. The old man remained still, and he studied her after this revelation; he then examined the photograph. When he finally lowered it, he stared at Marion long enough to at last understand the heightened consequences of her *quest* in Basque Country.

The old man stood up and he moved closer to Marion. There he reached out and placed one hand upon her cheek. He leaned forward to engage her eyes, and he then spoke softly, "You told me only that you were searching for your 'Father and his Brothers'. You did not ask me about your Grandmother. You are beautiful like she was, Marion . . ."

He reached up and touched her platinum hair, which was pulled back beside her temple, and he smiled at her, "This is *her hair,* Marion . . . No one else in the world has hair like you and your Grandmother . . ."

## SARRIA

Amaia waited for a long time until Marion was finally able to release her tight grasp of Sasha's hand, and she then hugged him once more before turning to leave. She walked slowly back toward the car, and then remained silent during the drive, until they were once more below Ubide. Amaia had learned enough about Marion today to give her this moment . . .

Only when they approached the lake country of *Legutio* did Marion speak again. She shared, "I didn't realize how beautiful this part of the world truly is . . . I won't be able to stay away for long." Amaia reminded her, "Well, it sounds like you will be back here in just a few weeks for some hiking." This refocused Marion, and during the remainder of their trip the two women made plans for her return.

Marion surprised Amaia when she asked her to stay on in her employment for the "foreseeable future." Amaia excitedly agreed, and Marion then asked if she would have time to gather more information about her Grandmother prior to their climb up Mt. Gorbeia. She assured Marion that she would, but then joked, "I have been worried about that climb actually, so maybe I should just ride up on the back of Sasha's *dog* . . ." and together, they laughed.

❀ ❀ ❀

Amaia's concerns resurfaced however, and she revealed that she had only done a little "car camping" with her family and while she was in college; she had never really owned the kind of backpacking gear which would be required for a climb up Mt. Gorbeia. Marion considered this and realized that *she too* would need new camping equipment. They therefore planned to return to the backpacking store the following morning.

Marion thought for a moment and suggested, "You know Amaia, tomorrow is my last day here . . . Do you suppose we might have enough time to find our way up to *Sarria* after we shop for our gear? If the clouds have lifted, I would love to see Mt. Gorbeia for the first time. It might be fun to visualize our trip, don't you think?"

Amaia was enthused with the idea, and she guessed that the travel distance couldn't be too far beyond Vitoria-Gasteiz. She then said she would print a map for tomorrow's trip when she got home. Both of them were tired after two days of pursuits, so they agreed to call it an early evening. Amaia dropped Marion off beside the hotel lobby, and the two new friends parted ways for the night . . .

❊ ❊ ❊

The following morning was sunny and beautiful as they found themselves traveling together on Highway N-622 toward Sarria. Sasha had indicated that this would be the departure point for their climb. Their shopping spree at the backpacking store was fun, and the same young clerk who previously assisted them with the topo map had been very helpful in steering them toward lightweight camping choices. He was impressed when he finally tallied their purchase, and he felt compelled to help the two women load everything into the car.

Nearly the entire area of Amaia's back seat (and the hatch) was now filled with new packs, tents, sleeping bags and clothing. They had acquired coats, pants, hiking boots, and socks, as well as two small camp stoves with cooking utensils. They also bought a water filtration device, and Marion acquired some dehydrated food packs while she thought out loud about meal-prep before the trip. The clerk might just have been flirting with Amaia, but his attentions amounted to a lot of extra time helping them consider how to distribute weight evenly between the two backpacks.

❊ ❊ ❊

The women shared their excitement as they envisioned their upcoming hike, and eventually Amaia turned at a sign which pointed them toward Sarria. From here, a dirt road led them another two miles into a deeply-wooded part of the terrain. They finally arrived at a clearing which revealed a small general store. Signage on the building indicated that they had arrived at their destination.

When they both stepped out of the car, however, they were confused to see only a continuation of the same stand of trees which had brought them here, so they decided to go into the store and inquire about the *location* of Mt. Gorbeia. The man behind the counter seemed amused when Amaia asked for directions to the mountain. He studied them above his reading glasses, and then pointed out through his window toward a sunlit meadow, visible two hundred feet beyond the store; he then instructed, "Walk into that meadow and look back in this direction," and he pointed at the wall behind him. They thanked him and made their way out toward the meadow.

When at last they stopped and looked back in the direction of the store, the impressive vista of *Mt. Gorbeia* could be appreciated for the first time. It towered in the sun beyond an old-growth tree line and surrounding grasslands, and it held close to it the wisps of small clouds that were the remnants of yesterday's rainstorm. Marion stared for a long time at the mountain peak, so vivid above the tree line. She then squinted to more closely examine the many granite outcroppings which characterized the landscape, and she wondered if someday soon she might find granite such as this rising up behind her ancestral home . . .

## RETURN FLIGHT

Both women were sad the next morning at the airport in Vitorio, as Amaia helped Marion organize her luggage. Marion felt acutely that she would miss her new friend, and she shared with Amaia that she had been surprised to discover how easily the two of them had traveled together—that being, *"the best litmus test* for a friendship." They agreed to talk frequently between now and the time of Marion's return, and then hugged before saying their goodbyes.

Amaia watched as Marion climbed the airstairs of the corporate jet, and she smiled when the captain extended his hand to help her step through the open hatch. Marion turned and waved once more to Amaia, and then she disappeared inside . . .

The Flight Attendant was there to help her get comfortable (again in the aft settee), where Marion anticipated, as before, dodging the ongoing business of the trip. She agreed to a flute of Champagne when it was offered, and then made herself at home in the back of the aircraft. The trip to Zurich would be quick, so she decided to keep her notes and maps hidden in the leather valise which she always carried during travel.

❊ ❊ ❊

At no time during the previous travel days had Marion arrived upon a plan to divulge to Bill that she now believed Frank was her *biological Nephew*. How could Bill, or *Frank* for that matter, be prepared for such a conclusion? Bill, given his skepticism after years of failed attempts to find Aguirre descendants, would certainly want to see birth certificates . . . And Frank, who knew almost nothing about her history, would be completely overwhelmed. She therefore decided during the plane's descent into Zurich, that she would wait for quieter moments at home before discussing these matters with either of them . . .

❀ ❀ ❀

Bill Bennett was the first passenger to board the jet in Zurich. He was happy to see his wife, and he made his way directly toward her in her settee. Marion stood to give him a kiss, and they hugged tightly while the other passengers boarded and took their seats. She studied him closely and commented, "Darling, your eyes seem *tired* . . . Was it strenuous carrying all of that *gold* around with you, or have you just been staying out too late with *'the boys'?"*

Bill laughed at this and said, "No, I have actually been fighting a chest cold; nothing serious, but I was hoping that we might just go straight home and skip our other travels. I have been feeling the need for your warmth and healing," and he leaned forward to kiss her again. Marion pulled him closer and spoke softly, "I will admit you immediately into the Intensive Care Unit once we are home," and she placed her hand on his butt.

They sat together in the settee, where Bill produced a small jewelry box from his coat pocket, "It's a memento to this occasion in Zurich." Marion smiled at him and opened the box, which contained a very pretty neckless that showcased a small rectangle of gold. She looked at it closely, and saw that the gold piece was officially identified as *Swiss;* Bill revealed, "The gold weighs 2.5 grams . . . At 'spot price,' plus the jeweler's fine work, you are looking right at *three hundred bucks . . .*"

Marion kidded, "Oooh . . . *big spender."* She leaned over to kiss him on the cheek as she squeezed his hand, "It *is* actually beautiful, but somehow I was under the impression that you came here to buy a larger quantity of gold than this."—He laughed and then quietly shared, "Well, there *is* that other $450 million in *bullion* which we will be leaving behind in Switzerland . . ."

They locked arms, and were smiling affectionately at one another when *Steve* boarded the jet as its last passenger. He immediately located Marion in the back of the plane, and when she realized he was staring at her, he pointed two fingers at his own eyeballs and then pointed them at her. Marion slumped comically to avoid his stare, and she whispered to Bill, *"Busted . . ."*

Bill waited until the plane was airborne before saying to Marion, "I am beyond intrigued by whatever it is that has compelled you on this secret mission to Spain, and I can't wait to hear all about it . . . But *first,* I have to tell you that I received some bad news from Hank when I got to Zurich, and I need to share it with you." Marion was concerned and asked, *"Oh no,* is it *Margaret?"* Bill shook his head, "No . . . I'm afraid this is about *Frank . . .* Something bad happened between him and his wife, and things have blown up back in San Francisco . . ."

# 19

## COWBOY UP

The best advice that Frank McClelland received in the months leading up to his divorce, came on the first morning after the incident at AT&T Park. Hank appeared early that Sunday to intervene on behalf of his friend. He was carrying a lot of food when he reached the top of Frank's stairs, and he stood there briefly to organize himself on the porch. Anticipating that he would have to knock, he freed up one hand by gripping a takeout bag in his teeth, and then he balanced the coffee and juice-tray with his other hand.

He was surprised to discover that the door had been left open, so he stepped into the entryway and listened for any signs of life . . . When he rustled the takeout bags, while setting everything down on the kitchen table, he heard a *snore* from the living room which reverberated off a hard surface. Hank silently moved in that direction and then stopped when he saw Frank, head lowered upon his forearms, asleep at his desk. He was relieved to see that there were no signs of discord from the previous night. The furniture was still neatly arranged and no whiskey bottles were evident, nor even any drink glasses indicating that alcohol had been consumed in excess.

Frank, however, was still dressed exactly as he had been when he attended yesterday's Giants game, and that moved Hank to sadness as he considered his sleeping friend. He moved one of the chairs closer, allowing him to sit directly across the desk from Frank, and he spoke to him softly, *"Hey buddy."* Frank startled a bit, and Hank continued, *"Hey . . . Good morning . . .* What do you say we get you up and moving? I brought you some coffee and juice, and some breakfast. I'll set us up over at the kitchen table."

Frank rubbed his eyes with both palms, then winced in pain before grabbing his neck and right shoulder. He asked, "What time is it?" Hank said, "It is *7:00 am . . .*

time to get up. Why don't you go splash some water in your face. Frank complied, and when he returned after a few minutes, he looked more awake. He drank some orange juice, and then took a large bite of the egg and cheese croissant that his friend had brought him . . . He was grateful, and soon he was able to speak, *"Thank you."* Hank smiled and answered, *"de nada,"* and they sat in silence for a while more.

❈ ❈ ❈

Hank studied him, and then offered, "So, the Giants *won* yesterday . . ." Frank turned toward him, confused, *"What?"* Hank continued, "Yeah, the Yanks tied it up in the ninth and they went into *extras*. Nate Schierholtz got Klesko in on a sac fly in the thirteenth; Giants beat the Yankees 6 to 5." Frank smiled and said, *"No kidding?"* Then ironically, "I was really hoping for a *positive takeaway* from yesterday." Hank (dry as ever), "You know me, the most positive Jewish man in America. I know how to deliver the good news." At this, they started laughing, and it gained momentum until Frank had to finally collect himself. He smiled once more at his friend, "Thank you Hank, I'm glad you're here this morning."

❈ ❈ ❈

Hank, now more seriously continued, "I do find it fairly *amazing* that you predicted this whole scenario with your wife—almost *verbatim,* by the way. Do you remember the day when you confided this to me?" Frank nodded, "Yep . . . It *sucks* being right all the time, doesn't it?" Hank chuckled, but then he added, "Well, I think you need to look back at it as a head-start on getting through this . . . Can I offer you some advice in this regard?"

Frank agreed, *"Fire away."* Hank began, "I have watched a lot of friends go through divorces over the years, and the ones who sat around and got stuck on the 'whys' and 'wherefores' came through it the worst . . . But the friends who just got after the matters at hand, and didn't look back, came out *far better* on the other side. My hope for you is that you will be among the latter . . ."

Frank nodded, "I may be a little shell-shocked this morning, but I do know you are right about that—funny, I was actually having a dream about protecting Marion's painting when you woke me this morning. I suppose I'll have to figure out what to do about that when people start combing through this place to move Cherise's things . . ."

❈ ❈ ❈

As the two men pondered this, they were interrupted by a loud knock on the entryway door. Frank opened it to find Stella standing there, holding a bag of groceries; she hugged him hard with one arm, and kissed him on the cheek, "Morning, Handsome . . ." She then moved with purpose toward the kitchen . . . Standing behind her was Richie, who was holding another full grocery bag. His grip on the bag revealed knuckles on his right hand that had been doctored with thin strips of white tape. He placed his untaped hand on Frank's shoulder and examined him closely. When he had studied Frank enough, he asked, *"How you doin?"* Frank answered back, "Good . . . How *you* doin?"

Richie laughed as he stepped in and then quietly warned, "I hope you're ready; she's been quoting *The Godfather* all morning. When they approached the kitchen table, Stella could be seen hugging Hank, and then conferring with him.

Stella quickly took charge, *"Okay, I'm here to cook* . . . I see that Hank brought you some breakfast, *which is nice,* but I'm going to make my frittata anyway; it's big, so there will be plenty of leftovers. Then, we've got the ingredients here for a pot of spaghetti. I'll make that up later today. We're *'going to the mattresses'* Frank, so let's make sure we have enough food to eat around here. Have you seen her yet?" Frank was puzzled, *"Hmm?"* Stella impatiently asked again, "*Charice?!* . . . Have you seen *Charice* yet?!"

Frank tried to come up to speed, *"Oh!* . . . No . . . No sign of her yet." Stella warned, "Well, *you are going to see her* sooner or later, so you better have a *plan*—it's actually good that you have possession of this house, so she can't just park her *sorry ass* over here anytime she wants. I always heard that 'possession is 9/10 of the law', and I'm pretty sure what that means is that *if you are in the house,* you have *control* of it." Hank agreed, "She's right Frank: A divorce falls under civil law, so if she thinks that she has a better claim than you to live here, she will need to prove it in court. That can take a long time . . . So, for the time being, you *are* in *control.*"

❀ ❀ ❀

Frank was still trying to catch up, but he agreed, "Yeah . . . I was just telling Hank that I have been worried about protecting Marion Bennet's painting, so I guess it's good to have some control over things." Stella looked at him and asked, "What *painting?*" Frank tilted his head and beckoned Stella and Richie to follow him out to the living room. Frank pointed at the painting, "That's a Monet . . . and this desk belonged to Voltaire . . . so I guess I need to buy enough time for Marion to return all of this stuff to MoMA." Hank remembered, "Bill and Marion are coming home from Zurich on Thursday . . . You probably need to buy at least a week to get that done."

Stella was still staring at the painting, "I can't believe you have a *fucking Monet* in your house! . . . We have to get a *locksmith* over here *now*, Frank!" Stella looked around at the three men, and each of them nodded in agreement; it was implied that they were all answering, *"Yes Ma'am."* She turned at last to Frank and instructed, "Why don't you start by finding a locksmith who can do this today, and then we can start making plans for everything else that has to happen here . . ."

❀ ❀ ❀

Hank needed not to have worried about his friend just sitting around licking his wounds. Stella's influence guaranteed that this was *not going to happen* on her watch. Following the arrival of the locksmith, she sent Richie and Frank on a mission to acquire enough large U-Haul boxes to pack-up all of Cherice's things. Hank helped Stella pack clothing and other belongings for removal from the premises . . . Frank was glad Stella took charge of that, and he and Richie eventually carried all of the full boxes down to the garage at street level.

### HANK STEPS UP

By mid-afternoon, as the spaghetti sauce was simmering on the stove, Frank grabbed some beers for a break on the patio. When Hank sat down, he asked Richie for the first time about his taped hand, "What the hell happened to your *hand*, Richie? If I didn't know better, I would say that your tape job looks like it was done by a *professional*—maybe even by someone inside the *boxing* trade . . ." Nobody said a word, as Stella and Richie and Frank glanced back and forth . . . Finally, Richie began, "I had a little run-in with Travis yesterday, Hank. It was unfortunate, but it was just one of those things that needed to happen . . ."

Hank looked at the three of them when they returned to silence, "From what I saw yesterday, Richie, it certainly was one of those things *'that needed to happen'* . . . Thank you for looking out after my friend here", and things got quiet again.

Frank had to say it again, "One last time Richie, I understand that you guys had history, but I am so sorry you got pulled into this thing between Cherice and I—if your career is fucked-up in any way over this, I will never forgive myself." Hank interrupted, *"Woah! Wait a minute! . . .* How could this possibly come back on *Richie?!* There were thirty people there from Icarus yesterday who saw what happened on that Jumbotron, and every single one of them knows who was at fault: This will come back on *Travis and Cherice . . . not on you Richie."*

Richie tried to reassure, "You may be right Hank, but you know what? Fuck it if Icarus HR gets this wrong. Lately, I'm tired of drinking the Kool Aid with assholes like Travis—and honestly, I'm starting to agree with Frank about this whole 'subprime mortgage' thing."

"Stella and I talked about it last night . . . I'm a year away from finishing my MBA at New York University—it took me a long time to get that far in their *online* program. So I'm asking myself, why not just take a year off and finish my degree back home?" He looked at Stella and they smiled at each other, "Truth is, we're both kind of missing *home* right now. So starting tomorrow morning, I'm gonna check into getting registered for the fall semester at NYU."

❈ ❈ ❈

Hank was suddenly on a mission: He stood up and reassured Richie, "That sounds like a great plan, but if there's any chance that Icarus comes down on the wrong side of this, I'm going to put a stop to it *right now*—regardless of your decision to stay or leave, you don't deserve a demerit on your resume." He pulled out his cell phone and started walking in the direction of the patio door. He explained as he left, *"I'm calling Larry Sewell . . ."*

# 20

## THE MOVE

Marion Bennett had not been home for more than an hour the following Thursday, when she called Frank to ask him to meet her at an address on *Jackson Street;* she told him, "That's in *Pacific Heights* . . . Just head up Laguna St. and turn left onto Jackson. The house is a few doors down on your left. Look for the big *Victorian* with dormers on the roof—it's an off-yellow color, with red terracotta stairs on the right side of the house. If you pass Lafayette Park, you've gone too far up Laguna . . ."

When Frank arrived at the beautiful old mansion, Marion's white Chevy Tahoe was already parked in the driveway—she was laughing in a conversation with an animated young man who sported fashionably-coiffed dark hair. He was holding a long black cat in his arms, and when Frank exited his truck to approach them, he could see that the recumbent feline was wearing a sparkling rhinestone collar.

The cat peered sleepily at Frank with one open eye. Marion turned toward Frank as he approached, and extended her arms. She hugged him tightly and then searched his eyes, "Are you alright?" He smiled and nodded his head, "Yes, actually . . . *surprisingly* so. Turns out I have some great friends." Marion smiled in relief, and then grabbed his arm to steer him back toward the young man . . . "Frank, I would like you to meet my *very* dear friend, 'Geo' . . . And Geo, this is *'Frank.'*" Frank extended his hand, but before Geo grasped it, he exclaimed, "You didn't say anything about him being this *beautiful*, Marion! . . ." as he accentuated his handshake with down-turned fingertips.

Marion laughed, *"Easy there Princess!* . . . Frank is just back from the relationship front lines, *Okay?!* . . . so let's dim the klieg lights a bit." Geo looked comically down his nose at Marion, but relented, "Don't worry Frank, we know all about 'relationship front lines' around here . . . So, if it's *R&R* you want, that is *exactly* what you shall have." He then turned his sleepy cat toward Frank and added, *"See?* . . . You won't find even the slightest bit of tension in Lady Windermere's body . . . We are peaceful creatures here on Jackson Street, aren't we *sugar?"* and he kissed his cat on its forehead.

Marion leaned in and hugged Geo, and then said, "Thank you Sweetheart . . . Please tell *Chris* that I was sorry to have missed him." She then grabbed Frank's arm and said, "I want to give you a tour of our first home in San Francisco . . ."

❈ ❈ ❈

Frank marveled at the restoration of the beautiful old building, while they made their way up two full stories inside the covered stairwell. As they climbed, Marion explained, "This home actually has four levels, but Bill and I turned the two upper floors into an apartment—that was just before our move to Belvedere, when we occasionally still entertained into the late evenings here in San Francisco. We had originally planned to rent out the bottom floors, but never got around to it . . . that is, until we decided to offer it to Chris and Geo. Chris is the 'Events Director' for Davies Symphony Hall, and Bill likes him very much . . ."

Marion turned the door key to the upstairs apartment and Frank followed her inside. As Marion turned on lights, Frank was struck once again by her grasp of style and space within the exquisitely decorated rooms. The kitchen, *of course*, was expertly equipped, and he let Marion know this fact wasn't lost on him . . . He slowly followed her into an expansive living room with a high Victorian ceiling, and then beyond it to two impressive bedrooms with separate baths at the far end of the first level.

Finally, they circled back to a balustrade, which led them up beside a living room wall and delivered them to a landing on the upper floor; here Frank was amazed to find a *library* which existed as the logical extension of a *large separate office*. He immediately felt Bill's influence here within these substantial and classic rooms. The library shelves featured rows of antique books, and the high dormer windows illuminated this upstairs space with streams of San Francisco daylight.

The office turned out to be uniquely impressive, as it could be enclosed by floor-to-ceiling mahogany doors; wooden grids framed the glass within these doors, which were finished to match the wainscoting and chair moldings that encircled the desk. A separate bathroom could be accessed from either the library or the office.

❈ ❈ ❈

Marion opened an exterior door on one side of the office, and stepped out with Frank onto a large deck, beautifully incorporated along the east side of the roof—this location offered a tree-top vantage which he had not expected. This was a wide, filtered sun retreat, protected along its eastern railing by the branches of a towering eucalyptus tree; the deck was large enough to allow for two chase lounges, and a wrought-iron table with four chairs. Frank leaned upon the railing and marveled, "This place is *amazing*, Marion. No wonder you wanted to keep it as an apartment."

She leaned on the railing too, and there beside him she breathed in a deep inhalation of tree-scented air as she lifted her face toward the sun. She confided in Frank, "I *do* love this place . . . When Bill and I first moved here from New York, we wanted to feel like we *belonged* somewhere, and this is just the quintessential San Francisco home. It felt to us like we had become a genuine part of *The City*, you know? . . . And I know it sounds crazy, because this place is *so big*, but we felt like we were *anonymous* here too; we were happy to just blend in with our neighbors . . ."

❀ ❀ ❀

She quickly switched gears, "Let's step back into the office for a moment; I need to talk with you about something, and Frank, I'm sorry that I don't have as much time today as I would like. Bill came back from Zurich a bit under the weather, so I need to leave soon and get back to him." Frank was concerned, "*Oh no!* . . . What's going on?" Marion shook her head, "He says that he just has a chest cold, but I don't like the way he's breathing . . . He said the long flights really got to him this time, so I made an appointment for him to see his Cardiologist tomorrow morning; I will certainly keep you up to date."

❀ ❀ ❀

Once inside, Marion turned two office chairs to face one another, "Here, let's sit." She began, "Frank . . . Please know that I was just devastated by the news of what happened between you and your wife, and I am actually still heartbroken for you as we sit here. When I first heard, I was completely beside myself at being out of the country and not able to help you at all. So, it was a relief to hear you say that you were surrounded by friends during all of that."

She got teary when she studied him, "Anyway, I'll just get right to it: Bill told me that he made some assumptions about your finances when you opened your Goldman Sachs account. He told me, *all things considered*, that he is presuming you will want to sell your house as soon as possible to settle your divorce, especially in light of the coming recession. Please forgive me if I am *overstepping* here . . . This is really not my style Frank, but Bill made me promise that I would address it with you."

Frank tried to reassure her, "No . . . *please, Marion* . . . Bill and I are completely candid about money matters, and actually that is *precisely* what I plan to do; I just haven't talked with Cherice about any of it, and, truth be known, I don't even know where to start." Marion nodded and continued, "Well, that brings me to my next topic: You know that we have run with the financial and legal circles of San Francisco for many years, so I brought you the name of an attorney whom I hope you will call. She is famous as a defender of men's rights in these higher profile cases, and I believe you need to address that now, considering the way that you were treated. Please call her today, and tell her that *I referred you* . . . And please, also tell her that you work for the Bennett Foundation."

"And regarding your negotiating directly with Cherice on the sale your home, or *anything else for that matter*, I am certain that your lawyer will advise against it . . . *Okay?*" Frank looked at the phone number and said, "Thank you. I'll call her today . . . the sooner the better, as far as I'm concerned." Marion again looked sadly at him, then finished, "All of these considerations Frank, lead me at last to this apartment . . . and *this* is why I wanted you to see it: Bill and I both feel that the timing is actually *perfect* for you to move into this place as soon as possible . . ."

❁ ❁ ❁

Maybe it was due to the fact that Frank had been walking around in a trance for six days, or maybe it was simply that he had been raised within a framework of *humility* where he could never presume to accept gifts on a scale such as this—but either way—he was not prepared to consider Marion's offer; he could only stare at her in stunned disbelief . . .

Marion recognized that she needed to make her case, so she continued, "Bill and I have *literally* not stayed here in years, Frank. We love our place in Belvedere, and our lives are just so different now; we're much more private than we were all those years ago. It's not that we don't *entertain*, it's just that we don't come into The City and party 'till the wee hours anymore."

"Also, you have to consider the very pressing concern regarding your need for a secure office. Bill said that this office, where you and I are now sitting, is already completely wired with dedicated lines and routers, and Steve wants you to know that it will only take a couple of hours for the Raytheon Techs to move your computers here and activate everything with new encryption. Both Bill and Steve asked me to convey to you that *neither* of them is comfortable . . . with all due respect . . . in any situation where you might be forced to leave your Marina home unprotected . . ." and Marion was careful in choosing her next words . . . "unprotected . . . considering the caliber of people who will soon be rummaging through that house."

❁ ❁ ❁

Finally, Marion implored Frank with a charged emotional attachment that she hadn't revealed to him before—something had changed within her since traveling to Spain, and it was reflected in her insistence that Frank should agree to this move. She pressed, "I have to tell you that I am really worried about Bill . . . Something is *not right* with him, and until we know for certain what is going on, all of us will be relieved to know that you are safely hidden away from conflict; we need to know that you *would not miss even a step*, should . . . should you have to . . . *assume control of The Bennett Foundation*. Will you please do this for me, Frank? It means so much more to me than I can possibly explain to you here today."

In spite of every tenet within him which would have otherwise driven Frank to resist—to try to prove his strength by finding some other solution of his own making. He found himself wanting to give Marion everything . . . He stammered, "Your . . . Your generosity is beyond anything I can comprehend . . . and all of these points that you are making ring *true* . . . Honestly, I have to admit that this would solve every problem which has kept me awake for almost a week now . . . So . . . Yes. Yes, I will . . . Thank you beyond words, Marion."

Marion's eyes welled into tears once again, and she hugged him for a long time. She at last turned his palm up and placed the apartment keys in his open hand. Lastly, before leaving for Belvedere, she told Frank, "Steve is waiting for your decision . . . Will you please call him as soon as possible? I believe he has an idea about getting Raytheon here tomorrow morning, while we are at Stanford seeing Bill's Doctor—And *Frank?* after that . . . please call your Attorney."

## **STANFORD HEART**

The next day at Stanford Hospital confirmed all of Marion's fears about Bill—at every diagnostic stop throughout the morning, it seemed that the conclusions were building upon an ever-more-serious reality. His chest x-rays showed diffuse *pleural effusions* (collections of lung fluid), which were now disrupting Bill's heart and lung mechanics. The echocardiogram still confirmed his history of *aortic stenosis*, but it also demonstrated that the aortic valve damage was now contributing to broader heart failure.

Bill's Cardiologist told him, "We've known for a long time that the valve was damaged during your childhood bout of Scarlet Fever; we now categorize that within 'Rheumatoid Valvular Disease' . . . but now your heart's 'ejection fraction' has fallen, and that has been backing up the blood in your pulmonary circulation; that's where this lung fluid came from." The doctor argued that the aortic valve needed to be replaced *as soon as possible*. "Given the rapid onset of your symptoms"— before scheduling it however, he first wanted to perform a thoracentesis to drain the lung fluid. If they could determine that there was no pre-existing infection in the pleural fluid, he wanted Bill to undergo cardiac surgery in the morning. So, all that was now left to do was to meet with his Cardiac Surgeon . . .

❈ ❈ ❈

Bill had already decided that Steve and Frank would make better use of their time today, by helping Raytheon connect the computers as quickly as possible at the Jackson Street apartment. As anticipated, that had taken only a couple of hours during the morning. Frank was relieved to quickly confirm that he was once again networked with the Belvedere computer, especially so after running a live systems check on the Goldman Sachs trading platform.

He and Steve were nearly finished loading Frank's belongings into the F-150 pickup bed, when Marion called to share Bill's developing news. Both men decided they should visit him in Palo Alto after delivering Frank's belongings to Jackson Street. Soon after that, they found themselves carrying boxes up and down the apartment's stairs.

❈ ❈ ❈

The late afternoon traffic made for slow going, as Frank steered his pickup toward Palo Alto. Once they exited Hwy 280 toward the downtown, however, he did have the advantage of knowing his way around Stanford—he and Steve soon found themselves at the *Cardiothoracic Surgery Unit* of the hospital. As they approached Bill's room, Frank remembered how impressed he had always been with the nurses and staff who worked in and around Stanford; even now, they continued to inspire confidence as they went about their work.

Steve knocked softly on the door, and he and Frank entered the room to find Marion sitting on the bed next to Bill. They were holding hands, and both of them turned to smile at their visitors. Marion was relieved to see them, and she stood quickly to hug them both . . . Frank joked, "Bill, you don't look sick enough to be in that hospital bed." Bill quipped back, "Just *sandbagging* . . . I'm playing the sympathy card for my wife."

Marion grinned at him and admitted, "You actually are looking much better since they drained that fluid from your lungs. But don't think for a minute that it will get you off the hook for what we need to do here." She and Bill then brought the two visitors up to speed on the events of the day, including the decision by the Cardiac Surgeon to replace the heart valve in a "TAVR" procedure, to be completed entirely by way of a transcatheter insertion. Bill happily reported that his Surgeon expected his convalescence to be much quicker than that which would have followed an open heart procedure, "He even said that he can switch me off of my anticoagulants to simple aspirin after recovering from the TAVR." I told him, "Make that happen and you can crew for us during the next Windjammer's Race to Santa Cruz . . ." Even Marion was able to smile at that.

Bill was pleased that the IT work had been completed, and he asked Frank about the apartment, "I trust that your new digs are to your liking?" Frank could only shake his head in wonder, "I still think I'm dreaming, Bill . . . *Thank you beyond words.*" Bill smiled and said, "Well, good! You are going to *love* that neighborhood, and I'm relieved that you are now fully ready to take the helm of our trading platform, whilst I enjoy my little vacation here—there is no one we trust more with the task, Frank . . . Isn't that right Marion?" Marion smiled back at him and concurred, *"Absolutely,* my love . . ."

With the appearance of Bill's Nurse, who announced that she needed to change his dressing, Marion leaned down to give him a kiss and tell him, "I reserved rooms over at the Stanford Park, so we will leave you for now. It sounds like this is a good time for us to check-in, and then I thought we might grab some dinner before coming back to see you . . ."

❀ ❀ ❀

Marion soon thereafter checked them into their suites at the nearby hotel (where everyone seemed to recognize her). Frank was impressed with the rooms, and especially with their patio access to the beautiful courtyards which meandered through the property. Steve threw his duffle bag atop the bed in his suite, but he had already decided he would spend the night in Bill's hospital room. He reasoned, "I should be there in case anything comes up, then I'll probably head back here in the morning for a nap . . ." Marion thought that was a good plan.

### BASQUE COUNTRY

That evening, Steve manned his post in a recliner next to the hospital bed, and Marion blew Bill a kiss before she and Frank exited toward the parking lot. When they returned to the hotel, Marion led them straight to the bar. She said, "I'm not even going to *apologize* . . . I need a glass of wine." Frank needed a drink too, so after collaborating with the bartender on a Manhattan recipe, he followed Marion outside to a private table, beside a masonry fireplace.

She started the conversation, "I have so much to tell you about my trip to Basque Country, Frank, and I fear this may be our last chance to discuss it for some time. I am relieved to know that Bill's doctor believes that a few weeks might be enough time to return him to health, but that stubborn man will require *watching*. That's going to keep you and I occupied right up until the time when Bill takes over again."

❀ ❀ ❀

She sipped her wine and studied Frank for a moment before jumping directly into her mission: *"Frank . . . I discovered during my travels through Northern Spain that your Mother and I were most likely fathered by the same man . . . and, if I can prove she was indeed my Sister, it will mean that you are my only remaining biological descendent."* After the absolute shock of that moved across Frank's face, Marion produced her old photo of "Ando and Baby Angelina." She then started at the *very beginning* to tell him her story . . .

Frank sat frozen in place, as all of the details were finally shared with him—her accounts of the Spanish Civil War, the lives of "Bixentia" and "Ando" and their separate escapes out of Spain (pursued by Franco, and eventually by the Germans), were beyond Frank's imagination. Finally, Marion's research in Churchill County, Nevada, which produced the Marriage License of Frank's parents, made these things seem so *logical*, and so *obvious*.

❁ ❁ ❁

In hindsight, he knew that he should have researched the license years earlier to learn more about his Basque heritage, and particularly about his grandfather "Andere Cenarrusa." This realization made Marion's stories resonate, and it brought her conclusions into sharp focus.

When Frank heard her speak the name "Cenarrusa," in fact, a childhood memory was immediately jogged. He asked Marion, "Did you learn in your research that Andere had *brothers*?" Marion's eyes widened and she confirmed, "Yes . . . two brothers: 'Matia' and 'Domeka'. Frank marveled, and he slowly shook his head . . . "Uncle Dom."

Marion was astounded, "What do you remember?!" Frank began, "I was very young, but I grew up with stories about my grandfather and his brothers: They had worked in the quarries of Spain when they were young, and after immigrating to Fallon to try their hand at raising sheep, they traveled to Elko and began working in the mines."

"They did some of their own prospecting while they were there, and apparently found a *legitimate* gold deposit. They eventually sold their claim to some big mining outfit, and that's how Uncle Dom bought his ranch in Lamoille." He turned toward Marion as these memories took shape. "I also remember hearing, because of that, my grandfather was able to help my parents buy the ranch in Austin. Mom said it had been his version of a dowry."

❁ ❁ ❁

"I think Matia followed his wife's people to Idaho, but my grandfather continued to prospect around Elko—everyone always said he was the *'real miner'* of the brothers.

But sadly, that is how he died; he was killed in a cave-in while digging . . ." Marion looked sad, as she and Frank quietly reflected upon it . . .

"All of that is what I recollect from stories I heard as a child . . . but before Mom got sick, I remember traveling to Lamoille a few times to visit Uncle Dom and his family—it was always fun for my brother and I . . . There were cousins *everywhere!* . . . and I remember the food being really, really good. I actually think I remember meeting her Basque grandmother there before she passed away . . . Mom always called her, 'Grandma Grace' . . ."

❊ ❊ ❊

Marion was as riveted during Frank's stories as he had been during hers, and she eventually turned to the inevitable. She described to Frank the narrow possibilities wherein they might at last prove that "Andere" and "Ando" had actually been "one and the same" man. She told him, "It can happen in only two ways: Either I will return to Basque Country and confirm that those rock outcroppings behind the Cenarrusa home are the same as those in my photo . . . or, you will travel to your family's ranch, and discover in your Mother's photo album that your grandfather is the same man holding 'Baby Angelina' on the porch of their home . . ."

Marion watched Frank process this information, and then she resigned herself, "But . . . given today's events, both of those journeys must now be placed on hold. You and I have to stay close to Bill until we are sure that his health has improved."

Frank continued to be stunned by these unfolding revelations, so he asked, "Have you told Bill . . . ?" Marion shook her head, "No . . . I planned to, but then he was obviously so ill when we returned from Zurich, that I chose to wait. Since then, it has been all about this day at the hospital." Marion thought out loud, "I made plans to return to Spain in as soon as two weeks, but now I'll have to call Amaia and ask that she tell our guide, Sasha, that the climb must be postponed . . ."

❊ ❊ ❊

They sat in silence, and Marion pulled her wrap tighter around her shoulders. She then studied Frank before asking, "What happened between you and your father?" Frank took a deep breath and looked down at his drink. He had learned that conjuring any part of that story was never a simple thing, and even though people were always kind enough to offer support after listening, he knew that he would only have to face his past all over again. And now . . . Marion, who had just presented reasonable evidence that she was his Aunt, would certainly be burdened by the hard truth . . .

Frank decided to shield her from that, but to do so would require excluding some of the details, "He blamed me for my brother's death. I know that's really at the heart of it. I mentioned to you that he had already withdrawn from me before that, when my Mom died . . . but Robby's death, only one year later? . . . that just sealed the deal."

"Robby jumped on my motorcycle one night after a rodeo—my dad *hated* that motorcycle . . . 'Too much noise around the livestock!' and he yelled at me a lot about it. Robby had been drinking, and I couldn't stop him. He had always been wild, and famous among his friends for doing crazy things. So he was showing off as usual, and he just rode it over the edge of a ravine . . . I have to convince myself every time I think about it, that he couldn't have known how far he would fall . . . and that . . . that, he couldn't possibly have done it on purpose. . . ."

❋ ❋ ❋

Marion reached over to grab his forearm, but Frank managed to press on, "My father arrived at the accident site when the Paramedics were putting Robby into the ambulance, and he just broke down . . . All I could do was watch him from a distance. It was then that a Sheriff's Deputy pulled my motorcycle up out of the ravine. When my dad saw it, I could feel his absolute hatred toward it . . . and then, when he saw me standing there watching . . . he turned that hatred toward me . . . "

Frank studied Marion's expression, and he knew that he had been right in choosing not to describe *every* image—the most painful images . . . the ones that only he and his father shared. Marion asked, "You were sixteen years old when this happened?" He nodded and continued, "My Dad and I never really talked about it afterwards. . . . I'm sure that's why we couldn't get past it. . . ." Marion moved closer to wrap her arm around him, and the two of them were quiet for a long time. . . .

❋ ❋ ❋

He was the first to speak, "I still think about it from time to time, and I am honestly surprised that so many years have passed between us . . . It's just that . . . it was such *a profound rejection*—directed at me—that I have never felt obligated to reach out to him again . . ."

Frank recovered, and he looked at Marion, "But *now* . . . your connection to my *Mom* . . . It changes everything, doesn't it?" He sipped his drink and concluded, "Of course I will go to Smith Creek as soon as Bill recovers . . . and I will ask my Father for that photo album . . ."

# 21

## LADY

When Frank awoke that first morning in his new apartment on Jackson Street, and realized it was 9:35 am, he struggled to remember the last time he had slept in so late—maybe once or twice back in his college days at the University of Nevada, but those memories were foggy. Of course, he and friends had broken through the fun barrier many nights at "The Wall," where they regularly tried to replace the *entirety* of their body fluids with *beer*. Yet even after those occasions, he still remained famous for being the first one up the next morning to make coffee for his maimed friends.

He was certain, right or wrong, that it was his father's regimental approach to each new day which had chiseled that routine into his consciousness. Before those long workdays at Smith Creek, Frank would invariably be the first one up, heading toward the barn to bring the horses to their grooming posts—through much of the year this required a flashlight, but he knew better than to resist. If Robby took longer than usual to wake up *(his Father had once turned the bed upside down with Robby in it)*, it might take more than ten minutes before the generator brought light to the horse stalls.

As he had disciplined himself over the years in a thousand opportunities, he chose not to think any more about Robby or his father this morning—free from that, he started his coffee. When he realized that his TV was still visible in one of the moving boxes, he kicked himself for not having the *tech team* install it when they had been here the day before . . . Accepting his oversight, he carried the TV upstairs to the office and placed it on top of a credenza, where he soon had it connected to his newly-encrypted Wi-Fi. Before long, he was watching the last segment of CNBC's *Halftime Report* and he smiled, knowing that order was once again restored to the Universe.

❄ ❄ ❄

Coffee in hand, he called Goldman Sachs in New York and touched base with his friend Nathan; he was point man there for the Bennett Company, and Frank had asked him prior to Bill's hospital stay to put together recommendations for "debt obligations" (absent exposure to "world banks"). Nathan came through with some strong offerings, and he promised that he would keep them coming. Frank researched the list for a couple of hours, and he felt good about adding most of them to the Bennett Foundation holdings, together with a growing list of US Treasuries.

Impressively, Bill's *Zurich purchase* of gold bullion was now appearing as a *'confirmed trade'* and it was being tallied separately in an adjoining Goldman account. Frank chuckled when he saw it, and shook his head as he counted the zeros in $450 million . . .

❄ ❄ ❄

When he at last decided to take a break, he made a tuna sandwich and grabbed some chips and a Coke Zero on his way to sit outside. The day was beautiful, and he fully understood Marion's decision to locate the patio table *exactly* where it was. As he took a bite of his sandwich, he caught the transient flash of something shiny atop distant branches of the eucalyptus tree . . . It turned out to be Geo's cat, "Lady Windermere," who was expertly navigating the tree limbs on a path directly toward Frank's deck; the athletic feline eventually leaped through the wrought iron railing onto the deck.

Frank was impressed, "Wow, *Lady . . . good job!* You are a long way above the ground here. . . ." The cat then quickly jumped up onto the table and rubbed both sides of her face against Frank's hand. When she inched closer to Frank's sandwich, he laughed, "Oh, *now* I get the picture. . . . This is a *lunch* date, because you smell my sandwich."

Frank tore off a portion of it and emphasized the tuna on a corner of the bread; he then placed it near the center of the table. After the cat had eaten this first offering, she turned back to inspect the sandwich once more. Frank prepared another small portion of his sandwich, where he again highlighted the tuna to share with his visitor.

This routine was repeated three more times, until the big cat had eaten nearly half of the sandwich. When she had at last consumed enough, she turned toward the sun and stretched out fully across the table; allowing for Frank's vantage, he would later confirm that he had faced the cat's raised posterior for a sufficient interval to positively identify the largest pair of *testicles* that he had ever seen on a domestic cat. The significance of this fact would be *repeatedly discounted by Geo*, but Frank remained forever certain that *Lady* Windermere had been the victim of *mistaken identity*. That aside, the sleek black cat curled up close to him, and Frank smiled as he scratched his new friend under *his/her* rhinestone collar. . . .

❊ ❊ ❊

Knowing that Marion and Bill were returning from the hospital today, Frank set about organizing his new dwelling—first and foremost would be his need to locate a nearby grocery store. He was pleasantly surprised to find a *Trader Joe's* right around the corner, where he procured food and supplies sufficient to last into the foreseeable future.

Stocking his own food choices for future meals (most of which would not have been condoned by Cherice prior to the ballpark betrayal) somehow felt meaningful to Frank. He smiled particularly when he considered his bulk purchase of *tuna*, in anticipation of future lunches with Lady Windermere . . .

After a later call to Marion to check on Bill Bennett's progress, he returned the office phone to its console. Frank then stayed at the desk for a while and weighed some of Marion's comments about prior days—she had observed that he seemed to be *'entirely unfazed'* in the aftermath of his life's recent upheaval— *"By anyone's measure"*, she had said, "the shock *alone* should have left you stunned in some visible way . . ."

He thought about that, and reconstructed the scale of his losses during his teenage years; he worried (as he had *many* times before) that maybe he had been dealt some irreparable blow to his ability to connect in relationships . . . Was he *damaged goods*, after all? By his own reckoning, both he and his Father had withdrawn mutually from one another for way too long following the death of his mother. The weight of that, together with all the other destruction, had certainly undermined his *marriage (*and his *life* really*)*. He now clearly recognized his own vacant emotional investment during the previous years . . .

❊ ❊ ❊

When his thoughts turned to Marion however, he was saddened to remember that she had never truly been part of a "family" at all; she instead was hidden away during the horrors of the War in France, where she never knew the joys a young girl might feel playing with her siblings or cousins. No wonder she had spent a lifetime trying to reconstruct some semblance of the family that *might have been . . .*

Frank felt guilty now, as he examined his own past motives which had led him to flee his father and the ranch . . . Considering what Marion had been through, would she under *any circumstances* have ever walked away from the remaining members of her family? He knew that someday soon he would be forced to reconcile his own past—especially if Marion was confirmed to be a member of his family. Frank weighed all that needed to be done, and he brooded for a long time over the collateral damage of death, and what it meant to life remaining.

❊ ❊ ❊

Eventually he found his way to the kitchen to make something to eat; he grabbed a carton of chicken stock and some Ramen noodles. . . . His "kitchen-sink" recipe for noodles included fresh produce, and he had purchased Bok choy today; that, along with sliced breast pieces from a still-warm rotisserie chicken, was perfect. It had been a long time since lunch, and food hit the spot.

After an evening of unpacking clothes and stowing his belongings from the remaining moving boxes, he showered and readied for bed. He eventually stretched-out with an antique copy of *The Idiot* by Fyodor Dostoyevsky, which had called to him from a library shelf, and he began to read.

## THE ASPEN GROVE

There could be no way of knowing how long he had been asleep, but he was awakened by a gentle tickling of his neck and earlobe—he swatted at it, and then wearily sat up and rubbed his eyes. He realized at once that he was now far above the ranch, and he was sitting in a familiar glade, at the edge of his favorite grove of Aspen trees; they had forever beckoned to him from this spot near the top of the Desatoya Range . . . . He had been napping beside Smith Creek, which was flowing quietly through the summer shade of quaking leaves . . . At first he was confused when he saw the denim cuff of his pant leg, and then the spurs which were fastened to his Roper boots (the same spurs and Ropers he had packed in his moving box) . . .

Remembering the Wranglers and the boots, he awoke fully to discover himself within the corporal essence he had embodied at the age of seventeen . . . Standing up now, he looked at his hands and then squinted toward the sun—its glare had gradually encroached upon him as it moved lower in the afternoon sky—When he turned to step back into the shade, he found himself staring in greater detail at his favorite stand of Aspens; they, for as long as he could remember, had been waiting for him together in this setting, and they never failed to acknowledge his presence . . .

Frank discovered at a very young age that when he focused obliquely at the spaces *between* the leaves (rather than at the leaves *directly*), he could share in a kind of communal movement of the grove as a whole . . . It was much later in life when he learned that, together, clusters of Aspens are actually a *single organism* connected by their common root structure.

❀ ❀ ❀

Today, they were welcoming him back again and smiling at him in unison, and he was suddenly overcome with joy in this homecoming. Frank took a few steps beside Smith Creek until he was once again protected beneath the trees' canopy, and he was startled to see two horses tied there. These were horses that he didn't recognize.

They were inexplicably saddled and secured with the familiar tack of the ranch, and they turned their heads toward him when he approached.

A tall chestnut gelding with a kind eye stood nearest to him, and Frank rested his hand upon its lowered muzzle as he studied the pretty bay mare standing beside him; she was tall as well, with a distinctive blaze, and she also seemed gentle and centered. Even with the saddles in place, Frank recognized their strong trapezoidal conformations, framed across their backs between withers and hips. These two horses were elite animals, and he wondered how in the world they had come to be here?

Instinctively, he bent down to grasp the gelding's knee and foreleg. His hand glided down toward the hoof, and the horse consented by bending his leg at the knee and pastern—this allowed Frank to examine the bottom of the hoof. He was impressed to discover that a new horseshoe was expertly secured in place, and someone had employed a 'hot-shoe' method in fastening it there; this farrier's technique was now mostly a lost art, at least outside the circles of racetrack expertise. . . .

❀ ❀ ❀

While still supporting the gelding's foreleg, Frank once again felt the tickle on his neck and earlobe which had awakened him earlier. When he spun away from the horses, he was immobilized by the sight of his Mother standing before him. She laughed at this mischief, and then grinned when she waved a long hawk feather at him to explain the tickle. Her eyes then poured out a fathomless love, and she moved in closer to hug her son.

When she at last released him from her embrace, she moved beside him and began lodging the hawk feather inside the band of his straw cowboy hat. While doing this, she was joyful, "I knew I would find you here at this beautiful spot of yours. . . ." Satisfied with her placement of the feather, she lamented, *"Oh, how I have missed you Francis* . . . Look how *tall* you are!", and she hugged him again.

Frank, still unable to move, could barely reply, *"Mom? . . ."* Smiling, she grabbed both of his hands and studied his face. She then said, "Come with me . . . I have something to show you."

Before he could ask for any kind of clarification, she untied the bay mare and spun up into her saddle; she nudged her horse forward and directed it to move more deeply into the shade beside Smith Creek. When she looked back at her confused son, she laughed, *"Well, come on slowpoke!"* Frank jolted out of his stupor to quickly untie the gelding, and he swung up into his own saddle; his mother was moving out briskly now in a westerly direction, and he was overcome by his need to catch up to her . . .

❀ ❀ ❀

When he prodded his horse to accelerate into a trot, his mother looked back and shouted to him, *"Find your seat, Francis Irvin!"* This instruction, along with the conjuring of his middle name (Gaelic for *'horseman'*), was her cue for Frank to relax in his saddle and allow his horse to welcome the connection between them. He remembered to just stop fighting the moment (a calming exercise which had served him well in many other settings throughout his life). Immediately upon feeling the comfort in Frank's balance, the amazing horse transitioned into an effortless rolling gallop, and Frank was at once linked in the smoother and longer strides.

※ ※ ※

His mother eased back a little as they made their way out beyond the canopy of Aspens. Frank recognized this terrain on the western slope of the Desatoyas; he knew they were on the Edwards Creek side of the range. Just when he had nearly caught up, his mother peeked over her shoulder and slapped her legs hard against the mare's side, and she rocketed away. Frank remembered this game, so he gripped his reins widely in both fists while he released tension on the bit. In one fluid motion, he lowered his head and tucked his chin down while he signaled for the powerful horse to engage. Instantly, he and his mother were racing in tandem down a slalom course outlined by healthy Jack Pines; the singular trees stood apart across the smooth terrain which was covered with a carpet of cheat grass at this higher elevation.

Precisely where the mountainside dropped off and became steep beneath a terrace, Frank shifted his torso back toward the hips of his strong gelding, and with one hand steadied behind him, they leaped together over the edge. Stirrups pushed forward, horse and rider were soon gliding downward in synchronized arcs of balance. It was during these steep descents that no one else in Frank's family could ever stay close to him, and today would be no exception. A long lost exhilaration suddenly returned to him, and it was magnified many times over by the physical gifts of his incredible, athletic mount; the two of them were soon flying together *as one* through the beautiful afternoon . . .

Only when Frank found himself upon terrain which leveled off above an arroyo, did he ease up enough to allow his mother to finally catch him. They eventually found themselves riding side by side again, and they laughed out loud at sharing their beloved game once more.

※ ※ ※

For some reason now, Frank didn't need to ask, *"Why?"* He just patted his horses' neck in overwhelmed affection, and moved in closer beside his mother. They smiled and remained quiet, but some moments later she pulled up and pointed to the hillside next to them, "Look . . . *'Chukars'!*" Frank could see that a covey of the partridge-like birds were flying out of a snarl of wild roses bordering Edwards Creek, only to scatter and disappear into the foliage of the mountainside. From there, the birds could be heard laughing their distinctive laugh at the folly of human attempts to confine them.

His mother gestured toward the wild roses and shared with him, "This is my favorite place. I believe this is the *Wellspring* of these mountains . . . can you see all of the life that is supported here?" She smiled as she gazed across the lush growth along the borders of Edward's Creek. Frank was not prepared for what his mother would say next: "Francis, you haven't yet found the woman who is meant for you, but please don't be disheartened."

"Someday *soon* you will meet her. . . . She also will recognize this place to be the wellspring of our mountain range, and that it is an uncommon and special gift*,* and in the moment when both of you can share that, she will forever be *bound to you* . . . and *you* to her."

His mother was somber as she studied her son's face, and then she quietly turned her horse toward an unruly, thorned branch of wild roses; once there, she reached out to pluck one of the many rose hips displayed upon it. She savored the smell of the fruit before she slipped a berry into her jacket pocket.

Frank paused as he tried to understand this, and then he followed her when she chose a trail which pointed them east. He caught up to her again, and realized that she was leading them toward a familiar mountain pass. His father had used this same wide trail every year during the fall months to return cattle to the lower elevations of the ranch. Frank also remembered hearing stories about the Pony Express riders seeking protection here during their perilous travels through Nevada.

## THE PASTURE

They soon arrived at a location just south of the ranch house, and his mother began traversing northward across a canyon wall which would take them down to their "deeded land." As he rode along, Frank remembered the pride in his father's voice anytime he reminded his sons of the *size* of McClelland Ranch: It was comprised of thirty-nine hundred acres of grassland property, which began above the home and its out-buildings.

The pasture bordered Smith Creek in a wide swath, starting from a large reservoir just above the house, and it fell far below into the Reese River Valley. The range permit—which had been appurtenant to that deeded portion of land for five generations of ranching families was *huge*. It encompassed half of the Desatoya Mountains; in total, it included nearly *two hundred sixty thousand acres* of Nevada public land.

The annual "beneficial use" of that public land and water, however, was administered by the US Bureau of Land Management, still an incendiary topic among ranchers, many years after the zenith of Nevada's Sagebrush Rebellion; a range permit of this size sustained approximately one thousand mother cows and their calves within the borders of the ranch.

❊ ❊ ❊

Descending by way of a well-established deer trail that brought them gradually closer to their "home place." Frank filed-in at a safe distance behind his mother's horse. They finally arrived at a gate which intersected mid-way along the southernmost fencing of the pasture. Frank remembered it to be a cascading field of fawn fescue and timothy grass, which flowed gently downhill until it disappeared far off in the distance.

Summer days spent irrigating here, amidst the diverted flows from Smith Creek, were times that he and Robby loved. They amounted to hours that never failed to be a welcome break from the dust and the heat of summer (a constant part of moving cattle around the mountains). To this day, he could easily recall the fragrant smell of healthy grass and legume, as cold mountain water spread out over the field. Those times amounted to days-off for the cow dogs as well, while they splashed through the water and relentlessly hunted the gophers that popped up from their flooded burrows.

Frank's father hoped the ranch might get three cuttings of grass hay each year before bringing the cattle back here from the high country. Spring, however, could not be even a little late for that to realistically happen. Whatever hay they were able to put up would have to be supplemented with more-expensive alfalfa, enough to feed the returning cattle throughout the coming winter months.

❊ ❊ ❊

After his mother jumped down to open the pasture gate, Frank rode forward into the field. He couldn't help but stare across it now in both directions, and he was stunned to find that it was in an advanced state of decline—what he remembered to be a border-to-border carpet of luxuriant green fescue had become a desolate span of weeds and dying vegetation. He could now only recognize some withered clusters of grass, but they were brown and dying from a long interval of neglect.

Sadness enveloped him as he rode slowly ahead, and this only got worse when he assessed the broad invasion of mustard and ragweed and nettle. When he rode toward the creek itself (midway through the pasture), he saw only a narrow remnant of green foliage; even that however, was overrun with cockleburs.

Frank shuddered to realize that it was almost July, and when he did the math, he knew that the ranch certainly could not by now have put up *any* of its own hay—nor would it be able to do so during the remainder of the growing season. His father would certainly be forced to purchase truckloads of expensive alfalfa for the entirety of the winter's feeding.

❀ ❀ ❀

His mother again took the lead, and she guided her horse straight ahead, eventually through Smith Creek, on a path that cut toward the opposite border of the field. Frank followed her through another gate until they approached a wide, elevated path just beyond the northern fence line. Here they found a tire-worn, dirt road which was formed after years of pickup and tractor travel. They turned left upon it to point toward the distant barns and out-buildings of the ranch.

Frank suddenly became distracted when he realized that he might soon come face-to-face with his father, and he began to lag behind. His mother sensed this, and she turned to study him. After reading his conflicted focus, she reminded him, "This is *your ranch too*, Son." When she encouraged her horse forward once again, Frank had to follow. . . .

Time passed too quickly, and they arrived at the tall, railed fences which framed the home corrals. Once inside the largest enclosure, he glanced around and recognized the livestock crowding pens and then a battered old squeeze-chute. He remembered the branding cables too, still connected to their faded innertubes which his family had used to stretch-out and doctor new calves each fall. Everything here brought back years of childhood memories.

Frank and his mother rode along next to the vertical railroad ties (standing tall and close together, where they served as fence posts within this fortified "sorting" area). They finally stopped at a gate located beside a steep loading ramp. The barn and ranch house were just beyond this gate, and Frank took a deep breath in anticipation of his exit toward it. He remained dismounted after he closed the gate for his mother, and then she too stepped down from her stirrups. Together, they walked forward a dozen yards, and then stood silently there beside their horses.

❀ ❀ ❀

Frank instantly became transfixed upon the man sitting in his familiar chair on the front porch: There was no mistaking the tall and angular frame of his father, Robert McClelland. It was just that . . . he looked *so much older*. Within the parameters of this dream, Frank knew that he and his mother remained invisible to the man. He could therefore look directly at him, and he saw immediately that there was a *sadness* about the man when he lowered his head in an apparent moment of reflection; this was clearly evident in his posture as well.

His father was a man who had worked hard all of his life, but he now appeared to be *broken* somehow beyond that. Frank had never seen him remain downcast for very long, even after the death of his wife, but now he just stared in silence at the porch beneath him. He held a sweat-stained felt hat in his hands, which he steadied with a knee.

When he finally looked up from the porch to the lawn beyond it, he sighed and tossed his hat onto the chair beside him—he then lit a cigarette. His first deep drag evoked a cough which erupted from cavernous reaches that only fifty-year smokers can carve into their lungs, and the rhonchorous cough didn't soon relent. Frank looked at his mother, who had always *hated* the smoking, but today she just stolidly watched. When Frank felt compelled to help his father, he was quickly held back by his mother's outstretched arm.

❀ ❀ ❀

It was then that they both heard (from behind them) the distinctive rhythm of a galloping horse; it was approaching the ranch house at impressive speed. His father at once stood up and squinted to see the horse and rider on the main road to the ranch. Frank thought he recognized the huge black thoroughbred, but he didn't recognize the rider: She was a very pretty teenage girl with a rope of ebony hair that was braided between her shoulders, and she wore the functional clothing which distinguishes authentic ranch girls from the sea of pretenders at summer rodeos.

Frank studied her circular hat, which embodied Spanish influence in its low Vaquero crown, and he recognized his mother's silk wild rag, knotted high around the girl's neck; she had expertly made the scarf her own.

She had eased up on her horse long before they actually arrived at the ranch house, and Frank smiled at this; apparently the young girl had learned about thoroughbreds—after getting up to speed, they don't want to stop running anytime soon. So, by the time she reached the lawn beyond the covered porch, she had already collected her horse into a spirited, yet manageable gait; this quickly transitioned into a cantor with flying lead-changes, as she showcased the big mare in wide figure eights for a sufficient time to cool the animal's jets. It was also enough time to completely mesmerize everyone watching the beautiful girl.

Frank's father, who moments before had been the picture of dejection, now stood tall as he genuinely beamed toward the young girl, "When you *ride* like that, you take fifteen years off that old mare. God only knows what you could do on a horse worthy of your skills." The girl giggled as she patted her horse's neck, "Oh, you're just prejudiced; real judges would think that I am nothing but an Okie from Muskogee." The old man laughed as he snuffed out his cigarette, and then offered, "Why don't you tie off that boney old mare, and come inside for some lemonade. We serve Okies in this establishment."

❀ ❀ ❀

Frank watched his beaming father (with hat in hand) open the screen door, and then hold it long enough to allow the girl entry into the ranch house—from there, they disappeared together behind the slamming door. When Frank turned around to ask questions, he discovered that his mother had stolen away; she was sitting atop her horse once again, waiting for him on the gravel road that exited the ranch. When he acknowledged this, she turned and began slowly riding away past the generator shack and the bunkhouse.

Just as Frank approached her however, she veered north onto the trail which he remembered would lead them toward *Basque Peak*, at the far end of the Desatoyas. This decision worried him, considering their late start, and he looked toward the sun to confirm that it was indeed falling lower in the distant sky. It didn't help that they would increasingly be traveling deeper into the shadows while they traversed the eastern slope of the range, but his mother was moving quickly now, and she didn't seem worried.

Frank's concern was to be wary of predators—this was mountain lion country, and he knew that the big cats could travel like ghosts through the half-light of dusk. He looked down and realized that his saddle had not been fitted to include a scabbard, nor his deeply scratched old Model 94 Winchester, which he otherwise would have grabbed before the start of such a late journey; his mother was not to be deterred however, and after a brisk ride she delivered them to within sight of the summit.

## BASQUE PEAK

It was nearly sunset by the time they reached a plateau beneath the northern face of Basque Peak. Frank dismounted and followed his mother around to a large bramble of Juniper, where they secured their horses—she knew where she wanted to go, and quickly began climbing up over the huge granite boulders which defined the peak. At last near the top, she sat down on a shelf of granite and patted the stone beside her to signal to Frank where she wanted him to sit. When he circled beneath the boulders to choose his own route up, he was suddenly distracted by the size of the sun that touched the earth on the western side of the peak.

He found himself staring across a vast playa which he knew did not belong so close to the Desatoyas; it reminded him of the prehistoric lake beds that he had once seen in northern Washoe County. A long time ago, he and Robby had discovered them together when they drew Mule Deer tags inside the Sheldon Wildlife Refuge. He squinted now, and held up a hand to shield his eyes. For one passing instant, Frank thought he glimpsed a massive stirring of people far off in the distance; the image was fleeting, however, and he quickly came to believe that it had only been a mirage.

❦ ❦ ❦

Darkness nearly enveloped him now, as he turned away from the western slope. He was suddenly confused to realize that the horses were nowhere in sight—looking up and listening, he was also unsure if his mother was still waiting for him at the top of the boulders. He climbed up in spite of this, and somehow found her granite shelf in the scant light that remained. When he circled to look in all directions, he realized that he was alone.

Remembering how his mother had been seated upon the granite shelf, Frank positioned himself where she had indicated. He looked forward to face the direction of his mother's choosing, and he was amazed to discover his unobstructed view of the entire northern horizon. Far below him to his right, he could just make out the lights being turned on in Austin, Nevada . . . and to his left, he could now see only the ink-blue remnants of today's sunset, at its lowest slice across the western horizon.

Frank could not remember ever being here, but he thought perhaps his parents had talked about it in years past, describing it as their favorite place to watch the annual Perseids Meteor Shower. This made him think once again of today's image of his father, and it saddened him. For Frank, it amounted to the first signs of frailty that he could ever remember seeing in him.

After he sighed and at last looked up, he recognized his place within the entirety of the Milky Way; it was revealing itself well beyond the synchronous framework of constellations that only central Nevada can display; Orion's place in the sky particularly made him feel as though he was home again. . . .

❄ ❄ ❄

What Frank then witnessed, with night's darkness now fully delivered, defied all of his scientific foundations. From the north, he began to see spiraling streams of light, first originating in shades of yellow and green and then blue; they were twisting higher and higher above the horizon. He recognized them to be a display of Aurora Borealis, even as his solidly-constructed id threw global latitude improbabilities at him, and then geo-positioning calcs which should finally have obliterated any possibility of this sighting . . .

More time passed and he confirmed that those calculations were only a *veneer* over what was now *real* in this place, and he was drawn further and further into this new vision, which now included him amidst the entire horizon. The sky was eventually framed along its lowest borders with a fan of red spires, exploding upward within the vibrant palate of first colors. The panoramic scale of it was beyond his imagination, but he yielded to it completely . . .

An unassailable calmness had now filled him; it was *welcome,* but not *familiar.* It had arrived at the cost of a deconstruction of his material edifice, yet in spite of that, he somehow felt more *complete.* As he continued to witness the fluid nature of the spires and the wide funnels and fans of morphing colors, Frank was infused with a certainty that some far-reaching conclusion had been gifted to him within this experience. Even though he couldn't now have spoken to its meaning, he knew with certainty it was something that he understood. When he laid back upon the granite and closed his eyes, a sensation of relief washed over him. . . . He could feel gravity pulling him down toward its center, while he spun (arms outstretched) in perfect synchrony with the Earth's rotation.

❀ ❀ ❀

He drifted there peacefully for a long time beneath his closed eyelids, until a low resonant sound brought him suddenly back to the surface. It had been a rolling bass note that trilled from the pharynx of a large animal, and Frank sensed that it amounted to a singular inquiry in his direction. He quickly looked around and was relieved to remember that his mother was gone, and that she had taken the horses with her.

He pushed himself back further to sit upright on the granite shelf. Here he became silent and heightened his senses to take in all sounds. His movement on the boulder had grated, however, and it caught the attention of the creature which now circled below him.

Another deeply guttural sound was tested in Frank's direction, as the animal was now clearly on a path toward the granite outcropping where Frank was seated. With an abrupt scattering of scree gravel, the creature leaped onto a boulder below him; Frank judged the distance it had jumped, and he knew immediately that he was being stalked by a Mountain Lion.

The moon, which was only a waning crescent, had risen high enough by now for him to see that the huge lion had identified his location, and Frank watched it crouch low atop a granite surface, to begin crawling toward him. Its resonant voice was now much closer, and there was no mistaking that it had become a malevolent growl. When the moonlight suddenly revealed the white flash of the lion's canine teeth, Frank was certain that he had only seconds before it would be upon him. In one desperate contortion, he threw himself higher toward the boulders above him.

Now *flailing*, he became hopelessly entangled in his duvet cover and the heap of pillow shams and bedding which had been piled next to his headboard—he was hyperventilating and sweating by the time he untangled himself. Only when he at last sat bolt upright to take stock, did he realize that he was in his bed! . . . *"Oh my God! . . . I'm in my own bed!"*

❀ ❀ ❀

After finally accepting that he would not be mauled, Frank glanced toward the foot of his comforter to find Geo's cat holding very still, but staring at him in considerable *alarm*. The animal had apparently been on a path to join Frank somewhere near the pillows, but he now seemed to be rethinking that plan. What had started out as a confident mission to strengthen the bonds between himself and the Honkey in charge of the tuna sandwiches, was now being second-guessed entirely by Lady Windermere . . .

Frank surmised that the sleek cat had just witnessed his fitful awakening, so he reached out and tried to offer support, *"Oh Lady!* . . . I'm *so* sorry. " Not worrying at all about how the cat had come to be on his bed, he spoke gently again, *"C'mere Lady . . . "* and eventually they curled up together and fell asleep to the sound of loud and resonant purring.

# 22

## CRÈME BRÛLÉE

The quiet of the surrounding neighborhood reinforced a Saturday feel to the morning, and Frank once again slept in. He awoke to find that Lady Windermere was gone, so he felt the need to check doors and determine whether or not the cat's sleepover had been real, or just another part of his vivid dream. The front door was still closed and locked, but his office door leading out to the deck had somehow been left ajar. He discovered that the door's alignment was off-kilter, so he grabbed a screwdriver to raise the latch and tighten it into place.

Establishing that the cat's visit had been *real* was a comforting thought, but the rest of the dream left him unsettled. When he finally moved into the kitchen, he began to consider last night's images: The growing clarity of his mother's communication in recent dreams was not something that Frank had experienced before.

Those dreams had started in his teenage years, but he remembered them only being obscure visions of his mother in unidentifiable settings—ultimately, they just reinforced his loneliness after losing her. Now, all these years later, she was appearing to him and imparting very specific messages. . . . This was something entirely new.

❁ ❁ ❁

While he was reflecting on the dream's itinerary, his phone began to ring. He answered it and heard Stella's bright New Jersey accent, *"Good morning, Gorgeous!* . . . Would you mind if friends stopped over for *cawffee*? We're dying to see your new place." She said they were close by and in fact, had ". . . picked up some nice cannolis on our way over." Frank smiled at the thought of seeing them, and he gave directions.

Stella and Richie soon appeared at his front door, where loud greetings and hugs were exchanged. Stella walked straight in and looked around with gaping jaw and wide eyes. Richie too was impressed, and he just shook his head while he tried to keep up, *"Wow . . ."* was all he could say, as Stella logged a full inventory of the kitchen cabinets and nooks—she stopped dead to stare at the commercial-grade range top. From there she cracked wise, "Oh, *poor you . . .* You have to live *here.*"

After inspecting the bedrooms and baths and the laundry, she returned to the living room and jabbed, "Okay, where's the *fucking Monet?!*" Frank followed her lead, knowing she would get the joke, "I decided it looked best in my office upstairs. I thought briefly about hanging it in the library, but that just didn't *feel right*, you know?" Stella brushed him aside on her way toward the balustrade and she quipped, *"Asshole . . ."* He and Richie grinned at each other, and they followed her up the stairway.

Frank explained the history of the house, while his awestruck guests considered the library books. He then guided them into the office and eventually toward the door which led them out to the deck. "This is my favorite part of the house . . ." he told them when they stepped outside.

The beautiful San Francisco morning only accentuated his tour, while he pointed out the gardens beneath them, and then the surrounding neighborhood and the park beyond. As Stella and Richie stood together at the railing to take it all in, Frank said "Let's have our coffee out here on the deck . . . and, did I hear correctly that you have come bearing *cannolis*?" Stella sprang into action, and by the time Frank returned to place the large coffee press on the table, she had already organized Marion's cups and service-ware (including linen napkins that Frank didn't even know he had).

❀ ❀ ❀

The morning was energized, with Stella and Richie happily bringing him up to speed on current events. Frank noticed that his two friends were increasingly expressing themselves as a "couple," and he smiled privately at this. When talk turned to the status of Icarus San Francisco, Richie surprised Frank when he said that he and Larry were now steering brokers and clients *away* from the mortgage bonds.

Richie said, "The collapse of those Bear Stearns hedge funds sent shock waves through Icarus, and somebody up the chain must be watching, because it hasn't been a big fight to turn away from the CDO's." Stella piped up, "Yeah . . . and word has it that the new 'mortgage team' in Phoenix has underwhelmed the C-Suite, now that classic fixed-income is back in vogue." This clear reference to Cherice and Travis failed to evoke any feelings at all, and when Stella saw that even Richie was unfazed by the reference, she lifted her coffee cup high and toasted, *"Good Riddance!!"* The toast was happily seconded, *"Good Riddance!!"*

Frank laughed and easily moved past it, "Those Bear Stearns funds were bad enough, but I expect we'll soon start hearing about entire divisions of *investment banks* suffering their own *redemptions*. Stay tuned . . ." In spite of this foreboding, the morning soon proved too beautiful to dwell on business for long, and the friends eventually wiled away their happy time together in the atmosphere of Frank's new deck.

❁ ❁ ❁

So the summer of 2007 was thus rung-in, and absent any second guessing of the changes in his life, Frank's uplifted mood eased him into a shared conviviality wherever he went. He was certain that a weight had been lifted off his back, and he came to believe for the first time since moving to San Francisco that he might someday even *belong* among its citizenry, that is, if he was ever meant to belong in a city.

People likewise responded to him when they felt his unfettered smile. Bill Bennett had certainly been right when he said, "You are going to love that neighborhood." Stella and Richie (and Lady Windermere, who had been awarded an upstairs cat-door), now shared many evenings together. When the friends weren't cooking for three or more in Frank's kitchen, they were joining others for dinner at nearby restaurants like Eliza's, or for brunch at The Grove—happy hours highlighted their weekends (and many *weeknights* as well). Those occasions were mostly celebrated at Palmer's Tavern, after Stella had determined that it was, "much too close to be ignored," and the happy cadre were quickly assimilated inside as regulars.

❁ ❁ ❁

Marion and Frank had kept to their plan to video conference as often as possible, and by the end of July, even Bill felt well enough to participate in portfolio decisions . . . Frank was introduced one morning to Amaia, who had joined Marion in Belvedere, and she shared new family discoveries with him: She had learned of the Cenarrusa's World War II escape by freighter out of Portugal. Frank found it fascinating that they had fled to a Basque colony in Uruguay, which was surprisingly close in proximity to the Nazis hiding in Argentina. Amaia had also determined that his family eventually traveled through the Panama Canal on a passage to San Francisco, where they initiated their steps toward US citizenship.

Marion expressed her feelings about the irony of it all, noting that Jose Aguirre and his brothers also hid in Uruguay as occupants of that colony—this would have likely transpired while Andere Cenarrusa lived there as well. She wondered aloud if her uncles ever realized that Andere was the same man they had chased away from her mother? . . . and if they were eventually forced to reconcile that *all* of them together had actually been allies during the Spanish Civil War . . . ?

❄ ❄ ❄

As Bill Bennet's recovery appeared seamless, Marion (aided by Amaia's professional references) had finessed him into the idea that there was a high likelihood that Frank's Mother had, in fact, been Marion's Sister, albeit supported with only the evidence discovered during their first trip to Spain. Both women shared with him their beliefs that an eventual return to Basque Country, particularly their climb up Mt. Gorbeia, would confirm once and for all whether Marion and Angelina had been sired by the same patriarch, Andere Cenarrusa. . . .

Shortly after those conversations, Marion invited Frank to Belvedere for a *smallish* dinner to celebrate her husband's "return to health." She had asked him to arrive early before the event, because her return to Spain was imminent and she wanted him to show her the painting that reminded him of his mother's album.

Before the arrival of guests, Marion took Frank's arm to lead him into the living room alcove, which featured her paintings. He immediately pointed to a landscape painting by Dario Regoyos and said, "These are the hillsides and hamlets that remind me of my mother's photo album." Marion was encouraging when she confirmed that Regoyos had spent a lot of time painting in the Pyrenees Mountains during the late nineteenth century.

She soon guided Frank through the histories of paintings by Fernando de Amarica and Aurelio Arteta, as she built upon her appreciation of "rural Utopias." This finally brought her to her *favorites*, by the Arrue Brothers . . . Marion spoke emotionally about 'Baserritarrak', painted by Jose Arrue and 'Fandango', by Ramiro Arrue. These led her to speak about the Basque theme of 'Arcadia', which she felt was best portrayed in the Arrue paintings. She believed that the Arrue Brothers brilliantly captured the pre-Civil War sentiment in Basque Country, where geographic and cultural "abundance" provided everything that its people could possibly need (*Utopias* in effect). Any reference to industry was always presented outside of the borders of the land's agrarian and cultural harmony . . .

Marion paused for a moment and shared that these paintings, joyous as they were, had ultimately built upon a sadness within her whenever she imagined the life that was stolen from her family during the Civil War . . . "I need to tell you that these two works are reproductions of the famous Arrue paintings. The originals had been separated for years, and I was eventually able to help reunite them again through my connections in France; a municipality there ("of all places") had been in possession of Fandango for years, and with the help of the Arrue family, we were finally successful in delivering them together to the Museum of Fine Arts in Bilbao . . . I'm proud of the small part I played in helping to restore the heritage of my Basque homeland . . .

❁ ❁ ❁

Of course the dinner party was fun, but Bill was visibly surprised during tableside conversations when he realized the extent to which his wife and guests had accepted the family connection between Frank and Marion. Witnessing this, Marion exercised a contingent plan—she was quick to take the lead in the clearing of place settings that evening, as part of a group dishwashing effort. With stealth movements, she isolated the spoons that had been used by herself and Frank during the enjoyment of their crème brûlée desserts. In the backdrop of noisy activity around the sink, she found that it had been easy to hide the evidence of her plot.

Then, during the frenzied days of travel preparation leading to her upcoming trip, Marion stole the two dessert spoons away to the Stanford Medical Genetics Laboratory.

❁ ❁ ❁

Once there, she parlayed her husband's stature among the Stanford Alumni Association to secure an introduction to the Laboratory Administrator—she in turn, introduced her to the Technologist responsible for "specific genetic testing." Marion articulated her belief that Frank's mother and she were sisters, and that both Frank and herself were therefore interested in searching Frank's direct maternal genealogy to examine those possible connections.

The Technologist took it from there, "Okay . . . we will start with 'mtDNA' studies: Those look at the mitochondria which Frank will have inherited from his mother, and then we'll examine your own." She continued, "And, once again, you believe that you and Frank's mother may have been conceived by the same father, albeit by different mothers?" Marion confirmed this, after which the Technologist decided, "I'll run 'autosomal' tests as well: Those will give us all of the ancestors, and that may be informative as well."

"Lastly, do you have reasonable confidence that you and Frank's mother share a common *geographic* origin?" Marion responded matter-of-factly, "Absolutely. We are both of Basque descent, from the provinces of Northern Spain . . ." The Stanford Technologist was jolted by this answer, and she looked up, *"Really?! . . .* That is not what I expected to hear when I came to work this morning! That will make these studies *very* interesting."

"Basque lineage is unique because of the isolation of its people within the Iberian Peninsula borders. Their genetic haplogroup can be traced back more than eighteen thousand years to the last *Ice Age! . . .* That is *extremely* uncommon in this modern era! There will definitely be a crowd around me when I study this."

The Technologist at last offered a caution of sorts, "We normally like to obtain inner-cheek scrapings from our test subjects, through a procedure called a 'buccal swab', but we can get around that if you are confident that these spoons will provide good samples." Marion laughed, "I can guarantee that both Frank and myself finished our servings of crème brûlée . . . *entirely.*" The Tech laughed, "Well . . . judging by the way my own mouth is watering right now, I'm sure we'll be fine."

## BNP PARIBAS

Six days after Marion's dinner, Frank awoke early in the morning and logged onto his computer. While it booted up, he realized that his cell phone had switched off. After connecting it to power, it vibrated nonstop through a long list of emails and texts. The first text he read was a Goldman Sachs "market alert"; it had been an overnight warning that the huge French Bank, BNP Paribas had frozen withdrawals from three of its investment funds tied to the sub-prime mortgage market.

He switched on CNBC and discovered that DOW futures were falling fast (presaging an opening decline of 387 points). Frank thought to himself . . . "This is it!" He quickly dialed Bill Bennett on the video conference console. Marion answered as usual, holding her cup of tea, "Good Morning Frank." Relaying his concerns, he stressed that Bill would definitely want to hear this news. Marion promised to wake him immediately and have him return the call.

During the interim, Frank read the other texts—most of them redundant in their degrees of *panic* . . . and then the emails, which were likewise mostly seeking Bill's advice. The one exception to this theme was the email sent from Hank Paulson, whose list of copied recipients staggered Frank in place: The message was a broad dissemination of details addressing, ". . . the concern now spreading through Europe."

Paulson then declared that he would convene, "the President's Working Group on Financial Markets, to bring focus front and center upon the complexity of the US mortgage model." He asked that all recipients of the document, "Please remain accessible to me in this regard." Paulson ended his message with the assurance that, "Treasury and all of its divisions will remain on high alert during the days ahead."

# 23

## THE QUEST

Marion at last knew that the time had come for her return to Basque Country. She summoned all of her courage and reaffirmed to Bill her detailed reasons *why*. Given her past history of failed efforts to find *Aguirre* relatives (and Bill's sharing in those sad outcomes), it was not a surprise when his reaction was one of strong disappointment.

He spoke with a renewed worry that only underscored his skepticism, "Marion. . . . I thought you had put all of these searches behind you! . . . They end in heartbreak for you *every time!* You know this better than anyone, and I shouldn't have to remind you that these *'intuitions'* of yours have even left you *clinically depressed.* We both remember that at least one of those occasions lasted for months on end. *Please* Darling, stay here with me in this lifetime, and stop *chasing illusions! . . . I beg of you!"*

His reaction could in no way dissuade her however, and she continued to organize her evidence to argue with her forever-skeptical husband. She had learned to be careful to avoid any mention of *metaphysical* signs—especially her belief that Frank's deceased mother had somehow steered Frank toward his long-lost aunt on Belvedere Island. But Marion was still effective in making her case.

❋ ❋ ❋

So . . . as much as Bill wanted to dismiss outright the odds of success in her latest quest, he eventually found himself at least intrigued by the Spanish Census Reports, as well as the Postal Records. Finally, it was her old photo, which Bill had not seen in years, together with the Nevada Marriage Certificate, which raised legitimate questions about "Andere Cenarrusa" and his child, "Angelina."

Could it actually be possible that Frank's grandfather, Andere, had been Marion's father, "Ando?"—surreal as that was to consider, Bill eventually had to soften his rhetoric. If this were somehow true, it would of course change *everything*. . . . So, in spite of his reservations, he was once again able to support Marion's decision to travel to Spain. This time to examine remote granite outcroppings, located somewhere behind the ancestral home of the Cenarrusa family.

Bill could not shake, however, his concern for Frank. The young man's family legacy had been so *tragic*, and this would certainly leave him vulnerable in the eventual failure of Marion's latest travels. He therefore reminded her, "As always Marion, you will once again have to face the reality that birth records have forever been lost in northern Spain, and proof of your family's descent will be no less impossible than it has ever been."

## GROUP DEPARTURE

The return travel to Basque Country materialized quickly. From the onset of planning, Steve had confirmed with Marion that there was ". . . nothing *funny* about that little *security stunt* you pulled on your last trip," and he informed her in no uncertain terms that he would personally accompany her and Amaia during their travels.

The basis for his concern was that Marion's family connection to the Aguirres might *even now* be exploited in Spain—especially given the modern separatist strife which was escalating in nearby Catalonia. He let it be known that any trip into the backcountry of northern Spain could be a security risk, especially given Marion's recent visibility in its surrounding communities.

After agreeing with Steve's concerns, Marion joked privately to Amaia, "Should we warn him in advance to bring some dog biscuits for this trip?" They giggled about it, but Amaia said, "No . . . It might be fun to watch him discover that for himself."

Frank smiled when he learned of the plans. He had no reason to doubt Steve of course, but his friend did appear to be showing a growing fondness for Amaia. Bill for his part, was actually relieved to know that Steve would be looking after them during their trip; he proclaimed that his own travels would keep him surrounded by ". . . an *army* of *security specialists*, traveling with the *'Working Group'* members around Washington." So, with those concerns behind them, Marion and her excited co-travelers (after three days of preparation), boarded their private jet for Vitoria-Gasteiz, Spain.

❁ ❁ ❁

On the morning of the expedition, Steve steered onto the dirt road which would deliver them to Sarria, and he smiled at the huge tri-colored dog lying beside him;

the Great Pyrenees was now sprawled entirely across the front seats, resting his huge head upon Steve's lap . . .

The day had started much earlier, so their guide *Sasha* could be collected at his home and then accompany them on the Mt. Gorbeia climb. When his excited young dog had once again collided with a passenger door (to the secret glee of Marion and Amaia), the women were shocked to watch Steve jump immediately out of the driver's seat and assume control.

Before the huge animal could intercept him in a race around the SUV, Steve whistled one loud piercing note and he held up his index finger. This halted the dog's advance at the front of the vehicle. Steve then whistled again, and stomped one of his special-ops boots hard on the ground between them. The dog was immediately calmed by this and he sat in place; from there, he stared up at Steve in obedient anticipation.

Steve held him still for a moment more, employing only his upturned index finger. He then leaned down to pat the dog's chest, and affectionately hug his neck. Incredulous, Marion and Amaia watched Steve then kiss the dog's forehead, before heaping on more approval, "Good boy! . . . You are such a good boy!"

❁ ❁ ❁

They only noticed Sasha (who watched everything from his front porch) when he broke into raucous laughter and shouted happily at Steve in his Euskara language . . . Sasha, still smiling, descended from the top step and approached Steve to more closely examine his faded military fatigues, and his black Navy tee shirt; when he reached down to tug on the fabric of Steve's camo pants, he laughed again.

By now, Amaia felt she could step out of the vehicle to greet Sasha and interpret, "He says you are the *biggest human* that his dog has ever seen, and also—judging by your military pants, it appears that we will be *safe* during our travels." Marion stepped out as well, and she hugged Sasha tightly when she greeted him.

After introductions, Steve placed Sasha's knapsack and walking stick among the other equipment, already organized in the cargo-hold of the SUV. Admiring Steve's well-used *Navy Seal* backpack—which was framed in desert camouflage. Sasha reached for it to feel that fabric as well. He studied Steve again and shared a conclusion with Amaia; she smiled at Steve and explained, "He says that we are in the presence of a *'warrior'* . . ."

Ready at last to embark, Steve stood near the rear hatch and signaled for Sasha's dog to jump into the cargo hold. The excited dog instead continued to leap over both rows of backrests, to arrive comfortably in the front passenger seat; everyone laughed (Marion most of all), and she quipped, *"Very well then* . . . It would appear that Steve has a new *co-pilot*." Sasha sat between the women in the back seat, and it was in this manner that they journeyed toward Mt. Gorbeia . . .

❊ ❊ ❊

Sasha directed them to continue further on the dirt road, which passed wide of the general store in Sarria. They traveled for another half mile or so at Sasha's instruction, and then pulled off into a small turnout next to the "Mt. Gorbeia Trailhead" marker. There were a few moments spent while Steve unloaded the gear. It soon became evident as he did this, that he was checking water quantities and assessing the weight and balance of each pack.

He then kneeled beside his own pack and unlaced an outer layer of webbing which connected four outboard storage compartments onto the pack's frame. Steve instructed them, "Take out some of your heavier items, and we'll transfer them here. Amaia, can you ask Sasha to do the same?" While everyone decided what to transfer, Steve centered the freed webbing and compartments over the back of Sasha's dog, which he then laced tightly under the dog's torso. His efforts were appreciated more when the climbers felt the new weight of their packs, and they were further impressed to see Steve balance their jettisoned cargo into the dog's pack.

He asked, "What do you call him, Sasha?" Amaia interpreted, and then giggled, "He calls him, 'Biscuit' . . . The Basque word for that is *gaileta*, and Sasha pronounces it, *Guyta*." Everyone laughed when Steve quipped, "Yeah, I'll bet this one can eat some biscuits."

❊ ❊ ❊

After asking Marion to retrieve her topo map, Steve cautioned her about "new boots and blisters;" he recommended that she and Amaia remove their boots, and then re-tie them carefully again after smoothing-out any wrinkles in their socks.

He meanwhile shot a GPS reading of the trailhead and recorded it on Marion's map. Sasha, at seeing the map, moved in close to Steve to reaffirm their location. Steve asked him to point out the course of their hike, and he then circled Arkarai and Berretin as he followed Sasha's planned path up the mountain.

Steve's preparation had been impressive, but there was no question about who would *lead* the expedition today. When the backpacks were finally adjusted, and members appeared ready, Sasha quickly turned and started walking up the trail. Trotting back and forth beside him was *Guyta* (who seemed proud of his new pack), and then Amaia, followed by Marion close behind. Steve brought up the rear, where he kept his eyes focused evenly above the horizon, scanning back and forth in all directions as he walked.

❊ ❊ ❊

They walked for more than an hour upon the trail, which protected them through the dense brush of the lower elevations, and everyone soon felt the day getting warmer. The trail was at first dusty from the traffic of summer hikers, but steps which had been formed between the rocks were soon increasingly prominent as the altitude increased.

In a clearing of poplar trees, Sasha veered onto a less-traveled path which pointed them toward the left, away from the main trail. Arriving at the fork, Steve glanced at the map to discover that there was no reference at all for this spot. He then quickly took another GPS reading and noted it on the map.

Before long, the hikers found themselves on a path defined by filtered sunlight; it led them beside glistening pools of water, visible beneath the cover of poplar leaves. Marion breathed in the archival balance which existed here in this gathering of ancient soil and flora. She once again felt a sensation of quiet ease as she savored the bouquet, and she commented, "Do you smell this place? . . . It is *so unique* to this part of the world, even as some of these leaves are starting to show their fall colors."

Sasha continued to guide them toward a stand of old trees, and then into a shaded opening which delivered them beside a mountain stream. Here they felt a pocket of coolness under the wide interwoven canopy of trees. The boulders were larger here as well, and they were prominent beside some very deep pools of water.

The old man removed his knapsack to sit atop a granite perch. Everyone felt that it was a good place to rest, so Steve called Guyta over to him and removed the happy dog's new pack. Marion passed out protein bars to the hikers, and they sat and enjoyed them while they watched Guyta wade in and out of a shallow section of the stream.

❀ ❀ ❀

Everyone soon felt refreshed, and Sasha urged them to continue. He led the way over a crossing of flat rocks, which took them out of the shade, to the west side of the stream. From there, they walked upward for some time along a narrow path, and watched as impressive cliffs of lichen-covered granite rose up vertically on the opposite side of the stream.

When the cliffs began to diverge and point northward away from the stream, Sasha once more asked them to cross. Here, beneath a dam formed by huge fallen rocks, they enjoyed the mist and rainbows of a summer waterfall. Delivered again to the east side of the stream, they quickly found themselves on a section of the trail that was noticeably steeper.

The slope now switch-backed its way up through granite remnants of the nearby cliffs. Progress slowed and breathing got heavier, as movement here required hand-over-hand climbing up through the boulders. When Marion at last approached the bottom of a cliff face, she looked up to see Sasha, standing on the ridgetop, aiming his impish grin down at her. He then pulled up his pant leg and *flexed his calf muscle*.

She laughed hard, but then wagged her finger at him as she accepted his challenge, "You just *watch* me, you *old goat!*" He laughed when he saw her quicken her pace up through an adjacent crevasse—at last, she stood (out of breath) beside him. There, standing upon the ridge, she turned to face him, and then she posed with two flexed biceps. Beside her, atop that difficult pinnacle, Sasha proudly applauded her effort . . .

## GORBEÌA'S CREST

After drinking water and sharing trail mix, it was afternoon before the hikers shoved off again, on what now appeared to be the final leg of today's climb. Steve retrieved the map to circle Igatz, and he recorded its GPS reading before joining them. He joked to Marion, "If I didn't know better, I'd say your little buddy up there was trying to kick your butt today . . ." Marion laughed and considered Sasha with affection, "We have *history*, he and I . . ."

Their ascent became steadier now, as they pushed themselves upward through a broad valley of native grass that was sprinkled with wildflowers; they soon realized this was pointing them directly toward the peak of Mt. Gorbeia. At this elevation tall conifers had begun to appear alongside the deciduous trees, which were now more dramatically showing their fall colors. The grass was particularly abundant in this glade, safely protected by the western slope of the ridge beside it, and Marion suddenly understood why this would be an ideal habitat for sheep.

Nobody seemed inclined to rest again, and the party sensed that the end of today's hike was near . . . so they pressed on. Steve determined that Sasha had led them to just below Arkarai, where the valley narrowed and turned them northeast toward a saddle, distinctly placed between two mountainous peaks . . .

❊ ❊ ❊

It was almost 4:00 pm by the time the weary hikers crested the saddle, where they emerged into a gnarled grove of wind-blown trees. Marion felt that they appeared prehistoric somehow; were they perhaps related to Bristlecone Pines? Beyond the trees, they at last found themselves delivered into a wide, rocky clearing. Here Sasha announced, "We are at Berretin. This is where we will camp tonight." From a nearby vantage, just above the tree line, the hikers turned in all directions and considered (for as far as they could see) the peaks of the surrounding Pyrenees Mountains; everyone was humbled by what they saw, and together they quietly shared in the beauty of Northern Spain.

Sasha stepped closer to Marion . . . He directed her view slightly toward the east, and then swept his hand over the distant peaks of the mountain range. She was amazed when he spoke to her in a French dialect, "*C'est la France . . . Au-dela` de ces montagnes.*" He had told her that, "France is there . . . Beyond those mountains."

She quickly pulled out binoculars from her pack, and scanned the beautiful, yet *extreme* terrain which characterized so many miles between here and France . . . In those moments, she understood, *for maybe the first time,* the courage of her mother's people in choosing that route for their desperate escape to safety. . . .

❀ ❀ ❀

Amaia had by now joined them, and Marion asked her to have Sasha point toward the location of the Cenarrusa home. Sasha reached for Marion's binoculars, and he looked through them in the direction of a distant ridgeline; after scanning the terrain more closely, he settled on an approximate location—Returning her binoculars, he leaned in close and began pointing as he spoke, "Follow this ridge below us . . . When that once again approaches trees, look straight above them to the cliffs of granite beyond." Marion did as she was instructed, until she clearly saw the granite cliffs off in the distance. When she acknowledged that she could see them, Sasha told her, "The Cenarrusa family lived there, just below those cliffs . . . We will travel to their home tomorrow." A kind of breathlessness suddenly overtook her, as hope materialized within her, that her father's ancestral home was perhaps less than three miles from where she now stood.

## PAGAZURI

Steve's military training emerged as he took the lead in determining the borders of their bivouac shelter. He soon dropped his pack on the edge of a circular clearing, protected on three sides by impressive boulders that he was sure would block wind and weather. Near the back of the campsite was a small tributary of cold mountain water, which fell in the direction of the stream far below them. Sasha approved, and he smiled at Steve when he too dropped his own worn bedroll onto the ground.

Marion and Amaia chose their locations in the campsite, and then giggled while they struggled with instructions to assemble their new tents—after spreading out poles and corner stakes, the Gore-Tex domes easily popped up. Marion had by now grown very fond of Amaia and was once again impressed with her resourcefulness; she smiled, knowing certainly that her San Sebastian family must be proud of her. Steve and Guyta meanwhile, had set off together in search of firewood, and soon enough, the capable group had a large fire burning inside a protective circle of granite stones.

Marion supervised the location of their tiny kitchen. She and Amaia had planned for a meal of Beef Stroganoff, made from a starter of dehydrated ingredients, procured weeks earlier in the Vitoria-Gasteiz backpacking store. Marion of course, had brought along several small bags of food-stores that reflected her own menu choices; this (as usual) took the meal to another level. Sasha also contributed during dinner when he passed around delicious pieces of lamb jerky, prepared for him by a Basque neighbor. Even Guyta shared in these treats, after wolfing down his dry dogfood.

❊ ❊ ❊

As night surrounded the campers and firelight danced off the granite walls behind them, Marion first marveled at the stars above her, and then at the features of this perfect campsite. Steve had earlier placed his Navy-issue 'alpine bivy' nearby to Amaia's tent, but Guyta quickly claimed the big man (who shared his jerky), and he was now sleeping atop Steve's bedding. That didn't faze Steve however, as he positioned himself closer to Amaia at fireside . . .

The collective trance which the campfire brought to everyone's eyes would easily have been enough tonight, but when Sasha began to sing an ancient Basque *abesti*, the setting grew transcendent. His soft and rich baritone seemed *lonely* at first; Amaia confirmed later that the ballad was an epitaph for his own lost loved ones. Why had he been moved to share these lyrics? Perhaps some memory had been unearthed; inspired by Marion's quest. In its ending, his song faded away on notes more *resigned* than *hopeful*, as they came from a place in Sasha's heart, scarcely less remote than the dialect which carried them.

❊ ❊ ❊

Before anyone else was organized the following morning, Steve was up with coffee already percolated, and eggs scrambling. Sasha had produced a bag of round oat dodgers, compressed solidly with mountain honey, and when they were added to Steve's fare, it amounted to a substantial breakfast. The hikers were excited, so they decided not to break camp until after they returned; when at last they set out, everyone was fully-engaged in finding "the Cenarrusa home."

Marion particularly, could hardly speak as she walked forward, in anticipation that was unlike anything from her past. She barely heard Amaia interpreting Sasha's recollection of the Cenarrusa land boundaries, but she was at least able to be overwhelmed by the verdant beauty of the terrain. Later, she would remember that Sasha had described flocks of sheep, numbering (long ago) in . . . "the many hundreds" . . . so the family was well-known because of that in the neighboring valleys.'

❊ ❊ ❊

Marion could not have recounted how far, or for how long they had hiked, but it seemed that they arrived quickly . . . Sasha described their location as, "Pagazuri."

When he at last crested a rolling upslope of grass, he stopped and turned (smiling) back toward Marion. He then extended his hand and waited for her to reach him.

There beyond them, perhaps a hundred yards below in a protected gully, stood the caved-in ruins of a wooden dwelling that was now gray with age. Something about what remained of the *porch* drew her eyes toward it. She finally realized that it was the roof's overhang, still being held upright at its corners by sturdy tree trunks, which now brought her hope that *this* had been her Father's home . . .

Sasha released her hand, and then he watched as she (fully entranced) walked toward the old building. Marion could not turn away until she at last stopped ten yards before it; standing still now, as she was only able to *stare*. When her plans finally resurfaced, she was at last able to look beyond the building for the granite outcropping which had bordered her mother's photograph.

She immediately recognized the ancient rock formation—illuminated in the gold light of morning sun, and more imposing than she had anticipated. She began to tremble, but she was somehow able to lower her backpack and retrieve her mother's black and white photograph. When she raised it up and framed it across the horizon, she immediately confirmed the porch overhang. She then moved her hand slightly, so the photo could approach the shape of the outcropping beyond it. All of the pieces suddenly took shape before her, precisely as they had always been, in the mosaic of her own history.

Marion knew instantly that this was the exact place where her father had cradled her newborn sister, Angelina, on the porch of their family home . . .

# PART III

# THE GATHERING

# 24

## REALITY CHECK

Bill and Frank met in Belvedere on the day following Marion's departure to Spain. It seemed to be business as usual for Bill, but Frank knew that this was urgent. "I'm still firming things up . . . Hank Paulson called again this morning to share agenda items, and to remind me once more of matters that are still growing in consequence. His need to convene the 'President's Working Group on Financial Markets' is now more important than ever, so I am asking members to plan first for a meeting with Treasury when we get to D.C."

### BILL'S WARNING

Bill then assumed a more thoughtful demeanor, "There is *something else* that I have been meaning to talk about, Frank . . . and it does not involve our work here. I'm afraid it's a more *delicate* subject than that." He was now choosing his words more carefully, "I am *worried* about you, Frank. I fear that you may have been drawn unawares into my wife's lifelong obsession to find lost family . . . Marion clearly believes that she and your mother were sisters, and she is therefore now certain that you are her nephew."

Frank didn't know how to respond. Bill stared at him for a moment more before continuing. "A few years after she and I were married, we had to face the reality that Marion would not be able to have children. This *devastated* my wife. Thereafter, she lapsed into a prolonged depression, and she reluctantly agreed to psychoanalysis only when I convinced her that I had gathered the very best people together on our behalf."

"It took *years*, but eventually she appeared to find closure. Sometime after that, she began to turn her energies *outward*, in the hope of finding missing family members—most of whom had disappeared during World War II. The psychologists believed that this was 'transference', inasmuch as it was an unconscious redirection of 'self' away from her heartbreak . . . toward building a family 'by other means.'"

❁ ❁ ❁

Frank watched as confiding got harder for Bill, "My dilemma over the years has been that my wife is happiest and most engaged in life when she can continue her search for family—and, because we have the money, she has been able to travel the world in that pursuit. Increasingly, however, there have been times when she was inspired to begin some past search, based solely upon her intuitions, or dreams even; method deviations that the psychologists caution might be 'delusional' . . ."

"Invariably, all of Marion's past searches ended in failure, and with each subsequent failure, she lapsed again into depression . . . sometimes for weeks on end." Bill continued to study him, "I think that *your* risk in all of this, Frank, is that you have experienced your own family tragedies, and I believe this sad fact leaves you vulnerable. I therefore want to ask you to prepare yourself, because Marion's new quest will certainly end, yet again, in disappointment."

"Beyond the improbability of her ever finding your family's home—which your grandparent's vacated *over seventy years ago*—you *too* will have to face the reality that most of the birth records in those Basque provinces were destroyed, either during Hitler's Blitzkrieg, or by Franco himself."

❁ ❁ ❁

Frank soon realized that he almost welcomed Bill's words, as an overdue reality check; he then tried to reassure Bill in tones which were measured to convey his detachment. This ultimately brought relief to both of them; truth be known, the idea that Marion might somehow magically be his Aunt had left Frank feeling unprotected, almost from its inception.

During all of those hard years, when he was alone and forced to accept that his mother and his brother were never coming back, he had arrived at a kind of peace in the finality of those tragic outcomes. . . . It eventually became safer to just resign himself to that certainty, knowing that *hope* of any kind surely posed a risk of upheaval.

Both men were relieved when they returned their focus to the business at hand, and after a brief mention of next week's travel together to Washington, Bill was once more pulled into a phone conversation with a "Working Group" member. Frank excused himself, and he waved as he left to return to his own work in San Francisco.

## CORY

He had not been at his desk long the following day, when he received a phone call from Stella. She seemed worried as she relayed the message, "Switchboard just called me to see if I knew how to find you, Frank . . . Your friend, Cory Ebert? . . . is trying to reach you. Someone from the Barrick Corporation apparently gave him our number. It sounds like this has something to do with your father . . ."

Frank collected himself and jotted the phone number onto a notepad, and then he thanked Stella. When he paused to consider that Cory was a ranching neighbor from the Reese River Valley, he grew more concerned. The Ebert Ranch was many miles below Smith Creek, and phone service between there and the valley was at times nonexistent.

He called Cory and was surprised when he answered right away. Cory began without hesitation, "Frank, I'm afraid that your Dad is in a bad way. He has been fighting pneumonia for a couple of weeks, and his breathing just pretty much gave out on him. My son, Logan, was visiting your ranch when this happened, so he drove him down to Carroll Summit. In the meantime, I called the Paramedics in Austin, and they met us there."

Cory's words became more tentative, *"Frank* . . . they put your dad on oxygen and started an IV before they transported him to Middlegate—that's where the Care Flight chopper met us. The flight nurse saw how bad he was doing, and she decided to put in a breathing tube. From there, they flew him to Regal Medical Center in Reno, and he's been on a ventilator ever since. I'm outside his room right now, and that's where I took your call. Frank . . . I have to tell you; everyone here is warning us that *he probably won't survive this. . . ."*

❧ ❧ ❧

In retrospect, Frank knew that he should have packed more realistic clothing than his usual attire from home. Reno sits at the base of the Sierra Nevada Mountains, at an elevation of 4,000 ft., and should he need to spend more than a little time at the ranch above Austin, he would be at 6,000 ft. or higher. Twenty years of living elsewhere had no doubt helped him to forget.

This was not Frank's first concern however, as he traveled east on Hwy 37 toward Vallejo . . . Bill had reassured him that the "heavy lifting" was already completed prior to next week's meetings in Washington, and now the agenda would rest solidly in the hands of the Working Group members. Even so, Frank was not able to escape his discomfort at the thought of being completely beyond the communication range of Bill Bennett.

When he protested that time spent at the ranch would *also* leave him disconnected from world financial markets, Bill reminded him, "Your first obligation now is to your Dad . . . Let me worry about the rest . . ."

Traffic on *I-80 East* was halting (as usual) in fits and starts, and that didn't help to quiet Frank's mind. He was struggling with the scenarios that might be waiting for him at the hospital in Reno. Would his father be conscious enough to recognize him? If so, how could their nearly 20-year estrangement be reconciled in that setting, especially if he was on a ventilator? What could he possibly say to bring his father comfort? What would his father want to say to him . . . ?

After weighing all of that, he eventually looped north to avoid downtown Sacramento, and he began to recount Cory Ebert's description of meeting Care Flight . . . He said that the Paramedics transferred his father at Middlegate; the place where Frank shared his last meal with his brother Robby, all those years ago . . .

## THE RODEO

The day leading up to that meal started early . . . The National High School Finals Rodeo was being held that year in Fallon, Nevada and the chosen venue was the Churchill County Fairgrounds. Frank and Robby were excited when they arrived that morning and saw all of the expensive haulers and horse trailers parked out front. There were license plates from as far away as Colorado and Texas and Oklahoma.

Their dad had chosen to travel with a Cattlemen's Association friend from Smokey Valley, and Frank was glad to have escaped the two hour trip with him. His father's lectures were always the same, and his absence today provided a rare opportunity for Frank to load his motorcycle into be back of the Ford dually. That would make it possible to race Robby at day's end, on the final fifteen miles of dirt road which delivered them back home.

❁ ❁ ❁

Frank knew with certainty however, that this reprieve from his father would only delay the inevitable; soon enough his father would find him on the rodeo grounds, and remind him once again that he didn't measure up to his brother. Those messages started at an early age, and had become unrelenting ever since Frank's decision to stop participating in rodeos. Truth was, Frank never really understood the connection between modern-day rodeos, and the realities of working your own cattle on a family ranch . . .

Almost nothing that could be witnessed at a rodeo would be tolerated by ranchers truly determined to keep their livestock safe and healthy—"calf roping," in particular, just seemed stupid and cruel. Every cow and calf on a ranch certainly represented income that would be precious to families hoping to survive until the next season.

His dad never wanted to debate that, however, and it only got worse if Frank even hinted that saddle bronc riding (Robby's chosen event) was now obsolete; the trend in horse training had years before turned away from "breaking" the animals, and now clearly favored the "joining- up" techniques taught by Monty Roberts and others.

While the McClelland family continued to follow Robby at those events however, Frank eventually did look forward to the "Ranch Rodeos," which could be seen in places like Winnemucca, or sometimes even in Reno. Contestants in those events had to be currently working on a Nevada cattle ranch, or on ranches within counties that bordered the state. The events were authentic: cutting and sorting, corral roping and team doctoring were realities on family ranches, and the horses had to be expertly showcased in reining and fence work.

The cowboys at those events were real "Buckaroos" from places like Deeth, or Starr Valley, or Tuscarora; their horses were older and more seasoned, and amazing to watch. They had to be smart and perfectly finished just to be competitive. Frank could be certain at those events to see his favorites: The "roan" quarter horses showcased from the remuda of the Van Norman Ranch in Elko County. Among them, he always looked for his favorite blue-gray horse, "Popsicle." Invariably he would tell himself when he watched, that *someday* he would *own* one of those horses.

❀ ❀ ❀

When Robby headed in the direction of the registration table, Frank spun off. He knew exactly where he wanted to go: the riding arena to look for his friend, Brandi. She would be limbering her horse there, as she loped in wide circles with this year's Rodeo Queen Candidates and Flag Girls from Churchill County. Brandi Ayala was the stuff of dreams for a sixteen year old cowboy. She was two years older, with flowing auburn hair and eyes and lashes that *devastated*. Her smile could paralyze Frank in place, and when he finally spotted her today, he was glad.

He had known her since early childhood, and he remembered staring even then at a tiny version of herself, as she guided her horses through pole-bending events at the junior rodeos; still close-friends, they had grown up together through the years. Today, however, he was suddenly struck by something different. There was now a lissome beauty about her from this vantage, and he realized that her sequined frame, sculpted by years of competitive barrel racing, had been altogether transformed.

❀ ❀ ❀

He watched her fly past on a beautiful horse (one that her father had no-doubt chosen for her), and Frank couldn't move even a step closer. When she at last noticed him and waved him over, he somehow found the courage to climb atop the arena fence as Brandi guided her horse toward him. She leaned away from her saddle and hugged him around the neck (something she had continued ever since his mother's funeral), and he felt himself blushing as he grinned at her, *"Look at you!"* he exclaimed. . . .

It was the first time he had seen her wearing her new sash and hat crown, which reflected her "Miss Rodeo Nevada" win earlier that year. "Of course you're *Queen* of the whole damn state . . ." he flattered, "Who else could it be, but *you*?" Brandi dismissed it with a modest smile, and she reached out to grab his hand, "It is *so* good to see you . . . Did you and Robby drive in together?"

Frank said, "Yeah . . . He's checking-in right now." She pressed him for more information about his brother, "What events will he be riding in today?" Frank tried to downplay her interest, "He's only going with saddle bronc today—we heard that those guys from Texas are supposed to have a champion PRCA horse here that they'll share in steer wrestling. Robby can't compete with that . . ."

"How about you? I saw that you qualified again in barrel racing . . ." Brandi nodded, "Yeah, but they've got the first event scheduled too close to the crowning of 'Miss Churchill Rodeo' . . . I sure hope I have enough time to change into my racing clothes." Just then, the leader of the Flag Girls held up a clipboard, and she walked into the center of the arena. From there, she called the group together . . . Brandi said, "I gotta go . . . *I'll look for you later today.*"

## THE TWINS

Frank sat mesmerized, as she turned and rode away—his infatuation would have been obvious to anyone watching, right up until the moment that a moist, round *horse turd* impacted the side of his face, and exploded! Giggles could be heard from a few of the Flag Girls who witnessed it, but laughter somewhere off to the side of the arena was *loud* and *unapologetic* . . .

Frank knew that laughter, and he jumped down off the fence to wipe turd remnants from his ear and the corner of his mouth. It could only be the Edurne sisters, Kellie and Shellie, twins whom Frank had known since they were all together in diapers. Frank was angry when he hit the ground, and he squinted at them now with vengeance in his heart, *"You cur mutts!* You're gonna *die . . . !"*

The girls, who were more than a match for him, had readied themselves while Frank jumped down off the fence. Shellie, with a hand on Kellie's arm, quipped, *"Oops!"* through stifled laughter. Both girls grinned at their angry friend and spun around to take off on an expert run for their lives! Bits of straw flew in the tailwind of worn cowboy boots, as the three teenagers raced past pens through the sheltered livestock pavilion.

Soon, the three of them were laughing hysterically (cheered-on by some appreciative *4H'ers*), and Kellie screamed when she realized she was going to be the first casualty . . . Frank dove forward to just get a hand on one of her ankles, and the two of them tumbled into a tangled mess of Wrangler jeans and straw. Frank got the early advantage when he pinned her to the ground. From there, he sat on top of her ribs and held her arms in place with his knees.

He grabbed a fistful of straw and began stuffing it inside the neckline of her shirt, "Here! Let's give you some *boobs!*" His triumph lasted only seconds, however, as he was hit full-force from behind by Shellie, who summersaulted him over the top of her sister. Before he could even clear his head, both of the Edurne sisters flipped like cats on top of him and returned the favor of pinning *his* arms to the ground!

This time, the straw was pushed mercilessly through his lips, toward Frank's clenched teeth—Shellie grinned down at him and yelled, *"Do ya give?!"*. . . We only came looking for you, because Mom wants you to come to lunch. Shoulda known you'd be over gawking at them rodeo queens. But you can forget about kisses from them, *Dummy!* with that *horseshit* on your face." Frank tried not to smile as he spit out straw, and then he reluctantly agreed, "All right . . ." That finally settled, the three of them jumped up together to brush themselves off.

❀ ❀ ❀

As they did this, Frank couldn't help himself, "I didn't *give*, ya know . . . I was taught not to *hurt girls* is all." Shellie snorted, *"Yeah, right!,"* and Frank then shoved Kellie sideways when he saw her grinning at him too. She giggled and shoved him back. The two of them had remained the closest of the siblings, since sharing their first kiss together years before, and they smiled at each other now as they made their way out of the Livestock Pavilion.

The twins' mother, Billie Jo Edurne, stood up and grinned when she saw Frank and the girls approaching the picnic table. She had been his mom's best friend since Angelina's earliest days in Fallon. When the Cenarrusa brothers began shearing sheep for the Edurne family, the friendship deepened—Frank knew, since his mother's death, that Billie Jo had adopted him on some level, and she was sure to check in on him at all of these events.

Today, she took stock of the tall and gangly boy and frowned, "What is that on your face, Frank McClelland?" He glanced over at the twins as she was wiping the green smear from his face and said, "That's a question for your daughters." When Billie Jo scowled at them, Kellie panicked, *"Shellie threw it, Mom!"* Her mother sighed loudly and ordered them to sit down, "Let's get you a plate, Frank . . . you probably shot up a foot since I last saw you. We're gonna put some meat on your bones today, young man."

Frank was grateful to sit with his adoptive family again, and he devoured the Carne Asada and baked beans that were placed before him, along with the fresh greens and tomatoes that only the Edurne Family knew how to grow in a garden. After finishing his Dutch Oven peach cobbler and ice cream, Frank and the twins raced off again toward the rodeo arena to watch the opening ceremonies.

❀ ❀ ❀

The day was fun, as always, with each of them reconnecting with friends along the way. Eventually, they became distracted and drifted apart. Robby had ridden well earlier in the day, and he was point-leader in the saddle bronc standings, going into the final rides of the afternoon. Frank looked for a seat in the grandstands that would give him the best vantage to watch his brother, and he spotted Shawna Casey sitting there by herself.

She and his brother had spent a lot of time together that summer, and although Robby fell short of calling her his "girlfriend," Frank suspected that it was so. She was pretty (like other girls encouraged by Robby), and her short dark hair was highlighted today with a novice-application of peroxide. This, together with her clothes, only confirmed that she didn't truly fit-in at a rodeo. Shawna was the same age as Robby, but she lived in town with her mother, and there was a hard edge to her that perhaps hinted at her family's past (which she kept to herself).

She did manage a smile for Frank today, but he thought that she seemed preoccupied. When he sat next to her, Shawna asked, "Did Robby tell you that you're giving me a ride home today?" He was obviously surprised, so Shawna answered her own question, "No . . . *of course he didn't!*" Frank smiled and tried to salvage the moment, "Austin's close by, so no prob . . ." He then remembered, "Robby's gonna want to eat though, so we'll have to stop in Middlegate for a burger, if that's okay?" Shawna nodded yes, and together they waited for the saddle bronc finals. . . .

❀ ❀ ❀

Robby and Frank were born with different body types; Frank was long and tall for reasons of lineage that he didn't yet understand, while Robby had a more compact torso, with muscular arms that suited him perfectly to ride bucking horses. During the ride which sealed Robby's finals win that day, Frank marveled at his brother's perfect balance. He had clearly leaned back farther, and raised his heels higher to spur his bronc during their eight seconds of chaos . . . Pride just poured over Frank each time he watched his brother ride like this, but today had been *special*.

At age eighteen, Robby was the consummate cowboy, and nobody Frank had ever seen could touch him. When at last, Frank and Shawna walked into the arena, they stopped amidst a gathering of family and friends to watch the awarding of championship buckles. Frank saw his father push in close to Robby, where he beamed alongside his Cattleman's Association friend during the presentation.

Brandi (wearing her Rodeo Queen attire) was there as well to award the buckles, but she had also taken a second-place finish in barrel racing, missing her own win by only a few hundredths of a second. As with other high school athletic events, the swell of vicarious pride from the parents was highly-charged within this circle. People lingered, so photos could be taken and hugs were shared, while bystanders mostly languished on the sidelines.

❁ ❁ ❁

Frank and Shawna stepped back after first congratulating Robby, because both of them were uncomfortable being trapped within the close scrutiny of crowds. Frank's father eventually spotted him inching his way back out to the periphery, so he walked directly at him. After sizing up both he and Shawna (with his signature disappointment), he challenged Frank, "That's all you have to do, Frank! . . . *You just get on the damn horse, and you ride it!*"

He then pulled out his wallet, and gave Frank two twenty dollar bills, "When he's done over there, get on the road. He's gonna need to eat, so stop in Middlegate. Carl and I are going to have a drink here with the Cattlemen, but we won't be far behind you." His dad then studied Shawna more closely, and he looked back at Frank, "No *funny business* on the way!"

❁ ❁ ❁

The two of them were embarrassed, but they stood silent for a long time and watched until the crowds finally began to thin. Frank felt Shawna tense up when she watched Brandi move in closer to hug Robby. From this distance it was evident that his brother and Brandi were comfortable together with that kind of affection, and Frank was surprised at the extent to which it lingered.

Shawna, however, was *not amused* and she scowled at Robby (who was oblivious to the fact that he was being watched). More time passed as the crowds dispersed, but Robby and Brandi stayed where they had been, in close proximity. At last, Shawna could not stand it for even another second, and she rushed forward to close the distance between herself and Robby. Brandi saw her approach but Robby did not. Frank could only stand frozen while Shawna then gripped Robby's elbow to spin him into the full impact of her enraged slap across his face, "Were you planning to tell *the Queen* here that your girlfriend has missed two of her periods while you were out playing cowboy?!"

Brandi fell back in confusion and stared at Robby. Robby flushed red, but he turned away to avoid her eyes. Shawna then stepped toward Brandi and threatened, *"What are you still doing here?!"* Brandi raised both hands and turned to walk away. She then noticed Frank standing in the background, and she veered directly toward him. As she sped past, she focused the full extent of her hurt and humiliation upon him, *"Did you know about this?!"* She didn't wait long enough to hear Frank's answer, *"No . . ."*

### ROBBY

Frank waited for a long time inside the truck, dejected on too many levels for a sixteen year old boy, until Robby and Shawna eventually appeared. Robby was carrying a Coke in a tall concession-stand cup, and he poured out half of it before opening the passenger side door for Shawna. Frank then watched his brother re-fill the cup with a long pour of *Crown Royal*, before hiding the bottle under the back seat.

Shawna didn't look happy about it, but she was silent now. She and Robby had apparently made their peace before their arrival at the truck. When Frank drove forward to point toward *Hwy 50*, Robby put his arm around Shawna and pulled her close. That's when he took his first big drink from the cup . . .

※ ※ ※

Robby dominated the talking between Fallon and Middlegate, where he claimed bragging rights about the "rank" broncs he had drawn, and all of the instances where the other riders had fallen short. He repeatedly brandished his championship buckle and held it up so the world could admire it—all the while draining his Crown and Coke. As he did this, he grew steadily louder . . . and to the added annoyance of Frank and Shawna, he eventually climbed over the front seat and then back again, after adding whiskey to his cup for a second time.

By the time Frank pulled into the gravel parking lot at Middlegate Station, Robby was clearly drunk. Shawna tried to settle him down before he went inside, and she finally pulled his arm over her shoulder to steady him. Frank saw this and warned him, *"You better cool it!* . . ." Dad comes here all the time, and these people will tell him if you're out of control."

Robby scoffed and held up his buckle, "Nobody's gonna mind if the saddle bronc champion *celebrates* a little." Frank shook his head, hoping that a hamburger might sober him up, and he then led them in through the front door toward a restaurant table A local rancher, who was sitting at the bar, recognized them and yelled out, "Hey! . . . there's the McClelland boys! . . ." Robby, not holding back, held up his rodeo buckle and shouted, *"Goddamn right! . . . with a new buckle to prove it!"*

The rancher laughed and lifted his beer to cheer Robby, "Good job! What did you win there?" . . . *"Saddle Bronc Finals!"* Robby proudly fired back, and a smattering of cheers and applause emerged from the bar regulars. Frank continued to guide them to the table, located farthest away from the bar, where burgers and fries were ordered all around. The waitress soon delivered them, but by now, she clearly recognized that Robby was *under the influence* and she peered over her glasses at Frank, "You gotta know that I'm not letting you leave here unless you can prove to me that your brother is not driving."

Frank quickly produced the truck keys from his pocket and jingled them at her." The waitress nodded, but felt that she needed to reiterate, "You know your *father* would kill you and me both if this one here (nodding at Robby) ends up behind the wheel . . . *Right?!*" In his most responsible voice, Frank assured her, *"Yes, Ma'am."*

# 25

## THE MOTORCYCLE

When Frank steered the Ford dually back onto Hwy 722, in the hope of reaching Carroll Summit before dark, he honestly couldn't tell if food had helped to inch his brother closer to sobriety. He at least seemed quieter, and he was now concentrating on pulling Shawna even closer. Nearing dusk, they crested the summit and the truck approached the westernmost access road leading back to McClelland Ranch. Robby saw the road and blurted out, *"Pull over here! . . .* I gotta pee before we take Shawna to Austin."

Frank needed to stretch as well, so he turned onto the dirt road and veered toward a line of power poles before stopping. This utility easement separated them from a cluster of nearby trees. When he saw Robby open the back door and once again go for the bottle of Crown Royal, Frank (exasperated) shook his head and reached back to remove keys from the ignition.

He was now *beyond tired* of Robby's act, and he suddenly felt the need to distance himself entirely from his out-of-control brother. He walked farther than usual away from the truck toward the trees, where he hoped he might find a break from babysitting. He did just find that moment of peace, but the sound of his motorcycle starting and revving threw him instantly into panic mode. . . .

❀ ❀ ❀

Frank spun around to discover that Robby had somehow unloaded the Suzuki from the pickup bed . . . Shawna could be heard loudly berating him, while he stumbled to escape. Frank was suddenly overcome, and he sprinted back to try to stop him.

His brother again laughed hard as he lurched forward (out of Shawna's grasp), onto a path that would take him easily beyond Frank's advance. Then, gears grinding, he settled upon the speed he wanted, and he tore away through the dirt in wide circles around the truck.

Reason abandoned Frank *entirely*, as he could only feel the violation in his brother's choices. He had for so long lived in Robby's shadow, that the motorcycle had become sacrosanct to him inside his world of diminished territory. To now have that *stolen* from him by his reckless brother had left a vacancy that absolutely unhinged him.

Full of rage, Frank searched the area around him for rocks large enough to do damage. He planned to bring to bear the full strength of his slingshot arm to hurl them at the thief. It took three tries before hitting Robby squarely on the ribs of his left chest (which bent him sideways in pain). After he recovered in a wide turn, Robby escaped toward the ranch road. Once there, he could be seen practicing "wheelies" off in the distance, where he was soon riding back and forth in long passes.

This only served to further enrage Frank, who had spent the better part of a year learning how to do wheel-stands on his motorcycle; his brother had mastered them *in under five minutes*. "Just like everything else," Frank muttered to himself. He and Shawna were then startled to suddenly watch Robby spin off the ranch road and accelerate back toward them at full speed. His chosen vector of travel appeared to be a direct approach to where they stood. . . .

❁ ❁ ❁

Frank was consumed for the first time ever by the idea that he *hated* everything about his brother. In that mindset, he welcomed a repeat chance to inflict harm. He then picked up another rock and stepped forward into position to confront Robby. When the motorcycle closed to within a dozen yards, he threw the rock as hard as he could at his approaching brother. In his heightened anger, he *overthrew it* and watched as the rock missed Robby's forehead by an inch.

Robby understood the close call, so he laughed wildly as he jerked the Suzuki up into one more wheelie, and then he veered it *directly at Frank*. In those final seconds, Frank considered knocking Robby off the motorcycle in one reckless tackle—When the bike rushed past him on its back wheel, however, he could only dive away to avoid being hit. This emboldened Robby finally, who then raised his cowboy boots high on either side of the Suzuki, to demonstrate the same unmatched physical skills which had won him today's saddle bronc event. . . .

❁ ❁ ❁

He was last seen tilting his head back fully as he hurtled forward on the back wheel, while grinning over his shoulder at Frank and Shawna. In spite of everything, Frank was once more awestruck by his brother's gift of perfect balance. This only left him to stare in dejection, right up until the instant that Robby dropped over the ledge, and disappeared *forever* from the face of the Earth.

## REGRETS

It had been a long time since Frank dredged up these memories in such detail, and as he descended the eastern crest of I-80, high above *Donner Lake*, he was consumed once more by his regrets. Certainly, a sixteen year old boy can't be held to wrap his brain around the sequelae of his brother's mortality, but if he had known Robby was going to *die* that day, Frank was now certain that he would have given him more measured signals. He of course, didn't *hate* his older brother in any ultimate sense that day, but Frank's haunting recollection was that he had tried to *convey* it. If Robby recognized that, did he believe in his last waking seconds that it was so?

Frank remembered a lifetime of quietly deferring to his brother, especially during his father's endless bragging about him. Robby's exploits always seemed bigger than any life that Frank might have imagined for himself. This fact had helped him keep a low profile, because he had been proud of his big brother and content in his presence, and Frank knew that he had loved him beyond any words. . . . From his earliest memories, he felt safest and most validated when in Robby's presence. . . .

❁ ❁ ❁

All of this was at the heart of what Frank feared he had lost that day, when he ran terrified toward the cliff's edge. The powerline easement was unfamiliar to Frank, and only when he reached the precipice, did he realize that the poles fell off dramatically toward the highway below—Robby had certainly driven over something *steep*.

Straining now to catch his breath, Frank peered over the ledge, and his eyes were drawn far below to a beam of reflected sunlight, which angled off a piece of chrome. It had come from the *motorcycle,* which now lay twisted and broken against boulders on the steep hillside—He scanned the surrounding area, and soon recognized Robby's boot and a denim pant leg, held up between rocks.

Frank immediately jumped over the edge, on a course that pointed him straight down toward his brother. He slid more that he walked atop the loose gravel of the slope, as he fought to steady himself with his uphill hand. More than once, he nearly toppled out of control. Finally, steady on his knees beside his brother, he focused first on Robby's head, which was turned to give the impression that he was looking downhill.

Frank was now desperate to search Robby's eyes—to ask him if he was *hurt*, or to determine if he *needed help*. Sliding further, Frank stopped close beside his brother's face, still illuminated in the last reaches of sunlight from the west. But when he moved in closer, he found himself staring into the dullness of glazed eyes, and fully-dilated pupils: There was no reflection *at all* of the light which inhabits the living.

❊ ❊ ❊

Frank jolted backwards in the horror of what he recognized. From this new vantage, he saw that his brother's neck bulged horrifically on one side—a localized purple hue had already permeated the swollen skin around the injury, while Robby's face seemed to be devoid of any color at all; just *pallid remnants,* after life seeped away. But, it was the realization that his brother's head was now wrenched a half-turn, and pointing backwards between his shoulder blades, that immersed Frank into the nightmare that would last for nearly two decades . . .

Frozen there on his knees, Frank was left alone to imagine how his once invincible brother could now be so mangled—only when Shawna Casey called down to him, did he emerge from this dreamscape to look up at her—She could see how far Robby had fallen, and she started crying, "Is he all right?! . . . *Frank! . . . Is he all right?!*" Lost now in his own purgatory, he could only stare up at her, and she became more frightened.

Shawna looked back and forth to find a way to make her descent, "How can I get down there?!" The thought of her seeing Robby like this suddenly prompted Frank to act. He pointed toward the Cat trail which had been carved into the slope to bring the utility poles evenly downhill, "Follow those poles, then traverse over to me. . . . *Be careful!*"

When he saw that Shawna had turned to run toward the poles, Frank was consumed with the urgency that he somehow needed to align his brother's body differently. "*Nobody should have to see him like this,*" he thought to himself. He then slid his arms under Robby's torso, and began to pull him off the boulders.

Nothing could have prepared him for the instant when his brother's head, which had been wedged between two rocks, swung free *in the absence of its skeletal connection*—all that was left to hold it in place was the soft tissue and cartilage of the throat, and he froze as his brother's head arced freely back and forth. This reality staggered Frank, and he was barely able to lower the body upon an upslope of gravel.

He sobbed uncontrollably now, as he lifted and pulled to straighten the lifeless body. He carefully realigned Robby's head and neck (as best he could) to lessen their grotesque appearance. Believing at last that nothing more could be done, he collapsed across Robby's chest and pressed his own face against his brother's cheek. He could only whisper to Robby now through streaming tears, "*Nobody should have to see you like this . . .*"

## THE DEVASTATION

The time that followed was clouded in a blur of surreal memories. First, Shawna's arrival on the hillside, and her utter collapse upon Robby's chest . . . and then her *wailing*. Frank kept his hand upon Robby's body as well, while he and Shawna were inconsolable together for a length of time that he couldn't later quantify. When he realized that darkness was gaining a foothold, Frank decided to tell Shawna, "You stay *here* . . . I have to go for help", and he moved across the slope of the hill toward the Cat trail.

He began to climb hand-over-hand up the steep embankment in boots not designed for that purpose, until he reached the top. From there, he sprinted toward the dually. He didn't know where to go, but he found himself speeding through the Reese River Valley. Eventually he turned onto a long gravel road, leading past a field of alfalfa with an irrigation wheel line . . . The road ended at a small single-wide trailer with its porch light on. There, a ranch hand gave him the phone to dial 9-1-1.

❁ ❁ ❁

Back on the easement road after directing two Sherriff's Deputies and the ambulance to the accident site, nothing was left for Frank to do but watch. After an eternity, the HASTY Team deployed their equipment to secure and retrieve his brother's body.

The timing of his father's arrival at the scene was still central in Frank's nightmare—his appearance out of darkness, into the flashing illumination of red and blue emergency lights was too vivid. If Robert McClelland had been staggered to find himself standing over his wife's grave one year prior . . . his destruction would now be complete . . .

Frank saw the Paramedics pull back the sheet to reveal Robby's face, and then he witnessed his father's anguished collapse onto both knees. His clenching of the transport gurney's siderail with both fists was all that kept him upright. The *Deputy* who had arrived in a department cruiser was his father's friend, and he kneeled beside him. When he placed a hand on Robert's back, he too began to cry. The *Paramedics* stood with faces contorted and staring down, their hands solemnly collected before them. *Losses in small towns are everyone's losses. . . .*

❁ ❁ ❁

Time passed, and it was inevitable that the second Deputy (with Shawna seated beside him) would drive up and over the ledge of the steep Cat trail—his truck's winch had been secured to one of the utility poles. In the background, he could be seen unhooking the winch cable before driving his truck around the site's perimeter, stopping finally beside the Ford dually. His actions were hypnotic, and those present couldn't help but watch.

Frank gasped when the Deputy dropped his tailgate and pulled the Suzuki into view from the Sherriff's Department pickup. From there, he struggled to push the twisted motorcycle forward, until he finally leaned it against Frank's truck. Frank knew what would happen next, and consumed with terror, he looked back toward the ambulance. The vulnerability in his eyes was all that his father needed to see to explain the tragedy, and he jumped up in a rage, to run screaming toward Frank, *"You fucking . . . !!"*

Both Deputies were stunned into hesitation, and therefore *too late* to protect Frank in the battery that followed. The *Father* lunged forward and tackled the *Son*, and then he raised his right fist high above him, before driving it down again into Frank's brow. Despite Frank's efforts to turn away, the concussion of the punch sent shockwaves through him, and when the blinding aftermath of the contact passed, his right forehead and eye twisted in pain.

Through tears and blurry half-light, Frank later remembered the two green shirts of the Deputies flying over the top of him, and he was freed from his father's weight. His last visual memory from that night was of one Deputy, with a knee into his father's back, while he pushed up hard on the elbow that was bent behind him. The other Deputy *(the friend)* was pressing the side of his father's face into the dirt, as he leaned down in an attempt to calm him, "This can't be right, Robert! . . . *This can't be right! . . .*"

When his father at last could no longer fight, he folded there under his own resignation . . . inhaling and exhaling deeply within agitated billows of dust, while he groaned out sobs, garbled as they were, *through the muddy snot and tears of his devastated life.*

# 26

## PRODIGAL SON

By the time Frank once more donned his certain blame for throwing the rock that had altered his brother's path forever, he found himself driving through Reno's outskirts—today's recollection of the accident still numbed him, but it had left him certain that he would be ready in the event of his father's death. An urgency remained, however, that he would still need enough time to deliver his long-overdue apology.

He had witnessed death before, and he knew that he was prepared to do whatever was required; to sell McClelland Ranch even, as just a final step in tying-up his family's affairs. In the aftermath of that, there would be nothing remaining of his childhood home (long ago reconciled by Frank as *inevitable*). Family would then finally and forever be extinguished, leaving only the irony that it should have fallen upon *him* to dispose of his father's legacy.

Beyond the obligation to Marion to find his mother's photo album, there would certainly be no other possessions remaining which had been nostalgic between him and his father. Likewise, obligations regarding the business of raising cattle had already disappeared into some ancient past; those matters would now be suited for anyone other than himself.

❀ ❀ ❀

In what amounted to a strengthening of his resolve, he called Cory Ebert for directions to their meeting . . . Memories of the medical center dated back to his college years, when it had already existed as *Washoe County Hospital* for more than a hundred years. The old buildings could be seen from the UNR campus, prominent near the center of town, and sometime after that era, it had been "taken private" and renamed, "Regal Medical Center." Frank was instructed to approach it from the east, and pull into the parking garage that fronted Miller Way. He was told to then walk to the nearby Tallac Tower lobby, where Cory would wait for him.

He was amazed as he drove toward a futuristic ten-story building, which looked to be in final phases of construction on the hospital grounds. He studied the winged-architecture which crowned this new tower, as he pulled into the parking garage and thought to himself, "Jesus Christ! . . . *Somebody here is making money.*"

Nothing, however, could have prepared him (referencing his recent impressions of Stanford Medical Center) for the *opulence* which greeted him within the Tallac Tower lobby. . . . Surrounding him were paintings and artworks which covered even the narrowest of walls, and juxtaposing them, were floor to ceiling windows which overlooked a courtyard garden of an acre or more.

The art was indeed breathtaking, and several of the huge pieces caught sunlight in their high suspension beneath a domed glass ceiling. In the center of this expansive waiting area was a gleaming baby grand piano, being played classically by a man in formal attire.

Frank struggled to reconcile how these first impressions might coexist in any focused healthcare facility, as he stared down into the courtyard garden below him. It was then that Cory quietly approached him and spoke, *"Hello Frank . . . It looks like you made good time."* Frank turned and smiled back at his friend, and he extended his hand, "Nice to see you, Cory. . . . I can't tell you how much I appreciate your help here."

❊ ❊ ❊

Cory Ebert was tall and thin, and in his Wrangler snap-pocket shirt, he had the look of a native Nevadan. Frank was thankful at the sight of his stalwart friend, who was born to a ranching heritage. The Eberts, like so many of the old rural families of Nevada, were LDS members who had raised cattle and hay for more than six generations; Cory's people traveled to the Reese River Valley during the 'handcart movement' of the 1850's, and after finding it, they never left . . . It was good to see his friend here now.

When Frank asked, Cory addressed the latest developments regarding his father, "He's still on the ventilator and he's not very happy about it. He keeps trying to pull out the breathing tube when they turn down his sedation, so that's been hard on him and everybody else watching. The doctors are saying that his pneumonia might be clearing a little, but x-rays are still showing that it's in both lungs . . . along with the emphysema from his smoking."

Frank considered this and pressed ahead, "You told me earlier that he might not live through this . . . Has that changed?" Cory was careful now, "The problem has been that when he stresses, his heart rhythm can change into something more dangerous. They had to shock him a couple of times after he arrived, to convert him back into a normal EKG rhythm; that's when they decided to move him into the cardiac unit . . . to be closer to the heart doctors." He watched for a minute as Frank absorbed the news, and then offered, "When I left his room to come down here, your dad had just been sedated again, and he was sleeping . . . Do you feel like you're ready to go upstairs to see him?"

❁ ❁ ❁

Cory led out of the elevator which had delivered them to one of the upper floors, and Frank followed him across the top of a long hallway with new hardwood flooring. They walked to an adjacent hallway, which together with the first, seemed to complete a huge circular workspace. Frank estimated that both halls formed a circle of nearly a fifth of a mile.

They passed only a couple of rooms before arriving at the one that Cory chose, and he lightly knocked before opening the door, "My son Logan is here with Jaycee. They've been at the bedside nonstop since your Dad got here." The comment didn't register with Frank, and he took a deep breath before following Cory into the room.

Near a tower of IV pumps beside the hospital bed, a handsome young man stepped forward and offered his hand, "Hello Mr. McClelland, I'm *Logan Ebert*. Cory's son." Frank managed a thin smile as he shook his hand, and then he stepped closer toward his father. The old man's thinning gray hair was damp and combed over to one side, and his deeply-wrinkled face seemed pale and vulnerable in the absence of his cowboy hat.

The old man's eyes were closed and he seemed peaceful enough, but there was a translucent breathing tube emerging from one corner of his mouth, taped in place—blue corrugated tubing connected that to a ventilator, which hissed through its cycles on the opposite side of the bed. Frank could only stare at his father's leathery face and then consider his diminished stature, now just a remnant of the man who had once owned the atmosphere in any setting that he occupied.

❁ ❁ ❁

The reality of his father's decline hit Frank suddenly, and he found himself reaching for the restrained hand which was closest to him. He placed his hand upon his father's, and firmly held it; there was no mistaking the calloused palm, or the steel-trap fingers, which together had thrown a million hay bales over a lifetime. The sudden welling of his own tears surprised Frank, as the irresistible weight of his link to this man rushed through him.

He stared in sad disbelief for a long time, before remembering that someone else was also there with him, on the opposite side of the bed. Frank glanced past the waveforms on the ventilator screen, and focused on the pretty girl who was standing beside it. He had *felt* that someone was staring at him while he considered his father. When he at last focused on her thick ebony hair, and then her beautiful young features, he stood breathless . . . He knew instantly that *this was the girl from his dream*; the *same* young girl who had raced past him on the thoroughbred horse. She smiled and said, "Hello . . . *I'm Jaycee . . . I'm your Niece . . .*"

❀ ❀ ❀

Frank struggled to attach that statement onto any component of his memory, and he came up empty, *"I don't understand . . ."* The pretty girl was patient, "I'm *Robby's* daughter . . . *I'm your Niece*." At this, Cory Ebert stepped forward in considerable alarm, "Good *Lord* Frank, *I am so sorry!* I assumed that you *knew!*" Jaycee smiled sadly at him, and reached down to take Robert McClelland's other restrained hand, "And, this is my *Grampa*."

Frank stared at her now, and in this close proximity, he was overcome by her striking family resemblance. The rising voices and the stimulation from the clasping of both hands suddenly woke the sedated patient. Robert McClelland's face grimaced, and he coughed a loud, rhonchorous cough through the ventilator tubing. A single alarm tone sounded in response to the spike of high pressure, and Jaycee leaned lower to stroke her grandfather's forehead; this calmed him, and she smiled at him until he settled down again.

She then spoke in gentle tones, *"Look who's here to see you . . ."* The old man, unsuspecting, turned and squinted toward the face of the man standing beside the opposite bedrail. He blinked at Frank, and tried to focus. Jaycee felt compelled to help him, "It's *Frank*, Grampa . . . *It's your son, Frank."* Frank managed a weak smile, and then gripped his father's hand tighter . . . He watched his father's eyes get wide with understanding, and Frank responded, *"Hi Dad . . . it's me . . ."*

His father's brow contorted into its deeply worn sorrow, and his eyes filled immediately with tears; *he gripped back on his son's hand* . . . Frank hastened, "It's *Okay*, Dad . . . I'm not going *anywhere*. I'm gonna stay *right here* for as long as you need me."

❀ ❀ ❀

Jaycee dabbed her grandfather's eyes with a washcloth that she had moistened at the nearby sink. When his father revived sufficiently, he turned to face Frank and then he pointed at Jaycee with his index finger . . . Frank nodded and smiled at her before turning back to his father, *"Yes, I just met her . . . She looks like* Mom, *doesn't she?"* His father teared up again, but fought through it. He signaled at Jaycee to adjust the bed, so his back could be positioned more upright. He then coughed again as he motioned that he wanted to write something.

Jaycee became stern when she *warned* him, "Every time we do that Grampa, you go for the ET tube! Your doctors have told us that you are still too sick to breathe on your own, and *you know that!"* The old man spread his fingers on both hands and slowly motioned them downward to indicate that he would stay calm.

She looked over at Cory and Logan, and both of them stepped in closer. Cory explained that they needed to stand beside the bed, because by now, he and Logan understood how the restraint ties worked. Frank watched as his father's hands were loosened, and Jaycee handed him a clipboard and pen . . . He was shaky, but he scribbled a few letters before motioning to Jaycee to get him his reading glasses; those in place, he continued to write in large print and then handed the clipboard to Frank when he finished. Frank turned the clipboard and looked at the writing; the message was succinct:

*"I WANT TO GO HOME!"*

Frank was unprepared, and he could only react, *"Dad . . .* It sounds like they don't think you're quite ready for that. Let me talk with your doctors and hear what they have to say . . . Then, we can decide from there." His father grew more adamant, and he reached for the clipboard again; when he did, he began to cough more and the ventilator alarmed as his movements reflected his agitation. He wrote again and handed the clipboard back to Frank,

*"I DON'T WANT TO STAY HERE. I WANT TO GO HOME."*

Jaycee looked at the writing, and it was evident that she had been through this with him before, *"Grampa,* we *talked* about this . . . Your doctor says you could *die* if that tube comes out too soon! . . ." By now, Robert was clearly unhappy, and the coughing spasms became more continuous. He pressed hard on the pen and wrote once more,

*"I DON'T WANT TO DIE HERE!*
*GET THIS TUBE OUT AND TAKE ME HOME NOW!"*

❀ ❀ ❀

When he reached toward Frank to pass the message back, he began coughing hard. A collection of yellow lung secretions could now be seen inside the ventilator tubing, and the alarm tones from the machine were getting louder; the old man panicked at not being able to pull a complete breath, and he raised his right hand toward the breathing tube. Cory and Logan knew the drill, so they quickly grabbed both wrists to return his hands to the bed. Jaycee pressed the "call light" button to summon her grandfather's nurse.

Frank felt helpless now (as he had in his dream), while watching his father cough without relief. Just as Jaycee began moving toward the door, a woman wearing dark blue scrubs entered the room and stepped quickly beside the ventilator. Jaycee recognized her, and seemed relieved, "Hi Susan. Thanks for coming! I think he needs to be suctioned again."

Frank saw on her nametag that she was from respiratory therapy, and she brought a calming presence to his father when she spoke to him, "Let's clear that tubing, Robert. It looks like that stuff is finally starting to break-up. . . . *That's good.*" Susan had dark maroon hair, which she tied back, and Frank recognized her kindness as she spoke in soothing tones. She skillfully removed the lung secretions through an enclosed catheter, and then she reset the ventilator controls.

She turned toward the sink to dampen a washcloth, and applied it again to his father's forehead. His father, who was still recovering with the aid of deeper breaths, nodded his appreciation. Susan at last turned to Jaycee and said, "We probably should turn up the vent support a bit; I have been trying to let him do more of the work today, but it looks like he's had enough . . ."

Jaycee thanked her again and introduced Frank, "Susan . . . this is Robert's son, Frank. He just drove up from San Francisco, and he will be staying here with us in the room." Susan was glad to meet him, and she shared that the nurses would be glad as well, "I know they were hoping your family could reach you." Before leaving, she turned to Jaycee and confirmed, "So, I'll just leave him on this increased ventilator support . . . I saw that you turned on the call light. If you see his nurse before I do, please let her know that he could use more sedation, and also that we are going to rest him overnight on the higher settings.

Frank and Jaycee were once again holding Robert's hands when the nurse stepped into the room to administer sedation . . . She told Jaycee that she had just spoken with the respiratory therapist about her grandfather. She was young and bright, and she introduced herself to Frank. He smiled when he noticed a *UNR Nursing School* emblem on the yoke of her stethoscope.

※ ※ ※

Cory stepped forward and suggested to Frank that he and Jaycee might take this opportunity to go somewhere and talk. He reassured them that he and Logan could, "hold down the fort" with his father. Jaycee looked up and agreed, "Why don't we go downstairs? . . . They have a garden on the ground floor, and it's nice there after the sun goes down . . ."

## JAYCEE

The garden turned out to be the one that Frank had seen from the lobby, and he followed Jaycee past a fountain which stood beside the stonework path. This led to a secluded table with two chairs, where they sat across from one another. He looked around and acknowledged, "This *is* a nice place . . ." Jaycee was glad for the small-talk, and she nodded, *"It is . . .* They call it *'The Wellness Garden'* . . ."

Frank smiled, and he knew that he had to start somewhere, "Jaycee . . . I am so, so sorry that I didn't know about you . . . When I look at you now, I can absolutely see my Mother in you . . ." Jaycee deflected it, "That's okay . . . Things can get *complicated* when someone leaves for twenty years . . ." Frank raised his eyebrows, but he didn't resent the bluntness. "Did your grandfather ever try to explain that to you?" Jaycee looked down, but knew she had to answer, "He said that he was pretty sure you *hated him* . . ." Her words startled Frank, and he shifted in his chair to address them, *"That wasn't my feeling at all, Jaycee* . . ."

"After your father died, I spent almost two years at home believing that your grandfather blamed *me* for Robby's death—that he felt it was *my fault.* I eventually came to believe it myself. So, I have been certain all these years that it was the other way around: That it was *your Grandfather* who hated *me.* . . . In fact, I hope that I have enough time to apologize to him. It got quiet for some time, as both of them weighed what had been said.

❁ ❁ ❁

Finally, Frank took things in another direction, "So . . . you have to be Shawna's daughter, right?" Jaycee nodded and began, "Yes . . . I was born six months after my dad died. My mother recorded my last name as "McClelland" on the birth certificate, but then she moved us to Las Vegas pretty soon after that. I grew up remembering us living in a lot of small apartments there, while my mom worked in the casinos as a cocktail waitress."

The story got harder for Jaycee, "When I was ten, the police came one night to get me, and they placed me in protective custody after she had been arrested for drugs. I don't remember where they took me, but Mom came and got me the next day. She had the car packed with my things, and she drove us all night . . . *straight through to the ranch.* When we got there, she told me to wait in the car while she went inside the house to talk with Grampa . . ." Frank sat quietly to let her finish . . . "When I look back on that time, I *know* she had probably been into drugs for a while; I remember loud parties, where she made me stay in my room all night . . ."

❀ ❀ ❀

Jaycee shook off those memories and was finally able to smile a bit, "I can still remember *Grampa* coming out onto the porch that first morning; he stood there waiting while my mom walked back to the car. I was so scared, but he never once made me feel like he didn't want me. He shook my hand when I stepped onto the porch, and he told me to follow him into the house to a room that he said was, *'your new bedroom'* . . . He told me it belonged to my *'Dad'* . . . and, in spite of everything, it made me feel for the first time *ever* that I finally belonged somewhere."

"I barely remember my mom driving away. . . . After we brought my things inside, he asked me if I was hungry, then he made us pancakes and bacon and eggs. He gave me my first cup of coffee that morning too; it was loaded up with cream and sugar, and it tasted so good." Frank was amazed, "And, you've been living there ever since?" Jaycee smiled and nodded her head *"Yes."*

Frank then asked her, "Do you still stay in touch with your mom?" Jaycee looked away, and answered more quietly, "No . . . She sent birthday and Christmas cards for a while, but a few years back, a Sherriff's Deputy came up from Austin to tell us that she had died. He brought her death certificate, and a few of her things. Grampa told me later that she overdosed on drugs." Frank reached over to take her hand, *"I'm so sorry, Jaycee* . . . but . . . I have to tell you how relieved I am, knowing that you have been with Dad all these years . . ." Jaycee teared up a little, and offered finally, *"He really is the best Grampa . . ."*

❀ ❀ ❀

Frank more carefully proceeded, "I could see when you were talking to him, that you know how stubborn he can be . . . Jaycee, you have to know he wants that tube out . . . and I don't think there's anything you or I can do about that. The hospital will determine if he wants to be resuscitated again in the event that he can't breathe after they take it out, and he will never agree to that. That means he could die sometime soon . . . maybe even tomorrow . . ."

Jaycee became sad again, and she stared out across the garden, *"I know . . ."* They became quiet again, and Frank finally asked her, "What do you plan to do if he dies?" She looked back and studied him, "I'll go home . . . You do understand that the ranch is my home, right?" Frank suddenly regretted his awkward words, and he stumbled, "Of course . . . Of course it's your home . . ."

# 27

# DR. HOLDEN

The topics finally lightened, and they sat and talked for a long time. Both of them eventually shared their stories of growing up on the ranch. When the summer twilight enveloped them at last, they returned upstairs to the hospital room.

Jaycee and Frank were quiet after returning from the garden, and Frank barely noticed when Logan took her hand and stepped closer to her—after which, they remained still as they stood together next to her grandfather. Cory motioned to Frank to follow him out into the hallway, where he informed him, "I assumed that you would want to stay with your Dad and Jaycee tonight, so I asked Robert's nurse to have maintenance bring us another recliner."

"With you being here, Logan and I decided to get a room over at John Ascuaga's, but we'll be back first thing in the morning to see what the plan is." Frank looked at Cory and confided, "You must know that my dad is asking to be taken off life support. From my earliest memories, Cory, I heard him tell all of us that he never wanted 'to be kept alive on machines' . . ."

Cory placed a hand on Frank's shoulder and offered his support, "It has been my experience with our church members, that this decision is easier for people who have reconciled their own passing—your father strikes me as someone who has already done that, presumably going back to the time when he lost his wife . . ." Frank nodded in agreement, and they stood in silence for a moment more . . . Cory eventually turned to look down the hall, and he said, "I think the nurses are getting out of their shift change, so let me make sure that the night shift got the message about your recliner."

# Nevada Son

❊ ❊ ❊

Frank leaned against a handrail and watched Cory walk down the long hallway toward the nursing station. . . . Suddenly, a man with quick movements emerged from one of the nearby rooms. He was wearing a white lab jacket with a stethoscope thrown around his collar, and he began to stride in Frank's direction. An emblem was sewn onto his pocket which identified him as a *Physician*.

When the man folded his notes and slipped them into a pocket, he looked up to see Frank watching him. Both men were immediately struck by the familiar appearance of one another. The M.D. was the first to speak. *"Francis McClelland! . . . as I live and breathe!"* Frank recognized the man's face as well when he put it together with the voice, *"Chico?! Is that you . . . ?!"* They stepped closer, both with genuine smiles, before shaking hands.

Frank's friend spoke again, "I just took report from my partner, and he told me that one of my patients is a big rancher from Austin, and that his name is 'McClelland.' I wondered if you might somehow be connected." Frank was amazed to hear this, "You are taking care of my Father?! That is amazing!" Chico smiled, "Well, let's hope so . . . I'm with the Pulmonology group here in Reno, and we follow patients on this unit whenever respiratory failure is part of the picture; your father has fallen into our world, I'm afraid."

He then stepped back to study Frank's San Francisco business clothes, and he marveled, "Look at *you*! . . . it appears that you've done well for yourself." Frank returned the observation when he grasped the nametag on his friend's jacket and read, "Charles Holden, MD . . . Yeah, we've come a long way since troweling foam off the tops of beer mugs at 'The Wall' . . ."

They both laughed, and Chico was able to recollect, "I remember that you headed to Elko for an internship with Barrick Mining . . . then I lost track of you when I moved away for my own Fellowship." Frank nodded, "Yeah . . . you talked about that. Where did you end up going?" Chico said, "University of Missouri at Columbia, for Pulmonology, and then I spent some time at Bethesda paying back my debt to the Navy . . . That turned out to be great duty, actually."

❊ ❊ ❊

Frank was relieved after thinking about old times, but he knew that he had to turn the conversation back to his father, "So . . . when can we sit down to talk about my dad . . . ?" Chico hesitated, "Look, I just got called to the ER, and I'm headed there now; it sounds like that might actually take a while. Tomorrow will be my first day back on duty . . . That's the start of a seven day stretch. I can tell you I heard in report that your dad was not able to wean off the ventilator today, most likely due to his underlying chronic disease . . ."

"In fact, RT just called to say they had to turn him back up on higher support, so he can rest for the night." Chico suddenly recalled, *"Hey!* . . . do you still wake up at those godawful morning hours like you used to?" Frank smiled, *"Yep . . ."* Chico continued, "Perfect. We're going to change your father's ventilator settings early tomorrow morning for 'spontaneous breathing trials,' and then I'll get some labs and an xray to see how he handles it. When I have those results, I'll come here first, to watch him breathe . . . then, you and I can go have some breakfast and talk about what it all means." Frank liked the plan, and he nodded his head in agreement.

❀ ❀ ❀

Chico then stepped back to study Frank's face for a minute more, and he grinned, "Seems to me I can recall a crazy night behind the Lakeridge Apartments, where we convinced some very pretty girls to participate in naked piggyback wars in the golf course sprinklers . . . I think that might have taken place on the eleventh green, actually." Frank laughed, "Jesus!, I still don't know why we didn't end up in jail that night . . . or why we didn't get shot by the greenskeeper!"

Frank asked his friend, "Who were you with that night?" "Gena," Chico answered, and then he waited. Frank visualized the memory and he nodded, "Ah yes . . . Gena! . . . I liked her." Chico grinned, "So did I . . . a lot! . . . That's why I *married* her." The memory was fun, and Chico finally quipped, "You probably don't need to share that story with my colleagues, however." Frank jabbed back, "Don't worry Charles, your illusion is safe with me."

❀ ❀ ❀

Later that night, from his recliner beside the IV poles, Frank watched Jaycee while she slept in her own chair. Her fatigue, following long days beside her grandfather's bed, had caught up with her; she had fallen asleep soon after Cory and Logan left for the night. Frank smiled to imagine his father teaching a ten year old girl how to ride a horse . . . or, teaching her *anything* for that matter.

He then remembered hearing a friend once say, 'Real men have daughters' . . . and he just somehow knew that his father's methods for teaching Jaycee had come from some kinder place; certainly, it would have been a different place than that which had been required for raising two rowdy sons. This moved Frank to reach again through the bedrail and take his father's hand.

❀ ❀ ❀

He soon slipped into his own fitful sleep, as he drifted through the images of his last dream, especially where Jaycee had expertly ridden that horse. He then remembered crossing the pasture with his mother, wondering why it had fallen upon such neglect—would the rest of the ranch show that kind of neglect as well? These questions took on heightened consequences now, as he weighed Jaycee's comments, "I'll go back *home*. . . . You do understand that the ranch is my *home*, right?"

In this realm of half-sleep, amidst the white noise of ventilator cycles, Frank's new worries allowed him only sporadic rest. Eventually he fell more deeply asleep, at about the same time that his father awoke to see his son there beside him, holding his hand. Robert studied Frank's careworn brow (thinking that it shouldn't be visible on someone so young), and he suddenly couldn't stop his own eyes from welling up in their years-long regret.

His tears flowed now in the absence of any witnesses, and Robert realized that they were soon speaking to the possibility of a better outcome than his life's trajectory allowed so far. He had not been expecting *hope* today, much less that he might be deserving of it, and he realized that he was glad no one else was present. Certainly his tears would be misunderstood, and perhaps some well-meaning person would be compelled to wipe them away again with a washcloth. His thoughts became privately defiant, "These are *my* tears, *goddamnit!* . . . I earned these tears, and nobody else has the right to wipe them away!"

## BREATHING TRIALS

At 4:00am, the night shift respiratory therapist appeared at the bedside to help radiology get a chest film. He then stimulated a cough and suctioned Robert's breathing circuit, before changing the ventilator settings to *"spontaneous breathing."* Frank and Jaycee stepped with the RT into a charting alcove when the xray was taken, and Frank asked him, "So, what's next?" The young man replied, "I'll be back in an hour to draw an 'arterial blood gas,' and Dr. Holden should be here soon after that to get *'weaning parameters'* . . . He wants to do those himself this morning . . . All of that together will tell us if your Father is ready to get the tube out."

Dr. Holden did arrive at the bedside an hour later, and when the RT joined him, things began to happen quickly. Lights were turned up bright, and he raised the head of the bed so Frank's father was in a sitting position. The Pulmonologist then coached Robert through some maneuvers which determined the volume of his forced exhalation. Next came a measurement of the negative pressure which his father could generate during inspiration, presumably as an indicator of Robert's muscular strength in drawing his own breath.

He considered Robert's cough, which sounded rattling and wet (in Frank's estimation), and after listening to his chest with an impressive sequence of stethoscope placements, Dr. Holden sat on the bed next to his patient. Seeing that Robert

McClelland did not look like a man who suffered bullshit, Chico proceeded, "I don't know why this pneumonia hasn't already killed you, Robert . . . and I'd be lying if I told you that this morning's chest xray looks much better."

"You're carrying around *way* too much carbon dioxide in your arterial blood, and the cardiologists are tormenting me about your heart rhythm. They want to laser an irritable focus inside your heart, before I even try to wean you further off this ventilator . . ." Robert signaled to the therapist that he wanted the clipboard, where he wrote clearly:

"I'M DONE WITH ALL THIS."

Chico pursed his lips, "You *do* know you might die if we take that tube out, right?" Robert nodded his head, and signaled with his fist and outstretched thumb that he wanted the tube removed.

❀ ❀ ❀

Chico looked at Frank and Jaycee, and then back to his patient, "Well, you are obviously a man who knows what he wants, so that decision should be *yours* and *yours alone* . . . If your family is ready for that, I will write to change your status right now to 'Hospice Care,' and then we can start the process of getting you ready to go home."

After he wrote his orders, he thought of the logistics, *"Jesus,* I just remembered that we're talking about *Austin* here . . . That's . . . *what?* . . . three hours away?" Everybody nodded. Chico then reasoned with Robert, "That's a long time to travel, Sir . . . You need to give me some time to get you oxygen for the road, along with all of the other equipment that you're going to need at home."

"Do you think you can *behave* long enough to let me arrange for all of that?" Robert thought the question was funny, and he nodded "Yes." Chico continued, "I'm going to call my friend 'Pat' about your equipment; he can get all of that stuff setup for you. Then we can try to get you out of here."

Robert, sensing progress, nodded in agreement. Chico then turned to Frank, "Is there someone who can guide Pat out to your ranch this morning, so the equipment can be set up there before your Dad arrives? Jaycee said she would call Logan to arrange for his help, and Frank was able to leave with Dr. Holden to talk further . . .

❀ ❀ ❀

Frank followed his friend through a lower hallway past a glittering gift boutique, where Frank found himself once again facing his incongruous reaction to "opulence" within a hospital. There was also a uniform store, and (amazingly) a large

Starbucks coffee shop, already bulging with a long line of presumed middle-managers at this early hour. Across from Starbucks was a restaurant with a sign that read, "Sustenance," and his friend steered Frank toward it.

Inside the entrance, Chico greeted some respectful acquaintances as he led Frank toward a table near the back of the room; here they would be isolated from the more crowded areas. It was soon evident to Frank that he was about to hear the professional assessment of a pulmonologist, and nothing resembling casual banter from a friend. Chico started, "I wish I had better news, Frank . . . Your Dad is still having a hard time doing the work of breathing on his own. His carbon dioxide levels are too high. His lung mechanics are just marginal, and the chest xray still looks like crap . . ."

Frank lowered his head as he took it all in, but then replied, "Well . . . you can see what we're up against: He wants that tube out, and he wants to go home *today*. Knowing him, there's no way around it." Chico sympathized, "You need to remind yourself that he smoked two packs of cigarettes a day for more than fifty years, so his fears about dying on a ventilator are *real*. . . . Your takeaway should be that our decision here today is academic, because sooner, rather than later, he *will* succumb to the ravages of his disease. . . . So, Frank, please tell me now that you understand it will not be your fault if he doesn't make it back to Austin."

Frank nodded, and both men got quiet while they ordered breakfast. Chico continued, "I'm really sorry, Frank. One small hope that I can offer you is that today's chest xray did show more than one plugged airway, so I'm going to do a *therapeutic bronchoscopy* right before we pull that tube. Maybe it will open up a little more usable space inside your Dad's lungs. . . . I doubt that it's going to be a game-changer, but it's all that I've got."

## BETHESDA

Frank was grateful for his friend's concern, and he conveyed that he was prepared for the worst. He then steered away from what was inevitable today, and asked, "Tell me about your time at *Bethesda* . . ." The topic change triggered a memory for Chico, who stared at Frank more intently, "Do you remember asking me back in my med school days about your Mother's kidney ailment, Wegener's Disease?"

Frank did remember and Chico continued, "I recall trying hard to explain its etiology back then, but I felt at the time that I wasn't really helping you. Well, a few years later, after I got to Bethesda, I took part in a study of some Wegener's patients who came to us from *Fallon*, Nevada. A small cluster of cases had appeared there, and because there is a Navy base in Fallon, the CDC brought it to Bethesda's attention."

"They told us the national incidence for that disease is 'one case per three and a half million of population', and Fallon at the time had only eight thousand people within its city limits. The troubling part of it was that *five* people from Fallon had developed Wegener's at the same time. Bethesda offered free medical treatment to those patients, so we could study them further and perhaps determine whether or not there was a connection to the Navy Base . . ."

Chico continued, "Nothing definitive ever came from those studies, although jet fuel pipelines were replaced between Reno and Fallon, in a cautionary move. People mostly wrote it off to the transient nature of Navy populations, where most of the sailors and their families had lived all around the world."

"But everything changed in the late 1990's. Between 1997 and 2001, seventeen childhood Leukemia cases were identified in Fallon, and that cluster came under national scrutiny." Frank nodded his head, "I followed that story. . . . That was awful." Chico continued, "Well, Hillary Clinton heard about it and ran with the story; she actually held a Senate Subcommittee Hearing at the Fallon Convention Center in April of 2001."

"Those efforts eventually brought about funding for a new, one hundred million dollar water treatment plant, but then everybody just packed their bags and left town." Chico shook his head, *"Typical of politicians:* After exploiting their fifteen minutes of media glory, no one bothered to follow up on the scientific studies that they had ordered during the investigation. Hillary, to her credit, did make 'childhood healthcare' a part of her campaign."

Chico zeroed in: "The University of Arizona School of Pediatric Medicine then entered into a study of 'airborne particulates' in the region. They were looking to determine if any of them had been factors in the Leukemia cluster. Their findings turned out to be a complete surprise: They discovered increased airborne levels of cobalt and tungsten in the Fallon area, with particles ranging in size from 1.0 to 5.9 micrometers. The EPA determined them to be 'anthropogenic' in origin . . . that is, 'not naturally occurring.' It turns out that cobalt and tungsten, when bonded together, are most likely carcinogenic, and when inhaled in particulates of that size, they become 'extremely problematic.'"

Frank could only shake his head. His friend continued, "The researchers then ordered tree ring studies in the Fallon area, where they found that from 1990 to 2002, the amounts of tungsten had quadrupled when compared to previous years. Worse still, some of those samples were collected from trees in close proximity to Fallon Elementary School. Based on those findings, urine specimens were also collected from area residents in 2003, and they too confirmed increased levels of tungsten."

"At that time, the results were reported out to US Health and Human Services, but nobody has uttered another word since. No one ever asked whether or not metallurgy emissions might still be occurring somewhere in Fallon's backyard." I'm convinced that those two disease clusters, both Wegener's and Leukemia, are connected."

Chico distractedly stared out of the window and said finally, "I have a friend there . . . an ER Doc at Banner Churchill Hospital, who swears that every time the wind blows in Fallon, the ER fills up with wheezing patients."

Frank was incredulous, but finally he was able to reveal, "My mother worked at that elementary school as a teacher's aide, starting when she was in her teen years. She continued to work there into her twenties, up until the time that she and my dad moved to the ranch ."

## CHAIN OF TITLE

Frank returned to his father's room after Dr. Holden left to arrange for the home medical equipment and prescriptions that would be needed. Before doing so, he asked Frank to get an 'advance directives' packet from the admitting desk, which would be needed prior to changing his father's status to hospice care.

Frank found his father alone and sitting up in bed when he entered the room. Robert turned and smiled at him, as Frank dropped the side rail of the bed to sit down beside him. He then placed documents on the clipboard, and held out his dad's reading glasses before speaking, "You need to fill out this stuff to make everything legal before they send you home. I glanced at it, and it just looks like you have to check some boxes and give them a signature, and then Dr. Holden will be back soon to get that tube out."

Frank struggled with a smile as his father nodded, "I'm assuming that the Eberts are helping to get your equipment out to Smith Creek—so, if they can meet the guy and his van here by 9:00am, that gives them a couple hours head-start on us." His father nodded, and they began to work together on the documents.

It really was a simple process to make his father's wishes known, and Robert managed a shaky signature and date. When Frank turned to the final pages of the packet, he was surprised to find a bold heading that read, "Last Will and Testament." Following it were two blank pages, apparently meant for hand-written text.

❋ ❋ ❋

Frank looked at his father and asked, "Do you have a will . . . ?" His father shook his head, "No." Neither man was ready for communication on the subject, but Frank at last said, "I want you to leave the ranch to Jaycee . . ." Robert McClelland stared at his son for a long time. His gaze was now more somber, and Frank was again moved to speak, "You have to know that my life is no longer *there*, Dad . . . but Jaycee's life *is*. That's her *home* now . . ." His father grabbed the clipboard, and wrote on its blank paper:

"IT'S NOT MY RANCH TO GIVE."

Frank was stunned, "What do you mean, *'It's not yours to give?'*" Robert wrote again:

> *"I ONLY OWN HALF. YOUR GRANDFATHER OWNED THE OTHER HALF."*
>
> *"THE CENARRUSA HALF."*
>
> *"THAT BELONGS TO YOU NOW."*

Frank was astonished at the revelation, but he was driven by the matters at hand, "Well then, you need to leave your half to Jaycee . . . That girl loves you, Dad, and you cannot leave this earth without her knowing forever that you loved her too; the ranch is the only home she's ever known, so let's figure out how to bequeath her the part that you do own." His father stared at him again, and wrote:

> *"PROMISE ME YOU WILL HELP HER."*

Frank didn't know how to answer that, but he smiled at his father and told him, "I promise . . ." His father smiled too and gripped Frank's hand . . . Frank gripped back and placed his other hand upon it. Father and Son shared a long-overdue moment of common purpose, and both of them remained still, as together they were glad about providing for Jaycee.

It took a few minutes more for Frank to compose the language necessary to bequeath the entirety of Robert's property to his granddaughter, then checking that dates and signatures were in place, Frank returned to the admitting desk to find a notary, and to make copies of the documents.

## THE ROAD HOME

Soon after completing that business, he and Jaycee worked to prepare Frank's pickup for their return trip to Smith Creek: Pillows were arranged in the back seat of the crew cab, and two oxygen tanks (one attached to a nasal cannula, and one to a mask) were secured on the floorboard. Earlier, Logan and Cory Ebert had stocked the truck with sandwiches and drinks, before gathering final belongings from the room. They had been able to leave two hours prior, with Pat following close behind in the medical equipment van.

The Pharmacy dropped off home medications, and by then the day shift therapist, an impressive guy named Dave had already setup the bronchoscopy cart. A pretty RN, carrying several vials of injectable medicine, joined Dave beside the hospital bed. She was reassuring when she spoke to Robert, "This shouldn't take too long once we start."

❀ ❀ ❀

Dr. Holden suddenly appeared and sat beside his patient; he explained the procedure, and then he told Robert, "The rest is going to be up to you. We need you around to keep an eye on *this guy,*" as he nodded in the direction of Frank. Robert smiled . . . and sedation was given. The Pulmonologist then guided a bronchoscope through remote lung anatomy to remove an impressive collection of mucous . . . a consequence of Robert's pneumonia.

After the procedure, Dave deflated a small balloon which encircled the breathing tube, and then he withdrew it. He quickly placed oxygen on Robert's face, and then began removing equipment from the room. When oxygen levels were stabilized, and Robert emerged from sedation, Dave and Frank lifted him into a wheelchair at the bedside and studied his breathing while he sat there.

When Dr. Holden returned from the charting alcove, following his dictation of the procedure, he shared goodbyes with Frank and Jaycee, and then he shook Robert's hand. Finally he wished him, "All the best to you and the McClelland family . . . I know we need to get you on the road Sir, so I won't keep you any longer." When he and the RT said their goodbyes, only Jaycee, Frank and Robert remained. Waiting around for hospital discharge personnel, and the delivery of a patient satisfaction survey, proved not to be a relevant part of the family's plan, so the McClellands decided to take matters into their own hands: Frank instructed Jaycee, "Let's get your Grampa down to the truck . . ."

❁ ❁ ❁

Jaycee wheeled her grandfather out of the elevator, which had delivered them down to the patient loading area at ground level. Robert breathed strenuously during his efforts to climb up into the backseat, but that continued only until he was able to arrange himself comfortably amidst his pillows. He fired off a joke about Frank's clean 'San Francisco pickup,' while Jaycee adjusted air conditioning from the dashboard controls.

Frank then pulled away from the curb, and he began driving them in the direction of McClelland Ranch. . . .

# 28

## CONSIDERING FAMILY

Marion Bennett had played phone tag with her husband ever since her descent from Mt. Gorbeia. Bill's messages conveyed that his time was still being consumed in protracted Washington, D.C. meetings. Hoping to spare her from panic in some remote part of the world, he avoided details about Frank's father, saying only that he needed to share some "very urgent news."

Unaware of this, a kind of happy complacency had overtaken Marion since finding the site of the Cenarrusa home; the home which she confirmed had belonged to her ancestors. By now, she had compared her mother's photograph many times to the images captured on her digital SLR camera, and she felt secure in her belief that it was *all true*.

With a lifetime of questions finally answered, she decided upon a quick flight to San Sebastian for the purpose of meeting Amaia's parents. Their daughter, after all, had agreed to move from Northern Spain, for permanent employment in the United States. Perhaps parental fears about her decision might be allayed if Marion (in person) could describe for them Amaia's future with the Bennett Foundation.

Marion smiled to herself when she overheard Steve's nervous questions about what he should wear during this first introduction to Amaia's parents. So, after checking into a hotel which was close to Amaia's family home, the three travelers ventured out for a brief time to shop for a shirt and slacks for Steve. Despite finding themselves in the beautiful mid-morning light of San Sebastian, they returned early to their rooms to shower away the camping dust prior to their visit.

Given the surprise notification of their arrival, a time had been agreed upon for an afternoon gathering with Amaia's family, but Marion insisted that she would host the evening's dinner at her favorite restaurant. When Amaia was overheard in a phone conversation to be encountering resistance to that part of the plan, Marion coached her, "Please tell your Mother that we have been extended a reservation at Restaurante Arzak . . . I am a life-long friend of the owner, and he insisted upon preparing our meal tonight." It quickly became evident that the objections had ceased, when Amaia and her mother were heard giggling together about that destination . . .

❃ ❃ ❃

Amaia's parents were relaxed and jovial, and they did seem relieved to attach Marion's elegant face to their daughter's career decision. The evening's extraordinary dinner was beyond belief, and Amaia's parents were awestruck when Juan Mari Arzak personally appeared at their table to direct the service. All eyes in the room turned toward him when he delivered a flower to Marion, and then kissed her on both cheeks.

He then offered flowers to each of the other women in the party as well, including Amaia's younger sister, who beamed when he doted on her. Marion addressed him only as "Chef," and it was obvious that the two of them were old friends who adored one another. The graciousness that he extended at their table built upon the already lasting warm impressions which had grown throughout the day. Amaia's father and Steve hit it off from the instant they met, and all present were impressed to later hear them discuss the historical intricacies of San Sebastian's inclusion within the "Basque Autonomous Community."

❃ ❃ ❃

Marion would easily have agreed to stay another beautiful day there on the Bay of Biscay (as suggested by Amaia's parents), had she not finally received Bill's phone call. She answered his call in the parking lot of the restaurant just as they were leaving. The group stood and watched her transition from a glowing happiness into one which was clearly more somber.

She listened in silence for what seemed like a long time, and before ending her call, she coordinated the date of Bill's return to Belvedere Island with that of her own. She then apologized to Amaia and her parents and explained that her husband had just relayed the news that, "My Nephew's Father . . . my Brother-in-Law . . . has taken ill, and I must return home to help." She glanced at Steve and further clarified, "Frank told Bill that he was driving his father back to their ranch, but I'm afraid the doctors didn't give him hope that he would live much longer. I need to leave as soon as possible, and join them in Nevada."

❃ ❃ ❃

In spite of the urgency that weighed upon Marion, she was grateful the following morning to see Amaia and her family in person at the San Sebastian airport. It had been decided that Amaia would stay behind in Basque Country to vacate her apartment and organize her belongings prior to moving to California. Steve, who remembered the remote location of McClelland Ranch, decided to accompany Marion there (following a brief reunion with Bill at home) . . . Steve would then, as soon as possible, return for Amaia in San Sebastian, when she had completed her preparation for the move.

## DIVISION

Bill Bennett arrived home in Belvedere several hours before Marion, and he smiled when she and Steve appeared together in the kitchen—to Bill, his wife looked more radiant than ever, and he concluded that "mountain climbing in Spain" suited her. Marion wasted no time after their embrace, and quickly removed her camera from its travel case; she positioned it on the counter next to her old black and white photo and cued a sequence of digital images for comparison.

Turning to her husband she said, *"We found it, Bill!* . . . Come see." She pointed to the details of the home, particularly the porch, and then to the silhouette of the granite outcropping behind it. As she scrolled forward, she beamed, "I found my *family,* Darling . . . I found them *at last."* His eyes got wide when he recognized the cabin's porch, and he turned to Steve, "And, you *also* believe this to be true?" Steve nodded his "no doubt" agreement and added, "That's definitely it . . . I took most of those pictures."

❀ ❀ ❀

It was evident that Marion was still on task when she asked, "Have you heard from Frank?" Bill shook his head and regretted, "Nothing in three days . . . When he left for Austin, he reminded me that he would be beyond communication up there on the ranch. I think they are literally near the top of a mountain range. It's somewhere out in the middle of Nevada.

Marion focused on Bill's face, "You know that I *have* to leave right away to help them . . . I need to be there for my nephew, and now as I have just learned, for my brother-in-law as well." In the pause that followed, Steve interjected, "How do you feel about me grabbing that satellite phone from the boat, so we can leave it with Frank? He should probably keep it while he's in Nevada." Bill absently nodded "yes," but agreed, "That's a good idea . . ." Steve then quickly disappeared to begin his own trip preparations.

❀ ❀ ❀

Things were suddenly moving too fast for Bill, and he was taken aback; his face betrayed it, and his plea to Marion was careless, "I do understand your feelings of urgency Dear, but don't you think you may need to move more slowly with these assumptions about *family?*" Hearing him finish, Marion spun around to glare at him . . . She could not fathom the words that he had just chosen, and a lifetime of struggle returned to her once again, "There are no remaining questions about my family's existence! I have just proven that to the entire world! You are the only person left who doesn't believe me!"

She seethed at Bill through growing tears, "If you cast a shadow over what has happened here, by dredging up your tired litany of 'lost birth records' in Spain . . . I swear to God, I will walk out this door and I will never come back!" Bill was suddenly overtaken by the scale of his mistake, and he reached out to hold his wife's arms and to engage her eyes. He could not remember a time when he had hurt her more, and he finally was able to say, "I am *so* sorry, Darling. Please, just give me time to absorb this new reality. Your trips to Spain have given you the advantage of a head-start . . . that's all."

Marion steadied herself, and her rage finally began to dissipate while she searched her husband's face. At last she could talk again, "Has this all along had something to do with your money?" Bill down-played it immediately, "Marion . . . you know that we are giving the money away." She didn't hesitate, "I'm talking about losing control of the money somehow . . . control even, of how we spend it when we give it away. Is that what this is about? You're afraid Frank might steal that authority from you?"

She remained at a loss while she stared at him, "I have never understood why you fail to recognize how important this is to me, Bill . . . You don't have a family *either*, yet even after that horrible scare with your heart valve, it still hasn't occurred to you to try to find them! What does that say about the differences between you and I?" Bill tried to collect himself and he looked down before answering, "I have never tried to find my family, Marion, because I didn't want to know who they were."

"You have forgotten that there are a lot of unspeakable reasons why children become orphans." Marion leaned in closer to place her hand on his cheek, "All the more reason Darling, for you to celebrate with me that we at last have Frank; he is this beautiful and brilliant young man, who somehow traveled through darkness to find us. A financial savant even, who cherishes his time with you in your work. You have even taught him how to sail, Bill . . . Truthfully, if I had ever been able to give you a son, can you imagine him fitting the part any better than Frank . . . ?"

❋ ❋ ❋

Husband and wife stared at one another until Marion broke the silence, "He is a member of our family Bill, and you need to find a way to open yourself to that fact.

At the minimum, you need to get used to the idea that he is now the rightful heir to our estate. I am going to pack now for my trip to the ranch in Nevada, and I've just decided that I'm going to stay there for as long as necessary. I would love nothing more than to have you join us . . . but, please . . . before you come . . . decide if that is truly what you want."

## THE MCCLELLANDS

As Frank traveled east toward *Fallon* on *Hwy 50*, he was reminded of how desolate some parts of the Nevada landscape can be. This occurred to him while driving beside the "Forty Mile Desert," and he wondered how overwhelming the heat and alkaline soil must have seemed to the pioneers? They certainly would have needed to accept on faith that the Truckee River actually did exist, and that it was waiting for them somewhere up ahead.

That important destination near Wadsworth (then called Rags Town) had been promised to them as an oasis of water and shade—supplies could be replenished there, and the exhausted livestock might at last be able to recuperate. From this junction, wagon trains would then either continue west over Donner Pass or turn north onto The Applegate Trail toward Oregon.

❋ ❋ ❋

Frank angled his rearview mirror to better reflect the image of his sleeping father. He was relieved to still find him breathing without distress in the back seat, propped up as he was on a stack of pillows. Jaycee was asleep as well, beside him in the front seat, and with her head tilted slightly back, Frank was able to stare at her and marvel once more at her resemblance to his mother.

Beyond Fallon, he pushed on past Sand Mountain and eventually to Fault Road. Here, he remembered the happy routine his father had invented, when he and Robby returned home with him after long days in Fallon. Robert McClelland would always include his sons in the conspiracy, and tell them that this was the place where, "We need to let the horses run . . ." And, given the scarcity of remaining traffic beyond this landmark, he would step hard on the gas pedal, bringing to bear the full roar of a Ford truck's 460 cubic inch engine.

As he did this, he never failed to recruit the responsibility of his excited sons to tell him *exactly* when they reached the speed of one hundred miles per hour. The boys' eyes would remain glued to the speedometer, and reaching that target never failed to elicit raucous joy from both of them. In the surreal wonder of feeling that speed, they would marvel as the scenery flew past. Robert would eventually back off and say, "That's probably enough for today," but he would invariably settle on cruising speeds somewhere north of eighty five miles per hour for the remainder of the trip.

※ ※ ※

Frank found himself smiling when he remembered this, something that had probably been necessary to mitigate boredom (resented *loudly* by young sons), and he suddenly couldn't resist his own impulse to accelerate. Glancing again at his passengers, he gradually increased the pickup's cruising speed until he settled upon eighty-seven miles per hour; a place where the combined speed and stability felt better to him than what he remembered of those old "one-ton" livestock haulers from his past. That balance endured and, sooner than imagined, he found himself turning off Hwy 50 toward Carroll Summit, and he was thankful that his father had so far remained comfortable.

※ ※ ※

The dirt access road pointing them toward McClelland Ranch was rough in places that had been washed away during untold winters, but that was not unexpected—seeing the rusted hulk of their old D-7 Caterpillar (abandoned along the wayside), however, explained more about why the road was in disrepair. This access artery was supposed to be maintained by the ranch, and it would not smooth out fully until they joined the wider main road (maintained for fire suppression by the forrest service), northeast of this location.

Frank was surprised when a kind of breathlessness overtook him during the final few miles of travel toward his home. He hadn't anticipated the kind of hold on this moment that the ranch was now exerting. When Jaycee awoke beside him and spoke, he felt relief from his cascading worry, *"Wow!. . . We got here in a hurry."* His father coughed and straightened his posture, as he too was now awake; he looked out his window and smiled, "Somebody must have let the horses run . . .," and he grinned at Frank in the rearview mirror.

# 29

# HOMECOMING

On some level, Frank recognized every detail of his birthplace when he approached the substantial mountain home, but he didn't allow himself the indulgence of staring. Knowing that his father would have to negotiate the tall steps leading up to the covered porch, Frank steered as close to them as he could, beneath the log and rock-framed entrance.

He studied the two young Border Collies who were happily checking him out and announcing his arrival. As if Frank needed further assurance that he was home, the vanilla fragrance of Jeffery Pine-filled air was waiting for him; that would be accented by sage and mountain grasses, comingled with his mother's lilac bushes, and it overwhelmed him when he opened his door.

Something else, which might have been missed by visitors, was his true homecoming—an indelible overlay upon the atmosphere, delivered by way of the huge breezeway barn which stood forty yards beyond him. It was the ranching legacy of sweet forage, emanating from sacks of rolled-oats that stood beside a tall stack of alfalfa hay (cut and baled while flowering), which now spirited his deep intake of breath, and the measure of how much he had missed this place.

### THE EBERTS

When he turned toward the rear truck door to assist his father, Cory Ebert and his wife Shelly appeared together on the porch. While Frank was greeting the trusting young dogs, Cory descended the steps and moved directly toward the truck. Soon after this, Logan Ebert emerged from the barn and jogged toward them. He called out to Shelly, "Mom, can you grab the wheelchair? I put it just inside the living room." When she rolled it onto the porch, Logan was there to retrieve it and deliver it down to the truck.

The Eberts were an irresistible force—every kindness had been anticipated by them (no doubt owing to their years of practice), and a grateful Frank was left only to step aside and watch. Cory and his son locked the wheels of the chair next to Robert's door, and then transferred him into it from the truck. Jaycee and Frank lifted the wheelchair leg-rests, as Cory and Logan carefully pulled his father backward up the steps.

Frank didn't have time to reminisce about his home's interior, as he remained a part of the procession. He followed Logan and the wheelchair down the long hallway which led them to a back bedroom. A lifetime ago, it had belonged to his parents; now it was converted for Hospice Care, complete with medical devices surrounding a hospital bed in the center of the room. Robert was wheeled toward the bed past a tall patient lift, standing ready at one side of the room, along with various other supplies.

Cory switched on an oxygen concentrator near the head of the bed, and replaced Robert's nasal cannula with a longer version that was attached to the machine. When the old man found himself positioned upright in the hospital bed, he said, "Jesus Christ . . . this feels serious." Shelly Ebert welcomed her neighbor home, and she quickly pulled a bedside table closer to him. She then placed a carafe of ice water and a glass upon it.

When she switched on a portable suction device and handed the oral wand to Robert, she told him, "This is where you *spit* when you cough stuff up, and here's your *urinal.*" Robert looked at it and scowled, "Well, you can forget about *that*, Missy . . . The day that I can't piss standing up is the day I'm going to end it all! . . . I've got a perfectly good bathroom right over there, and I'll use it if you don't mind."

Shelly was unfazed, and she countered, "Suit yourself, Robert . . . but for now, in the interest of safety, let's use this walker until you get your strength back." Frank felt compelled to jump in, "Dad, don't make this more difficult than it has to be . . . You're the one who wanted to come home before you were ready, so how about trying to work with us here?" Shelly deferred, suggesting to Jaycee, "Let's go to the kitchen . . . I have an idea about supper. We also stocked some food for you, so I need to tell you about the casseroles in your freezer."

❊ ❊ ❊

The afternoon passed quickly, as Cory conveyed information about pulse-oximetry, and Frank organized the long list of medications; his father had fallen off to sleep soon after receiving the day's final doses. Dr. Holden had been concerned about Robert's resistant strain of pneumonia, and he was emphatic about wanting him to finish his last course of antibiotics; that concern was enough to place them at number one on the med list.

All things considered, it came as good news during dinner when Shelly revealed she had been contacted at home by a hospice nurse from Austin. The nurse indicated that the Ebert's phone number had been provided to her as a means of contacting the McClellands, and importantly, that she had just received the orders for Robert's care. She told Shelly that she would begin daily hospice visits, starting sometime tomorrow morning . . .

After the Eberts left for the night, Jaycee offered to make Frank a cup of tea, but he declined; he had hoped instead to find his father's whiskey. He frowned when he found a half-full bottle of Kessler, hidden near the back of a kitchen cupboard, and his disappointment was confirmed when he saw the $15.89 price tag still stuck to the large plastic jug. Reading the brand's slogan, "Smooth as Silk," he thought to himself, "Yeah, *right*". . . and then decided to mix it with a Coke.

❀ ❀ ❀

He and Jaycee were finally able to relax after settling deep into the living room couch. The dogs had curled up earlier on a nearby rug, and now, especially in the sparse lighting of the room, Frank found himself staring at the fireplace and hearth before him. He recalled the responsibilities involved in keeping fires burning here, which he and Robby shared while growing up; the fires his family burned morning and night, throughout so many winters.

The tall fireplace was built entirely of "river rock," except for a laminated Sugar Pine mantle that was varnished and grouted into place, then seated horizontally above the opening. Frank remembered feeling the confidence that this mantle inspired in him. Larger rocks had been chosen to "coin" the fireplace opening, and they now revealed blackened edges from years of exposure.

Tonight, even in the absence of a fire, this location remained his favorite part of the house. He remembered his Mom bringing hot chocolate here, especially when winter storms raged outside, and that never failed to make him feel safe. Dinner had been a relief at the end of a long day, and Frank commented to Jaycee that the Eberts never failed to amaze him. She too was grateful, and she added that Shelly and a group of her church friends had descended upon the house, bringing the food with them, and then they cleaned everything before changing all of the bedding.

He nodded when he thought about it, "Your grandfather used to say about them, 'You shall know them by the fruits of their labors' . . ." Jaycee turned to Frank in surprise, "Really? . . . Grandpa is not a religious person. Why would he think to say that?" Frank chuckled before explaining, "When he was a boy in school, there was a LDS girl in his class who had eyes for him. He told me that they flirted a little, but all of that ended when your grandmother moved to Fallon, and she was introduced one day to his class."

Frank grinned, "I think the LDS girl's name was 'Betty,' and she was *not amused* when your grandfather turned his affections toward the new girl. As if that wasn't enough, Betty rallied her girlfriends, and they began teasing your grandmother mercilessly whenever they caught her alone at school. Mom was raised to be a very staunch Catholic, but she just never forgot or forgave that treatment . . ." Jaycee couldn't resist, "It seems funny to hear you talk about Grandpa as a young man . . . falling in love." . . . Frank smiled, "Be that as it may, I have a lot of early memories where I heard Mom grumble in no uncertain terms about, *those Mormons!*"

"But, your Grandpa was raised alongside Cory's father, and they were life-long friends who helped each other for years on both ranches . . . Whenever Dad overheard your Grandma's comments, he felt the need to add a little perspective for Robby and me; he told us many times that we needed to consider all people, '. . . by their actions, and not their words.'"

❊ ❊ ❊

Frank awoke early the following morning, feeling glad that a power line had at last been extended fifteen miles up from the Reese River Valley. He switched on a bedroom light, and examined more closely the familiar surroundings of his old room. There was still a Wrangler jacket hanging in his closet. He grabbed it and remembered that it was from his teen years. When he placed it back, he noticed his old straw hat, complete with the hawk feather which had been featured in his dream.

A pair of scuffed old cowboy boots were there beneath the hat as well, and he wondered why any of these items had been kept? He then stepped over to the dresser, where he examined a framed picture of his family; the photograph had been taken when he was perhaps twelve years old, and he studied the smiles of each family member. Returning the photo, he suddenly remembered his promise to Marion, so he stepped out into the hallway and walked quietly in the direction of his father's bedroom.

Robert was asleep in his hospital bed, which had been adjusted upward, nearly to a sitting position. The pulse oximeter at bedside was attached to a finger, and it showed his oxygen saturation to be 91 percent. All appearances indicated that his father had slept without struggle, and Frank was relieved.

He then turned toward his mother's vanity and mirror, and he was startled to see her hairbrush there, still in its place atop a matching porcelain hand mirror. Seeing a few long strands of black hair overwhelmed him with an instant sadness, and he couldn't help touching the brush. Time passed before he could bring himself to open her bureau's lowest drawer, where he was again surprised to find silk scarves (worn years earlier), along with a delicate, mint green sweater with tiny crocheted flowers that Frank could not remember ever seeing; it was neatly folded where it rested next to her jewelry box.

Organized beside those items were three photo albums from different eras, each covered with distinguishing cloth material, and trimmed with lace ribbons around the borders. One by one, he lifted each cover and glanced at the photographs within. It was the third album which held his mother's oldest photographs, her childhood history of the Cenarrusa family.

❁ ❁ ❁

With coffee now perking behind him in a vintage Corning pot, Frank sat at the kitchen table and studied every black and white photo in the album: The pictures, which presumably had been taken somewhere in the mountains of Spain, were mostly of three young men with identical black hair; he knew somehow that these subjects were his grandfather and his younger uncles, even though the photos had been taken over a span of many years.

The young men were featured in a variety of locations: Standing near a rock wall behind an unknown house, posing during occasions with family and friends, together in various settings in an old European town, or enjoying a seascape. There was one picture (most likely of his grandfather) which particularly intrigued Frank, where the subject was standing amidst the vaguely familiar landscape of mountainous terrain. Frank did remember hearing his mother describe one of the photos of herself, somewhere during a later era, as she stood beside Grandma Grace (presumably her father's mother), and he stared at it for a long time.

Frank studied picture after picture, until he at last made his way through the entire album. Although he felt a renewed appreciation for his heritage, certainly beyond anything he remembered from his childhood, he closed the album and lamented his search. Nowhere in the album had he found anything resembling Marion's photograph of her Basque father, holding an infant girl.

### THE TASK AT HAND

He poured another cup of coffee and stepped outside onto the porch. The two Border Collies were waiting there, excited to join him, and they moved in close beside him to wiggle their cropped tails at maximum speed. Setting his cup down, he scooped them both up in his arms and hugged them hard to smooch their faces, recalling how he had always loved this special breed of cattle dogs.

Remembering it now, he regretted that dogs with this much energy were not truly suited for life in San Francisco. On this particular morning however, these dogs could not be more appreciative of where they were, or who they were with, and he felt the need to savor their friendship. With heightened purpose, they all jumped down together from the porch and moved as a team toward the barn.

❂ ❂ ❂

Frank rolled back the breezeway doors fully, to gather as much light as possible—this placed him in the middle of the barn's enormous entrance. He was now standing where trailer-loads of hay had, for years, been delivered and stacked high for storage. Rarely was there ever less than thirty tons of grass and alfalfa hay available here for the horses, as well as for any other livestock, kept in the corrals for ranch-observation. He assessed the wide expanse of wooden pallets to his left, empty on the floor and revealing only scattered remnants of alfalfa legume and flower.

Near the back of the pallets was one badly depleted stack of hay bales (probably amounting to less than a ton). Frank suddenly heard the movement and nickering of a single horse. The greeting had come from one of the two opposing rows of enclosed stalls, which framed the middle of the barn. He spoke to the dogs, "Sounds like we have company," and then he heard the abrupt sigh and heavy footsteps of a second horse. He flipped on lights for the stables and walked down the barn's long center aisle toward the horses; he was soon bordered on both sides by eight stalls respectively.

On the wall that separated them, hung various lead ropes and halters. Frank recognized the bridles and bits, which also hung there on hooks above some old grain buckets; they had been placed beside a grooming step and brush. The first horse looked out over the top of a Dutch door and studied Frank. This was the big thoroughbred that Jaycee had ridden in the dream. He remembered the day his father brought this mare home from a racetrack in California; she was a lot older now, but still clear-eyed, and Frank stepped forward to stroke her long forehead and muzzle.

A second horse then peered around the next stall opening and snorted at seeing a stranger. Frank approached this horse as well and reassured it with calm hands as he stroked her forehead and poll. The horse turned out to be a tall sorrel mare, and when Frank recalled that his father liked his horses tall ("so they can cover some ground"), he presumed that it was an "Appendix Quarter Horse" . . . He quickly gained the horse's confidence, before stealing a closer look at her teeth.

❂ ❂ ❂

On instinct, Frank continued past the remaining stalls and determined that they were empty on both sides of the aisle . . . He shook his head and thought, "So . . . we have a fifteen year old quarter horse, and a thoroughbred who's probably pushing twenty two . . . Let's hope that's not the entire remuda." He then opened the tackroom door at the far end of the stalls and turned on a light. Two rows of well-worn saddles and bridles were organized on sawhorses, and Frank glanced across them.

He loved the smell of this place; it was equal parts linseed oil and tack soap, along with a remote history of lathered horses; still a remnant from the old saddle blankets. The room had always been used to store grain sacks as well (affording protection from deer mice), and he grabbed a worn coffee can which rested atop one of the sacks. Scooping up two thirds of a can of rolled oats, he stepped out of the room and grabbed a wheelbarrow.

He returned to the haystack and broke off two healthy flakes of hay, before steering back toward the horses. They were grateful for their early morning departure from routine, and they dove into their hay and oats, which was split equally between them. Frank would have added a selenium supplement to their feed as well (Nevada hay lacks it), but all that remained of it in the tack room was an empty container.

After filling water troughs, he felt the need to search for any additional livestock. Wanting to inspect the outside corrals, he walked past familiar grooming stations at the far end of the barn. On his path to open those sliding doors, he saw a disabled Case tractor, complete with backhoe and a large bucket. The hood was lifted to reveal work that had been started to replace its battery. A distributer cap and spark-plug wires had also been left to rest atop the radiator housing.

When the rear barn doors rolled open, rays of sunlight streamed into the dark enclosure. Frank then retrieved his coffee and walked together with the busy dogs in the direction of the corrals.

❀ ❀ ❀

The outer corrals were empty too, and deathly quiet . . . He made his way through the deep central enclosure, still framed by railroad ties, past the crowding pens and squeeze-chutes and loading ramps. Here also there were no horses, or cows, or calves to be seen anywhere. He also searched holding pens located on the periphery of the main corrals, and all of them were empty as well.

When he finally peered over the fence in the outer-most corral to examine the pasture, his worst fears were realized—there was no evidence of green foliage anywhere (as far as he could see), save a tiny thread of riparian growth which followed the trickle of water from Smith Creek. It was exactly as he remembered it in his dream; all that remained was a neglected panorama of yellowed and dying tufts of grass, rapidly losing any sustainable foothold to the desert weeds amidst the Nevada sand and silt.

Frank stood in silence, and he squinted once more to be certain of the scale of the disaster. His eyes swept across it now, until the yellowed field disappeared below the eastern horizon. He lowered his head, and wrestled with the reality that he had just confirmed.

❀ ❀ ❀

Overwhelmed as he was, he might have tried harder to imagine some kind of solution, but the dogs began barking in the excitement of Jaycee's approach, and they ran toward her. She was dressed in her ranch clothes this morning, and she spoke when she stepped up beside him onto the bottom rung of the fence, "I saw that you fed the horses, so I figured you might be out here."

They turned and looked together at the field. Frank struggled to find his words, "The condition of this pasture leads me to believe that Dad has been sick for a lot longer than just this bout with pneumonia . . ." Jaycee became somber, "Yes . . . It's been on and off really, for more than two years, but even on days when he feels better, he gets out of breath if he tries to do anything. The doctor at the clinic in Austin told him he needs to wear oxygen at these high elevations, but he won't do it."

❀ ❀ ❀

Frank stared again at the trickle of water in the center of the field, "What happened to Smith Creek?" Jaycee sighed as she stared toward it, "Not this past winter, but the one before it was big . . . We had so much snow! When it melted in the spring, the reservoir flooded over and washed around the headgates that supply the irrigation ditches. That just emptied the reservoir, and now we don't have a way to back-up the water . . ."

Frank did the math, "So, with no pasture here, the cattle had to stay in the high country." Jaycee grimaced, "They've been up there for two seasons now, with nowhere else to move them. Thank God last winter was light, so the cows could at least search for food. But now they've eaten all the grass down to nothing, and they're trampling the springs up in the high canyons. Those are the only places left where they can still find water and forage. The Feds are not happy about it at all!, and to make matters worse, they've entered into an agreement with the Sierra Club out of Reno to study the Edwards Creek side of the range. They're looking at the part that it plays in sage hen habitat, and the cattle are running all over it now to find water."

### THE HOSPICE NURSE

Jaycee watched Frank, as the weight of these revelations fell upon him, "We have a stack of mail from the BLM that I can show you . . ." The two of them stood together in silence for a moment more, then spotted the dust plume from an approaching car . . . Jaycee spoke first, "That's probably the hospice nurse. Let's head back, and I'll make us some breakfast . . ."

❀ ❀ ❀

The nurse was rough around the edges, like so many of the people drawn to rural Nevada. Her eyes gave a hard-set first impression, but there was kindness somewhere beneath that; Frank realized that her eyes were careworn. She had worked for years as an oncology nurse in Reno, then moved to Austin with her husband, " . . . to get away from the city."

While Jaycee and Frank listened, she introduced herself to Robert and then briefly explained her services. He seemed to like her, and both of them thought that perhaps they had met somewhere before. When she asked to spend some time alone with him, " . . . to get to know Robert a little better," Frank and Jaycee excused themselves to the kitchen.

❃ ❃ ❃

After organizing breakfast ingredients prior to cooking, Jaycee retrieved a bundle of letters and manila envelopes beside the kitchen phone and gave them to Frank. Most of the mail was letter-sized, but more than one was large enough to hold legal-sized documents. The bundle turned out to be correspondence from the US Bureau of Land Management, and Frank began to study the collection from where he sat. He thumbed through the letters to determine their postmarked dates, and then organized everything so he could start from the beginning; the earliest letters had been received as far back as two years prior.

Those early letters had been sent by, "E. P. Crocker, Range Biologist for the Battle Mountain BLM District." The theme of the first letter, addressed to Robert McClelland, was cordial enough, and suggested, ". . . revised grazing methodology can be shared with you to optimize the unique resources of your allotment within the Desatoya Range." Subsequent letters had been sent after intervals of several weeks each, and they amounted to entreating reminders that a meeting regarding "conservation specifics" still had *not* been arranged.

They went on to establish that, "techniques can be shared with you to optimize the watershed properties (and responsibilities) for both Smith Creek, and Edwards Creek, in our joint effort to re-enhance and extend the viability of the forage for longer durations."

❃ ❃ ❃

The tone of the correspondence changed abruptly on May 1, 2007, when E.P Crocker confirmed that, ". . . the district has become aware that the rotation of cattle populations is no longer being facilitated at all, as legally required within the borders of your grazing allotment, with resultant damage to the perennial flora, as well as to area streambeds and watershed."

"Further, any continuation of these practices shall result in the reduction, or loss of your AUM (animal unit monthly) permitted grazing totals." The final document that Frank examined, had been sent just two weeks prior to his arrival at the ranch: It was a legal-sized "US Government Notification," informing "Owners of McClelland Ranch, et al.," that it was the intent of the BLM District, ". . . to suspend the operational grazing allotment indefinitely, pending remediation of current use violations." Frank noticed with some dread that E.P. Crocker had apparently been promoted, and signed this last document as, "Interim Range Supervisor."

❀ ❀ ❀

Jaycee's breakfast was impressive, and when she finished cooking, she dished out a plate for her grandfather. Frank put tinfoil over the English muffins that he toasted and buttered and left them near the covered skillets. Before eating, the two of them together delivered Robert's breakfast to his room.

Robert appeared to be enjoying his visit with the Nurse. He was wearing new pajamas and sitting up in a chair beside the bed, where it became evident that he had also shaved and combed his hair. When the Nurse saw Jaycee holding the breakfast plate, she pulled the bedside table closer to her patient.

Frank was surprised, "You look pretty good there, Dad! . . . This nice person must know what she's doing." Robert grumbled, "I just needed to get out of that *goddamn hospital!*" His Nurse laughed and said, *"Amen, Robert!* You and I both agree on that." She then reached for two cartons of Camel non-filtered cigarettes—which apparently she had confiscated and placed behind her on a shelf. She handed them to Frank and said, "What this old cowboy and I can't agree upon, however, is whether or not he needs to be smoking while he has oxygen running."

She clarified, "It's really up to him and his family whether or not he smokes, but it absolutely has to take place outside, with his oxygen turned off." Frank smiled and said, "I think we can manage that, huh Dad?" His father scowled hard at him after he watched Frank assume control of the cigarettes.

## THE BLM

The nurse declined breakfast when it was offered, so after delivering two cups of coffee to the room, Jaycee and Frank returned to the kitchen. The food tasted great, and they both agreed that Robert looked surprisingly better over these past two days. When they turned to the subject of the BLM letters, Frank went first, "Their involvement here doesn't sound good, Jaycee. You do know that, although we *own* the cattle, the BLM sets the rules for grazing within our permitted range . . . Did your grandfather ever try to meet with them during any of this?"

Jaycee frowned and shook her head, "No . . . Every time I tried to bring up the subject, he would go off on a rant about, "not needing any federal idiots out here counting cow farts!" Then, he would start from the beginning to tell me all over again about the Sagebrush Rebellion, and how he and his friends took on Bruce

Babbitt and Bill Clinton to prove once and for all that, "state's rights still exist here in Nevada . . ."

Frank knew all too well that Robert and his friends detested the fact that the federal government administers the use of resources upon forty three million acres of grazing lands in the state of Nevada. He nodded his head in understanding, "The problem with that is, like it or not, that once they find you to be in violation of their rules, they can shut you down and seize all your cattle. Based on my last look at the cattle futures market, my best guess is that you probably have more than one million dollars walking around out there. . . ."

❋ ❋ ❋

Robert was still napping when Frank pulled a chair in close beside the hospital bed—from that vantage, he sat quietly and watched his father breathe. When at last Robert awoke to see him sitting there, Frank joked, "Well, it appears that you continue to defy the laws of medicine." His father managed a grin, "You know what they say about not being able to kill an old cowboy. . . ." Frank smiled and asked, "Can I get you anything?" Robert smirked and was quick to answer, "Yeah. You can get me those last thirty years back." They both chuckled and stared at one another.

Frank had to start somewhere, "Jaycee showed me all those letters from the BLM . . ." His father turned his head to stare out through the bedroom window, "Those worthless bastards . . . as if ranchers haven't taken care of these mountains for over a hundred years. . . ."

## ASHAMED

It got quiet for a minute, but Frank continued, "You know they always win in these situations, Dad. . . . Why didn't you let me know you were *sick?*" Robert turned more directly toward his son, "What the *hell* could you have done? You live in *goddamn San Francisco!* . . ." Frank didn't flinch, and he asked again, "Seriously . . . why didn't you tell me you needed help?" Robert squinted at him now, "You left, and you never came back, Son . . . I figured I already had your answer."

Frank started to speak, but his father held up a hand to wave him off, *"Save it (!)* . . . We both know it wasn't your fault." Things got quiet again as the weight of this subject changed the contours of Robert's face. "After you left, I had some dark days . . . *years* really, up until Jaycee came to live with me . . . And, when I finally sorted everything out, I just felt . . . *ashamed* . . . You never deserved the way I treated you, so what right did I have to ask you for anything?"

Robert looked out the window again, "I thought back to when you were just a little boy, and I used to tell myself that your mother *coddled* you, and that it wasn't the way a man ought to be raised on a ranch. . . . I did eventually come to accept why she loved you so much. She believed from the moment you were born that you were *different*. She used to tell me that you were sensitive to the world around you, in ways that she had never seen before. But, in spite of that, I resented from those earliest memories that her love for you was being given at my expense . . ."

He sighed, *"Then . . . she got sick . . .* and she used to fall apart when we were alone; she got it into her head that you were going to be too young to lose a mother. That idea just *consumed her* really, and I watched her try every day to somehow make things better for you.

After she finally passed, I spent a lot of time being mad, and I came to believe that she had forgotten to say goodbye to me—this is the woman who I believed was a gift from God. I imagined back then, in those miserable years, that *you* had used up all of her time, and I resented you for it, Frank . . . I understand now that I was *weak* to even think like that; it didn't honor how much I loved your *mother . . .* or how much I loved *you . . ."*

❀ ❀ ❀

The two men sat in silence for a long time before Frank was at last able to speak, "Well Dad . . . I'm here *now . . . and I'm here to help*. I'm not going to leave until you and I make all of this right again. So, let's start with you telling me what we need to do to fix this ranch for Jaycee. . . . That feels like a good place to start."

# 30

## THE WAY HOME

Marion declined Steve's suggestion that she should fly to Fallon, and then drive the rest of the way with him in a rental car. She was enthused instead about the idea of ground travel, believing that she would gain a better perspective for Nevada and for the location of McClelland Ranch within it.

Given their late departure, they decided to break up the trip with an overnight stay in Sparks. This allowed them an early start the following morning, so they wouldn't risk being lost somewhere after nightfall. Steve knew that negotiating the final fifteen miles of backcountry south of the ranch would be difficult enough, even in daylight.

He had printed a good Navy topo map, which showed the boundaries of the Bravo 16 Flight Range, and he was able to identify the Forrest Service road that led up to Smith Creek. The two travelers had also planned well enough to not make the same mistake as Frank. Steve remembered that Nevada's mountainous terrain can turn chilly in August, especially in the evenings, so he and Marion stopped at 'R Supply' in Fallon to acquire more durable clothing.

Marion settled on jeans, flannel shirts, and a vest, and Steve found a Carhart jacket and boots, which he remembered were standard issue for Nevada ranchers—he thought to himself when Marion modeled her new attire, that he had never seen her this excited; "giddy" was the word that came to mind. So, after grabbing a sandwich and drinks for the road, they sped off again on the final leg of their journey.

❁ ❁ ❁

Along the way, Steve referenced his Navy map, which kept them on Hwy 50 until just before Austin; from there, they turned into the northern portion of the *Reese River Valley*. Marion was impressed to see the scale of the alfalfa farming in this remote part of the world. After traveling a short distance more, they spotted a forrest service sign which pointed them toward Smith Creek and McClelland Ranch. By mid-day, the black Suburban was climbing up the final miles of gravel road which would deliver them to the ranch.

The road ended when it at last narrowed through an open livestock gate between fences, and over the noisy metal railing of a cattle guard. From here, the entrance passed beside corrals and outbuildings to just beyond an impressive barn. In the absence of any signs identifying their location, they decided to park beside the substantial log home.

Marion somehow knew with certainty that this was McClelland Ranch. Stepping outside at last, she and Steve were greeted immediately by the dogs. Marion petted them, and then turned to admire the wide, sloping valley which was bordered on each side by ridges of healthy pine trees. After marveling at the vistas in every direction, she approached the stairs which pointed her up to the covered porch.

❁ ❁ ❁

When she was midway up the stairs, the front door swung open, and a beautiful young woman stepped out to meet her. Jaycee was startled to find an elegant woman with luminous white hair standing there, and she stared for a moment. For her part, Marion was not anticipating the presence of this young woman, much less that she would possess a strikingly-familiar bearing, so she stared as well.

Finally, Jaycee asked, "May I help you?" Marion began, "Hello. I'm Marion Bennett, and this is my friend Steve . . . We are looking for Frank McClelland. Does he happen to be here?" Jaycee was surprised, "I'm afraid you've missed him this morning. He's meeting a friend today at the Austin Airport, and they're going to fly over the Desatoya Mountains. Frank didn't say that he was expecting anyone today . . . May I ask how you know him?"

Marion was still excited to hear herself say the words, "I am Frank's aunt." Jaycee was jolted by this, and in her confusion, she was unable to speak. Marion felt compelled to explain, "I am related on the Cenarrusa side of the family . . . I am Angelina's sister." Silence now defined the space between them, and when Marion studied Jaycee's wide stare, she at last had to venture, "And . . . may I ask who you might be?"

Jaycee was finally able to deliver her words, "I am Frank's niece . . . Angelina Cenarrusa was my grandmother. . . ." Marion's hands flew up to cover her mouth, and she stared at Jaycee. Her eyes welled as she struggled to comprehend. Jaycee was now astonished too, and then worried when she saw that Marion was overcome with emotion. She reached out to steady her, but Marion stepped into the gesture and pulled Jaycee close.

Only when Jaycee's shock relented, was she able to hug back, and the two of them embraced for a long time. Finally, while studying Marion's face more closely, she offered, "Please, come in. I think you and I need to sit and talk for a while. I'll make some *tea* . . . Marion smiled, "That would be wonderful," and she glanced over her shoulder at Steve, who waved her forward, and she then followed Jaycee into the house.

## THE FLYOVER

Robert's plan (which grew more daunting by the minute) had been to bring the cattle down from their highest elevations of the Desatoyas before the onset of winter. The ranch would be required to somehow feed and water them in the lower valleys during the five months that would deliver them back to spring grazing. This required identifying at least two viable springs on both sides of the mountain range, and "perfecting" them with pumps and troughs, durable enough to keep water flowing for more than one thousand head of cattle . . . And, in ways that Frank couldn't yet envision, store a winter's-worth of hay somehow in those remote locations.

These tasks were onerous beyond his experience, especially considering that everything had to be completed in about three months' time. Accepting that mountain foliage was surely grazed-off, and late-season declines in rainfall (characteristic of the arid West) would only make matters worse, he dreaded the coming of winter. "What if it arrived early?" He was going to need help, and he had no idea where to find it.

Frank's dread escalated when he realized there was an entire set of other problems, which existed beyond the immediate needs of the cattle: Disking and replanting the pasture could possibly be hired out to some big hay grower from Eureka or Fallon, but what about the damaged reservoir spillway? Was there a cement contractor nearby who could repair the damage on a scale such as that? If not, Frank was certain that the project would fall upon him, and it would consume the time he needed to gather and relocate the cattle . . . time which, he knew too well, had already been pledged to the Bennett Foundation.

❀ ❀ ❀

Ticking-off each of these monumental tasks left Frank unable to even think about acquiring more horses for the ranch—much less finding enough wranglers to help with gathering a thousand head of cattle. He had been absent for nearly twenty years, and other than his friend Cory Ebert, his connections in this remote part of the world had disappeared long ago.

Increasingly panic-stricken, he realized that all of these tasks would require money (during the time when accounts were frozen during his divorce), and he was certain that it would have to come from somewhere else. Would local bank accounts for the ranch still be viable, so loans might be obtained? Knowing that steers and culled cows had not been sold in at least two years, he assumed the worst about his father's finances. Then lastly . . . What did the fucking BLM have up their sleeve?

## JOE DALES

As he boarded the vintage Cessna 150 beside a dirt runway in Austin, Frank was certain that simultaneous projects (this far-reaching) had never been required of his father, and he conceded his own submersion into hopelessness. . . .

❋ ❋ ❋

Joe Dales' handsome face and jaw spoke to foundations of the 1930's Hollywood era of *Tom Mix*, and he was now at the controls of the tiny Cessna when they lifted off. Today he was wearing a tight bandanna that was knotted around his neck and pulled off to one side. Frank suspected that Joe didn't much like removing his cowboy hat for any reason, but he did so today for the sake of donning an aviation headset.

Joe and Frank's father had been friends for many years, and after hearing of Robert's failing health, he was glad to help—fifteen years younger than Robert, they had team-roped together for years, and they were notable in their success. During that time, they had grown to respect and trust one another, and Joe knew the McClelland Ranch terrain as well as anyone.

So, as the plane slowly gained altitude above the Smith Creek Valley, Joe said, "Let's go see how the water is holding up at Twin Springs, and then over at Porter Springs as well. Your Dad used to pump from both places in dry summers." Joe smiled at Frank and asked him, "Did you find your old baseball pitch-counter? You're gonna need it today to count these scattered cows." Frank smiled, "Yep . . . it was still there next to my mitt."

Joe was happy to confirm that those two springs on the Smith Creek side of the range were still viable, so he powered his old Cessna into a higher climb. He planned to bank back around the northernmost peaks in a wide arcing turn, then fly more closely beside the western slope of the Desatoyas. Frank's pitch counter had already begun clicking rapidly when he spotted the first livestock; Joe continued to point down, "Looks like you have a pretty good bunch there in Billie Canyon . . . Probably water and forage still there along upper Smith Creek, from the winter before last."

He grinned at Frank, "I'm seeing a lot of long-eared calves down there, Frank! Bet they haven't been touched in a couple years. . . . I hope you can find some big ole' boys to help you flop them come branding time."

❋ ❋ ❋

Joe banked the Cessna over Hwy 50, which marked the northernmost border of the range permit, and then steered them back toward Edwards Creek Valley. He wanted to assess Cold Springs, which was located far below Edwards Creek, and then another spring at the base of Rock Creek Canyon. They were glad to see that both of those springs remained viable as well.

Just as Frank was beginning to feel a bit more confident, the plane delivered them directly above Topia Creek, where Joe Dales looked down and exclaimed, "Sweet Jesus! . . . Looks like we found your cows!" Frank stared in disbelief as he realized that he couldn't count all of the cows and calves, and a quick glance at the pitch counter told him that three digits on the device would not be sufficient today. Estimating as he scanned the entirety of the terrain around upper Edwards Creek, he understood that the cattle would now total hundreds more than the thousand cow allotment.

The bad news was yet to come, however, and Joe had to break it to Frank, "Looks like this bunch has found their way smack into the middle of the BLM's Desatoya Mountains Wilderness Study Area."

❊ ❊ ❊

Frank fell silent, and Joe was sympathetic when he glanced over at him—he could see that Frank understood that having to involve the BLM (in any kind of resolution) here, was a problem of epic proportions. Frank somehow kept his poker face however, and he asked Joe, "Would you mind if we circle up and over the top here, so I can have a look at the reservoir? I need to assess the damage to that spillway." As the Cessna crossed over the pass, which was exposed in more direct sunlight, a powerful thermal rocked the tiny plane . . . Frank reached for the nearest bulkhead, and Joe tried to soothe his aircraft, "Easy there girl . . . we got this."

The plane once again returned to more laminar airflow as it passed over the ridgetop, but Frank nervously joked, "How *old* did you say this plane is?" Joe was unfazed, "She's a 1973 . . . That was a very good year for Cessna." They glided down more easily now, on a course which took them right over the top of the reservoir, and Joe pointed to it, "Here we are . . ."

When Frank raised his binoculars, he realized that the wide metal gates of the spillway remained solidly intact. It had been the earthen levees, washed away on both edges of the spillway, that had emptied the reservoir. He was encouraged to think that it would be an easier task to build up those levees again (perhaps with rebar and road base), rather than the spillway itself. . . . He remembered the mines close-by, and he wondered if he might even be able to find someone who supplied Bentonite, and pour that as a foundation for the levees.

Frank made a mental note to ask his father about their old backhoe, and when he lowered his binoculars to turn and face forward again, he caught a glimpse of a black vehicle parked beside the ranch house—he asked Joe to circle back around again, to give him a better look at the house, and when he recognized the *Suburban* from this perspective, he managed a smile, "Looks like we have company." When the Cessna passed more directly over the top of the house, he could see Jaycee and Marion standing together below the porch, waving wildly.

❀ ❀ ❀

Feeling calmer now, sitting at the kitchen table, it still felt surreal to Marion to be watching her beautiful niece brew tea, "Of course, you have to be Robby's daughter . . . How is it that Frank didn't know about you?" Jaycee explained, and when she delivered their tea, she asked, "Why is it that Grandpa has never mentioned *you* . . . ?"

Marion began, "As with your story, it's really about timing; Frank and I only recently began to research our family connection. In fact, I just returned from the Basque Provinces of Spain with new information, and I drove straight here. During that trip, I was finally able to confirm my sister's birthplace, which proves that we share the same father. Frank doesn't yet know about this, so the purpose of my trip was to tell him what I discovered."

"I'm afraid it will come as a complete shock to your Grandfather as well. May I ask how he's doing? Frank's messages didn't leave us much hope. Jaycee seemed relieved to answer, "Better than we thought . . . In fact, he has been telling us that the hospital was 'trying to kill him,' and now that he's home, he's 'right as rain.' We're pretty sure, however, that he doesn't really understand how fragile his health is."

Marion studied Jaycee for a moment, and then decided to change the subject, "Let me get my bag from the car. I want to show you some pictures . . ." When Marion returned with her camera case, she began to share her digital images of Angelina's birthplace, as well as copies of the Aguirre and Cenarrusa family records. She at last produced the black and white photo of her father and her sister, and then added that Frank had promised to search his mother's albums in an attempt to find the same picture.

Jaycee studied the photograph and said, "I saw yesterday that he had been looking through one of Grandma's old albums, but he didn't say whether or not he found anything. I need to wake Grandpa soon to give him his medicines, and we can show him that picture. I'm sure he would want to know that you are here, so let's go introduce you now."

❀ ❀ ❀

Marion was standing beside the bed the moment Robert awoke, where he first turned his head in the direction of Jaycee's voice . . . He was groggy, but when his eyes opened more, he realized that someone else was standing beside the opposite bed rail. Turning to study the visitor, he froze . . ."*Angel? . . . Is that you?!*" In shock, his eyes teared-up and he reached over the rail to extend his hand . . . Marion clasped it between both of hers, and she smiled down at him.

Robert's brow furrowed, and he couldn't look away, "Did I . . . die? . . . I don't understand . . ." Marion too was overcome with emotion, "Hello Robert . . . My name is Marion . . . I'm Angelina's sister—I didn't mean to scare you; Frank told me that I look like your wife, and I can see now that it must be true . . ."

❁ ❁ ❁

Marion explained enough about her link to the Cenarrusa family and her recent travels to Spain, that Robert at last became oriented. When she offered to retrieve her camera bag to show him the photos from her recent trip, Robert insisted that they share them together at the kitchen table. He asked Jaycee to make some coffee, and then said he needed a minute to splash some water on his face.

To Jaycee's amazement, it wasn't long before her Grandfather appeared in the kitchen, wearing his ranch clothing and pushing a portable oxygen tank beside him. Once there, he sat down to join them. Marion couldn't resist for even another second, so she unzipped a side pocket on the camera bag and retrieved the old photograph that she had carried with her for so many years . . . She gave the photo to Robert and told him, "Frank said he would ask if you had ever seen this picture, but he apparently looked first in an old album and wasn't able to find it."

Robert smiled at her and explained, "Well . . . he wouldn't have found it in those albums, because it's framed and sitting in a cabinet back in our bedroom . . . It was Angelina's favorite." The truth was now so easily shared by Robert, that it ran counter to the struggle of Marion's life-long quest . . . Pointing, he said, "This is her Father, 'Ando' . . . holding her just after she was born."

❁ ❁ ❁

And just as easily, Marion was left speechless after hearing his confirmation. Jaycee, however, jumped up and moved quickly toward the back bedroom. Once there, she opened the antique curio, where she knew her grandmother's things were still being enshrined. She immediately recognized and retrieved the framed duplicate of Marion's picture . . .

## BILL

In all of the years that Bill and Marion had been together, their time spent apart was never long in duration. This was because they had not once during their times of separation, ever agreed upon an option for return travel which was indefinite. That was the way they both wanted it from their earliest moments together. So, two nights of being alone in their bed would have been hard enough for Bill . . . But certainly, it was the not knowing at all when his wife might return which now brought him heartache not to be endured.

He tried to go about his business, but he quickly became restless and distracted. Why had he never been able to support Marion in her dream of reconstructing a family around her? Her history was compelling enough for even their most casual friends to understand her quest. Why couldn't *he* understand it as well? He suddenly felt alone and empty, and he could only sit at the kitchen counter and stare into his coffee cup.

That's when the intercom buzzed from the entry gate. He recognized the voice of his mail lady, "Postal Service . . ." Bill answered back, "Good morning, what do you have for us today?" She was cheerful in her answer, "Just a bundle of mail that we held for you while you were away. Do you want me to leave it here in your parcel box?" Bill agreed and thanked her, then he stood up and moved out toward the gate.

❊ ❊ ❊

It was a very large stack of mail, gathered together and tied with a string, and Bill carried it back to the kitchen counter. After cutting the string, he separated the letters and began dealing them like a deck of cards onto designated themes of correspondence. He stopped abruptly when he came to the letterhead for Stanford Department of Medical Genetics. Bill then pushed everything else away, and sliced open the manila envelope.

After skimming over an introductory letter, he held up the second page. It was a laboratory results template which presented the Matrilineal Study Conclusions. In it, the clinical subjects were identified, along with a corresponding list of tests and the results which were obtained. At the bottom of the report, a concise written interpretation was presented.

Bill went straight to the specifics and read: 'Based on study of the mitochondrial DNA samples collected, we have confirmed with 99.9% certainty that the participants . . .' Bill stared at the lab findings . . . and then re-read them over again (enough times to galvanize his worsening guilt), until he at last buried his face into his uplifted hands and lamented through his own regret, "Jesus Christ, Billy boy! What have you been hoping to accomplish here?!"

❊ ❊ ❊

He lifted his head only when he could accept that he needed to act. He then immediately contacted Steve by way of the satellite phone, and they agreed upon a time to meet at the airport in Fallon. When he was certain about the logistics, he called Hank to arrange for a ride to the Corporate Jetway in San Francisco.

## FAMILY REIMAGINED

Robert was spell-bound as he listened to Marion explain the details of her search for the Cenarrusa home, and then her accounting of the family's eventual immigration by way of South America. Steve had by now joined the gathering, and his stories of Sasha and Guyta brought color to Marion's pictures of the family home.

Marion was amazed to hear Robert reveal that Ando and his brothers had been forced to "silence" the fascist sentries at their port of departure; where they had been guarding against expatriate escape out of "the harbors of Portugal." Robert told her that the three brothers were big men, who were hardened by their years of work in the quarries of Spain. Marion was then astonished to hear him recollect Ando describing Franco's guards as "cowards, who we squashed like bugs."

Robert was silent for a moment, after which he told Marion, "That's where Angelina got her strength, you know . . . from her Father." Marion was wistful now, "I only wish I could have known her." Robert nodded toward Jaycee and smiled, "Well, if you want to imagine her in her younger years, you just need to look at this pretty girl sitting here with us now . . . Sometimes I have to pinch myself when I see her . . ."

They had only begun to touch on the details of Angelina's arrival in Nevada, when Jaycee heard the approach of the Cessna's engine. . . . She said to Marion, "That's Frank! . . . Let's go wave at him!"

## HEALING

There is no stronger elixir for a man, than being near a woman whom he wants to impress. So it was with Frank's father, as Marion hovered nearby. In the time leading up to Bill's arrival at the ranch, Robert announced, "I'm done with staying in that bed during the daytime." When he stood, his shoulders grew broader and his chest puffed out more. Only Jaycee could convince him to wear his oxygen, but that lasted just until he learned how to silence the oximeter alarm, allowing for stealth travel through the house.

It didn't take long for the hospice nurse to conclude (at least for the time being), that her services weren't required. She gave her phone number to Marion and told her to call for any reason, day or night. Before she left, Marion hugged her. Genuine kindness is not lost on someone who also practices it.

❋ ❋ ❋

Frank had been stunned to return to the ranch house and find the framed photograph of his infant mother and his grandfather displayed on the kitchen table. Robert most of all, had been amazed to link his memories of Ando with real images of his Basque homestead in Northern Spain, and he began sharing those memories (for the first time) with his youngest son. Robert and Marion, for their parts, would spend many hours together while details of her sister's life were shared with Marion.

In an instant, Jaycee and Marion were thick as thieves. following tours around the home, as well as the self-contained bunkhouse, Marion took inventory of the available food. She was impressed with Shelly Ebert's gift of casseroles, but when Jaycee opened a hidden "deep-freeze," to show her the treasure trove of Angus beef (that only an old rancher can covet), the two of them selected two large packages of tenderloins and set them out for thawing. Aunt and niece then departed immediately to shop for additional grocery items in Austin.

❀ ❀ ❀

Dinner preparation that night was everything Frank already knew it would be, and he sat still, silently grinning at his father, who could only stare at the unfolding spectacle. Marion had somewhere acquired wine that was worth drinking, and glasses were being kept full. With Jaycee close beside her at the skillets, the kitchen was soon reborn with wonderous aromas and the noise of happy family.

This pathway to a family dinner had been lost to Robert for longer than he could even recall, and when he heard an eruption of joyous laughter between Jaycee and Marion, a wide smile broke free from his habitual control. . . . It was only then that he remembered his smile could be something which existed for its own sake.

❀ ❀ ❀

Everyone seated around the table that evening fell into an afterglow, as they savored their coffee and a delicious pie, left for them by the Eberts. Marion knew that her husband had contacted Steve on the satellite phone while she and Jaycee were shopping, so she asked him, "When are you planning to pick up Bill?" That discussion led Frank to move onto the broader topic of "the ranch." "I'm glad he's coming; he and I have a lot to discuss." Marion could feel that Frank was burdened, so she asked him to elaborate . . . He began, "Well, for starters, I have to tell him that I need to stay here at Smith Creek well into the foreseeable future."

"There is no way of getting around that, and I can't imagine how it will be possible to work with Bill from this remote location. Dad and Jaycee are going to need me here for more than a year to help put this cattle operation back in order." He smiled at his father and made an effort to add, "There's no regret in that Dad. People get sick is all . . . and it feels good to finally be back home."

Frank then elaborated on the problems that needed resolution before the coming of winter, and he let it be known that all of it was dependent upon the ranch prevailing in its conflict with the BLM, "I'm going to meet with them in Battle Mountain tomorrow, to see where we stand . . ." This also led him to explain to Marion the decisions made by him and his father to bequeath the ranch to Jaycee, and therefore, his responsibility to stay on to help her indefinitely.

❃ ❃ ❃

On this topic, Robert interrupted, "I think you might be getting ahead of yourself there, Son . . ." Frank was confused, and he turned toward him, "What do you mean?" Robert began, "I mean . . . you are not yet one of the owners. Marion and I now own this ranch, at least until I'm pushing up daisies. Sure, I have already made my decision to leave it to my granddaughter, but Marion's decision will be entirely up to her."

Marion was stunned by the revelation, and she stared at Robert, "I don't understand . . . ?" Robert asked Jaycee to retrieve a folder from his desk. When she returned and placed it before him, he emptied its contents. Among them was an ages-old business envelope—the kind that wove red thread into a figure eight pattern around two riveted discs. Inside the yellowed envelope were various old documents; among them deeds, water rights contracts and grazing allotments. There was even a peculiar looking mining claim with an old Elko County wax seal.

Robert unfolded the deed that he had been looking for and then studied it for a moment. He spun it around, and slid it across the table to Marion. In a matter-of-fact voice he began, "It's all there . . . Your father and my father put the deal together. With Ando's cash to pay off the mortgage, added to my future equity, he and I bought this ranch from my father in a fifty/fifty ownership agreement, as 'Tenants in Common.' That's how Ando wanted it, so Angelina's interests would always be protected . . . From the start, he provided that it would include 'survivorship' for all Cenarrusa descendants on his side of the family."

"He made it possible for my wife and I to own this place outright, and that was his idea of a 'dowry,' back in the day. . . ." Robert then shuffled through the other documents until he found the "Last Will and Testament of Andere Cenarrusa." He studied it, and passed that as well to Marion, "Read down a little, and you can see his instructions, which were written to pass ownership down to his family. That now puts you first on the list of his descendants, Marion."

# 31

## ELLE

Before leaving the next morning for the BLM district office in Battle Mountain, Frank asked Jaycee to contact Cory Ebert, "See if he can join us here this evening, sometime after dinner if that's possible? . . . Let him know that we're all going to sit down tonight and make some decisions about the ranch, and we could *really* use his advice . . ."

❁ ❁ ❁

The Mount Lewis Field Office of the BLM turned out to be an expansive one-story building, that housed multiple divisions of federal oversight for land use in Nevada. Frank found his way to the Nevada Rangeland Management and Grazing Office, where he checked in with a businesslike secretary, "Hi, I'm Frank McClelland . . . I have an appointment with E.P. Crocker." The secretary said, "She's running a bit late. Go ahead and take a seat in her office, there on your left." Frank was surprised, "E.P. Crocker is a woman?" The secretary didn't even blink, "That won't be a problem for you, will it?"

Realizing his mistake, he back peddled, "No . . . *Of course not.*" His smile was definitely *not* returned, so he quickly slipped away toward the office. Frank was immediately drawn to the framed diplomas and various certifications, which hung on the wall behind a well-organized desk. He stopped before two diplomas from the University of California at Berkley—both of them were in the field of Biology; the first degree being a bachelor of science in conservation and resource studies, and the second degree being a master of science in range management. They had been awarded to Ellsbeth Penelope Crocker.

❊ ❊ ❊

In retrospect, Frank wasn't sure why he acted so carelessly (for the second time) that day. He might have easily blamed his indoctrination as a college student, where the school rivalry between Stanford and CAL was legendary but, when he looked more closely at himself during damage control, he regretted that his words certainly had roots in the laziness of old prejudice. Just before he spoke, he had been thinking, "How can this woman possibly know anything about my family, or the history of our ranch?" It was then that he spoke out loud in a clearly dismissive tone, "Perfect . . . a Berkeley woman!"

❊ ❊ ❊

The immediate response from a young voice, which suddenly came from behind him, was not resentful or confrontational, "Which part of that upsets you the most? My *institute of higher learning*, or my *gender*?" Frank turned toward the voice, but instead of launching into a feeble attempt to defuse his remarks, he found himself dumbstruck, and staring back in silence at the beautiful and healthy woman who had just busted him.

Stillness hung there between them (the result of surprise on both sides), and it finally ended when the young woman asked him with more of an *edge* this time, "What are you doing back there anyway? You must be aware that people put visitor's chairs on the opposite side of their desks for a reason, right?" Frank now wanted more than anything to just start over, so he decided to take the closest chair and agree, "Certainly . . . I didn't mean to intrude."

He felt the tallish woman *(maybe 5 ft. 9 inches?)*, in her pressed BLM Uniform, brush past him on a direct path to take her seat behind the desk . . . After sizing him up further, she spun a pink office memo pad and examined it, "This says you are here on behalf of McClelland Ranch, so I will assume by your business attire that you are an attorney representing Robert McClelland, and that you are hoping to legally forestall the suspension of his grazing allotment."

She began to speak further, but Frank stopped her mid-sentence, *"No!* . . . I am not an Attorney . . . I am Robert McClelland's son Frank, but yes, I am here to speak with you about the grazing allotment—first though, how should I address you?" The young woman answered, "My friends call me 'Elle.' "

She then quickly regathered her wariness to continue, "But, let's not jump ahead and say that you and I are *friends* just yet . . . *Where the hell* were you during the *past two years,* when I tried to deal *reasonably* with your father?! . . . To this day, all I ever get out of him is angry backlash, where he likes to refer to me as 'Smokey the Bear,' or my personal favorite, a 'Piss-Fir Willey.' And in at least one of his letters, he informed me that he would be 'waiting for me with his Winchester Rifle' should I ever 'lay my hands on his cattle,' a stance that the Federal Government does *not* take lightly, by the way. . . ."

Frank shook his head, imagining how difficult his father must have been over the years, since falling under BLM jurisdiction, and he tried to reason, "I am truly sorry for that, but I'm sure you must understand the history of why these old ranchers don't like taking orders from the Federal Government . . . especially . . . excuse me . . . if word has gotten out that you are from Berkeley, California . . . You have to admit Elle, you are a long way from home."

❀ ❀ ❀

Suddenly, there was nothing to hold her back, "What does *any* of that have to do with following 'the letter of the law'?! . . . much less, the greater responsibility of being stewards for these magnificent tracts of land, that the ranchers don't actually own?!" Frank had to interrupt, "Woah . . . Woah! . . . You have to know the courts have upheld that those grazing allotments are appurtenant to the deeded ranch property, right?"

Seeing her green eyes flash steely, Frank knew that he didn't want to go down that road. "Look . . . Elle . . . I didn't come here to fight with you. I am actually here today to apologize for my Father. The truth is that he has been sick for a long time, and I'm embarrassed to admit to you that I only recently learned of it. What I was hoping to hear from you today is that it's not too late for McClelland Ranch. Do you believe that we have any recourse at all to avoid the suspension of our grazing allotment?"

❀ ❀ ❀

Elle was cooler now as she studied him, "At the *minimum*, your cattle need to come off that range as soon as possible. And, judging by the amount of damage that has already been done up there, they will need to *stay off* of it until at least the middle of next year."

She continued, "I don't know if you are aware, but we have entered into an agreement with the Sierra Club regarding the riparian ecosystem that surrounds the Edwards Creek headwaters. Damage done by your cattle in that area needs to be reversed, and achieving it will be no easy task. Oversight for that has fallen upon *me*, by the way . . . and based upon what I have seen so far . . . I can't allow your cattle back into that area *at all* until remedies are in place."

Still fired-up, Elle looked him up and down before speaking further, "And, are *you* somehow going to be involved in setting things right on that allotment? . . . because . . . let's be honest here, you don't really look the part." Frank became defensive, "What's *that* supposed mean?!"—she was having fun now. "Well, let's start with your ridiculous shoes: I'm pretty sure that you didn't buy those in Austin, Nevada . . . You know, you were a little too smug when you lectured me about being 'a long way from home' . . . so, while we're on the subject . . . where the *hell* are *you from?!*"

❊ ❊ ❊

During his return trip, Frank felt fortunate that Elle had reluctantly agreed to issue an abeyance which would temporarily halt the BLM's suspension of their grazing allotment. It would be strictly conditioned upon compliance by the ranch in all the matters which she had defined during the meeting. Particularly, she stressed the unacceptability of any further damage to the riparian borders of upper Edwards Creek.

Her final caveat had been that *she alone* would design and supervise the installation of fencing around the headwaters of Edwards Creek, and approve (or disapprove) the restoration of vegetation in that riparian area . . . "before allowing the return of cattle for grazing by June 15th of the following year."

Relieved though he may have been, Frank felt a weariness following the long meeting, especially when he imagined his father's future participation. Had his father been present today (and able to keep his mouth shut), he might have concluded, "You had your hands full with that one." Nonetheless, Frank found himself still thinking about the pretty BLM Administrator, who turned out to be as worthy an opponent as he could ever remember facing.

❊ ❊ ❊

He eventually looked forward to a few days hence, when Elle planned to hand deliver the new BLM abeyance and collect signatures. She had quipped that it would be her first "ground visit" to the ranch house, and she sincerely hoped that your father's Winchester Rifle won't be around. He found himself smiling at her merciless ridicule of his shoes, but he had already conceded to himself that she had been absolutely justified to point them out. Prompted by that, he detoured into the city of Austin to update his inventory of Wranglers, and to buy some new Roper Boots . . .

## THE COUNCIL

Bill and Steve had arrived at the ranch by midday. Following introductions all around, and Bill's stunned affirmation that Marion's niece bore a striking resemblance to her, he seized an early opportunity to sneak away with his wife. As soon as possible, he found a private location where he could pull her close and kiss her like she had been missed. He then spoke with deep regret, "My love, I was such an ass . . . and finding myself without you has been the worst nightmare of my life." He then retrieved the laboratory report from his shirt pocket and gave her the positive genetic testing results.

"How could I not have been happy for you, that your search for family was at long last successful—*I am so, so sorry*. Will you please let me try to make it up to you?"

Marion smiled up at him and pulled him tighter. She then teased, "Just hold that thought for a very long time. . . ."

❀ ❀ ❀

Returning to the ranch in the late afternoon, Frank smiled at the surreal gathering of his family on the front porch—a family which was undeniably growing in size. His father was as animated as Frank could ever remember seeing him, while he appeared to be collaborating with Bill. Jaycee, Marion, and Steve (all attentive) were leaning in as well.

Bill was the first to stand after spotting Frank. With Marion right behind him, they merged together to greet Frank at his truck. Bill surprised Frank by lifting him off the ground with a bear-hug, and he was smiling broadly. "I'm glad to find that you don't look any worse for wear, all things considered, even though I am told that you have your work cut out for you here." Marion eagerly followed-up, "How was your visit with the BLM?" Frank managed a sigh of relief, "Well, for the time being, it looks like we may have dodged a bullet."

Marion seemed relieved to hear it, and then she steered him away, "We wanted to catch you to discuss your plans before you sit down with everyone. Bill and I both agree that it is truly remarkable for your father to have been able to hold onto this place at all, given the tragedy that befell him. You have to know Frank, that had I been involved here after my sister's passing, things would now be very different for all of us."

She put an arm around Frank and then Bill, and pulled them into a huddle, "Through some miracle, I suddenly find myself to be a part of my sister's life and legacy—however many years late to the game—and I want to make up for lost time. How would you gentlemen feel about banding together to save this ranch? . . . She grinned at them, "You have to know what I mean is that we should go big to accomplish it." Frank glanced at Bill (who smirked at him), "My advice to you Frank, is to just say, "Yes, Ma'am . . .""

Marion grinned, "Of course it will all go to benefit Jaycee someday, but I am only now realizing that this is the first family home I have ever had. I want to stay and help you Frank, and that will certainly include anything you need to make your plan work." Bill quickly added, "That being said, I have also realized that if I ever want to see my wife again, I will need to spend a lot more time in Nevada . . . emergency trips to Washington D.C. notwithstanding."

"Your father and I talked, and he has agreed to let me build a little addition onto your bunkhouse. Let's just call it an 'information center' here on your mountaintop, where you and I can remain in touch with the world, particularly so with our heightening responsibilities during the impending collapse of world financial markets. If you don't object Frank, I would also like to make that construction project a part of your plans . . ."

## A FAMILY INSPIRED

A palpable enthusiasm grew around the kitchen table that evening, as the energy imparted by Marion and Frank infused everyone in attendance. Joe Dales had been a late addition to the gathering, after Frank anticipated that his knowledge of springs and aquifers in the Desatoya Mountains would be invaluable. His authentic cowboy appearance and charm very much impressed the Bay Area Bennetts.

Shortly after his introductions, loud and happy greetings could be heard from the front porch, with the arrival of the Eberts. When he heard the commotion, Bill asked Frank's father, "Who's that?" Robert deadpanned, "That would be the Mormons." Bill's confusion lasted only seconds more, as Logan and Shelly and Cory steered directly into the kitchen with a huge tray of chocolate chip cookies, and two gallon jugs of milk. In retrospect, this proved to be the start of a lasting friendship between Marion and Shelly.

❀ ❀ ❀

The meeting's agenda became clear when Frank introduced Marion to the newcomers and she shared her intentions early on. The Eberts, especially, were stunned to learn of her Basque heritage which connected her to the Cenarrusa family, and to her sister, Angelina, directly. "My hope in being here is to make up for fifty years of lost time and return this ranch to a level of operation that is worthy of its history." When she thanked her "new partner" Robert for allowing her such as opportunity, he fired-off a favorite qui*p*, "I *warned* her that the best way 'to make a small fortune in ranching', is to start with a 'large fortune.' . . ."

❀ ❀ ❀

Marion's preface to the meeting led her to ask everyone for advice . . . "imagining the best possible restoration here at McClelland Ranch." During the course of those answers, help was volunteered, and many decisions were made. Frank (employing his father's supervision) would start immediately to repair the breeched levees at the reservoir spillway. Cory Ebert would arrange for "land-levelers" (from nearby Eureka) to float and replant the pasture. Steve, reminding everyone of his dairy connections in Minnesota, volunteered to oversee the installation of four covered hay structures, at valley locations beneath the Desatoyas; the sites for those metal structures would be determined by Joe Dales, depending on his choices for water tank locations.

Frank's father worried in the midst of planning, that storing hay so far away from the ranch would present new problems, "We're gonna need to transport it, and we'll need a truck to do that—one with a flatbed trailer and a piggyback forklift.

Jaycee looked at Logan Ebert and smiled, "Logan just got his Commercial Driver's License . . . so, if it might be something that he and his parents would agree to, McClelland Ranch could hire him to deliver and stack our hay this season . . . at least until we can put cattle back on the pasture again."

Logan was excited when he looked back at Jaycee, "That works for me! . . . and something else that you might want to consider . . . A commercial livestock trailer would make it possible for us to bring cows and calves back here to the home corrals. There's a lot of doctoring and branding to catch up on, and doing it here will be much easier, before we turn them loose again on the mountain." Robert liked the idea, and Marion smiled when she caught the affectionate glances between Jaycee and Logan.

## THE BUCKEROOS

After addressing those bigger problems, Frank found that he could at last breathe a sigh of relief, "That really just leaves us with finding some new horses, and the wranglers to ride them . . ." Marion sat up straight and raised her hand, "Sign this cowgirl up!" Everybody chuckled, except Bill, who suddenly looked nervous. When his wife noticed, she informed him, "I didn't come all this way to not have my own horse."

Frank tried not to grin, "Okay . . . together with Jaycee and Steve and myself (after we finish our projects) . . . that leaves us with four riders. Steve quickly added, "I talked to Amaia today—she is ready to come back from Basque Country, and I remember her telling me that she rode horses in dressage events while she was growing up. Let's assume that will make five of us." Frank nodded his head, "Great! Now we just need to find some horses . . . any ideas?"

Robert, Joe and Cory generally agreed that the quality of horses found at local auction houses would not measure up to the rigors of a mountain range the size of the Desatoyas. Frank suggested, "What about the Van Norman horses up in Elko?" His father smiled broadly when he remembered Frank's boyhood fascination with the roan horses from that ranch, "That is a *great* idea!" Frank then surmised, "We might start with two that have a little age on them—we do have beginner riders included, so let's find a couple of 'bullet-proof' horses to start with; you know . . . not resentful, but not dead either." Marion laughed at this. "Then, five or six more with some life in them . . . they all need to have experience on cattle. We can impress upon the Van Normans that these horses also need to be tall enough to cover some ground . . . two hundred sixty thousand acres, to be specific."

## DREAMS INTERSECT

Driving home with his father the next day, after their trip for tractor parts at the Austin NAPA store, brought an avalanche of memories back to Frank. Seeing his father smile in the sun today, as he rested his elbow outside the open truck window, was special beyond Frank's recollection. Color had returned to Robert's face during his recuperation, and he had certainly benefitted as well from the excitement of recruiting help for the ranch.

He suddenly spoke to Frank, "I have been at a loss about Marion . . . How in the world did you find her after all these years? Your *Mother* didn't even know she existed!" Frank shook his head and grinned, "I don't think you would believe me if I told you." Robert pressed further, *"Try me . . ."* So Frank began, "I have thought about this a lot, and I have come to believe that it was Mom who led me to her. . . . That sounds crazy, I know, but she has been coming to me in my dreams for a long time now . . . for years, actually."

"Finally, it was Marion who connected all the dots—she had literally been searching for her sister all of her life. She now *also* believes that it was *Mom* who put us together." Robert stared in amazement at his son, "Your Mother comes to you in your dreams?" Frank nodded his head, and is father soberly admitted, "She comes to me in my dreams too" This was beyond what Frank was prepared to hear, so he steered the truck over to the side of the road and stopped.

The two men stared at each other for a moment, and Frank saw in his father a new humility that he didn't recognize. Robert continued, "She told me that Jaycee was coming to me. In that dream, Angelina was standing on our front porch, holding a little girl's hand. Your Mom was smiling the most beautiful smile . . . It wasn't until Jaycee showed up here a few weeks later, that I realized she was the same little girl from the dream." Frank was stunned . . . "Mom let me know about Jaycee too. These revelations put Frank and Robert on a path of closeness that would last through the remainder of their time together.

### ALL HANDS ON DECK

On the day that *Elle Crocker* arrived at the ranch to obtain signatures for the abeyance, Frank was in the barn, re-shoeing horses. The noise from his Farrier's furnace was loud enough that he didn't hear her arrive in the BLM truck. When Elle heard the clanging of hammer-to-shoe upon a huge anvil, she headed toward the barn. She had not expected to find Frank there, much less to see him transformed entirely in his western clothes.

He was bent over (facing away from her), leaning against the black thoroughbred mare, who had lifted her hoof into the loop of a halter rope. Frank was expertly nailing a newly-fitted shoe onto the animal's hoof, as Elle approached him from behind. She soon realized that, in his Wranglers and boots, he was taller than she remembered. He was also wearing an old fringed-leather Farrier's chaps, slick after years of use. His tee-shirt, and his triceps in particular, were wet with the sweat and dirt from a morning of strenuous work.

She stopped to watch him and tried to reconcile this formidable man now standing before her, with her memory of the man she had ridiculed in her office. Just when she realized that she was staring at him, Marion Bennett's voice startled her, "Have you found what you're looking for?" Elle blushed, and Marion grinned upon witnessing it, "Is this Frank McClelland?" she asked. Marion answered, "Yes." She was wearing one of her sister's western hats and a bandana today, and she motioned back toward the barn doors. She smiled and added, "It looks like he's almost finished. . . . Let's wait for him inside the house."

The two women had just started walking toward the covered porch, when Elle broke the silence, "I don't know whether Frank mentioned it, but I have drafted a BLM abeyance, which requires some signatures." Marion was gracious, "He did tell us that, and thank you so much, by the way. But it won't require his signature on the document; his father and I are now the legal owners of McClelland Ranch." Elle was confused, "I wasn't aware of that . . ." Marion explained, "The ranch is now held jointly by Frank's father and myself. I am the senior-most descendant of the Cenarrusa family; Frank's mother was my sister."

❊ ❊ ❊

Marion said, "Come in. I'll make us a pot of coffee. Oh, by the way, Robert McClelland is also inside, but don't worry; Frank and I put the fear of God in him to behave during our signing. I think he finally agrees that you might actually be trying to help us here." Elle snickered and followed Marion into the house. Jaycee stood up to greet her beside the kitchen table, and Elle met the pretty young woman. Robert scrutinized the visitor's BLM uniform and cap, but he did manage to extend a smile when he gestured toward a nearby chair.

By the time Frank finished his work with the horses and he walked into the kitchen, Elle had already obtained her signatures. Marion was excited beyond memory to have signed her name for the *first time* as, "Marion Cenarrusa-Bennett." Frank was excited to see Elle, and he found himself grinning at her. She returned her own disarmed smile, with an enthusiasm that surprised them both. He nodded toward his father and kidded, "Did this cantankerous old coot keep his Winchester out of the proceedings?" Everyone except Robert laughed, but even he was able to smirk at the running joke.

❊ ❊ ❊

While Frank washed his hands and forearms at the kitchen sink, Jaycee beamed and shared the news with him, "Elle has offered to help us move cattle off the mountain, once the fences are up and Steve has finished the hay storage sites. He ordered the construction materials for those structures today, and then he left with Bill for Fallon. He's leaving from there to bring Amaia back from Spain" Jaycee beamed at Elle, "There's going to be a lot of cowgirls here on this Nevada cattle ranch."

Frank was surprised, and he looked back at Elle, "The BLM is okay with this?" She shrugged, " 'Rangeland' is now my division, and given your late start here, I thought it might be a good idea to get the cattle moving as soon as possible. Even 'Grumpy' over there agreed to it (nodding toward Robert). . . . Robert grinned, "Winter comes early up here; it didn't make sense to turn down help . . . and somewhere, Jaycee . . . your Grandma is smiling about this 'cowgirl crew' of yours." Elle grinned too and turned to Frank, "I was thinking . . . in the meantime . . . you and I should go figure out what to do about protecting upper Edwards Creek."

## THE NAVY

The meeting was suddenly interrupted by the approaching noise of a low-flying helicopter; it soon became clear that it was on course to land close to the ranch house. All who gathered on the front porch to watch the landing were in awe of the powerful Sikorsky MH-60S, the US Navy "Knighthawk" aircraft. Frank stood riveted, as the helicopter powered down and two passengers then exited through a side door. When he realized it was Bill Bennett and a Navy Officer who were approaching the ranch house, he had no choice but to head toward them from the porch.

Bill motioned for Frank to join them, when he and the Officer got closer to the porch. Meeting half-way, Bill stopped to introduce them, "Frank, I'd like you to meet Rear Admiral Nathan Reid of the US Navy. He is Commanding Officer of 'The Strike Warfare Center' at NAS Fallon." Frank enthusiastically shook hands with the man who was staring intently at him. The Officer wasted no time in leading the conversation, "When I realized that Bill needed a ride home today, I thought it might be a good opportunity to make your acquaintance. He and my old friend Steve have told me a lot of impressive things about you, Frank. . . . I'm glad to finally meet you."

Bill explained further, "When Admiral Reid learned of your advisement to myself and other members of the Working Committee—and more recently, of our plans to build an 'information center' here at the ranch—he indicated that the Navy would like to be a part of it." Admiral Reid quickly clarified, "With your consent of course. . . ." Bill continued, "Suffice it to say, the 'Defense Intelligence Agency' (DIA) oversees all threats to the United States . . . including those involving our economic stability, and they have recently ratcheted-up their scrutiny of current risks to the 'world monetary supply.' "

Admiral Reid then offered, "One of our crewmembers today is the Engineer in charge of Infrastructure at the base. Would you mind if I ask him to join us at the site where you and Bill plan to build the information center?" Frank was surprised, but answered, "Not at all . . . and we should probably include my Father, who will be a lot better than me at answering questions about that old building."

※ ※ ※

From the covered porch, Elle began to study the vaguely familiar man who was coordinating discussions between Frank and the Navy Officer. She was more confused than ever in her shape-shifting impressions about Frank, especially when Marion stood next to her and spoke, *"Good . . . it looks like my husband has recruited the Navy's help in building our little addition here at the ranch."* She then looked at Elle and realized, "I can see by your expression that I should probably share a few more details about my nephew . . . let's go back inside for a minute."

# 32

# A PURPOSEFUL LIFE

Frank's father would come to believe that his high point during the restoration of McClelland Ranch had been the rebuilding of the reservoir spillway, which he and his son had completed while working together. Bending rebar into foundation footings with the aid of the Farrier's furnace had been ingenious, and then the pouring of a Bentonite foundation around that framework had been Robert's first real look inside his son's mining expertise. In so doing, Frank also remembered once more how validated he had always felt when he was being genuinely useful in his father's work.

After multiple truckloads of crushed rock arrived to be poured atop their foundation, father and son both knew that their hard work had been successful. They then together marveled to at last watch Smith Creek fill up the reservoir . . .

❊ ❊ ❊

Soon thereafter, following Bill's return to D.C. (to prepare for the bankruptcy of Lehman Brothers), Frank had been surprised one morning to see his father driving the tractor toward the rear barn doors. Once inside the entryway, he lowered the tractor bucket and directed Frank toward a blue tarp, which covered something leaning against the wall. Frank knew that his father wanted him to load the object, but he did not expect to find a motorcycle beneath that tarp.

He turned to face his father and found only that their expressions matched completely in their degrees of profound sadness. There was no judgement or accusation from either of them that day, when Robert at last curled his finger to signal for

Frank to load the bike into the bucket. That task completed, he then motioned for Frank to climb up inside the cab.

### LAYING IT TO REST

Without speaking, Robert drove them to the gravel road which exited the ranch, and then he pointed the tractor east. The long interval of silence was difficult for Frank, and he fumbled to begin his long-imagined apology about the day of the accident—his father quickly dispelled his son's efforts. He was thoughtful now, "Jaycee's mother told her every detail of the day that Robby died, and my granddaughter eventually shared it all with me . . . Please, Frank, don't take the blame for what your brother did to himself."

❃ ❃ ❃

After traveling about a mile more, Robert veered off the ranch road and pointed the tractor up a gradual slope to a plateau that stood perhaps a hundred yards off the road. He then reversed course to position the tractor over the center of his chosen site. His plan became clear, "I'll get on the backhoe . . . You push that motorcycle around to me."

The Case backhoe quickly dug a hole that was big enough to dispose of the rusted and still-mangled motorcycle. It easily dropped into the pit, and Robert then circled the tractor to backfill and tamp the burial site. When finished, he and Frank could only stand silently, side by side, while they stared together at the ground beneath them.

### FRANK AND ELLE

Frank had been surprised on the day that he was scheduled to meet Elle for their inspection of upper Edwards Creek. She arrived in her BLM truck, pulling a small, but sturdy horse trailer that was painted and placarded to match US Government regulations. Frank stepped down from the porch in time to watch her expertly unload a big chestnut gelding (already saddled), and then secure him to the nearby fence.

Frank was impressed, "That's a nice looking horse you have there." Elle smiled as she patted her horse on the neck, "This is 'Fancy'. I bought him at an auction in Reno. He had a history of mountain trail experience, and that has helped us a lot. We work well together on the job, and he has gotten us through some pretty tight spots."

❃ ❃ ❃

The two riders soon traveled together past the reservoir and up beside the aspen grove, until they reached the still-defined Pony Express trail (which pointed them west). Frank was riding his father's appendix quarter horse now, and the mare was comfortable being in close proximity to Fancy. Riding side by side, Elle impressed Frank when she began to speak about the geologic history of the Desatoya Range, "The Desatoyas were formed during the volcanic activity of the Miocene Epoch . . . We might have seen Saber-toothed Tigers back then. That was near the beginning of a very long era of biodiversity in these mountains . . ."

Frank was suddenly wary, "Oh . . . Now I get it! Up until the time that cattle ruined everything! Is that about right, Ms. Berkley?!" Elle grinned at him, "Listen to you! . . . Defensive much?! . . . No! . . . I was just about to tell you that this area's history of biodiversity now includes twelve million years of ruminating animals living here in a symbiotic relationship with the mountains; those cattle hoof imprints are a necessary part of maintaining the permeability of 'capped soils' in these arid landscapes across the west . . . and that promotes the growth of natural vegetation; in your case: 'cheat grass.'"

❁ ❁ ❁

The grins that they now directed at each other were wide and mischievous. Elle made a face and she stuck out her tongue at Frank, and he laughed back at her. It was within this spirit of shared grins that they more-closely traversed the western slope of the mountainside. When they reached the downstream flows of *Edwards Creek,* they turned beside it to climb up toward the headwaters.

The higher they climbed, the more the terrain revealed itself to be a long, narrow valley of closely shorn, green grass; cows and calves began to appear in increasing numbers, and it was obvious that they were staying close beside the water. Elle speculated, "Somewhere above this elevation, the Sierra Club has asked us to build a fence that frames in the headwaters on both sides of Edwards Creek." Frank replied, "As long as the cattle can still reach these lower stream flows, it shouldn't be a problem."

He was less sanguine when he and Elle crested a plateau to discover a hundred or more Angus cattle crowded around water that was bubbling up in the middle of a muddy pool. Surrounding the pool, cattle were slogging through a wet border of black mud and flattened vegetation; a few of them jumped away when they were surprised by the riders.

❁ ❁ ❁

Frank immediately realized the extent to which Elle had been right about the damage done here. He said to her, "Let's see if we can push these cows out of here . . . maybe we can move them a couple hundred yards downhill; keeping them close to the stream will be important." He then circled his horse wide behind the pool of water and instructed Elle, "Help me try to frame them in on your side . . . If we can bunch them up in the middle, maybe the others will follow us downhill . . ."

Elle and Fancy stayed wide of the cattle, moving slowly back and forth to keep stragglers bunched up. As Elle did this, she was also watching Frank on his horse, *cutting back and forth* adeptly behind the central group of cattle, until they all began to move in unison downhill. Watching his horse flatten her ears, and crouch low to intimidate potential escapees, was an exercise in horsemanship that Elle had not been prepared to witness. So, there it was again! The enigma that was this handsome man (Marion had even called him a "savant" in his world of finance) . . . This same cowboy, who wore lawyer's shoes for their first meeting. . . .

❀ ❀ ❀

Riding back and forth below the headwaters, Frank and Elle had been pleasantly encouraged by their success in moving the cows—on their return uphill, Elle referenced a BLM map while they agreed upon the design parameters of a fence (one that they would soon build together) to keep livestock out of the 'riparian borders' of upper Edwards Creek. When Frank approached the pool of water once more, however, his eyes were drawn to a collection of trampled vines that could now barely reveal themselves through their mud-caked struggle for existence . . . Sadly, it hit him: These were the same wild roses that his mother had so loved . . . the ones with "healing properties."

Elle watched silently as Frank stepped down from his horse, to walk toward the trampled vines. He showed no regard at all for the mud that existed between himself and the threatened plants. Only when he reached into the mud to begin lifting the wild rose vines up from their entrapment, was Elle finally compelled to speak, "What on earth are you doing?!" Frank was despondent when he gazed for a moment around the pool, "This was a special place to my Mom . . . She called it the 'Wellspring' of these mountains, and she once told me that the rosehips from these plants have healing properties. . . ."

Elle was suddenly moved to step down from her own horse and join him, "It sounds like your Mom was a wise woman . . . I should tell you that we track this spot by satellite—we think the water comes from an 'artesian well', but our geologists have no idea where the water originates, given this high elevation." She grabbed her canteen, and walked through the mud to stand beside Frank. She then lifted one of the freed vines and poured water over a cluster of berries. . . . Frank understood, so he retrieved more vines and handed them to Elle. He watched her clean and pluck enough rosehips to fill both outside pockets of her jacket. When there was no room left, she filled Frank's jacket pockets as well.

## ELKO

Elle grew to love her time spent with Frank at the ranch. As they built their fence together to protect the artesian source of Edwards Creek, it became clear that Frank loved it too. He quickly grew to appreciate her strength and endurance on the long days required during their construction project.

That collaboration amounted to the organic embodiment of Elle's vision of a purposeful life. Her years spent in school had included field studies and labs, but never this vivid reality that she was now sharing with Frank. They soon discovered that they loved working together, and Frank spoke often of his appreciation for her help; it would especially help during the gathering of cattle from the high elevations. He warned, "I'm relieved by that, but you and Jaycee and I will be the only riders with any experience moving cattle. My father is no longer up to the task, and everyone else will be novices . . ."

"So, I have been thinking . . . I need to ask if you might want to come along on a trip to Elko this weekend to buy some new 'cow horses' for the ranch . . . I have this idea that Marion might be safer when riding 'Fancy', if that's okay? While you and Jaycee and I need to find horses with better cutting and sorting skills. . . . We will have a chance on Saturday morning to look at the sale horses and pick out the ones that we like, and then the Van Norman and Friends sale will take place at 1:00pm at the Fairgrounds. You and Marion and I can ride there in my Ford, with Logan and Jaycee following us in the semi and livestock trailer."

Frank was relieved to hear how quickly Elle agreed to the trip, so he added, "There's no reason why it can't be fun . . . We'll be loading the horses and driving home on Sunday morning, so I made a reservation at 'The Star' in Elko for dinner on Saturday night . . . Have you ever had Basque food in Nevada since moving here? The Star is my absolute favorite . . . They've been there since the early 1900's, and I made some friends there during my mining days . . . Marion is excited to see it too." Then with a wicked smile he added, "I'll buy you a 'Picon Punch' . . . That will tell us whether or not you are a real Nevada Cowgirl . . ."

## THE BUNKHOUSE

Marion had early on convinced Elle to stay in the bunkhouse during the completion of her work (which now included moving scattered cattle from the lower elevations), while Fancy and her treasured new roan horse were easily cared for in the barn; Jaycee (and eventually Amaia) began joining her on those mornings to groom their new horses as well . . .

With Marion's expert help she had settled in for a longer stay, anticipating the gathering of cattle from the upper mountains. From the start, Jaycee had joined her there, and they often talked together at night amidst the stars and the quiet nights at that elevation; and sometimes, Jaycee wanted to talk to her about

Logan. Things became livelier when Amaia and Steve moved in following their return from Spain.

Early one morning, while the visiting wranglers were sleeping, Elle was awakened by the sound of subdued clacking on a computer keyboard. It was still dark outside, but she sat upright and was immediately drawn to the blue LED light that emanated beneath the nearby door. When she peeked inside the adjoining room, she discovered that Frank was at work before three large computer screens. She then rolled an extra chair beside him and smiled before sitting down next to him.

She studied his trading platforms for a moment and pointed to a long column of stock "call signs." "What are these?" Frank explained that they were stocks that were being managed in the "Trust Accounts." Elle countered, "I thought you said that you sold your stocks before going into this recession." Frank smiled at her and explained, "Not these stocks . . . These are in a sector called 'Consumer Staples.' They amount to companies who sell things that people can't live without, even during recessions."

Elle pointed to the screen and asked, "What are these companies?" Frank said, "Procter and Gamble, Clorox . . . Campbell's Soup . . . among others. Elle pointed to the stock symbol 'MO' and asked, "What is this one?" Frank answered, "That's Phillip Morris . . ." Elle immediately turned her chair to face Frank, and she studied him in disbelief, "Phillip Morris . . . the cigarette company?!" Frank could only return a defensive grin when he was met with her glare of profound disapproval.

Elle finally shook her head back and forth and grinned at him, "You are going to require so much work . . ." When Frank then leaned forward on a path directly toward her lips, he toppled both chairs at once and spilled them together to the floor . . . The crash of their chairs and their uncontrolled laughter woke up everyone next door in the bunkhouse.

## ARCADIA

On a day of rest, following concentrated efforts to prepare everyone for the gathering of cattle from the upper mountains, Marion planned for a picnic above the ranch. Robert had spent many hours with her in the corrals and he had been successful in teaching her to be an accomplished rider aboard "Fancy." Jaycee and Amaia, meanwhile, had polished their heel roping skills nearby upon their spirited new 'working cow horses' from the Van Norman sale. Amaia had indeed been well-prepared as a teen growing up in San Sebastian, and she impressed everyone with her horsemanship skills.

Frank led the group on horseback that day to his grove of aspen trees above the reservoir, and he was happy to discover that the picnic would be surrounded by the still-golden leaves of his "quakies." The early fall had remained nice, and today would be no exception, so the attendees spread out their blankets within the beautiful glade, while Marion passed around her sandwiches and other lunch choices.

Everyone participating was surprised to then see *Robert* arrive on his appendix mare, and an eruption of cheers rose up among them. Those who loved him most were amazed to see him riding (at all) and they welcomed him again when he stepped down to allow his horse to graze with the others. He shared broad smiles all around, and his smile lingered when he saw that Frank was sitting close to Elle.

There was a moment when Marion looked around while everyone was enjoying this happy gathering, and she was suddenly taken by the aspen leaves as they shimmered in the sun and a mild breeze. She was astonished to feel that they seemed to be conveying their approval to her. When she turned toward Frank, she discovered that he was staring directly at her. He then smiled and proclaimed quietly, "Arcadia" . . . and she smiled back.

### PIES AND TEA

The family had planned for a big reunion on Thanksgiving day; Stella and Richie were attending too; Richie and Steve had worked well together to stretch out and ready the calves (many of them big after an extra year of wandering). Everyone on the crew took their turns inside the corral during the vaccination and doctoring and branding . . . While this transpired, Marion sauteed the "mountain oysters" (much celebrated by the San Francisco visitors) in a skillet over the branding fire . . . And "especially for Frank," she slow-cooked her new recipe for "Angelina's Red Beans" in a cast iron pot which hung beside the same fire . . . this new tradition would be celebrated year after year.

❀ ❀ ❀

Elle had joined Marion and Jaycee one day prior to the holiday, for the baking of pies. Elle was by now embraced entirely within this family (especially by Robert), for her tireless direction in the moving of McClelland Ranch cattle down to the four valley locations. There . . . new fencing, alfalfa hay and water had awaited their arrival.

She used her BLM satellite photos each day to carefully locate stray groups of cows and calves, before helping to move them all downhill. Jaycee, during these efforts, realized her vision when the "girl Buckeroos" (herself, Marion, Elle, and Amaia) accomplished most of the wrangling needed for that monumental task. This amounted to weeks of saved time, while work on the wells and hay storage sites were completed in the Desatoya Mountains.

❀ ❀ ❀

So it was, within the spirit of relief and celebration, which followed such an accomplishment, that Frank and his Dad sat together at the kitchen table, waiting for pie dough trimmings from the oven (baked and sprinkled with sugar and cinnamon). Of course, the coffee pot was always perking in this kitchen, but when Elle produced a Mason Jar full of dried "rosehips" and she and Marion discussed them while retrieving Angelina's stainless mesh "tea ball," Robert stood up in disbelief.

By the time he was able to stand beside Elle and confirm her ingredients, the rosehips were turning the teapot water a red mahogany hue. Frank also moved close beside her, just in time to hear his father say, "My wife would have loved you." She was overwhelmed, and she hugged Robert for a long time. Elle had been surprised by Robert's words, not understanding that he knew (better than anyone else) that love is stronger than pride. When she was finally able to turn back to face Frank, she nestled her head inside his shoulder, and pulled him close. This now-favorite posture allowed for the essential completion of an embrace that fit them both perfectly.

## TWO YEARS LATER

Frank and his young companion were quiet in the saddle, atop a tall working cow horse. The blue roan gelding had a long chiseled face, and a forehead that emphasized his intelligent and confident eyes; he was "the kind" that belonged on a Nevada cattle ranch.

Frank beamed down at the old felt cowboy hat and chaps of his helper, and he smiled at him when he realized that his son was staring intently at the cattle just beyond them. They were eating the grass and alfalfa hay that Jaycee and Logan had earlier distributed across the field. Robby was just one year old, so he couldn't have known how much work had been required to restore this home pasture, now brimming with fall cow and calf pairs . . .

Just as Frank was confirming (for the first time) that healthy perennial grass can also boast late-season color changes, he heard his wife call out, "Hey! . . . Are those my two cowboys?!" She was posting toward them on her athletic roan horse, and Frank could only smile when he stared at her. . . . Elle was more beautiful than ever with her loose, sun-kissed hair, and transformed entirely in her signature western hat and clothes; apparel choices (more function than form) that had been collectively arrived upon by herself, Marion and Jaycee.

She opened her eyes wide when she leaned down to share a twist of pie crust with her young son, "Auntie Marion made something really good", and Robbie gripped it in his fist, to take a bite. Elle then leaned over to kiss her husband, "Here . . . you have to try this too . . ." and she shared another sample of pie crust, "Marion added a glaze of confectioner's sugar that she brushed on the hot pie crust, just out of the oven."

Frank tasted the delicious pastry, and reacted, "Yumm! . . . That's good!" So, when their one year old son lifted up his own sample in a gesture of celebration, Mom and Dad could not hold back their joyous laughter. . . . Elle then said, "Let's get back to the house. Marion has pies waiting for us, and you know how much she likes having her family around her. . . .

# ACKNOWLEDGMENTS

No expression of gratitude could fairly measure the contributions to Nevada Son made by Larraitz Ariznabarreta, Editor of the 'Basque Book Series' at CBS Press. Her courage and commitment to publish a novel of historical fiction uniquely sets her apart and her creative oversight absolutely strengthened the fabric of my story; particularly, her knowledge of pre-Spanish Civil War art and its depiction of 'Arcadia' amidst settings of cultural and pastoral abundance has been invaluable. It was her introduction to Jose Arrue's painting, Baserritarrak, which entirely reshaped my book's ending. Finally, my fortunate collaboration with Alrica Goldstein, CBS Press Coordinator, brought the sustained energy required for a strong finish.

I must also thank family members and friends too numerous to mention who encouraged me during the four years of writing and one year of editing required to complete this novel. To all of you, I will remain forever indebted…Eric and Jo Ann, gratefully raised together by our dear parents Frank and Joyce, we are forever linked in those beautiful memories. Now particularly, my own children and grandchildren remind me each day that all of life's real gifts are centered among family.

The creative process which ultimately led me here now dates back forty years to include my friend Greg Hunn, who still helps me realize through quantum entanglement that I need to write everything down as soon as it is imagined. It is also fitting that another stalwart friend, Pat Bailey, would be instrumental along my path to becoming a published author; it was his daughter, Johanna Moxley and her affiliation with the University of Nevada Study Abroad program, who steered me toward the Center for Basque Studies. And thankfully, this circle of beloved people introduced me to Carlos Brandenburg, whom I now count among my most valued friendships.

To Chuck and Jeanne Held, instigators of nearly all of my most dangerous lifetime exploits, you still make me smile these many years later. To the Egbert family of Fernley, I am a better man for having known you. Special thanks to Joe Dahl, who turned me loose upon what would become my best horse ("Red

Bluff"), as we pushed cattle together through the Desatoya Mountains; Joe will forever be the real cowboy in this story. Kellie Jo Snow, you are precisely what is best about Nevada. And these numerous ranching themes would be less authentic if I did not reference my "old Pard" Stephen Milstein, who memorably taught me which end of the cow to preg check.

And finally, this story could not have been completed at all without the perspective I have reclaimed during my friendships with Dave Millsaps and Curtis Morrison. Our time spent at Millsaps Ranch has effectively brought me back full circle to my best memories of home, owing to you and the landscapes that we still navigate in rural California.

*In Memoriam*
*Dr. John Andrews MD*

Milton Keynes UK
Ingram Content Group UK Ltd.
UKHW040259181024
449757UK00001B/138